Best Enemies

Lynn Emery

ISBN: 0983335745
ISBN-13:978-0983335740

DEDICATION

This book is for all of the smart, strong, creative, and sassy women I've known, and the men who loved them- or foolishly crossed them and lived to regret it..

Chapter 1

Willa stared at the pile of papers on Jack's desk and started crying. Not dignified dainty tears. Willa's face quickly became a soggy mess as the one tissue she could find in her purse became soaked then shredded. No matter how she tried, Willa couldn't pull it together. This was crazy since she'd threatened to kill her estranged husband more than once.

Four days ago someone had done just that. Willa tossed aside the destroyed tissue then glanced around. Jack's office reflected his personality, controlled chaos. Piles of books, manuals and papers were stacked around in what looked like no particular order. In frames along one wall hung Jack's pride and joy, his degrees and licenses. On the opposite wall were framed pictures of Jack with various famous and infamous people of influence. Shining success mixed in with unsavory choices.

Jack Crown had paid for one last bad decision with his life, wandering around late at night in a bad neighborhood. Not smart, and not the way Willa's mother had predicted either, by an outraged woman he'd screwed literally and figuratively. As if on cue the screen saver on Jack's notebook clicked on showing a woman in a sexy pose. Swearing, Willa broke a fingernail hitting the keys changing it to a bland picture of daisies.

Willa stared at a photo of Jack standing next to his prized car, a metallic green Jaguar. Four days ago an unknown executioner had killed him for a few dollars on a dark street. So unfair. So horrible. Willa clenched her hands into fists. She had not even had the satisfaction of a farewell knock down fight. Some no good murderer had deprived her of one last chance to nail him with a piece of his family's fine China. She snatched up a plaque on his desk and threw it. The sound of it hitting the wall sounded good, but it didn't break. She'd broken quite a few plates during their marriage. Her sobs dried up. And yet...

The sight of his usual stack of files, his messy office habits, reminded her of their brief period of good times. His flair, wicked wit and grace enthralled her within five minutes of meeting him for the first time. His mess used to be cute. And the way he teased Willa about her penchant for color-coding and organizing everything used to be cute. Jack Crown could tilt his head to one side and make a woman believe he only had eyes for her. And God what beautiful eyes, clear and the color of honey. Willa sighed. Of course he knew his own power. The bastard. Willa started to cry again.

"Damn you, Jackson Phillip Crown." Willa gave her nose one last determined swipe. Tackling her purse again she found a fresh pack of tissues. She dabbed her eyes then took a deep breath.

"He did have that affect on people," his secretary said from the doorway.

Only her head was visible at first. When Willa nodded the rest of her came into view as she entered Jack's office. Kayosha Singletary, who liked to be called Kay, walked in, but did not sit down. Her smooth young face appeared eager to help. Still she was reserved around Willa, her deceased employer's almost ex-wife. Today was the first time Willa had stayed in the office more than a few hours. Being there had felt eerie and she'd had to adjust to the fact that she was still Jack's next of kin.

"This office is a hot mess," Willa said around a few more sniffles. She pulled herself together so Jack's secretary wouldn't think she was completely nuts. "How he got anything done is a miracle."

"Actually his system sorta made sense. Everything that he was working on stayed piled on his desk. Cases on hold for any reason are stacked over there." Kay pointed to a corner near the window facing east. "Closed files got dumped in this stack next to the filing cabinet. Once a week I filed things away."

"Okay." Willa glanced at the folders. She still only saw chaos despite Kay's explanation. "I'm surprised he let you into his office."

Kay laughed. "We had an understanding. I only touched what he told me to touch, and he didn't touch the files I put in order." Her smile faded slowly. "It's a shame the way he—"

"Yeah," Willa replied.

Neither needed to finish the thought. Crime in Baton Rouge since The population surge after Hurricane Katrina seemed to be an unstoppable force. Yet it was unreal that someone she'd known and at one time loved was a victim. One more senseless murder added to grim crime stats for the city. Jack had been murdered for what mounted to pocket change while withdrawing cash from a convenience store ATM machine.

"Now what?" Kay said, breaking into Willa's bleak train of thought. She studied Willa as though looking for clues.

Good question, Willa mused as she rocked back and forth in Jack's expensive leather executive chair. Crown Protection Services employed forty-five full-time employees and almost as many part-timers. Kay was posing the question on behalf of them all Willa felt certain.

"I'm not sure. My lawyer will have to advise me on what I can do legally. We were about to sign the final divorce judgment when... this happened. Jack may have changed his will in the last six months since we separated."

"Uh, I'm not trying to get in your personal business, but— " Kay stopped as though waiting for a signal.

"I realize that my personal business affects Crown Protection. I just don't have any solid answers yet," Willa replied.

"Well what I'm saying is Mr. Crown never changed his will." Kay sat down in one of the two chairs facing Jack's desk. Then she moved a stack of papers so she and Willa could see each other better.

"How do you know?" Willa stopped rocking and leaned forward.

"Okay, I may have only worked here for a couple of years, but we clicked fast once he hired me. Not like that I mean," Kay added quickly. "Strictly professional. He wasn't my type."

"Right." Willa wondered if she meant arrogant, lying womanizers weren't her type. But she didn't want to speak ill of the recently departed, at least not out loud.

"Right," Kay said, her lips curving up slightly for a few moments. "Anyway I took care of some of his private business, too. His lawyer advised Mr. Crown to change his will, but he didn't."

"That's weird. I would think cutting me out would have been his first priority. Jack may have kept a messy desk, but he was meticulous about his bottom line." Willa gazed at a framed photo of Jack on the wall. He wore a custom suit and proudly held up a local business award he'd won seven years earlier.

"Despite what it looks like Mr. Crown could put his hands on anything he needed like that." Kay snapped her fingers.

"True," Willa agreed. Administrative assistants and wives knew men best. "So I'm shocked he didn't carve me out of his will the minute he realized the old charm wouldn't work anymore."

"He used to talk about you a lot."

Willa gave a snort. "I'll just bet he did."

"Okay, not all of it was, er, complimentary. But he also said you were one of the few women he'd trust with his money and his child."

In spite of everything he'd put her through Willa's heart skipped at hearing that. Damn that Jack Crown. Just when she thought his magic had lost its hold. One simple statement brought back the happy memories. They'd shared six months of blissful courting followed by seven good years of marriage. And Jack had embraced Anthony like he was his son. Willa cleared her throat and closed her eyes to fight off a crying jag.

"He wasn't all bad when it came down to it. He bragged on Anthony all the time." Kay pointed to one wall of the office covered with pictures of Anthony. "He called that Anthony's wall of fame."

Willa laughed hard, and Kay joined her. Seconds later they both took a deep breath as they exchanged a glance. "So you think he put off changing his will because he trusted me?"

"Mr. Crown respected you as a person, Mrs. Crown."

"Call me Willa."

"Sure." Kay smiled at her. "And yes, he definitely trusted you unlike, that string of hoochies he had in the last year or so."

"Terrible taste in women, present company excluded of course," Willa said with a grin.

"Actually he agreed with you about his taste in women based on a couple of comments he made about being too stupid to stay married to a good woman." Kay nodded.

"Thanks for telling me." Willa wanted to shed more tears but managed to stay dry.

"Anyway, one of his last lady friends came here and made a scene. After she left Mr. Crown was cussing like crazy about crazy heifers and how he needed to get his you-know-what together, etc."

"Uh-huh. Notice he never changed," Willa snorted. "Oh well. That was Jack up and down."

"He said something about how the only smart thing he ever did was to not marry to any of them or change his will." Kay smiled at her and shrugged when Willa's mouth fell open.

"Considering I was wife number three that's saying something." Willa rocked the chair back again.

"So you're in charge. Boss." Kay gazed at Willa as thought expecting to get a set of instructions.

"I have good news and bad news then. The good news is you won't have to work for one of Jack's crazy mistresses. The bad news is I don't know a damn thing about running a security business."

Kay waved a hand as though Willa had mentioned a minor detail. "Cedric may be a bit full of himself."

"What an understatement."

Cedric Robinson was Jack's chief of operations. He'd let it be known he expected to be left in charge. He even dropped hints about buying the business. Aside from that he seemed a bit too starched. Maybe being ex-military accounted for that. In any event Willa had decided she didn't like him. He was condescending and humorless.

"I'm surprised he and Jack got along. Jack was Mr. Charm and had that dry sense of humor. Cedric doesn't have either," Willa said.

"Yeah, but opposites not only attract they make good working partners."

"I'll try to remember that," Willa replied with a grimace. In just a few short weeks she'd butted heads with Cedric over several issues.

"Hello," a deep male voice boomed from the foyer.

Yes, sir. I'll be right with you." Kay scrambled from her chair and straightened her skirt. "Probably our new client dropping off some paperwork. Jai won't be here until after lunch to man the desk." Jai Henderson was a full-time student with an undergrad degree in criminology. They always worked around her schedule

"Maybe we need to hire a temp receptionist to help you out." Willa frowned over one more decision she had to consider, and possibly fight with Cedric about.

"More hands around here would be a nice change. Besides Jai graduates in a week and she already has a job."

Willa sighed. Six clients had bailed on Crown Protection after Jack was murdered. Having the man who is supposed to provide protection die violently could shake your confidence. Luckily the agency had contracts that would cost the clients money if they tried to jump to another security firm. Willa's challenge was to inspire them to stay with Crown. To do that she needed experienced employees. She needed Cedric. And he knew it.

***

Two hours later Kay knocked once on Willa's half-open office door, said "I'll be right back," over her shoulder and came in. She shut the door firmly then crossed to Willa's desk. Her entrance combined with her wide brown eyes gave Willa a start.

"What the— "

"Police Detective Armand Miller is here to see you," Kay broke in. "Maybe they've arrested Mr. Crown's killer."

Willa doubted it. The last she'd heard from the police they had no leads, no suspects and a lot of other crimes to chase down. "Well let's hear what he has to say then."

Kay nodded then left. Willa heard her voice seconds later, high pitched with contained curiosity. A deeper voice thanked her then heavy footsteps approached. Willa worked hard to appear calm and in control, to fake her way through one more interview with him. She stood and came around the desk to greet him.

"Hello, detective."

Detective Armand Miller strode in wearing a serious expression. She judged him to be six foot two inches talk, two inches taller than Jack had been. Detective Miller didn't have Jack's smooth pretty boy good looks, but he definitely could hold his own when it came to appearances. Might help if he smiled more. It's not like he didn't have good teeth or anything. Willa liked his rugged "I can bench press two hundred pounds and catch the bag guys" aura. Detective Miller held out one wide hand. Yes, he definitely inspired a sense of confidence in law enforcement. She shook his hand feeling safer just at the solid heft of it. Before she knew it she'd smoothed back her hair with the tips of her fingers once she let go of his hand and wet her lips. When one of his dark eyebrows twitched up she stopped both actions. She blinked rapidly feeling a bit like one of Jack's hoochies.

"Good morning, Mrs. Crown. Thank for taking time out to talk to me last minute." He glanced around the office then his gaze settled on Willa. Detective Miller managed to appear alert and relaxed at the same time.

She crossed her arms to assume a business-like pose. "Don't worry about interrupting my day. I'm still feeling my way along. Thankfully Jack has knowledgeable and efficient employees."

"Is that right? Well, that must make things so much easier for you. I mean, taking over a business that your ex-husband started. Or did you work for him at one time?"

"Nothing more than answering the phones a few times while we were married. I had my own career of course." Willa gestured to a chair and watched him fold his hefty frame into it.

Detective Miller crossed his long legs. "Yes, paralegal and notary public. Interesting, working for that big criminal defense firm I mean."

Willa knew police officers had a tendency to like criminal defense attorneys as much as they liked their clients. "I'm afraid my job with them was quite dull, legal research mostly."

"Research that helped them build cases," Miller said.

"Right." Willa sat on the edge of the desk. Her light gray skirt inched up causing Detective Miller's eyebrow to go up once more. Clearing her throat Willa returned to the safety of her desk

She had worked as a paralegal for the law firm of Craft, Mouton and LaPlace part-time after the divorce. The income from her small business as a notary didn't come close to paying the bills. She was sure Detective Miller knew all about her, including her family background. Willa sensed he was taking in every detail and building a mental file on her beneath that genial exterior. She smiled as she added to her own file on him.

"I see. I wanted to get a few more details from you about Mr. Crown's activities in the months before his death." Detective Miller pulled a small PDA from the chest pocket of his neatly pressed sky blue dress shirt.

"You made any progress on locating a possible suspect? From the evidence found at the scene, I mean." Willa kept smiling when he glanced at her sharply. His cocoa eyes sparkled as if to say, "Nice try, but I'm not talking."

"We're following up on a few leads. Nothing I can discuss, of course." Detective Miller held the PDA as though he'd forgotten it for the moment. He studied her.

"Of course. I'll help in any way I can naturally." Willa watched him nod in approval. Then he favored her with a smile for the first time. He took care of his teeth. Put that in the plus column.

"When we first asked his operations chief, Mr. Robinson, about the murder he said the business didn't handle any cases that might be dangerous, mostly just security for private events and employee background checks." Detective Miller used his small stylus to touch the screen of his PDA.

"Right. Actually Crown Protection did as much valet parking as protecting," Willa quipped. "Not exactly high intrigue from what I've read through the files."

"Someone who didn't get a job or lost a job because of a background check might have become upset with Crown Protection." Detective Miller looked up at her. "I'll need a list of folks who might have had dirty drug screens or background checks that revealed unsavory histories."

"Wow, that's a good idea. I'll have Kay pull the database and give you the list of our clients. You can contact them directly." Willa picked up the phone and hit the button to ring Kay. "Can you come in?"

Kay blurted out a fervent "Yes" then seconds later appeared with a pad and pen. "What do you need, Mrs. Crown?"

"Detective Miller would like a list of unfavorable employee background reports. Someone who didn't get or keep a job might have had a grudge against the agency," Willa said.

"Sure. Mostly the employers didn't tell us what personnel action or hiring decisions they made though. So I'll give you the contact information for the businesses we contracted with. I'm thinking maybe go back at least six months?" Kay glanced from Willa to Detective Miller.

"That's a start. Thanks," he replied with a curt nod.

"Of course most of them probably wouldn't know we were the source of the background checks. At least seven other agencies in town do that sort of thing. Not to mention freelancer investigators and New Orleans agencies," Kay said.

"Really?" Willa was impressed with Kay's knowledge. She decided to spend more time having Kay tutor her in the fine points of the business. That should take Cedric down a few inches from that high horse he was riding.

"Yes, ma'am."

"But existing employees might know who their bosses use for security and background checks," Detective Miller countered. His dark brows drew down as if unhappy that amateurs were trying to play cop.

"Good point," Kay said as she aimed her ink pen at him. "I'll pull that list together right away." The phone in the outer office rang and she left like a woman on a mission.

Detective Miller watched her leave then turned back to Willa once the office door bumped shut. "By the sound of that ringing phone it might take her a few minutes. I can ask some other questions while we wait."

"Sure. Let me get you some coffee." Willa went to the credenza along the east wall of the office. A coffee pot with fresh Louisiana dark roast sat on a tray. She looked at him over her shoulder. "How do you like it?"

His staid expression relaxed. "Cream, no sugar. You seem to have settled in around here."

"No choice. Of course Jack's parents aren't too thrilled about it. But then I'm sure you know they don't like me," Willa said as she handed him the cup of coffee. She knew Miller had already talked to her former in-laws. A good bet that Miller got an earful of "Miss Bea's" ideas about Willa's shortcomings, aka motives.

"I gathered." Miller nodded his thanks for the coffee as he accepted it.

"As far as Miss Bea was concerned Jack hung the moon and stars. He was perfect in every way. But then mothers tend to have a blind spot when it comes to their sons." Willa felt a sharp pain in her gut at the thought of her child. At fifteen Anthony was trying to be tough, trying to take are of her. She bit her lower lip to keep it from quivering.

"Your son was close to his father?" Detective Miller had an eye for details as well. His smooth segue also showed he was good at following them.

"Step-father technically, but Jack and I had been together for two years before we got married. Anthony was just five when Jack and I met. But yes, they were close. Except for the last two years." Willa inhaled deeply and let out a slow breath. "Kids always know what's going on. Not that our fights didn't get loud toward the end."

"Anthony took sides, your side specifically," Detective Miller said.

"Mrs. Crown told you that I suppose," Willa replied with heat.

Miller's impassive expression confirmed her guess. "Several family members mentioned some conflict between the two."

"I didn't want him to, but yes. Anyway, Anthony still loved Jack deeply. I'm sure of that. Jack was working hard to reach out to him." Willa marshaled her defenses so she wouldn't cry. "They were talking."

"So Anthony was home the night Mr. Crown died?"

"At a friend's house. He and Greg are on the soccer team and..." Willa blinked back from her inward musings. She looked up to find Detective Miller gazing at her intently. He'd put the cup of coffee down and his pen was poised above a little note pad.

"And?" Detective Miller prompted.

"And he loved Jack. They were as close as a biological father and son," Willa said through clenched teeth.

"Anthony has had some problems with anger. There was an incident where he actually punched Mr. Crown." Detective Miller spoke in a steady yet relentless monotone.

"My son would never, <u>never</u> kill anyone. Certainly not the only man he ever regarded as his father." Willa struggled to calm her own anger. She knew Detective Miller was looking for a reaction along with information that might become a lead. After a silent count to ten Willa lifted her chin. "Call Greg and his family to confirm where my son was that night, all night."

"This is routine. He's not a suspect." Detective Miller's tone suggested the "yet" was unspoken.

Willa picked up an ink pen on her desk. She wrote down the phone number, address and names of Greg's parents. The strokes were so firm the notepaper had indentations. "Stephanie and Robert Bellmont will be happy to speak with you, as would Greg. We have nothing to hide."

"Thank you. These questions are routine and need to be asked especially under the circumstances." Detective Miller lifted his dark eyebrows. "The sooner we cover all bases with family and friends the faster we can proceed down all other avenues."

"Hmmm," was all Willa could trust herself to say. Having the detective check her alibi that night hadn't caused even a twitch when he'd questioned her three days ago. Her protective instincts kicked into overdrive when it came to her child.

He took the lined note pad sheet Willa thrust out toward him. "I appreciate your not getting overly emotional about my questions. As I said— "

"Yes, routine," Willa cut him off. She just wanted him to leave, now. "Do you need to know where my baby girl Mikayla was that night?"

Detective Miller smiled. "Your little girl was with your mother, ma'am. We talked to Mrs. Wilson when we— "

"Checked my alibi of being at Mama Ruby's house for supper later that night," Willa finished for him, though the detective had never used that loaded term "alibi." He kept referring to placing everyone's movements around the critical time.

Detective Miller rose to leave. He extended a hand. Willa barely touched the smooth brown skin before letting go. His unruffled expression indicated that he was used to hostility. The antipathy radiating from Willa bounced right off his broad shoulders covered in crisp blue cotton.

"Yes, ma'am. I appreciate your time and patience. I'll be in touch. Call me if you think of any information that could be helpful," he said, pointedly not offering to keep Willa informed.

"I most certainly will be in touch," she replied.

He nodded at her then smoothed down the front of his shirt. "Have a good day, ma'am," he said the left.

Willa rolled her neck to ease the muscle tension Detective Miller had inspired. She knew her former in-laws still had connections despite the elder Crown's past mistakes. Detective Miller would no doubt keep Mr. and Mrs. Crown informed. In the meantime Willa worried about Anthony. She only hoped that he had indeed stayed with his friend this time. Before she could continue down that bothersome path of Anthony's troubling teenage defiance Kay appeared at her door again.

"Is everything okay?" Kay glanced around as though the office furnishings would give her a clue.

"Yeah," Willa stretched her lips into a smile.

"I gave Detective Miller a printout of the recent checks we've done for employers. Here is a copy." Kay came to the desk and placed sheets stapled together at one end on Willa's desk.

"Wow, that many." Willa leafed through six pages of neatly typed names with employers and contact information.

"Cedric kept working our same client list. I mean, you've had a lot to handle since... it happened," Kay offered. "Cedric decided we should just keep doing our jobs like normal, if we could."

"Right. Right."

Willa no longer saw the pages before her. Instead she had an image of Anthony filled with rage the day he'd struck out at Jack. They'd been at a family picnic. Everyone could feel the strain between her and Jack, but as usual her family worked around it. However when Jack made a sarcastic comment about Willa's wide hips she snapped something back at him. Jack patted Willa's butt and she knocked his hand away. Out of nowhere Anthony appeared shouting at Jack not to touch her again. Three of her cousins and two uncles had to wrestle Anthony to ground. Jack tried to appear untouched, yet Willa saw the pain in his eyes. The next day Jack had moved out for the last time. After twelve years, six affairs and numerous lies neither of them bothered with the usual kiss and make-up ritual. Anthony as a suspect. Willa fought off the budding panic that tried to get a grip on her gut.

"Sure you're all right? Maybe you can leave the rest of this stuff for another day. I can organize everything." Kay gazed at Willa with concern in her cinnamon brown eyes.

"Fine. Uh, call Cedric and ask him to meet with me Wednesday at 10 AM. Please," Willa added when she realized Kay was eyeing her dubiously. Take control, Willa said, mentally repeating the mantra her Aunt Ametrine favored.

"Sure. I'll also run over to the accountant's office and pick up the paychecks for your signature. One more thing Mr. Crown took care of, instructions in his will. Lord, bless his soul," Kay said quietly. She sniffed a couple of times as she went out the door.

"Humph," Willa retorted once Kay closed the door. She looked around the office feeling Jack's aura in the baseball memorabilia and photos from his days of playing the game in college. "Jack Crown, if you want some kind of divine second chance to redeem yourself and avoid the fires of hell you'd better send me some kind of message about your murder now, because they're questioning Anthony."

Silence. No rush of wind lifting up a page with a promising lead. No eerie whisper with a cryptic message containing a clue. Nothing. Willa picked up the phone to call Stephanie Bellmont and check Anthony's alibi. As she tapped the keypad Willa silently prayed that Anthony had not picked that night to sneak off and get into trouble again.

***

Ruby Wilson stood behind the waist high bar in her nightclub on Alligator Bayou. She wiped glasses, popped her gum and nodded her head to an old Bobby Blue Bland song blaring from the speakers above her head. At sixty years old she didn't look a day over fifty, as her husband Elton loved to brag. Willa entered the cool dark room with a sigh of relief. She crossed the bare wood floor then sat down hard on a bar stool with a red cushioned seat.

"Fix me the usual, Mama," Willa said and slapped her purse down onto the scarred dark wood that topped the bar.

Ruby reached behind her and turned down the volume on the sound system. "How you holdin' up, baby?"

"Other than dealing with my mean as a snake mother-in-law, a business I know nothing about and a cop who thinks Anthony is a suspect, I'm doing good." Willa crossed her arms on the bar then rested her forehead on them.

"What the hell? That child wouldn't hurt a fly. Let me call my friend Judge Henderson. No, better yet I'll call Deputy Devine." Ruby already had the cordless phone to her ear.

Willa stretched across the bar and snatched the phone out of Ruby's hand. "Please. The last thing we need is a battle of the local politically connected Black families. That will only get our names in the newspaper. Again."

Ruby put her hands on both hips. "I hope you don't think that's the only phone I have, or that I'm gonna let them frame my grand-baby. Be damned if I will."

"You need to calm down." Willa heaved a sigh. As usual Mama Ruby lost her temper when it came to her "babies", no matter what their age. "You sit down and I'll fix us something to drink."

"I don't need no drink," Ruby huffed. Still she sat down as ordered on a carved oak stool behind the bar.

"We both need a drink." Willa walked around to the bar and pushed through the small swinging door on hinges. She reached inside one of two mini refrigerators. As she expected there were two pitchers of iced tea.

"It's just two o'clock in the afternoon. Don't be puttin' no liquor in my tea either." Ruby drummed her fingers on the bar. "Now tell me what idiot cop thinks Anthony would have killed Jack. He loved that man."

"He also hated that man." Willa found a store of fresh mint leaves and added those to each glass of sweet tea. "No amaretto added. You watched me fix it."

"I wasn't watchin' you. I'm thinkin' 'bout my baby. And he didn't hate Jack, he was just mad as hell at him for being a screw up and hurtin' you." Ruby frowned at the glass Willa put in front of her. Her nut brown face had few lines, which made her look younger than sixty-two by a good ten years.

Willa took a long slow drink of the tea savoring the sweetness. The kick of strong mint added just the right flavor. Sugar always soothed her nerves. She sighed again, this time with satisfaction. "Listen, Detective Miller— "

"Yeah, from up north? Now what does he know about us anyway? Just cause folks in Chicago— "

"Philadelphia," Willa corrected.

"Where ever. Just cause them people done lost their minds up there don't mean Black folks down here killin' their own daddies." Ruby pointed a finger at Willa.

"That logic perfectly sums up your bias, Mama Ruby." Willa shook her head.

"Humph, I lived up there back in the sixties. Most folks thinkin' moving north was like goin' to the promise land." Ruby's face took on the strained look talking about her time in Chicago.

Ruby had been seventeen with a singing voice that rocked Sweet Home Missionary Baptist Church. In defiance of her parents she'd run off with a boyfriend to become the next big singing sensation. Seven years of hard times had knocked those dreams down. Mama Ruby still had never told Willa the details of what she'd gone through. Yet Willa knew some of the story from Aunt Ametrine, the family historian. Family gossip was a more accurate description.

"Detective Miller is just doing what police officers do, look at the family and friends first. Most crimes are committed by someone close to the victim," Willa said, repeating what she'd learned by watching police reality shows.

"Girl, you have lost your mind! The man is tryin' to pin a murder on your first born and you up in here defendin' him," her mother's voice boomed.

Used to Mama Ruby's "bark worse than her bite" ways, Willa faced the anger head on. "Will you stop freaking out, please? I'm not defending him. Once I stopped trippin' I realized his tactic. He wanted me to get upset and blurt out something revealing, a promising lead. Miller knows about that time Anthony punched Jack at the family picnic. You remember. The one where you invited Jack hoping to get us back together."

"And?" Mama Ruby ignored Willa's dig at her failed attempts to help them reconcile.

"What I should have done was keep cool and find out why they don't think Jack was killed by a mugger." Willa sipped more tea.

"What the— " Ruby picked up her glass and sipped from it as well. She lowered the glass. "Yeah, you got a good point. This detective what's-his-name— "

"Miller," Willa replied. She watched the wheels turning behind her mother's black coffee eyes.

"Right, Detective Miller would have questioned Anthony if he thought that the child really could have done it. Did he start out asking about Anthony or lead up to it?" Ruby glanced at Willa.

"He led up to it."

"You're right. He's fishin'. Which makes me wonder. Jack had just been to one of those ATMs when he was shot.

His wallet was gone." Ruby blinked as she considered the few facts they knew.

"Along with his 18k gold Rolo link bracelet and gold Kappa Alpha Psi ring," Willa added and let out a loud hiss. "After everything that happened he was still wearing that damn bracelet." A gift from his mistress and the links that led Willa to find out about the latest in a string of women he'd had.

"Yeah, so somethin' has Detective Miller goin' down another road. We just need to find out what he's found out." Ruby nodded.

"No."

"What?" Ruby arranged her cute features into a look of pure innocence. "As members of the family it's only natural that we should have questions. After our terrible loss I mean."

"Do not make phone calls or start snooping around," Willa said stabbing a finger in the air between them. "We're going to stay cool, let the police do their jobs and take care of business."

"You're right, baby. I'm just sayin', if you get a chance call up Detective Miller and ask if there's been any progress on the case." Mama Ruby gave Willa a sweet maternal smile. She got up and went back to arranging glasses on the shelves behind the bar.

"You gave in too quick," Willa replied. She crossed her arms as she watched her mother. "So you're promising me that you won't use your connections or get mixed up in Jack's murder investigation. Even if they bring up Anthony's name again."

Mama Ruby's mouth twitch at the mention of her beloved Anthony was the only sign that she might be lying. Still she kept her voice steady. "Naturally that frightens me, but I won't get all in a tizzy and make a move without talkin' to you."

"Good." Willa had to be satisfied with that much. Yet she knew Mama Ruby well enough to suspect she had a game plan in mind anyway.

"What did this Detective Miller say about Anthony anyway?" Ruby kept her voice calm. She glanced at Willa sideways.

"He wanted to know where Anthony was that night. I told him he was with his best friend Greg."

"And was he?" Mama Ruby stopped polishing the over-sized glass beer mug in her hand.

"The Bellemonts are on vacation in Orlando. I left a text message on Stephanie's cell." Willa looked at her glass of tea and considered adding a dollop of peach schnapps to it.

"And she'll get back to you with the assurance that Anthony was at her house all night. He was most likely playing video games and doin' whatever kids like to do these days," Ruby said.

"Yeah, what kids like to do," Willa repeated. She tried not to think of less childlike activities that attracted Black teenage boys these days, including Anthony. With a final prayer that Stephanie would call her back soon with good news, Willa helped Mama Ruby set up for the Friday night crowd.

Chapter 2

Willa watched her daughter with a smile as she fixed a plate of sub sandwiches at the kitchen island. Seven-year-old Mikayla sat at the breakfast table. Late afternoon sunshine coming through the bay window to her left brought out the red highlights in her sandy brown hair. Mikayla screwed up her small face just the way Jack used to as she colored the picture with a marker. She restrained herself from crossing the room to scoop Mikayla into a bear hug. Soon to be eight, Mikayla had decided she was a big girl and didn't like spontaneous babying from adults. No doubt Willa could thank the latest rump shaking female teen pop star for that change.

"Do you want mustard on your baloney sandwich, baby girl?" Mikayla shook her head no. "Pickles?"

"Yes, please," Mikayla said softly then stared out of the window, her purple marker poised on the paper. "Me and daddy liked pickles on our sandwiches. Anthony doesn't."

Willa's neck muscles tightened as she struggled not to cry. Seeing her kids in pain felt like a knife slicing thin pieces of flesh from her body. She stopped making the sandwiches and went to the table. Taking Mikayla's small hand that rested on the table Willa kissed it.

"I know, sweetie. Daddy loved pickles. Bet he's up in heaven at a deli stuffing his face on roast beef sandwiches piled high with pickles."

"But I don't want him up in heaven. If I ask real nice maybe God will send him back." Mikayla turned to Willa, her big dark eyes pleading for the answer she wanted to hear.

Willa knew all about facing harsh reality at a young age. By the time she arrived at Mama Ruby's house as a foster child, Willa had stopped believing in happy endings. Now she felt like a failure. First Anthony had to feel the pain of his biological father's broken promises. Now he'd lost his surrogate father, too. Maybe the world was like an intricate mechanical device. Change one event or decision and the entire machine turned in a different direction. Maybe if she hadn't been so angry with her ex, Markus, he wouldn't have distanced himself from his son.

Maybe if Willa given her marriage to Jack one more chance they would have been together as a family that night. Jack wouldn't have been at that ATM machine. He would have been home playing video games with Anthony, or reading Mikayla's favorite fairytale for the thousandth time. Or if she'd just pretended to believe his lies Jack would have been with his mistress. At least he'd be alive. And Mikayla wouldn't have to ask God to undo what could not be undone.

Before Willa could answer Mikayla pulled her hand away. Her expression said she knew asking would be in vain. "I'm not hungry anyway."

Anthony walked in with the earpiece to his slim MP3 player draped around his neck. When Mikayla walked by with her head down he put a hand on her shoulders. "What's up, baby sis? Hey, you walk outta here and I'm eating your sub and mine."

"I don't care." Mikayla shrugged. "You can have it."

"Won't be any fun if I'm not sneaking it from you," Anthony said and tickled her on the neck.

Mikayla tried to smile but failed. "You eat up everything whether you sneak it or not."

"What you talkin' about, girl? You better take that back."

Anthony tickled her all over as Mikayla wriggled to get away. When she made a dash for the door he chased after her. Moments later Willa heard her little girl squeals of delight. Willa felt a rush of love for Anthony as he teased away Mikayla's pain if only for a little while. Willa prepared sandwiches on a plate, covered them with plastic wrap to keep them fresh. Her children's laughter had died away. She moved quietly from the kitchen and down the hallway to the large family room. Pausing, Willa listened to them talk though she couldn't make out their words. Mikayla's lilting voice like a delicate little bird, then Anthony's deeper responses. Willa decided to retreat. Maybe one child could give guidance to the other better than an adult. At least that was the excuse she made. Despite therapy and Ruby's healing love Willa was still no good at talking about tough subjects.

She went back to the sunny breakfast nook to wait for him. Staring out of the window Willa tried to think of what Mama Ruby would do. Ten minutes later Willa was no closer to channeling her adoptive mother's wisdom. Anthony came back into the kitchen and went straight to the food. She watched him wolf down one meatball sub standing at the counter.

"So, Mikayla is okay?" Willa watched his square jaws working on the spicy meat and bread.

Anthony nodded as he swallowed then turned to the refrigerator. He took out a bottle of strawberry soda, his favorite. After a deep gulp he started toward the door food in hand. "Playing with the Bratz dolls Jack gave her. Going to shoot some baskets at Bernell's house."

"Wait, baby. We need to talk," Willa said quickly before his long legs carried him out of the house. Anthony seemed to always be walking away from her these days.

He let out a hissing sigh through his full lips. "Look, Ma, Miz Kennedy is trippin' ah-ight? Me and the guys was just jokin' around in the cafeteria. Cry baby Tiffany Kendricks made a big deal about a little catsup on her blouse. And then— "

"I'm not talking about some horseplay at school. By the way I totally agree with Mrs. Kennedy." Willa made a note to call the assistant principal to get the details. "And you just told me about your latest escapade before she did."

Anthony put the soda and sandwich down on the counter. He covered his eyes with one large hand. "Ah man."

"Sit down. This is a serious talk. Real serious." Willa patted the cushioned seat of the chair next to her.

He dropped his hand, looked at Willa for a few seconds then sat down as requested. "Okay."

Willa cleared her throat. "The police came by your dad's office today while I was there."

"You planning to sell Jack's business soon?" Anthony looked at her.

"I haven't decided yet. Kinda caught me off guard that he made me his main beneficiary and executor of his will," Willa replied.

"I guess Jack owned you that much," Anthony retorted. He folded his arms across his chest.

"We weren't sworn enemies, Anthony. I mean one thing we shared is wanting the best for our kids." Willa leaned toward him.

"Uh-huh." Anthony's jaw muscle tightened, but he said no more.

"We both made mistakes, okay? A failed marriage is the responsibility of both partners. I know your dad— "

"Jack liked women, weed and liquor so don't try cleaning it up. I'm not Mikayla," Anthony said firmly.

"I'm not trying to treat you like a kid. I— " Willa blinked at him rapidly. "What is this about Jack smoking marijuana? I never. How would you know such a thing?"

"Guys talk. I know some people that know some more people who like to hang out at the clubs. That's all." Anthony's gaze skittered to the opposite side of the room. "Anyway I know Jack wasn't exactly squeaky clean so don't try to make him sound that way."

"He had his faults when it came to women," Willa began.

"Yeah, big time," Anthony put in.

"But don't listen to rumors about him using drugs. I knew Jack a lot longer than you did. He liked to drink, but drugs? I don't believe it." Willa shook her head slowly.

"Ma, weed ain't really considered a drug nowadays. Just like takin' a drink. Part of the club scene, little party ain't hurt nobody," Anthony said with a shrug.

Willa stared at him hard. Although he spoke the words, she felt sure they came from another source. She pointed a forefinger at his nose. "Stop talking like those thugs from the bottom. I lived that life back in the day so don't play tough boy with me. You don't know anything about it. You and your little bourgie friends acting like you're so damn bad. If I even think you're into anything illegal I will knock you back into the land of the righteous. And stop talking in that stupid Ebonics. You hearing me good?"

"Yeah, I hear you," Anthony grumbled, eyes flashing with anger.

"Say what? I missed something," Willa spat and returned his gaze with her own dose of fire.

"I meant to say, yes, ma'am."

"Damn right that's what you meant to say. Okay, you wanna be grown then let's talk like grown folks. Whatever Jack did as my husband he did to *me*. I got a right to be pissed, to dog him out about being a pitiful husband." Willa grabbed Anthony's shoulder hard. "But he kept right on doing for you and Mikayla no matter what anybody says. He loved *both* of you. Jack felt bad about you being so angry with him, but he said he understood that it was his fault."

Anthony's tough exterior cracked. His eyes glistened with tears. His voice shook and he covered his face with one hand. "I didn't mean…"

"He knew you loved him back. Nothing you ever said or did changed that, baby. Nothing," Willa said, her tone softened by the raw pain on his face.

She rose and hugged him to her like he was a little boy again. Still seated Anthony buried his face against her body, both arms wrapped around her waist. He cried quietly for several minutes. His shoulders shook with the effort not to let go completely. Willa stroked his tightly curled wooly hair as she murmured words of consolation. Seconds later Anthony pushed away from her. He grabbed a napkin from the holder on the table and wiped his face.

"I'm going' over to my friend's house like I said. If that's okay," Anthony added. His tough face had returned.

"In a few minutes. Detective Miller is checking up on alibis as part of the investigation. Part of the routine is looking at the family first, then friends and so on." Willa paused as she considered the best way to continue.

Anthony scowled. "Yeah, like on those TV shows. Is he saying' you're a suspect? Cause if he is— "

"Miller considers everyone a person of interest until he eliminates them," Willa cut him off. "So I have to ask you about that night. You were at Greg's house all night, right?"

His eyes blinked then went wide as the realization of what she was asking sank in. He stood up with force making the chair scrape the floor. "You think I could kill Jack? Just cause I called him out on the crap he pulled? Damn, mama. That's messed up."

"Of course I don't think that. Sit back down," Willa shot back in a tone that pressed home her right to have respect. Anthony eased back onto the chair seat with a stony glare at her. "Detective Miller wants to know where you were. And I don't want any surprises. So before he finds out tell me the truth. Did you and Greg stay at his house all night?"

"We were together the whole time," Anthony said.

Willa's eyes narrowed at she looked back at him. "That's not what I asked you."

"Fine, sure. We were at the house all night. Ask Mrs. Bellmont. If you haven't already." Anthony pursed his lips then looked out of the window.

They were back to being opponents. These lightening fast teenage mood swings were wearing her out. "I wanted to hear it from you."

At that moment the phone rang once. Before Willa could get to the kitchen phone Mikayla bounced in. "Mama, Greg's mama wants to talk to you. She said you called her."

Anthony let out a grunt of disgust. "Yeah, right. You wanted to hear it from me. If that's all then I'm gone. Call Bernell's mama if you don't believe me."

Before Willa could react Anthony had taken three long strides to the back door. He slammed it shut behind him. Mikayla gasped at the drama unfolding then rushed to the bay window. She watched him walk quickly down the driveway past Willa's Honda Pilot. Seconds later he disappeared down the sidewalk going east.

"Anthony is going to be in trouble now. Where is he going?" Mikayla craned her neck to keep watching him.

"To Bernell's house," Willa said. She hissed out some of her frustration before picking up the cordless phone. She hit the "on" button and talked to Stephanie Bellmont. Ten minutes later Willa hung up the phone and had three more things to worry about, Anthony's guilty behavior and his troubling account of rumors about Jack. Last but not least, Stephanie had left the boys alone for a good four hours the night Jack was murdered. But Stephanie was sure they hadn't left the house because Greg told her so. Right. Detective Miller was probably licking his chops at the juicy leads he was no doubt uncovering.

***

Two days later Willa was back at Crown Protection. She and Cedric Robinson sat at the round conference table in one corner of Jack's office. They were wrapping up a meeting that laid out all of the jobs scheduled for the next few weeks. Willa had to admit that Cedric had a handle on the business operations. Good thing, too. Her mind kept wandering to her children, her in-laws and Jack's other life that she apparently knew nothing about.

"So that's it. The contract to provide security at two state owned office buildings means we'll have steady revenue for twelve months. Positive cash flow while we take on short-term assignments. I think we should try for more long-term contracts just like it." Cedric nodded as he tapped the neatly arranged paperwork in front of him.

"Right, right. Long term contracts," Willa echoed.

"I realize you've been stressed by these events." Cedric placed a hand on the back of her chair. "If you have any concerns about Crown Protection let me assure you I'm on top of things. As chief of operations Jack relied on me heavily. I'm going to make sure the agency doesn't suffer."

"I know you will. I'm grateful for the hard work you've been putting in, and for being patient with me while I learn," Willa replied quickly. She rubbed her eyes for a few seconds.

"No problem at all. This all has been dumped on you in a very dramatic and tragic way." Cedric paused for a few moments. "Kay told me Detective Miller spoke to you a couple of days ago. He talked to me, too."

"He's just doing his job." Willa frowned as she once again debated calling Miller. She wanted to know what he'd learned about Anthony and Jack. Somehow Willa had to get Anthony to trust her and spill the truth about where he was the night Jack was killed. The fact that she had not heard from Miller only added to her anxiety.

"Right." Cedric paused. "Listen, I don't want to get in your personal business." He paused again as though waiting for a cue.

"Go ahead and ask," Willa replied with a smile and shake of her head. "I'm used to personal questions from men

I hardly know, namely the police. Besides you knew Jack pretty well. I mean you two worked so closely together.”

“Yes, well.” Cedric rubbed his chin and frowned, as though considering how to proceed. Then he looked at Willa. “I’m sure you’ve heard talk about Jack’s personal habits.”

Willa tossed the ink pen in her hand onto the table and leaned back in the chair. “I didn’t know specifics about his ‘personal habits’ in the last year or so. Mainly because- A: I didn’t care. And B: I didn’t want to know. But if anything is going to come out that will hurt my kids then tell me.”

Cedric sat straight like a man clear on his duty. “Of course. In the last two years Jack got, er, distracted by his non-business pursuits.”

“Okay, let me stop you right now. I’m not like Jack’s mama, a siditty upper class black woman who tiptoes around the real deal. I’m from the ‘hood, bounced around foster care when my crack-head mama finally abandoned me and six more kids.”

“Yes, ma’am.” Cedric still had a bit of southern gentleman starch in his collar.

“Forget the formality. Call me Willa,” she said with a smile.

“Okay, Willa. So I’ll just lay it out. I was doing most of the work when it came to day-to-day operations. Jack was mostly attending business luncheons and doing customer relationships type socializing.”

“Oh I know how much Jack enjoyed socializing,” Willa retorted. “So you were actually running the agency. Jack was playing Mr. Big Shot.”

“That’s one way to describe it, yes.” Cedric cleared his throat. “Not that I’m criticizing him, you understand.”

“You, Kay and the other full-timers were loyal to Jack. Otherwise you could have let this place go to hell and just collected your paychecks. Or worse.” Willa meant Cedric could have stolen Jack’s best clients and struck out on his own. In fact, she wondered if he still might. As she gazed back at him she knew that was an unspoken question between them. She took his silence on the subject to mean the answer was “maybe.”

"I've got too much pride in my work to do such a thing. Besides, I really liked Jack. It was hard not to." Cedric's staid demeanor faded a bit. His mouth curved up at one end into a faint smile.

"Tell me about it," Willa replied with a shake of her head. Jack had charisma to spare. She'd been married to the rascal for five years before the blinders fell from her eyes. Even then it was easy to forgive him. Too bad his charisma had been useless against a determined killer.

"The famous Jack Crown charm, his biggest asset and weakness. He started to party hard, even for Jack. He had a lot of anger, too. I think a lot of it was left over from what happened to his father."

"Probably. He always talked about how his father was left hanging by his big time political buddies. Mr. Crown hasn't been the same since he spent time in that federal prison on corruption charges." Willa didn't add that mostly Jack was bitter about the loss of prestige. His anger was directed at the elder Crown as well for getting caught.

"Jack had this thing about becoming big time. He loved flaunting his success in front of the people who turned their backs on them when Mr. Crown was convicted," Cedric said. "But he couldn't get loans from the banks. Other agencies with less of a track record got them and won choice jobs"

Willa grunted. "Let me guess, white owned agencies."

"It was a combination of things, but race played a part. Even so I told him Crown Protection could still be a player. He kept saying the white man was determined to keep us on the chitlin' circuit." Cedric said the words "chiltlin' circuit" as though they tasted sour in his mouth.

"Oh yeah, I heard him say that a time or two," Willa replied. "But you think he made too much of that?"

"I'm not into that victim mentality. Besides, we had a lot of support from black businesses and several white business leaders reached out. Frankly that's why we've done so well." Cedric tapped the folders containing proof of their success.

"But Jack couldn't see past his bitterness. So he found affirmation of his manhood in women and partying."

"I hate to say it, but that's pretty accurate," Cedric finally admitted after hesitating.

"Cedric, did you have any reason to think Jack was doing drugs?"

"You've heard that, too?" Cedric sighed as though relieved the news hadn't come from him. "In the last few months he'd slipped from recreational use toward a serious problem."

"His daddy is a heavy drinker." Willa thought about how the proud Crown family lived in denial.

"Honestly, I was worried about where we were heading. Not that Jack had a public image problem. He always had it together at business functions."

"For sure. His daddy is no falling down sloppy drunk. Just gets quietly soaked and manages to maintain his dignified air." Willa had endured enough family holiday affairs to know.

"I just wanted you to be prepared for anything the police might find out." Cedric seemed ready to drop the subject.

Willa wasn't though. "Is there any reason to believe his death wasn't because of a robbery?"

"Did Miller say that?" Cedric asked sharply.

"Not so much in words, but he's asking questions about who had reasons to harm Jack. He's even asking about my son." Worry stabbed into Willa's gut like a giant sick pin.

Cedric rubbed his square jaw as he frowned at nothing in particular. "Yeah, Jack told me about Anthony's strong left hook. But I wouldn't worry about it. Let me see what I can find out."

"You think Miller will tell you something he wouldn't tell me? You're probably a person of interest, too, you know. He could say maybe you wanted to take over Crown Protection." Willa got a surprise when instead of expressing outrage he dismissed the idea with a wave of one large hand.

He shook his head. "I could have walked off with Jack's business without killing him. Jack was his own worst enemy."

"We definitely agree on *that*," Willa said with a nod.

"Naturally I know Miller won't be forthcoming, but I have sources." Cedric gathered up the files he'd brought in. "You just hang tough. Take care of the kids. We'll get through this."

Willa felt a surge of warmth at his protective stance. She hadn't had a man offer to take care of her for a long time, especially one that didn't have a hand on her thigh as he was making the offer. So maybe she had misjudged the guy. Today he didn't seem like a tight-butt who was trying to grab control of the business.

"Thanks, Cedric. I really appreciate that. I've been feeling a little overwhelmed."

"Miller is following the usual police procedure. They first have to eliminate the family so they can concentrate on real leads." Cedric spoke with confidence as he smiled at her.

"Yeah, you're probably right." Willa felt the tension start to ease from her midsection.

"Look, why don't you let me handle all these details." Cedric swept a hand out gesturing to the file folders. "Most of this stuff is routine, day-to-day dull stuff. I do this on auto pilot."

"You know what? You're absolutely right. To be honest I'm still clueless about the details of running this place." Willa shook her head slowly. "I haven't had a chance to read the state regs, let alone Jack's internal procedure manual. Which by the way shocked me. I had no idea Jack could be so meticulous."

Cedric laughed. "Jack paid attention to detail up to a point. Actually I wrote the manual. Even have a short pamphlet format to train employees."

"Wow, you really do handle your business. Between you and Kay things seem to be rocking along."

"We're committed to Crown Protection, Willa," Cedric said with a crisp nod. "Not that I want to burden you with one more detail."

"No, please. What is it?"

"As I said I really value this company. So I'm willing to make you a very good offer for the company." Cedric nodded again and wore a sympathetic smile. "One less complication for you to deal with, Willa."

"Buy Crown Protection."

Willa turned the idea over in her mind. For weeks she'd had to put up with her snippy, snobby in-laws. Then two of Jack's former skanks had appeared like twin harpies claiming they should have part of his estate. Everything coming at her had put Willa in no mood to be bossed around by an employee, *her* employee according to the will. Willa had fought Cedric on general principle. She'd turned her anger toward men in general, and Jack in particular. Silly really now that she thought about it. The man was right. She didn't know anything about running her own business, much less a private security company.

"Just think it over." Cedric smiled at her. "You've got plenty of time to decide. Settling the estate will take at least a few months."

"Let's hope it won't take long," Willa said with a frown.

"It shouldn't be a big deal. The will is clear and well executed. No other heirs can put forth a claim that will stand up." Cedric leaned toward her. "His family might not be thrilled about it, but there's nothing they can do."

"You don't think?" Willa blinked at him in surprise.

"We've dealt with clients who had estate disputes. Those cases are the most interesting. Anyway, I became fairly familiar with succession law." Cedric shrugged.

"I would think the suspicious spouse investigations would be the most interesting." Willa remembered some of Jack's extramarital exploits and the fireworks they'd caused between them.

Cedric waved a hand dismissing her description. "Mostly the same old, same old. Spouse goes on the Internet then meets someone in a newsgroup or some forum. On average two weeks later they meet face to face. The rest is predictable."

"Well when you put it like that it does sound downright dull," Willa said dryly. "Except of course if you're the wronged spouse."

"Ahem, right." Cedric blushed then changed the subject. "As I was saying though, the succession fights can get really interesting. But since your divorce wasn't final and you're the mother of his minor child it's just a matter of going through the legal process. Parents and siblings have no standing as far as the law is concerned. They might make a lot of noise—"

"I see you know my in-laws," Willa quipped.

"Yes," was Cedric's restrained reply. He grinned back at her. "But the bottom line is they can't do a thing. I'm sure your lawyer will tell you that."

"I haven't gotten around to sitting down with him yet," Willa said with a sheepish expression. "Not about the succession. There was the funeral, my kids, and Jack's condo to deal with. He had it on the market. Anyway, I haven't even been inside. I just handled paying the rent at the office. I can't bring myself to go in there."

"So police say it's okay to move things?" Cedric looked at her sharply.

Willa nodded. "They took his notebook, but they must not have found anything on it. Not that Miller has been chatty with me about anything."

"Hmm. Well, I'll find out as much as I can." Cedric only needed one wide hand to scoop up the files. He stood towering over her, a solid wall of assurance. "In the meantime, don't worry about the business. I've got your back on this."

"I appreciate it, too. Thanks again, Cedric." Willa placed one hand on his muscled forearm. He glanced at her hand then looked into Willa's eyes.

"Er, of course. Excuse me. I have to meet with Charles Wilkinson about security for the high school football play-offs." Cedric fidgeted with the folders as he stepped away from her.

"Sure." Willa drew her hand back. She cursed herself for making the guy feel uncomfortable. Lord, she didn't want to come off like a love-starved widow. The last thing she needed was a sexual harassment complaint. Awkward silence stretched between them as Cedric cleared his throat three times.

"Listen, I didn't mean— " Willa broke off unsure what she should say.

"Not a problem. In fact, I— "

Cedric turned toward her, his gaze drifting from her mouth down to the top button of Willa's silk blend blouse. Willa realized that the first two buttons were undone. The lacy top of her matching champagne camisole peeped out at him. Had she done that in anticipation of this meeting? Hell, maybe she was a love-starved widow. She hadn't had a date in three months, and she'd been separated from Jack for over a year. Thankfully Kay chose that moment to interrupt. After one knock the secretary pushed through the door. When Cedric stepped back Kay glanced at him in surprise. Then she looked at Willa.

"We just finished the meeting." Willa started to button her blouse up to her neck. She stopped when Kay saw the motion.

"Right," Kay replied with a twinkle in her eyes.

"You need something?" Willa crossed her arms.

"There's someone here to see you." Kay pursed her lips as though sucking something bitter. She looked at Cedric. "MiMi Landry."

"Oh crap," Cedric blurted out. "You tell her."

"What is the matter with you two?" Willa looked at him then at Kay. When neither spoke up Willa frowned, started to ask if they'd lost their minds then stopped. "Wait a minute. One of Jack's women."

"And this one is a true blue ribbon b— " Kay bit off the word when Cedric shot her a disapproving scowl. "Sorry, sir."

Cedric merely lifted a dark eyebrow in response then turned to Willa. "I'll talk to Ms. Landry and gently show her the front door."

"Oh please, let me do it," Kay blurted out. "I know how to deal with a loud-mouthed, classless woman like her." She took a deep breath and let it out. "You two have more important things to deal with today. I can take out the trash."

"Kay, really," Cedric admonished. "I know you and Ms. Landry have a history, but— "

A steady rapping on Willa's office door interrupted the back and forth. "Hey, Miss Secretary. I meant sometime *today*, all right? Just give me the files and I'll be on my way. Thank you."

"I told her you weren't in, but I would check your calendar to see when she could come back," Kay whispered.

Willa grunted. "And you thought that sounded like the truth? I've had experience dealing with Jack's women. I got this."

"No, I don't think the office is a good place for..." Cedric seemed to struggle with a way to finish.

"A bloody cat fight? I wouldn't break even one fingernail on Jack's latest bump in the night. He had more miles on him than a Greyhound bus. I'd have spent every waking hour fighting some hoochie if I had tried." Willa yanked open the door as Cedric and Kay gasped in unison.

MiMi Landry blinked in surprise then flashed a dazzling perfect white-toothed smile. "You a new secretary? If so, then it's nice to meet you. I just need one tiny little file then I'll be on my way and out of *your* way. Then you can go back to doing... office things."

MiMi stood with her right hand on her hip. She wore a royal blue cotton knit tank dress and three-inch strappy white sandals. A white and metallic silver handbag swung from her left shoulder. What looked like two-inch sterling silver hoops gleamed beneath the florescent lights of the office. Willa took a moment to covet the fabulous hobo style purse then she smiled back at her.

"No, I'm not the secretary. I'm Mrs. Jack Crown." Willa allowed her smile to freeze in place as she stared at MiMi.

A kaleidoscope of emotions flashed across her smooth brown face. Shock, uncertainty, anger, calculation all took their turn as MiMi obviously worked out what to say next. She must have finally settled on a strategy because she nodded and sighed.

"Yes. How horrible for Jack to lose his life over pocket change. I hope the children are okay," MiMi said with a solicitous expression.

The heifer had nerve. Willa glanced back at Cedric, who cleared his throat and looked down at the top of his spit shined shoes. Kay muttered something under her breath. Then Willa turned to face MiMi again.

"They're holding up as well as can be expected given the circumstances. Thank you for asking. Now how may I help you?" Willa crossed her arms to signal she should bounce on out of there.

MiMi appeared in no mind to take a hint. She adopted a business-like manner. "Jack and I were seeing each other. Now I know this is awkward, given you two were still married. Though you were estranged." Seconds ticked by as they studied each other.

"Hmm," Willa's said. She had no intention of giving this woman more information.

"If we could speak privately," MiMi said, lowering her voice.

When Willa turned to Kay, the secretary mouthed the word "No." Cedric looked like he wanted to be anywhere else. Yet he didn't move. He put the folders he held down onto the table.

"Exactly what is it you need, Ms. Landry?" he said and stepped forward to stand beside Willa. Just then two security guards came in laughing loudly. They waved at him.

"Mornin' everybody," one called out with a grin. The other one merely waved good-naturedly.

"Kay, take the guards to your desk and give them their paychecks and their next assignment. Cedric, I'm sure they want to give you a report of how security went at the art gallery event," Willa said and nodded for them to leave.

"Uh, right." Kay glanced at MiMi once more before she left.

"I've spoken to the event coordinator for the art gallery. Things went fine." Cedric tugged on his necktie when Willa's right eyebrow went up at him. "But I can get a report from them as well. I'll check back with you later to let you know how it went."

"Thanks. Close the door, please," Willa said as he walked out. He paused in the doorway, looked back at the two women then pulled door behind him. When Willa realized he'd left the door open an inch or so she walked past MiMi and shut it firmly.

"I realize you must be very busy, so I won't take up more than a few minutes of your time." MiMi took a seat without waiting for an invitation. She looked around the office as though trying to memorize the new layout.

"How can I help you?" Willa sat at her desk, now thoroughly organized. MiMi seemed to have noticed the lack of clutter as well.

"This is kind of awkward. Under the circumstances I mean." Despite her words MiMi did not appear to be all that nervous.

"You mean the wife meets the mistress kind of circumstance? Yes, I can agree that it's an 'awkward' moment. At least it was the first three times. After that I got used to it." Willa flashed a big smile at her. "The reason for your visit?"

MiMi stopped looking around the office and focused on Willa. She exuded attitude as she lifted her nose in the air. "Listen, I'm not looking for drama. I mean the final divorce decree was a formality."

"True," Willa shot back at her then waited.

"What I mean is— " MiMi affected a congenial expression. "I was saying that there is no reason for us to be angry at each other. I wasn't with Jack before you two separated."

Willa bit off a retort that she only had MiMi's word for that. Instead she nodded. "Believe me, I moved on emotionally from Jack several years ago. Now you came here for a reason?"

"Right. Well, this is the truly awkward part. You see Jack owes me money…, owed me money. You see I helped him out in a business deal and I was supposed to get back my investment plus thirty percent. He had a file with the name Strafford, Inc. on it. It has a gold circle around a blue logo. Maybe you've seen it." MiMi leaned forward.

"No, I haven't. Cedric didn't mention any such business deal to me." Willa gazed back at her, figuring the matter was settled.

MiMi frowned back. "I doubt Cedric had anything to do with this venture. Jack wouldn't have shared something so sensitive with a subordinate."

"First of all Cedric is chief of operations, much more than a subordinate. Secondly, Jack went into business with you?" Willa crossed her arms and continued to stare at MiMi.

"Okay, I'm not just here trying to run a game," MiMi shot back, her upper-class manners slipping. "Now if you let me look for the file, it's probably in that second cabinet, then I'll be outta here."

"I'm not going to let you search my office, Ms. Landry," Willa said in a 'you must be crazy' tone.

MiMi blinked rapidly then smiled. "Of course you're quite right. What was I thinking? Kay probably knows where the old files are now and can— "

"And Jack's estate has to be settled. If you have a claim then have your lawyer send the written agreement you had with Jack to my lawyer. I'll give you his name." Willa pulled a note pad toward her and started to write.

"Written agreement. Well, that's the thing. Jack and I, well, you know our relationship was close, special. We didn't need to put things in writing. We were engaged. Practically," MiMi added when Willa glanced at her left hand looking for a ring.

"Hmm. Witnesses?" Willa stopped writing and looked up at her again.

"We were alone. Look, we're talking about a lot of money. Now things have changed drastically and I need that money. I'm sure he had the details somewhere about the deal and location of the money."

"Even if I wanted to, Ms. Landry," Willa said, making it clear she didn't want to give MiMi even a nickel. "I can't just write you out a large check from Jack's estate. As the executor I have a responsibility to handle things correctly. Not to mention minor children are involved, and both are beneficiaries of the estate."

"But— "

"Just so I can document your claim and discuss it with my attorney, how much money are we talking about?" Willa said.

"Three hundred thousand dollars. Part of that is the equity in the home Jack and I bought," MiMi blurted out. "I have to get that money back to pay the mortgage, insurance, the lawn service..." She blew out a gust of air in exasperation.

"I can see why you're so anxious to find out about this deal. Did you buy the home in both your names?" Willa affected a sympathetic tone.

MiMi started to answer then stopped. Her flustered state quickly changed to a wary one. "The home is mine. I really need to have this matter settled. If you just let me copy the file that would help."

Willa didn't believe her. She wondered how to find out about this sweet valuable asset that just might be part of the Jackson P. Crown estate. "I can't do that, Ms. Landry. However, if you give me information about the house, the loan you took out and any other details it will help. You can document your claim to this estate debt and maybe we can expedite the matter."

This time it was MiMi's turn to look skeptical. "Sure. Listen I have rights under the law. Let's keep this civil, shall we?"

"Under Louisiana law I can't do anything until the will is probated. At that time you can present evidence of this alleged debt— "

"Alleged?" MiMi yelped. Her mouth worked like a gold fish sucking for air and finding nothing.

"And we'll take it from there. Now this may take several months. Of course it could be longer if some other woman contests the provisions of the will." Willa rocked the leather executive chair and watched MiMi with amusement. "Years even."

MiMi pressed a palm to her forehead. "Kay knows. She was here that day when I met with Jack."

"You said you two were alone," Willa reminded her, her voice cool as water dripping from an ice cube.

"In his... I mean your... in this damn office, yes we were alone. But when we left for lunch to celebrate she must have overheard him thank me. Get her in here." MiMi jabbed a finger at the phone on Willa's desk.

Without answering Willa picked up the receiver and hit the button that connected her to Kay's phone. "Kay, step in here a minute. Thanks."

Kay broke some kind of secretarial speed record getting back into the office. Willa saw Cedric out in the foyer across from Kay's desk. He craned his neck for a look into the office but Kay shut the door blocking his view. Not before Willa saw him mutter an expletive.

"Yes, ma'am." Kay kept her gaze on Willa as though MiMi did not exist.

"Ms. Landry claims she had a business arrangement with Jack. Do you happen to recall hearing anything at all about this?" Willa asked placidly.

Before Kay could answer MiMi stood. "It was about ten months, maybe a year before Jack died. I came to his office with an envelope. Okay, so maybe you didn't see it. I had it in my purse when I came in." She chewed her lower lip.

"You were here several times," Kay said. She blinked at MiMi as though puzzled then shrugged. "Sorry."

"Okay, okay. Now think. Take your time. I had on that turquoise wrap silk blend top that Jack bought for me at Neiman Marcus, and a black pencil skirt. We went to Houston." MiMi turned to Willa. "Not that he dressed me as a rule. I was not that kind of mistress, uh, woman."

"Hmm," Willa replied.

"Doesn't ring even one bell," Kay said with a smirk she couldn't conceal.

"Shit," MiMi blurted out and stomped one Gucci sandaled foot.

"Thanks, Kay." Willa smiled at her.

"If you need me again just call." Kay smiled back at Willa. She shot MiMi a smug glance before she walked out.

So as I said before, file a petition with the court to be listed as a debtor to Jack's estate." Willa stood as a signal that it was time for MiMi to leave. "Sorry I couldn't be more help."

MiMi shot her a dirty look. "Paralegals aren't real lawyers, so please stop tossing out legalese as if you're one."

Willa wanted to know more so she pushed down the urge to body slam the heifer. "You know more about me than I know about you, Miss Landry. What is your profession?"

"Beauty consultant and fashion coordinator for a major retail outlet." MiMi squared her shoulders and lifted her nose in the air.

Willa figured that translated as cosmetics counter salesgirl. "I see. Well, unfortunately that's about all I can do for you right now. Unless you can give me a lot more details about the business venture and the house in question."

"Okay, listen. All I know is some of Jack's creditors won't be so patient. Let's just say his other investors aren't as polite as I am. If we can pay them back..." MiMi blinked rapidly. Beads of sweat on her forehead glistened beneath the ceiling lighting overhead. Without looking MiMi yanked a tissue from the box on Willa's desk and dabbed her face dry.

A cold shiver crawled up and down Willa's back. The woman was obviously scared out of her wits. Willa thought about Detective Miller's questions. Maybe he wasn't just asking form questions because it was procedure. What had he found out?

"Could these impatient creditors have had something to do with Jack's death?" Willa asked quietly. MiMi's reaction caused the cold shiver to spread all over Willa. Her cinnamon brown skin went sallow. Suddenly Willa didn't want to know the answer.

"That folder is *my property*. When you find it you'll see that, and I want it back. I'll call you in a few days. Give you time to look. Trust me, you really want to just give it to me" MiMi spoke fast as she snatched up her purse from the floor. She started to leave then changed her mind and spun around to face Willa again. "No need to discuss this with Detective Miller either. I mean this is a civil matter like you said, involving probate and the will and all."

"Conceal information from the police regarding a murder investigation?" Willa raised an eyebrow at her.

MiMi let out a combination hiss and groan as she seemed to realize she'd said too much. She whispered a cuss word. "I'll be in touch. Bye."

Cedric must have met MiMi going as he was coming into the office. The door to Willa's office was still open when he strode in. "What is this about MiMi claiming she was in business with Jack?"

"So you don't know what she's talking about either?" Willa answered his question with her own.

"Nonsense. She's just upset that her little private line of credit and cash source has dried up." Cedric frowned as he studied Willa's expression. "What?"

"Let's find out more about Ms. MiMi Landry. I mean that is what we do here. Background checks." Willa gazed at Cedric.

He blinked rapidly for several seconds then a slow smile spread across his face. "We sure do. I'll be back in two hours. Three max." Cedric started out but stopped. "Anything else I should know?"

"I'll fill you in later."

Once he left and closed her office door behind him Willa picked up the phone. She planned to do exactly the opposite of what MiMi wanted her to, talk to Detective Miller. MiMi Landry was no friend of hers and she sure as hell wasn't going to take her advice.

Chapter 3

Two days later Willa sat in the office of Bradford F. Craft of Craft, Mouton and LaPlace. The law firm where she worked had offices in Houston, Memphis and Washington D.C. Brad, as everyone called him, fingered her written resignation. He read it, tapped a finger on his desk then pursed his lips. All this was part of Brad's thinking process.

"Yes, I know what I'm doing." Willa answered the question she knew was forming on his lips. "I've studied the financials of Crown Protection. The business isn't in the best shape, but with help from experienced staff I think it can turn around."

Brad nodded causing a lock of reddish blonde hair to fall across his forehead. He absentmindedly brushed it back in place. "You, you, you. It's not all about what's good for you, ya know. What about me having to train a new right hand? Huh? What about me?" He faked a frown then grinned at her.

Willa laughed at his antics. "Oh boo-hoo. Poor Brad has to promote that buxom secretary who just finished the paralegal program at LSU."

"I'm not that superficial," he quipped then quickly added, "and don't mention Ingrid."

"The fact that *you* did speaks volumes as they say," Willa said. Ingrid had stolen Brad's heart for six months and ended his second marriage. "But seriously, beside this chance to be my own boss I feel like I owe it to Jack. I mean the whole last wish thing from the departed is pretty powerful. I feel like my kids would think I'm killing off more of his memory if I just sold the agency."

"Or maybe this is a way for you to hold on emotionally. You two were together for almost ten years," Brad offered. When she didn't answer he nodded solemnly as though knowing he was on the right track.

"You're no Dr. Phil, okay? I wasn't even angry at Jack anymore, well not much." Willa waved a hand dismissing the notion. "No, I didn't hate Jack, but I wasn't in love with him anymore either. Just disappointed he couldn't get his act straight. But back to the will."

"Right. Did you know about the amendment, or codicil?" Brad opened a folder with the faxed copy sent over by Jack's attorney."

"No, the other attorney just told me in general what it said and that he would send it to you." Willa leaned forward with a scowl. "What did that chump pull on me?"

"Thought you weren't angry at Jack," Brad replied and flipped to last page of the document.

"I said not much. Now about this codicil?" Willa said. A headache was forming starting at the back of her neck.

"Who is MiMi Landry? Anyway, Jack went to his lawyer a couple of weeks before his death and added that she should have a twenty-five percent interest in net income generated from a contract with Strafford, Inc. That's odd." Brad tapped his fingertips on his expensive desk again and frowned.

"Her debt," Willa said, remembering the flashy woman's visit.

Brad's frown cleared. "Makes sense if she invested in the business. The wording of this amendment could be problematic, but I wouldn't worry about it. So I take it you've met Ms. Landry."

"She showed up like a couple of Jack's other 'lady friends', but her game was unique. She claims she invested money in the business and wanted to be paid back." Willa looked at Bradford. "Can she hold up the will?"

"With the law anything is possible, you know that. Just because a claim is ridiculous doesn't mean the claimant won't have his, or her, day in court."

"While the legal bills pile up," Willa added. She blew out a gust of air at the thought of more complications in her life. Jack Crown left her a legacy of drama. Great. "She also said something about other shady investors, but she wouldn't be specific. Makes me wonder just what the hell Jack had gotten himself into."

Brad's frown returned full force. "Crap. You better tell the police."

"I'm on my way there once I leave here." Willa took the check out of the purse in her lap and reached it to him. "Your fee, sir."

"Forget it. You're getting the kinfolk deal," Brad said after reading the amount.

"Listen, I know what good legal representation costs. I took those funds from the company account. As executor I'm exercising my duty to protect the assets of the estate," Willa said in her best professional voice.

"Exactly. That's our story and we're sticking to it." Brad took the check with the boyish grin that melted female hearts. "And you don't pay any debts until we probate the will. Then she'll have to prove the amount of this debt."

"I know. Thanks for your help, Brad. I mean as busy as you are right now with the Henderson case and — "

Brad waved away her words. "Don't be silly. Besides, this looks like it's going to be interesting."

"In other words you're thrilled to be getting all up in my business," Willa tossed back with a grin.

"Exactly. After all, what are friends for? I'm going to file with the courts to get the succession process rolling."

Willa stood. "Fine. Now I'm on my way to see Detective Miller. What fun I'm having."

***

Twenty minutes later Willa sat across a messy desk gazing at Detective Miller. She could have called him, but Willa wanted to read his face. Not to mention she wanted a look at his workspace. She'd found that observing people in their natural habitats was almost as good as a background check. Detective Miller gazed back, reading her as well. Willa smiled. He smiled, too, as though acknowledging the game they were playing.

"Well I really appreciate your giving me this information. Could still just be a simple robbery gone bad. That ATM at Ray J's convenience store is in a rough part of town, you know. Had three robberies in six months last year. Things had calmed down there until this." Detective Miller tilted his head to one side.

Willa nodded back. The area known as Brookstown was worse than bad. Drug dealing, shootings and prostitution made just walking the streets risky. Since the population swell in Baton Rouge after Hurricane Katrina things had become Wild West. Why Jack had chosen to stop at Ray J's, or why he was in Brookstown at that time of night was a puzzle. Detective Miller must have been good at reading people. Naturally. Willa had decided he knew his job. Being fine didn't hurt either. She bet his looks had gotten more than a few female suspects to relax and talk too much. A fact she should keep in mind.

A beefy man the color of dark chocolate came toward them. He had the rolling gait of a professional wrestler walking across the ring. Although his white shirt and tan pants were neat enough, his big frame seemed stuffed in them.

"This is Detective Don Addison," Detective Miller said without looking at the big man.

"How ya doin'?" Addison said in a gruff voice as he nodded to Willa. He reached out a hand that would intimidate even a rough gang-banger.

"Hi," she replied meekly.

She'd confess to *whatever* if he grilled her for any length of time. Yes, sir. In sixth grade I deliberately tripped Quaneesha Butler down just like she said, Willa imagined herself saying. Then she'd list every other wrong she'd done, including putting the dent in Mama Ruby's battered old Oldsmobile Cutlass back in 1990. Willa allowed her puny hand to get wrapped in Addison's meaty grip. He gently held it for a moment then let go. She wondered if this was some kind of tag team act. But Addison took a seat at the desk next to Miller's. He became engrossed in reading paperwork. Or at least that's what he wanted Willa to think.

"So, Ms. Landry implied that your late husband made some enemies of a business nature," Miller went on.

"Yes." Willa cleared her throat. By now Miller must have found out that Jack had plenty of enemies of a personal nature as well. No surprise given his penchant for chasing women regardless of their martial status. "But Jack was a smart man, Detective Miller. So I would guess anyone who pulled him into a shady deal would be just as smart. Maybe even a professional scam artist."

"Really?" Miller stopped writing and looked at her.

"Yeah. You probably know Jack had a reputation as a player when it came to women. I'm sure you can line up a few husbands or boyfriends that have reason to hate him." Willa shrugged. "Most of his ladies came from upper-class families."

"Interesting." Miller crossed his arms and leaned back. He shot a glance at his partner who looked at him. Addison's response confirmed that he was indeed paying attention to what was said. "How did you two meet?"

"You mean a girl from da 'hood? I'm sure you've checked into my background." Willa smiled when he started to explain. "Don't worry, I'm not sensitive. I was still attending Baton Rouge Community College and took some courses at Southern University. Jack was doing his big man on campus, frat boy thing at SU. We met in a business class, hit it off and the rest is history. His mother was not pleased, but Jack didn't care."

"I see."

"Anyway, most of the husbands of those former debutantes are educated, see themselves as civilized. They wouldn't be going after him with violence. At least I don't see it," Willa said.

"Never can tell," Miller said.

"You should check into it. That kind of thing can be a powerful motive." Willa ignored their barely concealed amusement at her amateur sleuth insights. "I know these so-called society folks better than you. I had to deal with them while Jack and I were married."

"Must have been hard, not being totally accepted into their world," Miller said. Addison had gone back to supposedly minding his own business.

"I didn't give a damn what they thought about me ninety-nine point nine percent of the time," Willa said mildly. Addison let out a laugh then tried to cover it by clearing his throat. Miller smiled at her.

"What about Mr. Crown's family?" Miller asked.

"Call him Jack. He was a friendly kind of guy so he'd probably tell you that. It's weird hearing you call him 'Mr. Crown' all the time." Willa shifted in her chair into a more relaxed position.

"Jack it is then," Miller said with a nod. "So Jack's family wasn't all that welcoming?"

"You've talked to them so I'm sure his mother says I did it, right?" Willa wasn't worried about his suspicions about her. She had an alibi. But Anthony was another matter. Her chest tightened at the thought of her son being handcuffed.

"Mrs. Crown was rather, dramatic." Miller waited for Willa's reaction

"You don't know the half, detective. Not by a long ways." Willa let out a snort. "But I've been blissfully distant from her for the last three years at least, except a few times a month when my daughter visits her. But Jack usually took the kids."

"So they had a relationship with both your kids?" Miller seemed surprised.

"They're not all bad," Willa admitted grudgingly. "Before I had Mikayla they were sweet to Anthony." No need to mention they lavished attention on their "real grandchild" leaving Anthony feeling abandoned.

"And after?" Miller asked picking up on her thoughts.

Willa shelved thoughts of family issues and went on guard again. She flashed an easy smile at Miller. "By that time Anthony was into his own life: skating parties, laser tag, you name it. He had a full social calendar."

"I'll bet." Miller seemed about to go on.

"MiMi Landry?" Willa said, steering him back on the track she wanted to follow.

"Yes, ma'am. We'll check it out. Could be nothing, just an affair or sugar daddy kind of deal. So far we haven't found any evidence that Mr. Crown, Jack I mean, was into anything illegal."

"I see."

Willa caught and held onto that useful nugget of information. Miller had shared precious few. So far no evidence that MiMi Landry's melodramatic behavior had any basis in fact. Relieved Willa looped her purse over one shoulder and stood.

"Thank you for seeing me on such short notice. I know the police have plenty to do without me taking up their time." Willa held out her hand to him. She wondered if Miller picked up on her subtle message not to waste efforts looking at her or Anthony.

"Not at all. The first forty-eight hours are critical. But even though we're long past that timeframe on Jack's murder the investigation is still active." Miller shook her hand then walked her to the lobby.

"Thank you. I know from watching television that the odds are slim you'll find out who killed him," Willa said as she faced him.

"It gets tougher the longer time passes. But you'd be amazed. Eventually somebody talks." Miller nodded at her as though sure there was more to find out.

"I hope so. The thug who robbed and killed an unarmed man needs to be off the streets." Willa pretended not to hear the double meaning in his words. She gave him a cool parting smile. "Goodbye."

***

Two days later a long black car pulled up to Willa's house. She stood at the window with Mikayla, both hands on her daughter's slender shoulders. Anthony, dressed in a dark blue suit, pulled himself off the sofa to join them. Morning sunlight glinted off he polished chrome of the Lincoln limousine. It was one of five family cars for Jack's funeral. Rhodes, the name of the funeral home, was etched in discreet, tasteful silver letters in a corner of a side window.

Mama Ruby bustled in from the kitchen having stored numerous casseroles from her family. Her sisters Ametrine and Beryl followed moments later. All three of the older women seemed to know why Willa and her children stood frozen.

"Okay, babies. Y'all come with us so we can go on out to the car," Aunt Ametrine said in a composed, gentle tone. She took one of Mikayla's hands. She brushed a speck of lint from Anthony's shoulders. Her way of mothering him because she knew he wouldn't hold hands like a little kid.

"Yes, ma'am." Mikayla didn't move. Instead she glanced up at Willa as if asking if she had to go.

Willa wanted to respond. She even opened her mouth to give encouragement, but a sob caught in her throat. Shocked that she felt such an intense reaction Willa put a hand to her chest. Anthony glanced at his mother then put a hand on the top of Mikayla's head.

"Come on, kid. Mama's going to meet us in the car in a minute." When Willa could only nod in response he walked out between his great-aunt and sister, a long arm around both.

"Can't this day just be over?" Willa closed her eyes and put a hand to her forehead.

Aunt Beryl came over and gave Willa a quick hug. "We'll be right there with you, sugar." The white feathers of her hat bounced as she moved. She tucked a black clutch purse under one arm, patted Willa's back then went to the car.

Mama Ruby came with Willa's purse and the house keys. "Now, baby, I know this is hard, but the children need a chance to say goodbye."

Willa had debated, forcefully in fact, against letting Mikayla and Anthony attend the funeral. Mama Ruby, Willa's adoptive father and both aunts had advised for their attendance with equal force. They argued that the children needed a chance to say goodbye, to feel apart of family and doing so was a vital part of the grief process. In a rare moment of unity with her side of the family, Jack's parents had agreed. The real deciding factor had been when Mikayla showed her mother the dress she'd chosen to wear.

"The one with pink and purple flowers. Daddy bought it for me last Easter," Mikayla had said in a strangely grown-up way.

And Willa knew. Mama Ruby was right. The children had to learn the ritual of loss. She'd always imagined one of their older relatives would be the first lesson of course. Even with Jack's crazy love life Willa never would have imagined him leading the way to the grave. Mikayla disappeared into the limo right after Aunt Ametrine. Aunt Beryl followed with Anthony holding her arm.

"Right. Just get through this," Willa whispered and pushed herself forward. She welcomed Mama Ruby's sturdy arm around her waist.

An hour later they were seated in Mount Olive Baptist Church in a sea of relatives. Willa sat with Mikayla and Anthony on the third row pews between two of Jack's female cousins. Mikayla had not wanted to be close to the front, facing her father's casket. Mrs. Crown had tried, but Mikayla refused to sit on the first bench. Her grandmother had only succeeded in making Mikayla clutch Willa tighter. Willa's family had shown up in force to support her, knowing that the Crown family still regarded her as an interloper. Yet Willa forgot everyone but her two children once the organ started playing "Nearer My God to Thee." For the next two hours she concentrated on comforting Mikayla and Anthony. Her son held up well until the end. After going to look at Jack in the casket with other family members he returned with tears streaming down his face.

"Mama, I'm so sorry," he gasped then buried his head into her shoulder.

"That's okay, Anthony," Mikayla said. She left the pew and hugged him around the knees. "Daddy knows you didn't mean it."

"That's right, baby," she said, not wanting her daughter to bring up the fight between Anthony and Jack. Willa froze when she saw a familiar face. Detective Miller stood in the line of mourners filing by. He transferred his intent gaze from Anthony to Willa then nodded. How much had he heard and what conclusion had he drawn from what Mikayla said? She shuddered to think. Seconds later the line moved passed them.

Mama Ruby appeared in the crowd with Willa's adoptive father right behind her. Elton Wilson was a compact man of five feet eleven inches. With powerful arms from working at the docks few men challenged him. He gave Anthony a manly clap on the shoulder and murmured something to him. Anthony nodded and leaned on his grandfather. People closed in on her to offer condolences. Kay and Cedric managed to get through after a while then left. Cedric went on to continue his duties as a pallbearer. After a few minutes Willa pressed a palm to her forehead. She felt dizzy.

"You okay?" her father said with a glance toward the detective. Miller stood at the edge of the crowd.

"Sure, Daddy. Why don't you take the kids out for a minute for me, okay?"

"So y'all not going to the cemetery? Well, I think that's best for the kids," Elton nodded to his wife and a silent message passed between them.

"Come on with me, baby. You need some fresh air, too." Mama Ruby put a protective arm around Willa.

"Maybe you're right." Willa heard her own voice sounding far away.

"Excuse us. Pardon me. Sorry, but Mrs. Crown and her children need to get through." Mama Ruby waved a hand at those around them urging them to move.

Soon Willa realized two of her brothers and her half-sister, Jazz, were helping Mama Ruby by shouldering their way ahead of them. Dion and Shaun, at six feet six inches, stood out the most. His sheer size made a dent in the throng. Shaun wore his characteristic charming smile to help move people. Jazz did her usual, gave them a dirty look that communicated they'd better get out of her way or else. The sedate upper-class folks shrank away. Even so it took Willa and her family a good ten minutes to find their way down a hallway to the church annex, or Fellowship Hall as it was caused. A long table held buffet servers filled with food at one end of the spacious hall. Tables had been reserved for the family. Her father was the first to sit down. Anthony took the chair next to him.

"Y'all just wait here and I'll get you something to eat," Mama Ruby said briskly, ready to take over. She looked around to get her bearings. "There's plates and silverware on that table.

"No food," Willa said quickly, a hand on her stomach.

"Me neither, Nana." Mikayla shook her head. Instead she climbed on her grandfather's knee and rested her small head against his broad chest.

Willa's brother Shaun glanced at Willa and the rest of his adoptive family. Appearing satisfied they were secure for the moment he eyed the food. "I could go for some of that pasta and shrimp."

"I love that stuff. Smells good, too," Dion agreed following his brother's gaze.

Willa gave a short laugh. "Just like always. Twin bottomless pits when it comes to eating."

"Like they didn't just eat at the house," Mama Ruby said and shook her head at them.

"Hey, Anthony. You want some?" Dion tapped Anthony's shoulder.

"I dunno. I'll look at it." Anthony followed his uncles. All three had the same dip and roll hip-hop motion to their stride.

"Look at 'em. Three peas in a pod," Daddy Elton said with a grin. He planted a kiss on Mikayla's braided hair. "You sure you don't want a little bit of something, sweetie pie?"

"No, thank you," she murmured.

Mama Ruby had gone over to inspect the food. Church members came from the kitchen to serve them. She spoke to them briefly then came back to the table. "Nice enough folks. Least they're not acting stuck up like those Crowns."

"Now Ruby," Daddy Elton said gesturing discreetly at Mikayla. "They're kin remember."

"Humph," Mama Ruby replied. Still her expression softened when she looked at her granddaughter. "Anyway, I'll get you something later, Elton."

"I can serve myself. You just relax." Daddy Elton rocked Mikayla gently and hummed his favorite gospel tune.

Dion came back to the table with a plate and sat down. He was about to eat when he stopped at a look from his mother. He whispered a quick prayer over the food then dug in. Shaun joined him moments later.

"I saw that policeman," Shaun said to his brother.

"Just doing his job." Dion shrugged. As a firefighter and certified emergency medical assistant he felt kinship to the police.

"We'll see." Shaun gave a grunt then dug into his food. He didn't even seem to notice Mama Ruby's disapproving glare.

Jazz strolled back from the buffet tables with a dissatisfied air. "I don't eat from folks I don't know," she said loudly.

Several of the church ladies gasped then whispered to each other. Two male church ushers observed her as well, but with a different kind of interest. They watched the swish from east to west of the deep purple flared skirt as Jazz's hips moved. Willa mused that her sister had provided days of gossip for the Mount Olive hospitality ministry. Her aunts appeared talking animatedly, no doubt comparing notes on who was among mourners that they knew. Dion glanced as if to make sure the rest of their family was preoccupied. Then he leaned over to Willa.

"Anything wrong? I'm just saying that detective looked mighty interested in us," Dion said, his voice low.

Shaun leaned as well. "Yeah. Mama told us he's askin' questions about Anthony. You know I can get the boy a lawyer."

"I don't need help. And Shaun, I worked with top attorneys," Willa replied, her voice low as well. "Not that Anthony needs one."

"Those Ivy League white dudes you work with are smart. I'll give 'em that. But they used to dealing with corporate fraud and stuff. All those rich dudes got connections. Most of them don't even do time." Shaun snorted. "And they steal a helluva lot more money than any small time thief I know."

"What Shaun is trying to say, Willa, is you need lawyer who knows our world," Dion said sharply, then nodded at his twin brother. "Now shut up about it. Anthony is coming."

Anthony returned with a plate loaded with nothing but Swedish meatballs. Willa hoped his appetite was a good sign. With the keen sense of radar most adolescents had Anthony eyed them. He seemed to know he'd been the topic of discussion. Still he said nothing as he sat down farther from the rest of the family. Papa Elton nodded at him from his seat across the wide round table. Anthony tried on a brief smile that didn't stick. He examined a meatball then nibbled it cautiously.

"Pretty good, huh?" Shaun said patting his mouth with a napkin.

"It's awright," Anthony replied after a few chews.

Mikayla perked up as she watched her brother eat. She slipped from her grandfather's knee and went to her brother. Anthony shoved her away when she reached for a meatball. Mikayla shoved him back with a baby sister pout. Her big brother grinned, then he speared one on a fork and held it up for her. Soon they were giggling and poking each other with elbows. Three young cousins wandered in and the two of them joined them in horseplay. Willa sighed with relief.

"Maybe they'll get through this day without too much trauma," Willa said leaning close to Dion.

"They'll be fine," Shaun replied then licked buffalo wing sauce from a finger.

"Sure they will," Dion echoed. He paused from eating long enough to give Willa a quick hug of reassurance.

"Look at those three. Up in here trying to take over." Willa nodded toward the buffet line.

Aunt Ametrine had somehow managed to join the Mount Olive members. The family came in first. Under her direction they were seated and served. Beryl wore clear plastic gloves and put hot rolls and corn muffins on plates in an assembly line. Mama Ruby came back with their purses and sat down. Papa Elton followed her with a plate in each hand for both of them.

"Ametrine knows some of those ladies in the kitchen. Wouldn't you know it, she's found a way to boss folks around." Mama Ruby shook her head as she dumped three purses on the chair next to her.

"Humph. I noticed Beryl's got next to some of the Mount Olive brothers who are serving." Papa Elton jerked a thumb over his shoulder without looking around at the subject of his comment.

Shaun, Dion and Willa followed the gesture. Sure enough Aunt Beryl, forty-nine and never married, was beaming at a man standing next to her. His white hair made him look quite distinguished. Seconds later she leaned over to comment to the shorter, plumper man to her right.

"Looks like Auntie B has her own buffet line," Shaun quipped with a grin. He bit into another boneless buffalo wing.

"Lord, have mercy look at Jazz." Willa hissed sotto voice so as not to alert the children.

Jazz tossed her long vibrant auburn weave and laughed. The dark-suited man next to her blushed with pleasure at her reaction to his words. Jazz leaned closer as though to make a point. Willa suspected it was to give the guy a better view of her décolleté dress. Another man joined them. Then another. Her half-sister stood at the center of three attentive men. A group of the Mount Olive church ladies served food and scowled at them.

"Probably some of her admirers from the Candy Girls club," Shaun blurted out with another wide grin.

"Please don't talk so loud," Aunt Ruby said with a light swat to his left shoulder.

"What? It can't be a secret that Jazz does 'interpretive dance' at Candy Girls," Shaun said in an exaggerated whisper then laughed.

"Humph," was Papa Elton's only response. Still he shook his head in resignation. "We tried, Ruby. And Lord knows Ametrine was hoarse from preaching to the girl."

"That sanctimonious naggin' probably pushed her over the edge into dancing half-naked," Aunt Ruby replied, her long held argument with Aunt Ametrine rising again.

"Let's change the subject," Willa mumbled when she saw Anthony approach. Then she smiled at him. "Your cousins invite you over to swim in their new pool?"

Anthony dropped down onto the chair next to Shaun. "Ain't my cousins."

They all grew quiet. Willa shot a glance across the room. The Crowns and extended family seemed to have enveloped Mikayla into their midst. Mikayla nodded at something one of Jack's sisters, said then looked around for Anthony. She waved for him to come back. Sharon, Jack's oldest sister, distracted her with a piece of cake. With outrage bubbling to the surface Willa stood and walked toward the table where Jack's parents sat. Her mother was at her side in seconds.

"Don't start anything in here, Willa. This is the man's funeral. He can't rest in peace if you start a fight." Mama Ruby huffed with the effort to keep pace and talk, too. She gripped Willa by the arm and stopped her progress. Then she plastered on a smile at those who had glanced at them.

"Anthony needs to feel accepted and loved, especially now. Jack meant just as much to him as he did to Mikayla," Willa shot back.

"I know that, baby," Mama Ruby said through the smile. "But we don't want Detective Miller to get any ideas." Without moving she shifted her eyes to the left.

Willa followed her glance. Sure enough Detective Miller stood with a plate chatting, but his gaze was fixed in their direction. Even though it made her cheek muscles hurt Willa forced a smile. Then she continued walking toward the Crown clan. MiMi appeared from behind a column like a magician's assistant. What now?

"Girl, I saw the whole thing. They treat me the same way. Tell those Bs and Bs where to get off," MiMi whispered while smiling as though they were exchanging pleasantries. "Just not here with everybody in the world, God and the policeman watching."

"Excuse me, where the hell did you come from, and why do you think I'm your new best friend?" Willa shot back at her.

"Not now, baby. Bad idea," Mama Ruby whispered in a singsong warning. "Who is this?"

"MiMi Landry, ma'am," MiMi broke in before Willa could speak. "I'm so happy to meet you. Lovely service wasn't it? We'll all miss dear Jackson so very much."

"I'm Ruby Wilson, Willa's mama. Yes, we will," Mama Ruby smiled back at her in gratitude. "Won't you join us?"

"You are so sweet to ask. Thank you," MiMi gushed.

Before Willa could object she was guided away from the Crown family. With MiMi to her left and Mama Ruby to her right Willa would have had to make a scene to stop them. The two women batted chitchat across Willa like a ping-pong ball as they walked. Since everyone was clustered at or near the food Mama Ruby steered them to an empty corner.

"Now what did you say your name was, sugar?" Mama Ruby bathed MiMi in a warm glowing smile.

"MiMi Landry. Actually my name is Mionne Loren Landry. My granddaddy owned Landry Laundromats for years." MiMi lifted her nose with pride.

"No! I remember back in the day when all they had was that one little laundry place on East Boulevard. Didn't your daddy work there?" Mama Ruby seemed not to notice Willa fuming next to her.

"Every summer from the time he was twelve until he got out of college. That's where he met my mama." MiMi gazed around the room as she talked.

"Right, your mother Pauline." Mama Ruby's glow faded a bit as she stared at MiMi.

Willa stopped fuming long enough to read her mother's expression. She could almost see wheels turning. She started to ask a question, but Mama Ruby gave a slight shake of her head. The gesture meant she would tell her later.

"So how do you know each other?" Mama Ruby said in a careful, neutral tone.

"MiMi was Jack's *friend*." Willa twitched an eyebrow up at her mother, a signal that MiMi caught.

"We were also business partners. As a matter of fact since Willa has inherited Crown Protection we're partners now," MiMi replied with a nod when Mama Ruby's mouth formed a wide circle.

"No, we're not," Willa said in a voice like a finely honed filet knife. "Mama, would you mind giving us moment?"

"Sure. Nice meeting you, Ms. Landry." Mama Ruby blinked at Willa then MiMi.

"MiMi to you, Mrs. Wilson. Bye-bye." MiMi gave her a fond pat on the arm as Mama Ruby wandered off glancing over her shoulder every few steps.

Willa worked to steady her temper and her nerves. She hardly knew where to begin. "First, how dare you just sashay in here like you are— "

"Like what? Like someone who cared deeply for Jack, yes, even loved him? I needed to say goodbye. I didn't read anywhere that this was a by invitation only funeral." MiMi dabbed at a corner of one eye with a tissue.

"Girl, please. We both know you were digging for gold when you latched onto Jack," Willa shot back. "And he was, well it's obvious what *he* wanted."

"True, I have never been one to date broke men," MiMi replied with no trace in her tone or expression that she was offended. "The Lord was good to me in the looks department, and men like what they see."

"Yeah, and you give them a good look, too."

Willa nodded to the form fitting deep blue knit dress MiMi wore. The faux wrap front dipped just low enough to show a hint of generous cleavage. The fabric and style draped her figure in an elegant sexy way. The hem stopped at the knee revealing Vegas show girl legs. In truth Willa stifled a pang of envy that MiMi could carry off that look so well.

"You may not believe this, but Jack came to mean a lot more to me than a pay day," MiMi said with a sniffle. She searched her designer clutch handbag then pulled out a tissue.

"I don't believe it," Willa answered.

She was about to go on to express more of what she thought but stopped. They were being watched. Detective Miller said something to the beefy man next to him. His partner glanced in Willa's direction then nodded. Miller headed straight for them. Mama Ruby and Aunt Ametrine waylaid him. The man gave them a brief polite smile, a few words then started off again.

"Have you spoken to Detective Miller?" Willa plastered a fake smile on as she asked the question.

MiMi paused in her sniffles. Her expression sobered for an instant as she looked sideways in his direction. "He's left me a couple of messages. I've been busy," she said through her own fake smile.

"You really should have called him back," Willa added quickly before Miller came too close.

"I had to do more research before I could, er, have a little talk with him," MiMi whispered then faced Miller as he arrived. She flashed a dazzling smile at him. "Hello and thank you so much for coming."

"Hello, sorry for your loss," Miller said to her then blinked hard. He transferred his gaze to Willa. "I mean, Mrs. Crown so sorry for *your* loss."

"That's quite alright, Detective Miller. We know each other," MiMi said.

"We know *of* each other," Willa corrected without looked at MiMi. "We only recently met actually."

"But we have no reason to be anything but friendly. In fact we're business partners," MiMi added. "By odd coincidence."

"Really? How interesting. Well, you'll both be happy to know we're making some progress on the case. The store security video camera footage shows several people entering the store around the time Mr. Crown was there. We have to locate them, not an easy task. Still we did get lucky." Detective Miller watched their expressions as he spoke.

"Lucky how?" MiMi spoke up first to Willa's annoyance.

"The store also has an outside camera so we have a few full and partial license plates. That should help us find those folks. At least some of them." Miller nodded.

"Oh good," MiMi replied. She cleared her throat.

Willa couldn't help but notice her happy tone seemed superficial. "That is wonderful news. I hope you track down the crooks and lock them up for a long time."

"We're going to do our best, ma'am. Again, my condolences." Miller left them. He headed for the door. As if on cue his beefy partner crossed the room to meet him. The men left nodding to other mourners as they moved through knots of people.

"Damn," MiMi mumbled. A church member strolled by with a tray full of plastic cups filled with red punch. She grabbed one and drank from it.

"Trouble?" Willa smiled, for the first time happy to be standing next to MiMi.

"Listen, we need to talk about Jack's activities. Things neither one of us want Miller to find out about until we can." MiMi looked at her. All traces of the giddy mistress gone from her serious expression.

"Oh? Since I wasn't in bed with Jack when it came to business, then I don't see why I should care." Willa patted her hair into place and grinned at MiMi.

"Because it could destroy the company he took so long to build. And because of your son," MiMi said, her voice barely above a whisper.

Chapter 4

Willa rubbed her eyes. They burned as though grains of salt had been sprinkled in them. MiMi's ominous words kept bouncing around in her head. She glanced at the clock for the fifth time in ten minutes. Cedric had promised to meet her at seven. Since she'd been unable to sleep, Willa got to the office at six thirty. She had finished off two cups of coffee already. Her Aunt Beryl had spent the night to give Willa support and help with the kids. An early riser, Aunt Beryl would clean up, cook the kids breakfast and get them off to their respective schools without breaking a sweat.

"Hey, boss lady," Cedric strolled in with a white paper bag in one hand. "You're a real go-getter to be here earlier than me."

"Beats staying at home not sleeping and pretending nothing's bothering me." Willa brushed her hair back. She'd spent less than a minute making sure it looked decent. Cedric's smile faded a he gazed at her. "What?"

"Look, you just buried Jack two days ago. Why don't you let me handle the business." Cedric put the bag down on her desk.

"In other words I look like hell and should stay home so I won't scare away clients." Willa grabbed the bag and opened it. She took out a cinnamon roll wrapped in wax paper. "Thanks. I need sugar and carbs. Loads of creamy icing on top. Heaven."

"A big mug of coffee will round out our nutritious breakfast." Cedric poured two mugs full from the pot Willa had prepared. He handed her one and sat in one of the chairs facing her desk. "You okay?"

"Ah yes. The universal male question that means, 'Please don't go all girly on me and start bawling'," Willa quipped. She licked creamy icing from the end of her finger then plucked a napkin from the stack he'd provided. "Don't panic. I'm not going to."

"Right, tough girl." Cedric sat down with only a cup of coffee.

"Lady, tough lady, thank you very much. Ah, now you're worried that I'm going to be abrasive and pushy." Willa savored a small piece of the cinnamon roll and sipped coffee. The combination of flavors was a pure delight. She swallowed and sighed. "Like I said, heaven."

"Mickey's has the best donuts, cinnamon rolls and biscuits in Baton Rouge." Cedric gazed at her with a small smile on his broad face. "So you've got us males all figured out, huh?"

Willa laughed out loud. "Please. Would I have married Jack if I had the answers to the mysteries of men?"

"Just because he was crazy enough to lose you doesn't mean you were at fault," Cedric said quietly.

His comment, but even more than that the look in his eyes, caught Willa off guard. She gulped more coffee to gain a moment and to craft a response. His gaze unsettled her thoughts too much. She mumbled, "Uh, thanks."

"I liked Jack as a friend. Respected him as businessman and my boss, but his personal choices were less than admirable." Cedric went on in a more business-like tone. "Which brings us to MiMi Landry."

"Right, right," Willa said quickly, grateful for the change of subject. Maybe she had imagined that look in his black coffee eyes. "Mionne Loren Landry of the Landry Laundromat empire from back in the day."

"You've been doing your own research I see." Cedric looked at her in surprise.

"She graciously shared that at the funeral. Which reminds me. My mama knows the family I think," Willa replied and glanced at the clock. "Eight o'clock in the morning is way too early to call mama."

Mama Ruby had given up being a foster mother four years ago deciding she was too old. Children arrived on her doorstep with challenges that she'd felt were just too rough on a woman her age. After twenty-three years of working hard to heal broken kids Willa figured she deserved a rest. So her mother concentrated on running her restaurant and lounge these days.

Cedric put down his coffee mug then pulled a note pad from his shirt pocket. "I've got pretty good info. The family has been in Baton Rouge since the early twenties at least. She was born here. Like you said, the grandfather opened a coin operated laundry business back in the late fifties. The family ran it until the early eighties. Neighborhood changed, crime became a serious problem. The original storefront was robbed three times in one year.”

“Ah yes, the rise of crack in the black community. Lovely history.” Willa shook her head.

“Few jobs, lots of street drugs,” Cedric said with a frown. “Not a good combination. Anyway, business was a struggle and that didn’t help. The kids convinced the old man to retire. Sold off the equipment and closed the three small stores.”

“Well, grandpapa did something right. He had three locations. Must have known how to handle his business. So they’ve got money?” Willa nibbled more cinnamon roll.

“There was some kind of family scandal back in the day. Seems to have been around the time her grandfather retired. I can’t find anyone old enough who knows the details.” Cedric frowned at his notes as though irritated with the information hole.

“That’s where my mama comes in. Between her and the Amen Chorus I’ll bet I can find out,” Willa grinned at him.

“The who?”

“Her older and younger sisters. My aunts will give up the goods all the time professing not to be gossips.” Willa waved a hand in the air. “My daddy is a gold mine of off the record facts, but I always start with the ladies.”

Cedric laughed. “You will turn into an ace private eye yet.” He went back to his notes. “They sold one location to a chain of dry cleaners. The kids went on to become even more educated than the parents. Two daughters are doctors. Three sons own businesses and one works for a Fortune 500 company.”

“Which is MiMi’s dad?” Willa asked.

“That would be Hillary Landry. He’s the fourth son. He worked for the state of Louisiana for twenty-eight years. Got pretty high on the food chain until, then there was a shake-up back in eighty-nine. He got dumped into a dead end job. Some political stuff. Retired four years ago. He and his third wife live in Houston." Cedric flipped a page. "MiMi is the middle child."

"Oh-oh, middle kid syndrome." Willa smiled.

"Daddy's girl sounds like. Anyway, she went to Spelman University. She's AKA. Came back to Baton Rouge after a month or so of grad school. Too much partying, too little studying," Cedric flipped the notebook closed.

"Mama and Daddy found out and cut off the funds."

"Exactly. She's worked in retail since ninety-two. Apparently met Jack at some social function. They it off and..." Cedric shrugged as though reluctant to go on.

"You don't have to be delicate about it. I know the drill. So how 'close' were they?" Willa had to admit she liked his old southern gentleman manners. His mama raised him right.

"According to Jack's best pal Roderick pretty close."

"You got Roderick Carrington, IV to talk? Damn, you're good. Those old frat boys generally keep a tight lip, especially the old family types." Willa blinked at him. She'd been on the receiving end of their snobbish tolerance of her more than she cared to remember.

"I'm Omega Psi Phi." Cedric shrugged again when Willa's mouth dropped open. "Poor kid from the Oklahoma Street projects makes good."

"Apparently," Willa murmured. His stock went up a few more ticks in her mind.

"Thanks. Anyway, they were pretty into each other according to Rod. Not that Jack didn't sample other products. I mean.— " Cedric coughed.

"So that's what you men are calling it now. I'm not a bit surprised. There were only a few good-looking women Jack met he didn't 'sample'. Inherited that from his daddy I hear." Willa grunted. His two older brothers weren't exactly examples of morality either. One had made a pass at Willa once.

Cedric exhaled nosily. "Moving on. That's about it for the personal business. Jack and MiMi did the usual stuff. Attended Greek social functions, ate out at nice restaurants, went on trips to the Caribbean."

"Humph." Willa knew the drill indeed.

"Trips to Hong Kong and Paris— "

"What? That chump never took me to Paris!" Willa scowled at Cedric as though it was his fault. "I've always wanted to see Paris. Don't even tell me he took her on an expensive VIP tour of Africa."

"Not that I know of," Cedric said and pursed his lips.

"Right, right. I'm not going to trip. Go on." Willa decided not to press him even though his answer didn't ring true.

"I can't find anything in our company files about this Strafford, Inc. MiMi talks about. It's weird. I'm not saying Jack told me everything, but why would he do something like that?" Cedric shook his head slowly. "Just doesn't make sense."

"Maybe she was holding something over his head. Let's find out if she's got some connection to a Strafford, Inc. Maybe her family or friends. Could be she owns stock in the company or something." Willa rocked the chair back and forward hard. She fished around until she found an old battered pack of gum in Jack's desk. She absentmindedly polished off the sticky sweet cinnamon roll.

"I don't know. Ms. Landry doesn't strike me as the business mogul type," Cedric replied and sipped more coffee.

"Willa patted crumbs from her lower lip and swallowed. "Hell yes. That heifer is more into *doing* the business mogul types."

"Uh, yeah. I was going to say something like that. Anyway I did dig up information on that company. They have three main divisions. One makes shipping boxes, mainly for companies overseas. They seem to deal with retail products manufactured in China, Pakistan and Indonesia."

"Huh? What's that got to do with security guards?" Willa reached into the bag and got a donut.

"Not sure yet. Maybe he was negotiating with them to do their security systems in plants here. We talked about branching into that or maybe even e-security. Internet and intranet security is big these days." Cedric nodded as though sure Willa would understand.

"I'll bet." Willa had no clue except that she knew the value of a good firewall.

Cedric's handsome face had the shadow of a smile. "I'll explain it to you more one day."

"Didn't fool you one bit, eh? Go on, Mr. Know-It-All." She flipped her fingertips at him.

"Nope. Anyway, Strafford, Inc. also has a division that ships recycled materials for construction and electronics. According to the company website they're just starting that one." Cedric picked up another folder and flipped it open. "Mostly what I've found are press releases and not a lot else. I'll try digging deeper."

"You think maybe some of his old frat brothers hooked him up with Strafford?" Willa took a sip of coffee and wrinkled her nose.

"I hadn't thought that far ahead yet. Good idea. Several of his classmates from college are in the corporate world now. You have an instinct for investigating." Cedric took the mug from her. He went into the private restroom and dumped the cold coffee out. Then he came out, poured her a fresh serving and handed the mug back to Willa.

She took a minute to appreciate a good-looking man serving her without a second thought. <u>It's good to be the boss lady</u>. "Thank you."

Still following his own train of thought, Cedric only nodded then sat down again. "Now MiMi comes from one of the prominent black families in town. All those folks run in the same circles."

"And she's Alpha Kappa Alpha." Willa thought back to the parties and lunches she'd attended. "Kinda made me claustrophobic seeing the same faces all the time. Those people dropped names so much I wanted to scream."

"And discuss their vacations, business perks, etcetera. I know." Cedric grinned. "They're not so bad when you get to know them."

"Yes, they are," Willa shot back. "You socialize with that crew, a poor kid from the projects?"

"Frat brother, remember? They're very loyal and clubby that way, even with my background. Married into the circle, too." Cedric shrugged.

"Where's your ring?" Willa blurted out then pressed her lips closed. He'd taken her by surprise with that one.

"Divorced three years now. Two sons."

"Didn't mean to get in your personal life." Willa suppressed a sigh of relief, and then wondered at her reaction.

"Not a problem. Besides, I know quite a lot about your personal life. Only fair I think." Cedric smiled at her and Willa smiled back.

"I don't know about you, but Jack's family tolerated me at first. Then we had a few run-ins and well." Willa let out a sigh at the memory of tense holiday dinners with the Crown family.

"I got along with the family a whole lot better than I did with my ex-wife," Cedric quipped. "Anyway, I'll keep looking to find out more."

"Sure would help if we could find this mystery file MiMi keeps talking about. You don't have any ideas where Jack might have hidden it? No wall safe or hidden door leading to a secret room?" Willa swung her chair around looking as she spoke.

"That would be great but, no." Cedric shook his head and wore an amused expression.

"Been watching too many suspense movies, I guess. Okay, then we keep looking."

"Right." Cedric tapped closed the file but did not stand. "Have you done any thinking long-term? About the business I mean."

"I've been just trying to keep my nose above water at least with everything going on at once. But sounds like Jack and you had good ideas about where to take Crown Protection."

"Thanks. When you're ready we can talk about future directions once the estate is settled. Remember, I am interested in buying the business. Of course if you're not ready for that we can discuss other options," Cedric added with a crisp nod.

"Other options," Willa echoed. She gazed at him steadily.

"Sure. I'm willing to run the business for a period of time, with you as a partner of course. That way you can preserve your interest in the business while I grow it. I'll increase the value of Crown Protection. ” Cedric looked at Willa with a kindly expression. “Being a parent I know you’re thinking of the future of your kids.”

“Right. Well you’ve given me food for thought,” Willa said, her throat tight with restrained anger. The cinnamon rolls and coffee were a ploy to soften her up for this pitch?

“I have a proposal if that will help. I know how much is on your plate now. I outlined the options so you can weigh which one is best for you. No rush.” Cedric stood. “Be right back.”

“You’ve already got it all written up?” Willa blinked at him hard.

“Rough, real rough draft. I’ll e-mail it to you. Oh, and get on this Strafford thing while I’m at it. Need anything else before I go?” Cedric seemed energized, eager to get the ball rolling on his future.

“No thanks,” Willa replied mechanically.

“Talk to you later then. Bye.” Cedric strode out, and had the nerve to whistle as he left.

“Yeah, bye.”

Willa stared at the closed door and listened to the quiet ticking of the fancy clock on her wall. Her paranoid evil twin spoke up. That other Willa had been born out of necessity when she was a kid. She’d survived more times than she could count because of her “twin.” First a crack crazy mother, the predator men that came in and out of their lives, four foster families and more. Willa had finally suppressed that constantly angry, suspicious part of herself after two years with Mama Ruby and Elton. But every now and then that twin popped up to help her out of a dicey situation. What if Cedric was lying about the Strafford file and knew more than he was telling? She hit a key on the computer to stop the abstract screen saver from twirling around. Time to do some of her own research.

***

By seven-thirty that night Willa had finished a days work. After Aunt Beryl and Mama Ruby both assured her the kids were fine with them, Willa decided to visit her sister. Jazz lived in a section of the city that used to be nice. After a series of changes in the neighborhood, the area around North Blackwood Boulevard had become wild. Instead of hardworking blue-collar families, the enclaves of apartment buildings and duplexes now housed way too many who had no jobs and too much time on their hands. How they filled up the hours was the problem.

Willa punched in Jazz's phone number and spoke into the intercom. The electric gate rattled opened thirty seconds later. She pulled into one of the two parking spaces in front of Jazz's townhouse. The Tudor styled two-story homes looked neat and quiet. The residents paid a price to keep it that way. Willa resisted the urge to wave at one of several security cameras installed strategically under the eaves of the buildings. When she got out of the car, a tall woman was walking a pair of fox terriers with matching lilac ribbons around their necks. Frankie wore her auburn weave pulled back into a long ponytail. Her white T-shirt had the words "Total Woman" in fluorescent pink across the chest. Dark blue Capri leggings hugged her muscular legs.

"Hey, Frankie. How's tricks?" Willa waved to the statuesque transsexual.

"Girl, please," Frankie shot back. "If tricks was any good I'd quit that stupid day job I got. How you doin', baby?" She gave Willa a brief sisterhood hug.

"I'm doin'," Willa replied with a shrug. "I refuse to complain."

"Amen. No room on the pity pot around here. You just keep hangin' in there, sweetie. Have they caught the no good little thug what killed Jack?" Frankie pulled on the leashes to keep Paris and Milan in line.

"Not yet."

"Well, I'm keepin' my ears open. If I hear anything at the club I'll give you a call." Frankie co-owned a dance club called Juke Joint across town.

"Thanks, Frankie. I appreciate it. How's Howard doing these days?" Willa looped arms with Frankie as they both walked in the direction of Jazz's front door.

"Stubborn and asshat crazy as always. Love me some Howard though." Frankie laughed and shook her head. They had been together for fifteen years, ever since Frankie had the operation to become a woman. "Girl, let me get back home before he comes looking for me. He's got some stupid idea that this guy in building twelve wanna get with me. I'm like, 'Howard, please. That man is gay. I'm a girl now. Okay?'"

Willa burst out laughing. "He thinks a gay guy wants you?"

"Nah, that man ain't gay. I just told Howard that to finally shut him up. Brother is fine, too." Frankie fanned her face to indicate the man in question was hot.

"You better behave. Don't mess up a happy home for a little excitement," Willa warned, shaking a finger at her.

"Girl, you right. But Howard better quit talkin' before he gives me ideas. See you later. Look, there he is now." Frankie waved at her significant other. "Tell Jazz I'm gonna call her later."

"Hey, Howard," Willa called out and waved at him.

"Afternoon. Hope you takin' good care of yourself," Howard called back.

"Doing my best." Willa smiled at him.

She watched Frankie and Howard meet each other halfway then walk toward their home. She went up the short walkway to Jazz's door and rang the doorbell. A hip-hop rhythm bonged through the walls. Seconds later Jazz opened the front door and waved her in. Jazz tapped the wireless headset she wore to indicate she was on the phone. She wore a flowing caftan with a revealing slit up the front. The rainbow colors of the fabric matched her painted toenails and fingernails. Rhinestones glued to each nail completed the look. Yet somehow the style did not look overdone on Jazz. Her long flowing hair, a weave, was piled high on her head.

"Yeah, Lorraine, I heard you. You need to just fire her ass, all right? Nah, I don't wanna hear that sh— " Jazz glanced at Willa then gestured with one hand. "Get yourself something to drink and eat. You know where everything is. I'll be with you in a minute."

"Sure."

Willa walked through the spacious living room to Jazz's kitchen. She wanted to hear the rest of that conversation with Jazz's boss at Candy Girls, but her half-sister went upstairs with the phone. After getting a plastic bottle of iced tea Willa leaned against the counter top and looked around. Dirty dishes sat stacked in both sides of a double sink. Several cups with cold coffee were scattered around and corn flakes littered another portion of the counter.

"Geez, the maid has the year off," Willa muttered.

She went back to the living room. Willa grunted at the contrast. This room was fairly tidy, if you didn't count the sequined thongs and skimpy halters scattered on the sofa. To be safe Willa selected to sit on the matching small sofa. A hard object poked her in the ribs. Moving away from the source of her discomfort, Willa glanced down at something round and shiny. She pulled out a set off handcuffs. Willa used the tips of her fingers to pick them up. She dropped them into a wicker basket next to the sofa. The rest of the room was stuffed with an odd assortment of bric-a-brac, including a dozen collectible dolls. Mardi Gras masks decorated one wall. A portrait of Jazz in one of her costumes hung over the fireplace.

"Aunt Ametrine would have a stroke if she saw this place," Willa whispered. Then she giggled as she thought up schemes to make that happen.

Jazz came back at that moment. She gathered up the lingerie into a ball and tossed them onto another chair then flopped onto the sofa. She propped her long brown legs on the sofa cushion next to her. "So what up?"

"Everything, including the rent," Willa quipped.

"I heard that," Jazz retorted. She reached down and came up with a glass of wine that had been on the floor. "Sorry about all the crap that went down for you and the kids. Life's a B."

"Yeah." Willa took a swig of tea from the bottle in her hand.

"So what brings you to Sodom and Gomorrah, pray tell?" Jazz swept a hand out.

"Don't start. Besides, that would be Candy Girls," Willa said. The club where Jazz performed her "erotic interpretive dances" was supposedly an upscale gentlemen's club.

"Now who's starting something?" Jazz threw back at her. "Every year you sound more and more like Ametrine."

"That's going too damn far," Willa tossed a small round fringed pillow at Jazz's head.

Jazz laughed as she batted it aside. "Uh-huh. So tell me the truth. To what do I owe this unexpected pleasure?"

"Can't I visit my baby sister just because?"

Willa shrugged leaned back against another larger pillow at her back. She frowned then pushed it aside. The room was crowded with things, like the rest of the townhouse. Jazz seemed intent on making up for not having her own possessions as a child. The result was any place she'd ever lived was crammed with an odd assortment of stuff. Although the dolls gave Willa the creeps, she knew what they represented to Jazz.

Her sister snorted and emptied the wine glass. She went to a small bar in one corner of the room and poured more wine into it. "Yeah, right."

"Look, this thing with Jack— "

"Him being dead you mean," Jazz broke in sharply. Never one to dodge the real deal, Willa's retreat from facing harsh truths grated on Jazz. When Willa flinched, Jazz stopped before drinking more wine. "Hell, I shouldn't have said that. Just habit."

That was the closest Jazz had ever come to apologizing, to anyone. Willa nodded and looked down at the strange orange carpet. "Anyway, you never know. We should be closer. And I got stuff coming at me so fast I don't know who to trust."

"Ruby, Ametrine and Beryl. They always did care about you," Jazz replied. She perched on one of three leather bar stools.

"And they care about you, too." Willa looked at her.

"Uh-huh." Jazz's expression implied she did not want to have that old argument again.

Willa did not want to go there either. Jazz had bounced from home to home while Willa had been adopted. Though Mama Ruby had tried to help her, Jazz had proved too much of a challenge. "I'm just saying you and I should do stuff together."

Jazz sighed and put the glass on the bar. "Yeah, okay."

"What?"

"Nothing. That's fine. We'll do lunch or something ever so often. Feel better?" Jazz took a large clip out of her hair. The weave cascaded down.

"I mean it, Jazz."

"I said fine." Jazz flipped thick waves over one shoulder. "Lunch, diner, a movie. Whatever."

"Okay, great," Willa pressed on forcing cheer into her tone. She wanted to say more, to hug Jazz and talk about their past. A big lump of fear anchored Willa to the sofa cushion. Maybe one day.

"And I'm worried about Anthony. You know, he's hanging out with these kids from the hood, getting into trouble. Nothing serious yet," she added quickly when Jazz opened her mouth to ask. "I'm just saying. You know how fast nothing serious becomes a whole lot of something real bad."

Now she had Jazz's attention. Anthony and Jazz had always had a special bond. When Jazz had learned her seventeen-year-old sister was pregnant she'd been one happy eleven-year-old kid. Once Anthony was born his tiny feet hardly touched the floor or ground for Jazz carrying him on her hip. She'd decided to be a very hands on aunt.

"He's awright. Just don't ride his back about it. Ain't nothin' pushes a kid to the street faster than *that*." Jazz spoke with the voice of experience. "I mean a few scraps at school ain't too bad, and..."

"How do you know?" Willa cut in.

"Girl, please. You know I specialized in trouble on the few days I showed up at school." Jazz waved a hand.

"No, I mean how did you know he'd been in trouble at school? I didn't mention exactly what he'd been up to." Willa squinted at her.

"Well, uh. What else could it be? I mean that's common with kids these days." Jazz looked around at the array of bottles on a shelf behind the bar. "Want some of this wine? It's an expensive red something or other. This guy gave it to me."

"I don't want any wine. Jazz, has Anthony been talking to you?"

"No, well maybe he mentioned something about it. That principal is a tight-butt. Mrs. What's-her-face. She's a combination of your mother and your Aunt Ametrine."

Willa ignored the dig at her adoptive family. "Jazz, the police think Anthony knows something about Jack's murder. They asked for his alibi."

Jazz went very still. "So? He was at home or with a friend."

"He lied about where he was. Did Anthony talk to you about this?" Willa leaned forward.

"I don't wanna get in the middle of this. Besides, you always freak out. I mean, good God almighty. You wanna wrap those kids up in some freakin' antiseptic black bourgie fantasy life," Jazz blurted out in a rush then took a deep breath and let it out.

"Oh. I see." Willa put the bottle of tea down hard on the glass coffee table in front of her. "So you're in a damn position to critique my child-rearing methods now?"

"I'm just sayin' you need to loosen up and let Anthony breathe. He feels like you've got all these rules and standards that you keep revising every minute."

"It's call life, Jazz. I don't want my child to become another paragraph in the newspapers crime reports. Young black male arrested or sixteen-year-old found shot to death. He's so angry, so bitter and it's too soon for him to feel that way. I want him to feel like he's got a future to look forward to." Willa's voice got louder as she spoke.

"He's a typical kid, and just like a lot of typical kids he's gonna buck authority, girl. If you push his back against the wall he's just gonna keep pushin' back. I oughta know." Jazz fished a pack of small cigars from a pocket of her caftan, took one out and lit it with a lighter shaped like a naked couple. She sucked in deeply then let out a stream of smoke.

"So what? Just let him do whatever? Oh hell no. I'm fighting to keep him from having a negative label stuck on his back." Willa shook her head. "No, I won't let it happen."

"Jack always said you were too jumpy when it came to Anthony. Willa, your kid isn't like our brothers. Okay? He's not like our father either. You trippin'.

Both women stopped talking at the mention of their two biological brothers and father, all in prison. Willa pressed a shaky hand to her forehead. Jazz jumped off the bar stool and paced for a few minutes. They avoided looking at each other. Willa sucked in a few ragged breaths. This conversation reminded her too much of her childhood. The thought of Anthony being in any juvenile system would keep her awake another night.

"I'm just so scared, Jazz. Detective Miller is asking about Anthony. And Anthony is being stubborn. He won't tell me where he was that night and— "

"And nothin', girl. Anthony probably wasn't doin' anything more than chasin' after some teenage booty.." Jazz took another puff from the slender brown cigar. She sat down again and grinned. "You could be a grandmother as we speak."

"Damn, I'm serious," Willa spat back. "This is a murder investigation and Miller is asking about my child!"

Jazz stopped grinning and waved the hand holding the cigar around in the air. "Hell, take it easy, all right? Look, I've got more experience with this than you."

"Umph," was Willa's only response.

Jazz had been arrested a few times for public indecency, shoplifting and possession of marijuana. No felonies, but her boyfriends had been another matter. The last two were gangsters, both suspected of drive-by shootings. Willa worried that Anthony was identifying with his young aunt in the worst way, seeing her lifestyle as exciting or cool.

"If Miller was truly building some kinda case on Anthony they'd at least drag his long tall butt down to the police station for questioning. He's a minor so Miller's got to be careful. They don't have any evidence, but he's fishing. Miller is hoping to push the right buttons and flush out some details. Just tell Anthony to keep his mouth shut, don't talk to no cop unless you're with him and things will be fine."

Willa took a turn pacing the space in front of the long sofa. "I guess you're right."

"You need more than some tea, girl." Jazz went to the kitchen and came back with a glass of white wine. "Here. Now just chill for a minute and think about what I said. I wasn't tryin' to make fun of you bein' all worried or nothin', ya know?"

After accepting the goblet Willa gulped a mouthful then sat down again, this time in a chair next to the sofa. She took in a few deep breaths. The chilled wine tickled her throat as it went down. Since she hadn't eaten, Willa briefly worried about the effects on her senses and driving home. She allowed herself one last sip then put the glass on the cocktail table.

"Thanks," Willa said and cleared her throat. She rubbed at the dull thudding ache that had taken root in her forehead. "I shouldn't have freaked out like that. My nerves are just scraped raw."

"Hell yeah you got bad nerves. Your man was gunned down for pocket change; the cops are nosing around and who knows what kind of funny business Jack got into at that agency. Just keep your cool and talk to them fancy lawyers you work with. They'll school you." The tip of the cigar glowed red as Jazz pointed it at Willa to emphasize her advice.

"Thanks."

Willa knew this was the real reason she'd come to Jazz. Their relationship was complicated and difficult at the best of times. Certain issues they might never resolve, or even be able to talk about. Yet in a pinch they always turned to each other. Oddly enough Willa did feel better. Jazz had experience with the criminal justice system from the wrong side. Mama Ruby was Willa's rock. Her aunts would always stand with her. But Jazz and she had a connection that drove them to each other when bad trouble came up. Few others understood, except Mama Ruby.

"You want some more wine?" Jazz nodded at the goblet. She hadn't poured much into the glass and Willa had consumed half of that small amount.

"No, thanks. I guess I better get home. Maybe I'll try talking to Anthony again. Seems like my child turned into somebody else once he hit thirteen." Willa shook her head slowly.

"He did. Turned into a teenager. You remember what that was like." Jazz let out a sharp laugh. "I seem to recall you wasn't always Miss Proper-Manners. You sneaked out with that nineteen-year-old dude when you was only fourteen."

"Police picked me and him up at that nightclub. Whole lotta grown folks got busted that night because of me." Willa winced at the memory. "Girl, don't make me re-live those days. Besides, you hit thirteen and did stuff I had never even dreamed of doing."

Jazz lifted her nose in the air as though proud. "Had a hell of a good time, too."

"Really? I don't remember having all that much fun. The partying, boys and drinking was more a way to keep from thinking too much," Willa said softly. She glanced at Jazz.

Her sister took one last puff of the slender cigar then lit another one. Jazz blew a series of smoke rings. "Speak for yourself, sistah. I was havin' some serious, straight-up fun. Just bein' a kid, ya know. Anthony's no different. Sure he's got stuff on his mind, but he'll be okay."

Willa wavered for a few moments, wondering whether to talk about the horrors that pushed Jazz into being wild. She was about to try when Jazz's phone rang. Jazz picked up the cordless phone on the bar. After a few minutes of a cryptic conversation , Jazz hung up. She wore a troubled frown then shrugged off whatever was bothering her and poured herself a shot of brandy.

"Something wrong?" Willa squinted at her. She could smell the smoky scent of a fire brewing, trouble in the wind.

"No. Anyway, like I was sayin' you shouldn't worry about that cop. Anthony and Jack had made up months before Jack got killed. He told me so. They was spendin' time together and everything. I'll bet that cop has already found some witnesses that saw 'em together having a father and son day."

"See, that's what I mean. Why didn't he just tell me so? I'm his mother." Willa huffed in irritation.

"Because he's being a hard-headed kid and just because you asked he's not gonna tell you," Jazz said with a smirk. "I was the same way."

"Times ten," Willa retorted. "But he should be talking to me about these things. Not that I don't want him to feel close to you. In fact, I'm glad he feels he can come to his Auntie Jazzmonetta."

"Yeah well. Anyways, Jack said they'd worked it out like two men, hashed out what was botherin' Anthony and everything was cool," Jazz said.

The achy tension eased across Willa's forehead. "Girl, you're right. Even I didn't know Jack and Anthony were hanging out. There must be some other people that saw them together. Wait, that might be why Miller hasn't been coming on so strong about Anthony." Willa sank onto the sofa with a loud sigh of relief. "Jazz, you don't know how glad I am I came over here."

Jazz patted her weave. "Sure. Whenever you need to sort out some of your drama just guide your Honda SUV right over here. We specialize in drama on this side of town."

"Don't I know it," Willa tossed back. Before she could say more Jazz's phone rang and Jazz picked it up.

"Hey, Rico. Yeah, baby." Jazz waved goodbye to Willa, engrossed in what sounded like her latest male enterprise.

Minutes later Willa was on her way home. She drove through thick evening traffic. Flashing police lights behind her turned the night blue. Adrenaline rushed to Willa's brain as she watched two police cruisers weave across lanes and go past her through a red light. They hit their sirens as a warning. Cars stopped allowing them through.

She thought about the night Jack died and how those lights had probably flashed then, too. At least she could sleep better tonight knowing there was a way to keep them from her son. Anthony and Jack had made up. Willa sighed noisily and turned up her radio. Somehow she had to figure out a way to make Anthony confide in her again. She shouldn't have to find out information from Jazz. Why hadn't Anthony just said something? Then a giant switch went off in Willa's brain. Jazz had talked to Jack, the man she'd never liked, had ignored since Willa's wedding day. So when, and most importantly, why did they start having heart to heart chats?

Chapter 5

"Jazz, call me." Willa slapped the button on the phone keypad ending the call. "Damn caller ID."

She took off the wireless headset and tossed it onto her desk. Here it was three days since Willa had been to Jazz's house and she still couldn't get her to return her calls.

Willa swiveled the chair around so she could stare out of the window of her office. What had been Jack's office had been transformed to Willa's taste. She'd moved his certificates and softball trophies out. Most of them were in either Mikayla's room or had been sent to Jack's parents. Instead of the gunmetal gray furnishings and blue paint on the walls, now the office had soft green walls with a new sofa and seating area furniture. Framed black art prints were on the walls. Two plants made the office seem softer, more inviting, in Willa and Kay's opinion. Cedric had been more restrained. Probably because he was hoping she'd be gone by now. But the new décor did nothing to help her mood. Jazz knew the deal and was ducking Willa. She considered going by her place again. The one time Willa had tried, Jazz didn't answer the buzz to open the electronic gate.

"I'm going to whip her butt when I finally do get close enough," Willa muttered and let out a string of expletives once again.

There was a knock then Kay came in. When Willa spun the chair around to face her Kay took a step back. "Uh, maybe you're too busy for this visitor. I'll just tell Ms. Landry it isn't a good time."

"Show her in," Willa said sharply.

"You sure?" Kay pursed her lips.

"Positive," Willa said and smiled.

Kay's expression said she was not reassured, but she nodded and headed back out. "If you say so."

Moments later MiMi came in. Her thick hair was pulled into a French roll with curly tendrils trailing down both sides of her face. She wore a black fitted cropped jacket and her light gray skirt hugged her figure. Apparently her guise today was Ms. Takin' Care of Business. Willa and MiMi gazed at each other in stony silence. Kay looked from Willa to MiMi then back at her boss.

"Holler if you need me," Kay said. She raised an eyebrow at MiMi to indicate she too meant business.

When the office door shut with a discreet thump MiMi snorted. "Please. Like you need a guard dog to protect you from me."

Willa tilted her head to one side. "She was talking to *you*."

MiMi flipped a manicured hand in the air. "There is no need for us to be enemies."

"Say what?" Willa took her turn at letting out a snort.

"Other than the obvious reason, but that is now a moot point. Our source of feminine conflict is..." MiMi paused then took a tissue from her purse and dabbed at the corner of one eye. "He's no longer with us."

"What do you want? Other than a piece of this business and my late husband's estate, which you won't get," Willa added with such fierceness that MiMi stopped her grieving act. She lifted her chin.

"Your estranged almost ex-husband. And my lawyer says differently. But— " MiMi held up one palm to cut off Willa's retort. "We can't afford to have a smack down over this. Remember I told you about the Strafford, Inc. contracts?"

"I'm glad you brought that up. My lawyer says since we can find no record of such a business deal your claim is shaky at best." Willa wore a genuine smile for the first time in the last few days. "So this little visit was wasted."

"Not so fast, missy." MiMi dug a large envelope from her wide leather purse.

"Did you just call me 'missy'? My granny doesn't even use that phrase anymore." Willa blinked at her then at the envelope MiMi waved at her.

"I got this in the mail. A letter from Jack with a bank deposit box key."

Willa stared at the envelope and sat very still. She felt a chill along with a jumble of emotions. Anger, hurt, jealously flashed through her gut, all unpleasant reminders of how Jack had made her feel during their marriage. Even in death he managed to push her buttons. She finally admitted to feeling that hollow abandoned sensation at losing his affection to another woman.   And fear. A message from beyond the grave?

"That's impossible," Willa finally managed to rasp from her bone dry throat.

"Scared the crap out of me, too, when I saw the return address. Then I opened it and saw the letter. Girl, it was creepy. I could hear his voice, almost smell his cologne as I was reading it," MiMi said, her voice a whisper. She stared at the envelope as she spoke.

"Escencia," Willa said, matching MiMi's muted tone. Jack had favored the designer cologne with hints of oak and leather.

"He had his own style for sure." MiMi's eyes went glassy, this time with what seemed to be real tears.

Willa snapped back to reality. Having a nostalgic moment about Jack with his last mistress was crazy. She shook off the haze that had muddled her brain for a few moments. "What does this alleged letter from Jack say?"

"It *is* from Jack," MiMi shot back with a sniff. Apparently her moment was over as well. "He wants me to have some security, and he talks about the Strafford agreement. Here is your copy. My lawyer already has one. He mentions a safe deposit box and left this funny looking key," MiMi added and held it up.

For a few seconds Willa looked at the sheaf of papers MiMi extended without touching them. When MiMi shook them at her Willa finally accepted copies. She read through them. Strafford, Inc. had hired Crown Protection to provide secure courier services for important papers and guards for two warehouses. The arrangements seemed pretty straightforward. So why didn't Cedric know about it?

"Something is up with this whole deal. I'm getting a weird feeling, like I'm being followed. Then some guy called me the other day asking about the money." MiMi nodded when Willa looked at her.

"What money?"

"I don't know," MiMi squeaked. "Which is what I told him, but I don't think he believed me."

"Okay, so go look in the box since you got the key. Get the money and give it to him," Willa spoke slowly as though talking to a not too bright child.

"Don't you think I would have done that already? He didn't tell me where it is," MiMi squeaked again and actually stamped a foot. She seemed on the edge of a temper tantrum.

The entire scenario suddenly seemed ridiculous. Willa tossed the papers aside and laughed. "You had me sucked in for about a minute. Coming in here with this cloak and dagger mess. I have to say the mysterious key to an unknown box was a nice touch. Consult your lawyer and I'll see you in court. Go to the police if you feel threatened." Willa waved at the door. "Goodbye."

"I didn't tell my lawyer everything, and I don't want to talk to the police. You don't want me to either. Not until we find out just what Jack was into." MiMi bit her lip as she frowned at the papers.

"What do you mean 'we'? Look, we're on opposite sides in this. If Jack got involved in something shady…" Willa took a deep breath to calm down.

"You don't want the children to get hurt. Right now he's a victim of a terrible crime. Before we unravel something nasty I say we find out more on the down low. Just for now." MiMi tapped the toe of one pump on the carpet.

"Stop saying 'we'. There is no you and me." Willa had lost her momentary fragile hold on her temper. "Listen, I'll do my own investigation without *you*, thank you very much. Now goodbye."

"Willa— "

"Mrs. Crown to you, heffa," Willa yelled back and stood. "You come waltzing in here announcing to me that you've been sleeping with my husband."

"Ex-husband," MiMi corrected again. "Will you slow your roll long enough to listen?"

"Then you have the brass-ass monkey nerve to claim you own a piece of this company. Well, honey, you better go back and get that job at the cosmetics counter in the department store. Ain't gonna be no pay day up in here." Willa put both hands on her hips.

MiMi fanned her face with the envelope. "Lord, a lot of hot air is what's up in here."

"You're about ten seconds and two feet from a beat down, girl," Willa shot back.

Cedric pushed through the door without knocking. Kay followed right on his heels. Through the open door Willa saw several employees and at least one client in the lobby stretching their necks to see the drama. Kay quickly shut the door.

"I think this meeting is over now, Ms. Landry," Cedric said firmly. He positioned himself in a spot between the two women.

"Fine." MiMi stuffed the papers into her handbag and stood. "I can discuss Anthony and Jack with *Mrs. Crown* some other time. Or maybe her sister will fill her in." MiMi ignored Cedric and stared steadily at Willa.

"I don't understand." Cedric glanced at Willa with a slight frown.

"I'm not here to start a fight," MiMi said, her gaze still on Willa. "I really think you need to hear me out."

The icy chill that moved through her body instantly cooled down Willa's hot rage. "Give us a minute."

"But— " Cedric started to continue his protest but stopped when Willa looked at him.

"Please." Willa nodded at him and Kay to leave. Once they were gone she crossed her arms. "What are you talking about?"

MiMi eyed her cautiously. "You calm now? I mean, I don't want you jumping across that desk on me. I just paid almost two hundred dollars for this suit at Dillard's. "

"Tell me about my son. Now," Willa said through clenched teeth.

"Anthony is a smart boy, and handsome, too. When we met I almost thought maybe Jack was his daddy after all. Of course I know he wasn't, but— " MiMI inched back when Willa started around the desk. "Okay, okay. Anthony and Jack had sort of healed their rift. I mean it was slow going at first. Jack used to brag on Anthony so much. He even said he was grooming him to be a businessman instead of somebody's employee."

"Sounds like Jack," Willa admitted. She batted away her irritation that Jack had introduced his hoochie to Anthony. "Go on."

"I think Jack was mentoring him to maybe take over this company one day. He would take him along to visit job sites, go over contracts with him and things like that. It was really sweet. Anyway I think Jack told Anthony about this Strafford, Inc. deal."

"So?" Willa didn't like the way the chill deepened into her bones.

"Look, you figure it out. That file is missing. Jack's right-hand man didn't know about it. Something smells about the whole thing. I thought those guys looked a bit too slick that time we met." MiMi's eyes narrowed at the memory.

"You met representatives of the company?" Willa forgot to be irritated with the source of this new information. She dropped her arms to her sides.

"Yeah, girl. The lawyer was smooth. High tone hired gun is what he is. That guy with him, the vice president of something or other, looked like his manners were newly acquired. You know what I mean?"

"Street?"

"What do I know about street?" MiMi flipped her acrylic nails in the air. "I can tell you he didn't pledge any fraternities or grow up in *my* circle of friends. His name is Ike Nelson."

"La-dee-da," Willa said dryly. "Get back to the part of this story that I care about- my son."

MiMi gave a hiss of annoyance but went on. "Jack had some custom suits made for Anthony and they went on business meetings a couple of times. You know, for experience. Anthony played the part of business intern perfectly. He was so cute with his little lap top and everything."

"Funny how they both kept it from me. Are you sure about this?" Willa squinted at MiMi. "It occurs to me that you might be making this up."

"Didn't Jack pick up Anthony a few times after their big blow-up?" MiMi asked. She crossed her arms to wait and let her question sink in.

"Yeah. Come to think of it Anthony went with him a few times. But I thought..." Willa frowned as she searched her memory. Since Anthony hadn't said much or seemed to changed his attitude she had assumed there was still tension between them. "But why would they be secretive?"

"Jack asked him not to say anything to you. Said you'd just worry since he was in the security business." MiMi shrugged. "Actually you weren't getting along too well with Jack back then. Maybe he was afraid you'd turn Anthony against him again."

"I never slammed Jack to either of the children," Willa protested with enough heat to melt glass.

"Hmmm," MiMi responded. "Anyway, Anthony knows about some of Jack's business dealings. Those Strafford people know this, Willa. If they're sweating me about the money, well you figure it out."

"What money?"

"Jack got a large cash deposit for services that were never rendered or something or other. The money is missing." MiMi wore a grave look. "A chunk of which is my money and I want it back. Of course I'll be willing to consider giving up my percentage of the agency in return for— "

"You have no percentage," Willa broke in.

"If you pay me back the amount I invested. Thirty thousand." MiMi cleared her throat. "Plus the interest Jack promised. And the profit. That brings the total to around seventy-five thousand."

Willa burst out laughing while MiMi gazed at her. She picked up a folder from her desk and fanned her face to cool off. When she finally gained control Willa sat down at her desk again. "I can't be angry with a woman who is clearly off her medications and delusional."

"Girl, I'm not playing with you, not about my damn money." MiMi waved a forefinger in the air as she spoke.

Willa barked out another laugh then covered her mouth. "Sorry, right. I see you're serious." Still she giggled one last time.

"See, I'm trying to be reasonable. But you can bet your life them other folks won't be. Think about Jack and if you really want to make that kind of bet," MiMi said with grim expression.

Willa squinted at her. "Threats don't scare me."

"Well these people should. I don't think they're your everyday same old-same old businessmen." MiMi tapped a foot nervously. "They called Anthony yet?"

"Okay, don't keep pushing that button. Even if what you're saying is true there's no reason for them to think Anthony knows anything." Willa tried to keep the worry from her expression.

"You hope," MiMi shot back. "We both have an interest in finding that money and giving it back to those guys. Of course we could just do business with them as usual. At least we'd find out what the heck Jack was up to. What do you think?"

"The same thing I did a few minutes ago-- that you're crazy," Willa replied. "First, all this is just what you say, and news flash- I don't trust you. Second, if, and this is a big if, Jack was dumb and greedy enough to hook up with gangsters we'd be even more stupid to do the same thing."

MiMi did the hand flip again to sweep away Willa's comment. "Listen to my logic. Jack was business smart. He must have brokered a smart deal with minimum risk to him. We could complete this one transaction, get paid and then shut it down."

"Living at that deluxe address is expensive, huh, sweetie?" Willa wisecracked.

MiMi gave Willa the evil eye for a few seconds as she huffed in anger. Finally she took in a deep breath and let it out slowly.

"If I want my money this bad just think about those other guys and what they're willing to do to get it back."

"Okay, that's enough. I'm done visiting your version of fantasyland. Some whacked-out crack addict killed Jack for pocket change. There is no big conspiracy and you don't own a piece of my company. This has been an entertaining break in my day. Now it's over." Willa waved goodbye to MiMi and pointed to the door.

"You best wake up, Mrs. Crown. We need to handle this before they show up on our doorstep." MiMi stood. She gathered the papers together and grabbed her purse.

"Yeah, sure. Have a nice day." Willa turned to her computer screen and opened a file.

"One last thing, you better hope they don't decide Anthony knows something. So I suggest you find out if he does." MiMi stomped to the door and went out then came back seconds later. "I'm sure you'll be in touch with me. Since you've probably done a background check, you have my phone numbers and my e-mail address. You have a nice day."

The door slammed shut hard and loud making Willa start. Her heart and mind raced as she considered the firebomb MiMi had tossed as she'd left. After a short knock Cedric came into her office.

"Is everything okay?" Cedric glanced around office as though checking for damage.

"Yeah," Willa replied, though she wasn't at all sure. "I didn't break any furniture over her head or commit a felony assault. Thanks for asking."

"So did she know anything about Strafford, Inc.?" Cedric placed his hands on his narrow hips. "We really need to find out more."

"No, she didn't— " Willa stopped cold and then closed her eyes. "Damn."

"That sounds like bad news." Cedric's dark eyebrows pulled together as he gazed at Willa.

"She claims Jack left her a safety deposit box and hinted the answer is in there." Willa threw up both hands when Cedric's frown deepened. "I know. She's so annoying my brain stops functioning and the urge to slap her crowds out rational thought.

"Yeah, well learn to tolerate her, at least until we find out what we need to know. So I'm guessing she wants to form an alliance with you." Cedric walked to the window and gazed at the scenery outside without really seeing it.

"Something like that," Willa replied.

"Smart move." Cedric glanced at Willa over one shoulder then looked through the window again.

"And my reaction wasn't. You don't have to say it," Willa put in when Cedric turned around to protest.

"Since she's willing I say get in touch with her, but not right away," he added quickly. "Best not seem desperate or she'll use that to her advantage."

"Just the fact that I call her will let her know she has a valuable bargaining chip," Willa replied. She rocked her chair back and forth thinking.

"You were pretty hard core with her, huh? Look, when emotions are involved it's hard to be all cold and logical. I mean she and Jack were... involved. "

"I don't care if she and Jack swung from chandeliers. I was done with him long before he died."

"I'm just saying— "

Willa let out a long-suffering sigh. Just like a man to assume two women would always battle over one of them.

"For the last time, I'm not mad at MiMi cause she was with Jack. She's the type that I dislike-- spoiled bourgie Black princess who thinks the world tilts on her axis." Willa snorted. "I had to deal with her kind in high school and college."

In fact, girls like MiMi had made Willa's life hell. Willa's adopted parents had helped her get an excellent education when they'd enrolled her in private school. Papa Elton had joked, "Well look at it this way, you'll get plenty of practice using them anger management skills." College had been another rich source of practice. Cedric's throat clearing brought Willa back from her school daze.

"About this whole deal with Strafford, Inc., I'm still tracking it down. I've got a couple of leads. I don't want to jump to conclusions, but I'm starting to think I'm chasing shadows."

"What do you mean?"

"This company has a few offices, and seems to put out a couple of products. But all those divisions, foreign branches— looks like a set of stage props to make them seem like a real company. I'm tempted to fly to Hawaii to check out their headquarters." Cedric wore his intense investigator expression.

"Whoa, we don't have that kind of expense account cause if you go I'd have to come along," Willa joked with a sideways grin.

"That wouldn't be a bad idea. How are your surfing and snorkeling skills?" Cedric's lips curved just enough to suggest a sexy smile.

Willa looked into his eyes, deep and black as coffee. She had to remind herself that like MiMi, Cedric had his own agenda. Still that buttoned-down version of sexy tugged at her gut. He was looking at her as though he imagined them both in swimsuits on a tropical island. Willa shut down that hot image in her head. She affected a forced laugh.

"We better find a faster and more cost effective way to deal with Ms. Landry's claims." Willa straightened her spine to appear more like a boss rather than an overheated desperate housewife. "MiMi keeps saying Strafford is some kind of shady outfit. So we have two possible threats to this business."

That seemed to jerk Cedric's attention from the beach. He scowled. "Yeah. We deal with agencies in other states. Not Hawaii, but I'll bet Jay with J & J Investigations in Los Angeles can recommend somebody."

"Really? We farm out work?"

Cedric nodded. "Like you said, we're cost effective. Computers, phones and e-mail go just so far. Sometimes there is no substitute for direct observation."

"I know what you mean. That is true for talking to people. Face to face you can read body language. Sometimes that gives you as much valuable information as what people say." Willa thought back to her talk with Jazz. Her baby sister hadn't told her everything. She didn't need MiMi to tell her that much.

"Back to MiMi," Cedric said, cutting into Willa's thoughts.

Willa turned from one troublesome female in her life to another. She hissed her displeasure. "Right, MiMi. Jack sure loved flashy troublemakers."

"Ahem, with one exception," Cedric put in.

"Thanks," Willa replied with a restrained smile. She looked away from his smoky topaz gaze. "Guess she was right. Looks like I have to call her."

"You can bet she's going to use that key as a bargaining chip," Cedric said.

Willa nodded and rocked her chair for a few seconds. She stopped and smiled at Cedric. "But she doesn't know where the box is. Otherwise she wouldn't have come to us. So why not go hire another private investigator to find it?"

"Yeah. She either knows or suspects they might uncover something illegal."

"So?" Willa glanced at him.

"No investigator will risk his license and keep his mouth closed if he uncovers a crime."

"Except an investigator who wouldn't want that information to come out anymore than she would," Willa replied. Her gut tightened. Jack wasn't much by most standards, but he was everything to Anthony and Mikayla. And the last thing she wanted was her kids exposed to scandal and danger.

Cedric crossed his arms. "I know you want to protect the kids, but we have to follow wherever this thing leads us. Otherwise we risk losing this company. Without a license this place will close. Period."

"Yes, of course we have to do the right thing," Willa replied and closed her eyes. She rubbed her temple in an attempt to ward off a giant headache. "But MiMi doesn't know that. So let's do it."

"And if Jack did get into something illegal?"

"I know, I know. We report it to the authorities. But only if we have solid evidence indicating he committed a crime. Not that he might have but never got a chance to. Agreed?"

Cedric shook his head slowly. "We can't play chicken with the truth, Willa."

Willa stood. "Don't be such a tight end, and I'm not talking football. Do you see any colors other than black and white?"

"Very witty," Cedric clipped. Still his rigid wide-legged stance and taut expression made him look like an uncompromising drill sergeant.

"Who's to say Jack wasn't on the verge of going to the cops but he was killed first?"

Cedric blinked as he considered her words. "Okay."

"Right, and— " Willa tossed around for a way to convince him. "We shouldn't be too quick to hurt the agency. We'll bleed money if even a rumor gets out Jack was into something shady."

"You have a point, a fine one, but still. However if we find evidence of criminal activity we have to report it." Cedric let out a long slow breath. "Then deal with whatever hits the fan."

"If we find hard evidence of crimes we'll absolutely do our duty," Willa replied with a sharp nod.

"Because the alternative is a crap load of trouble way beyond losing business," Cedric said and pointed at her. "Agreed?"

"Yes. But if we only suspect something fishy after putting two and two together." Willa started to go on but Cedric held up a palm like a traffic cop.

"We report it," he finished for her.

"Cedric, my kids need Jack's good name and good memories more than they need his money," Willa said quietly. "If we're not sure Jack was involved..."

Cedric followed Willa's gaze to the large photo on her desk. Anthony and Mikayla sat posed for the camera in their best clothes. Anthony had a protective big brother arm draped around his sister's slender shoulders. Willa looked back at Cedric. His stony expression had vanished. He pulled a large hand over his face and sighed again.

"Yeah. Let's do this." Cedric headed for the door.

"Thanks," Willa called out.

Cedric turned around and walked back until he stood close to her. "I'm doing this for the kids, and you."

Willa gazed into his eyes. He was breaking one of his rules for her. That's what she read in his face. She also knew he didn't break his rules for just anybody. Unable to take the heat she took the nearest exit out of the kitchen. She looked away and he left.

***

That night over instant macaroni and cheese, rotisserie chicken and salad Willa tried to make life seem normal. Willa considered having her serious talk with Anthony, but figured a frontal assault would only make him rebel. Maybe what they all needed was a break from serious. So instead she asked the kids about school. Anthony did his usual monotone short sentence answer then shoved another yeast roll in his mouth. Mikayla gladly filled in his vacuum. She gave what seemed like an hour by hour account of her day, including some story involving a kid named Justin and a salamander.

"And all the girls were screaming like crazy. I just told them to stop acting like squealing idiots. Then I helped Justin catch Sal."

Willa blinked hard and stopped sneaking looks at Anthony. "Sal?"

"Justin's salamander, Mama," Mikayla replied with annoyance in her tone. "Are you even listening?"

"Yes, ma'am. I hope your teacher made you apologize for calling your friends idiots. That's not very nice." Willa moved into the role of vigilant mother with ease.

"Mama, I didn't call them idiots. I said they were acting like idiots," Mikayla reasoned. "There's a difference."

"Not by much, little lady. So don't try that precocious line of logic on me. I'm not— " Willa stopped before completing the sentence.

"I know. You're not daddy. He would have just laughed and said, 'Baby girl you're gonna be a lawyer'." Mikayla did her best effort to imitate her father's baritone voice.

"Yeah," Anthony said and laughed. "You sound like him."

Mikayla grinned at him. "You do it, Anthony. Talk like Daddy."

Anthony launched into one of Jack's favorite lectures about kids being too spoiled. He imitated how Jack would stutter when confronted with the fact that he was a spoiled brat growing up. Then he did his imitation of the elder Mr. Crown. Anthony had them laughing until they were breathless as he went on to mimic both men.

"Then old Mr. Crown would chime in with, 'You kids don't know anything about earning a living'," Anthony finished in a gruff, irascible tone. Then he pretended to cough loudly and hitch up his pants like Jack's father.

"You better not let Grandmother see you doing that," Mikayla finally gasped.

"That's enough now. We shouldn't make fun of Mr. Crown." Willa managed to stifle another round of the giggles as she dabbed at tears in her eyes.

"Yes, ma'am," Mikayla and Anthony said in unison then winked at each other.

"You have an assignment, baby girl. No playing video games first," Willa warned.

"I promise," Mikayla replied and bounced from her chair then skittered off full of energy. "I'm doing a paper on dinosaurs. It's fun looking up stuff on that!"

Since it was his week to help in the kitchen, Anthony got to work clearing the dishes. He shook his head at his sister. "Hey, KayKay. Don't forget, no making fun of the idiots."

"Promise," she called back. Mikayla turned around to wink at him one last time. She giggled with one hand over her mouth then continued on her way

"That girl is weird. Happy to do homework." Anthony let out a snort.

"Yeah, well you could do with some of that weirdness, mister man," Willa retorted. She wiped the table with a damp cloth the worked on the counter tops.

"Yes, ma'am. Hey, I'm doing better. You haven't gotten any calls or notes from the teachers. Right?" He glanced at her over one shoulder.

"Knock on wood." Willa smiled when he scowled at her remark. "Okay, okay. Credit where credit is due. Your teachers report that you have a better attitude."

"Thank you." Anthony finished dumping leftovers from the plates. He started loading the dishwasher.

"Now I'll be doing back flips if you bring those grades up by the next nine weeks report." Willa used a kitchen spray to clean the cook top.

"Man, will it ever be enough?" Anthony heaved a long-suffering sigh.

"Sure. When you get a law degree, a PhD or graduate from medical school the pressure will be off," she joked. "Mama will let you take it from there."

"Dang," Anthony muttered. "Cut a young brother some slack. Darnell's mama is happy he just shows up for class and gets Cs."

"You want to be average?" Willa replied, gathering steam for a lecture on achievement.

"Read the memo, Mama. I *am* average. Just an average dude trying to get by." Anthony went to a small closet near the pantry entrance. He took out a broom and dustpan.

"Something we continue to disagree on, baby. You have better than average potential. There is no reason that Anthony Jarrod Alexander should settle for second best. When you were three years old— "

"I could recite nursery rhymes from memory. I used to count out my blocks way before the other kids," Anthony cut in and finished for her.

"That's right. You're smarter than the average kid. This whole choosing to be an underachiever culture with kids is crazy. You know it, too. You just hate to admit it and agree with me."

"I'm a teenager. Being a jerk and lazy is my job," Anthony wisecracked. He kept his lopsided grin even when Willa glared at him.

"Then you're going to change careers fast, young man," Willa shot back.

"Yes, ma'am." Anthony finished sweeping up the crumbs Mikayla had left around her chair.

Willa seized on the subject at hand to move onto the subject of Jack. "Your father had a lot of dreams for you, too."

Anthony dumped the crumbs into the trash then put away the dustpan and broom. "I know."

Without needing to say it both knew Willa meant Jack. With all his well-documented shortcomings, Jack had been a loving father. In fact, he was the only true father Anthony had ever known. Anthony once asked Jack about his biological dad when he was seven years old. Whatever Jack told him had only cemented their bond. Until the separation and divorce drama created the first crack.

Willa gazed at Anthony. He was well on his way to being a man. Now she blamed herself for the wedge that had grown between her son and husband. Anger and pain had caused Willa to say too much too often about Jack. Willa folded the dishtowel in her hand and dropped it on the counter. She crossed to Anthony and gave him a hug.

"What was that for?" Anthony tried to maintain his cool. Still traces of his boyish smile broke free.

"For a job well done. You pulled your act together in spite of your buddies."

"Huh?" He looked at her with a puzzled expression.

"I'm sure they're still trying to pull you back. Maybe they even make fun of you for following rules, being polite, listening to your mother." Willa put a finger under his chin and gazed into his dark hazel eyes.

"Whatever. They always making noise 'bout something." He shrugged off the teasing. He leaned against the counter and folded his arms.

"Good attitude. Don't let anybody try to control your mind and drag you into doing wrong." Willa took a deep breath and let it out. "Speaking of Jack, Jazz tells me you and he were on speaking terms again."

"Yeah, we were talking every now and then." Anthony looked away from her. He seemed to find interest in something on the wall.

"You never mentioned it," Willa prompted.

"I didn't want you to get upset. You know you'd think I was taking his side or something." Anthony went from staring at the wall to examining his fingernails.

Willa sighed again. "Look, I know I was upset about some things Jack did."

"Like the women, gambling, clubbing," Anthony said filling in the details. "I'm not a little kid like Mikayla, Mama."

"Okay. All that is true. But I should have been careful not to let my feelings about him as a husband spill over to you kids. None of that meant he didn't love you and Mikayla. And don't for a second think there was a difference either." She stabbed a finger at him.

"I know he loved me," Anthony said quietly. "I miss him a lot."

"Just remember the good times, like when he took you on business calls," Willa probed. "You went to some important meetings, I hear."

"Yeah, Jack said with my brains I could take his business to another level." Anthony lifted his head with pride.

"He was right," Willa added, every bit the proud mother. "Did you remember details about a company called Strafford, Inc.?"

"Uh, I'm not sure. We talked about lot of stuff." Anthony shifted from one foot to another. "Why?"

"One of your dad's— " Willa tossed around for a way to describe MiMi. "One of his associates told us about this contract with them, but we can't find the paperwork."

Anthony shrugged. "Must have been one file Kay didn't manage to clean up off his desk. She had a time keeping that office straight, ya know. I better get to work on some calculus problems. I didn't finish all the worksheets in study hall."

Willa exhaled in relief. Of course Anthony wouldn't know anything. Silly of MiMi to think he did or Jazz to suggest he might know more. Willa brushed a hand through his wooly locks.

"Sure, future business tycoon. Learn all you can so you can take care of your mama one day." Willa smiled at him.

Anthony faced her with an intense look in his eyes. Then he embraced her tightly for a moment before letting go. "I'm going to do that for sure, Mama. I'll be in my room."

"Okay, baby."

Willa watched his leggy stride in baggy jeans as he left. Assured that Anthony didn't know anything, Willa felt better. Jack would never have knowingly put Anthony in harm's way. Now all she had to do was beat off Mimi's attempt to cash in, keep the cops from suspecting her son, hold onto the company and resist her insane urge to flirt with Cedric.

"No pressure on me," she said to kitchen appliances.

***

After a good night's rest Willa felt refreshed. She went to the office the next day ready to take on the world. When Kay placed three messages from MiMi on her desk Willa smiled. She put them aside. Let MiMi simmer in her own juices for a little while longer. She had no intention of letting Miss Thang think she had the upper hand.

For most of the morning she felt like take on the world was exactly what she'd done. She spent two hours on paperwork, had a conference call with Cedric and a potential client, and a late morning meeting with another client. Reverend Lawrence Fisher was the pastor of a growing mid-city church. He wanted security for church functions.

"We're growing so fast. We have Bible study two nights a week. Three of our choirs have practices three nights a week, a drug abuse support group on Tuesdays." Reverend Fisher ticked off the events on thick fingers.

Willa nodded and smiled. She blinked at the way light danced on the gold jewelry that decorated both his hands. "Your ministry is prospering."

Reverend Fisher dipped his head in what seemed a practiced show of humility. "Yes, indeed. We're sowing seeds for the Lord."

"Well, we're glad you chose Crown Protection, Reverend," Cedric put in.

"Yes, well our success has angered Satan. He's sending these young brothers to burglarize our cars and steal church property." He shook his head in dismay.

"Terrible," Willa agreed. She was tempted to suggest he not flash all that gold around. Instead she matched his serious expression.

"Our security guards are well trained, Reverend Fisher. I had two of our supervising security staff come in so you could meet them. I'll see if they've made it." Cedric left them alone.

"How thorough. I like that. Yes indeed." The reverend nodded his approval at Willa.

"We were sure you'd want to meet members of our team. After all you're putting your trust in us. We take that very seriously."

"More confirmation that we've chosen wisely." Reverend Fisher assumed a sincere expression. "And may I express sorrow for your loss. I spoke to Mr. Crown only once a few weeks ago. He seemed like a very nice man."

"Thank you, reverend," Willa replied.

"I know the pain of such a loss. My dear Elnora passed away almost two years ago. Such a loss of companionship is hard." Reverend Fisher turned to Willa and his knee brushed her leg.

Willa glanced to make sure she saw both his hands. She inched her leg farther from his. He leaned toward Willa spreading the scent of his heavy aftershave. Willa was on the verge of putting the good pastor in check when Cedric returned. Reverend Fisher sat back quickly, his pious façade firmly in place once more.

"They're right on time, Reverend. Good men." Cedric wore a pleased smile. "Kay will show you to my office when you're ready." He left again.

"Excellent." Reverend Fisher stood and buttoned his suit coat again. He extended a hand to Willa. "I look forward to working with you, Mrs. Crown."

"Same here. We plan to take good care of your security needs." Willa stood and gave his hand a firm shake.

Reverend Fisher gave it a little extra squeeze as he gazed into her eyes. "We'd love to see you at one of our services. The doors of Abundant Love Ministries are always open."

"I'll remember that," Willa said. She would also remember not to be alone with him.

"I think we will have a long, rewarding partnership," he intoned and held onto her hand tighter.

Willa pulled her hand away, yet kept smiling. "Cedric and our guards will make sure of that."

"Your late husband— " Reverend Fisher stopped. "He was actually your ex-husband. As I was saying he and I discussed a lot of ways enterprising men, and women of course, can prosper."

"Really?" Willa was about to brush him off, but something in his tone stopped her. "Such as?"

"Real estate, courier services and other means. We had very enlightening discussions. I hope we can have the same rapport." Reverend Fisher's smile seemed hungry, and he had the mistaken notion that Willa was on his menu.

"Are you familiar with Strafford, Inc.?" Willa replied, ignoring his subtle invitation.

He blinked rapidly at her, thrown off for a few seconds. "Strafford? Uh, why yes. They've generously supported our ministries. One of my deacons works for them. Why?"

"How did Jack meet your deacon?" Willa pressed on. She took a step closer. The move had the desired effect.

Reverend Fisher's dark eyes gave Willa a full body scan. "Why for several months before he died Jack attended our church. After years of living in the flesh he heeded the call to come home."

"Right." Willa tried not to burst out laughing. No doubt he heeded the call to make business contacts with Fisher's prosperous congregation.

"How inspiring. What's the name of your deacon again? The one who works for Strafford, Inc., I mean." Willa put on what she hoped was a fetching smile. "I want to reconnect with all of Jack's important business contacts, like you."

Fisher beamed at her. "Naturally. Deacon Isaac Nelson."

"A fine biblical name. What exactly was his position at Strafford?" She waited expectantly.

Eager to maintain their friendly momentum Fisher fell right in. "One of their operations managers I believe."

Willa managed her own operation. Keeping him at arms length she learned more about Nelson, how he'd met Jack and when he'd introduced Jack to his boss. Reverend Fisher even gave her Nelson's business card. Fisher bragged about how many contacts he had that were influential in the city and state.

"I'm so glad we will have a chance to further our... partnership." Fisher's voice dipped low as he gazed at Willa. "I think we can help each other a lot."

"Of course. Well it was so nice to have met you," Willa said.

"Yes, I— "

"Cedric must be patiently waiting and here I'm delaying both of you." Willa took his arm and before he knew it marched him out to the lobby. "Kay, show Reverend Fisher to Cedric's office."

"Sure. The guys are in there with him, but they didn't want to interrupt you." Kay stood and came from around her desk. "This way, Reverend."

"Uh, yes. Goodbye, Mrs. Crown. I hope to see you at Abundant Love Tabernacle one Sunday." Reverend Fisher flashed one last smile then followed Kay down the hall.

Willa took a deep breath. She made a mental note to ask her mother and Aunt Ametrine about the good pastor and his church. If anyone knew the real deal about him it would be those two. Aunt Ametrine was the CNN of church life in Baton Rouge. Kay came back with a smirk.

"Reverend Fisher sure isn't into chastity. Playa had the nerve to hit on me." Kay rolled her eyes. "Again."

"I'm devastated. Here I thought I was his one true love," Willa quipped.

When she heard voices she and Kay exchanged a glance. Then both rushed into Willa's office. Kay shut the door firmly. They listened through the door until they heard Reverend Fisher say goodbye. They waited a few seconds then returned to the lobby.

Cedric wore a satisfied smile as he looked at the guard supervisor, Emerson. He clapped a hand on the man's shoulder. "The schedule you worked out looks great, man. Thanks for taking the initiative."

"Hey, that's my job. I'm gonna work on filling those gaps at the game schedules. I'll be in my office if you need me." Emerson noticed Willa. "Mornin', ma'am."

"Hello, Emerson. You're definitely doing great work. I appreciate it," Willa said.

Emerson's nut brown faced cracked into a wide smile. "Thank you, ma'am. You're too kind." He nodded at them then walked off with his chest out.

Cedric shook his head slowly. "Can't beat a woman's touch even in business. Reverend Fisher was considering another agency after Jack died. You impressed him."

"Yeah, that's one way to describe it," Willa said and pursed her lips.

Cedric lifted one eyebrow. "I know his reputation."

"Well earned, too," Kay put in then went to answer the phone.

Willa beckoned for Cedric to follow her and headed to her office. Once Cedric closed the door Willa gave a snort. "Reverend Fisher's been fooled into believing he's irresistible," she said.

"I have no doubt that you handled him well," Cedric replied.

"If he had rubbed his big bony knee against my leg one more time." Willa simulated a slapping motion then a backhand. "Bam. Down for the count, preacher or not."

Cedric took a step back. "I'm scared of you."

"I prefer peaceful solutions, but I'm a graduate of advanced self-defense courses. I know some kick-box moves, too." Willa put both hands on her hips. "A girl can't be too careful."

"Thanks for the warning. I'll be sure to put some distance between us if I ever make you mad," Cedric said. He wore a half-smile.

"Wise man," Willa quipped. "But the good pastor gave me a clue about Strafford, Inc."

"Reverend Fisher?" Cedric's eyes widened in surprise.

"Seems Jack saw the light and was going to his church." Willa grinned at the dubious expression Cedric wore. "Yeah, I thought the same thing. He was making business contacts."

"And he found a Strafford contact at Abundant Love Tabernacle?" Cedric sat on the edge of Willa's desk. "Now that's one place I would never have thought to look."

Willa dropped down into one of the leather chairs facing her desk. "Jack wasn't the church-going type. Besides, his family is family's church is very dignified."

"Right." Cedric rubbed his chin in thought.

"They might even have rule against folks shouting 'Amen!' in that fancy church the Crowns attend." Willa sat straight and rigid in imitation of Mrs. Crown.

"Smart of you to find that lead. Wonder why none of his frat boys knew?"

Willa glanced at him. Cedric didn't look like he was ready to celebrate. She squinted at him. "I don't know, but it doesn't matter."

"Right, right. I'll get to know this deacon... What did you say his name is?" Cedric looked at her.

"I'll talk to him. Besides, Reverend Fisher gave me a very personal invitation to share the love at Abundant Love," Willa said.

"Oh. Right." Cedric stood as though about to leave.

"Speaking of investigations and intrigue, let's talk about something else. I really like being here, running Crown Protection. You want to buy this company, and I'm not sure I want to sell. In fact, I'm pretty sure I don't want to."

Cedric nodded slowly after a few moments of thought. "I thought you were leaning that way."

"If you want to go off on your own then, hey, no hard feelings. Let's just put our cards on the table, know what I mean? I want us to have a good working relationship. No unspoken tension or agendas." Willa studied his handsome face, but his expression remained neutral.

"I won't lie to you. I've been considering my options. But I'll promise you this; as long as I'm working here you'll get my best."

"I never thought you'd do less," Willa said and beamed at him.

The faint shadow of a pleased smile lifted his full mouth at the corners. "You'll be the first to know what I decide."

"Thanks."

"Now about Reverend Fisher and this deacon," Cedric said, back to all business. "I makes sense for you to follow up. Just stay far away from Fisher's hands."

"Don't worry. If he tries spreading the wrong kind of love, he'll be sorry," Willa quipped. Then she picked up the small stack of yellow phone message notes. "But before I pay him a visit, I'll talk to MiMi. I think she's simmered in her own juices long enough."

Chapter 6

Willa stared at the manicured lawn of MiMi's lovely home. And muttered a few curse words. Jack seemed not to be worried much about money if he'd bought her this spacious two-story home. Painted a light green with dark red wood shutters, it blended in with the carefully tended plants landscaped around it. She had been curious ever since MiMi had mentioned it. As if reading her thoughts Mimi swung open the door wearing a smirk.

"I knew you were dying to see my place," MiMi said.

"Good afternoon."

Willa gave her a frozen smile, furious that she'd been read so accurately. She walked into the foyer past MiMi. She was about to deliver a witty insult, but instead Willa stared at the artwork on the wall. The painting faced the wide entrance into the house. Vibrant colors made Willa gasp as each detail sank in.

"Yep, it's the real thing, Jack said it's a John Biggers painting circa 1959. Famous Black artist I understand. That's a Caribbean market scene or something. Worth a bucket of cash. Jack bought it as an investment."

"No, it's the Ghana Harvest Festival. I thought there was only one." Willa dropped her purse on a side table and went to look at the painting closer.

"Really? Then that means it's worth even more than I thought? Hallelujah and thank you Mr. Biggers."

"Biggers pioneered a new painting style rooted in the Mexican mural movement. He— "

"Wait, let me write this stuff down." MiMi darted off. She continued talking from another room. "I've got a note pad somewhere. Ah, here we go. Now you said something about Mexican morals?"

"Lord have mercy," Willa muttered. She snatched her purse from the table and spun to face MiMi. "The Mexican Mural Movement. You have no idea what I'm talking about, do you?"

MiMi started to speak then stopped. She scribbled notes. "Murals, famous black artist. Got it. I'll do an Internet search and become an authority."

"Lord have mercy," Willa repeated and shook her head.

"Okay, look. Art isn't my thing. Jack bought it— "

"As an investment. By the way you shouldn't have it here. The sunlight will affect the paint. Too bright in this foyer." Willa felt the creep of envy up her spine. She'd long coveted having even a few pieces of fine art by leading black artists.

"Thanks, girl. I'll move it today. What about in here. The living room doesn't get all that much light." MiMi chattered on as she led the way into a large, beautifully decorated room. A baby grand piano sat in one corner.

"You play?" Willa said, interrupting the flow on some subject she didn't care about in the least.

"Oh yeah. My mother made me take lessons. I actually started to like it after a while. To get back at her I started playing low down dirty blues songs instead of Chopin." MiMi giggled. "What about this wall?"

"That should do. If it's too dark at night you can buy a small light to mount on the wall beneath it. You know like they have in art museums." Willa winced at the color scheme, lime sherbet green and pink clashed in her view. Obviously MiMi didn't agree.

"Right, right. Let me put that down," MiMi mumbled to herself as she scribbled again. "Come on to the kitchen. I'll fix us a couple of diet sodas. Got some low fat popcorn I just made."

"Hmm." Willa took in her surroundings as she walked.

MiMi also liked paisley. The draperies in the living room had a subtle pattern that repeated several chairs. She wondered where MiMi had managed to find a sofa in that funky shade of lime green. The hallway leading to the kitchen was lined with more prints, mostly landscapes. A staircase curved up. Double doors indicated a closet underneath it. The polished dark wood of the stair handrail gleamed. Willa could imagine decorating it with a long garland for Christmas. Mikayla would sneak downstairs in her cute nightgown trying to catch Santa by surprise. Okay, that fantasy would never be. Mikayla now considered herself a big girl who didn't believe in kiddie stories. But still. The acute green attack of envy intensified. The beautiful kitchen made it worse.

"Damn," Willa blurted out as she looked at the honey oak cabinets. The refrigerator and dishwasher both had oak doors.

"Thanks, girl. Jack and I..." MiMi's voice died away. "Look, I'm sorry about the way Jack treated you. I mean men can be such dogs."

Willa rolled her eyes. "Oh don't even try to have a "girlfriend, can we talk" session with me. I know you."

"No really. I'm for real. And Jack really cared what you thought." MiMi waved her hands when Willa sputtered. "I'm serious. I heard him telling his brother and father off when they criticized you. He never talked about me with that kind of, you know, respect I guess is the word."

"Right. Respect that didn't include our marriage vows or my feelings when he was screwing half the city." Willa sat down on a bar stool along one end of a breakfast counter.

"He respected you as a strong woman and a great mother." MiMi cast a glance at the kitchen. "Sometimes I think I was just window dressing."

"Window dressing," Willa echoed.

MiMi picked up two glasses. She filled them with ice from the refrigerator ice dispenser then poured cola from a large bottle into both. She nodded as she put a glass in front of Willa along with a napkin. Willa almost laughed. MiMi juggled being the perfect hostess while faking a reflective moment.

"Sure. The right look." MiMi smoothed a hand over her curvy body. "From the right family. He put me up in the right neighborhood, in the right car."

"Hold on. Don't tell me you're driving a BMW silver sports coup. I'll toss my lunch if you do." Willa sat still with her glass halfway to her mouth.

"Sorry," MiMi whispered.

"Damn you, Jack Crown. That's my dream car. And frankly this is my dream house. Well, minus that pukey color scheme." Willa grimaced.

"Hey, those are my sorority colors. Alpha Kappa Alpha proud." MiMi sniffed her indignation.

"Delta Sigma Theta all the way." Willa smirked. "And those colors suck."

"Girl, when did you pledge? You should have come over to the right side," MiMi teased and slapped Willa on the arm.

"I was a freshman. My aunt's friend sponsored me." Willa stopped and mentally shook herself back to reality. "I'm here on serious business, not to be your buddy."

"Hey, since we're going to work together we should get to know each other." MiMi shrugged.

"Let me say this one last time. We're not on a team, you and me. Got it?" Willa put the glass down. She didn't want to get chummy with Jack's mistress. "About the safe deposit box."

"Okay, okay. Back to business. But like it or not we are a team, even if temporarily," MiMi added quickly when Willa hissed a sigh. "Now where do we start?"

"With the banks here in Baton Rouge of course," Willa retorted.

MiMi took a turn hissing in frustration. "Willa, I'm not that stupid. I already tried Jack's bank and all the major ones."

"If he gave you that key then he must have put your name on it, too."

"No. I would have had to fill out the signature card. You have to sign each time you open it," MiMi said with a smirk. "See? You don't know everything, Miss Just About Perfect."

"Did Jack ever have you sign a bunch of papers?" Willa ignored her dig.

"Sure, for the house and a bunch of other stuff to set me up with a couple of certificates of deposit." MiMi scowled. "I don't want to pay penalties by cashing them in early to pay my house notes."

"Get a job," Willa said. "We need to check all the branches of any bank Jack used."

"That could take me forever. Can't you and that sexy guy that works for you get your staff to get on it? I mean that's what you pay them for, to investigate." MiMi flipped one of her elegantly manicured hands.

"Our employees are paid to provide security to our customers. If they didn't we wouldn't have any business. I can't just pull them off jobs." Willa shook her head at the depth of MiMi's clueless state.

"You've got a point. Well, we can see why Jack left you in charge of the company." MiMi patted Willa on the arm. "Okay so what should we do?"

Willa looked at MiMi for a few seconds then gave a short laugh. "This is unreal."

"You know, under different circumstances we could be pals," MiMi said and sipped more cola. She reached for a large bowl. "Popcorn?"

"No. We could not be friends. And no thanks, I don't want any popcorn."

"Hmm." MiMi munched for a few seconds, sipped then patted her lips with a napkin. "Maybe not. You're a little judgmental."

That did it. Willa slid from the bar stool and found the note pad. "Here. Write down banks you know Jack visited. As executor of his estate the banks will at least tell me if he had accounts or a safe deposit box."

"That's smart. Let's see." MiMi wrote down three banks and a credit union.

"Of course if you don't fight the succession I could be granted even more authority. That might help me find this account faster. If it exists. You would get the money back faster, too."

"If I don't raise objections," MiMi said. One exquisitely shaped eyebrow went up.

"We both get what we want." Willa nodded.

"Hmm, best not to rush things. We're still pretty emotional after our terrible loss. Let's just look for the safe deposit account and deal with that later." MiMi smiled at her.

Willa pursed her lips. She could say a few choice things about MiMi. But dumb wouldn't be one of them. Not that Willa's move was all that subtle.

"Fine. I'll let you know what I find out. I won't open the box if I find it without telling you first." Willa picked up her purse."

"I trust you. Besides, if my name is on the account the bank won't let you anyway." MiMi smiled at her. "It was so nice of you to stop by."

"Yeah. Whatever." Willa endured a trip past the bad color scheme living room on her way out. "I'll call you."

"Please do. Bye-bye." MiMi waved cheerfully as though they'd had girly-girl tea party.

"Give me strength," Willa said as she strode down the driveway to her SUV.

***

Two days later Willa and Cedric had come up empty on every turn. No bank they visited had a safe deposit account in Jack's name. Armed with Jack's will, bank managers had been cooperative. For all the good it had done Willa. After another frustrating day of searching Willa was glad to be home. Almost.

She sat on the floor in her den in the middle of Jack's papers. She'd gone into his condo using MiMi's keys. Jack's mother had insisted she didn't have a set. This in spite of clear instructions added to his will saying he'd left duplicate keys with his parents. As usual after any encounter with the elder Crowns, Willa had a headache. She took turns massaging the tense spot at the back of her neck, sipping wine and plowing through the details of Jack's life. With the bits and pieces, his daily routine came together. Unfortunately Willa hadn't found the one part of the puzzle she wanted. A rustling sound near the door made Willa look up from a stack of credit card statements. Mikayla stood in the door holding one of her workbooks.

"Hi, baby girl." Willa blew her a kiss.

"Hey, Mama. I'm not coming in 'cause I don't want to mess up your homework. But what does the word 'sen-si-tive' mean?" Mikayla lifted a knee and balanced the workbook on it. She held a pencil in one fist ready to write.

"It means something has to handled carefully because it's easily hurt or maybe even has already been hurt." Willa shuffled more of her homework as Mikayla called it.

"Like Cassidy," Mikayla replied nodding her head.

"Who?" Willa glanced up at Mikayla with a frown.

"This girl at school. She wears a thing on one of her legs to help her walk." Mikayla sat down on the floor

"A leg brace."

"Yes, that's what the teachers call it. Kids make fun of her because she walks funny. If you just look at her sometimes she cries." Mikayla shrugged.

"Because the kids have hurt her feelings so she's sensitive. I hope you haven't joined in making her feel bad." Willa looked up at Mikayla.

"No. Well, I might have laughed once when Brandon Goff hopped around like he was Cassidy," Mikayla confessed finally when Willa continued to stare at her. "But I never did anything like Brandon."

"If you laughed then you most certainly have made fun of her. You don't have to say a word to hurt someone's feelings."

"But I've never said anything mean to her, and Brandon was jumping around looking silly," Mikayla replied defensively.

"You encouraged other kids to make fun of her, Mikayla. Y'all encouraged him by laughing. Honey, just remember how upset you were when kids teased you."

"Yes, ma'am. I won't do it again." Mikayla turned her attention to her workbook for several minutes. Then she looked up. "Mama?"

"Yes, baby." Willa suppressed the urge to curse when she saw how much money Jack had spent at Victoria's Secret.

"Anthony is sensitive about Daddy, isn't he? I mean sometimes he cries when he doesn't think anybody is around. I cry, too, but I don't care who sees me. Boys are different."

Willa's irritation at her dead ex-husband dissolved. The image of Anthony crying alone in his room tore at her. "Yes, baby girl. Big boys especially don't like people to see them cry."

"But I try to make him feel better. I told him some jokes I learned at school." Mikayla wrote more in her book as she talked.

Willa swiped away a couple of tears and cleared her throat. "That was really sweet of you, Mikayla. Did he laugh?"

"Nope. He just said they were dumb baby jokes then he tickled me until I laughed. Boys are wonky." Mikayla grinned. That was her word for the mysterious or messed up.

"Oh my little darlin'. Just wait until you grow up. You'll find out just how wonky the male species can be." Willa sighed as she looked at a receipt for sex toys. *Best to make sure that doesn't fall into curious kid hands.* She stuffed it into a metal file box with a lock on it. The doorbell startled her.

"Got it," Anthony yelled. His heavy athletic shoes clomped toward the door.

"Look first and don't open the door if you don't recognize the person," Willa reminded him.

"I know, I know," Anthony replied, his tone dripping with exasperation at being treated like a kid.

Moments later she heard Anthony's voice and a deeper male one. Then Cedric stood in the doorway. He patted the top of Mikayla's head.

"Evening, ladies. Hard at work I see." Cedric smiled down at Mikayla then nodded at Willa.

"Yes. I'm pretty sure Mikayla is making more progress than I am," Willa complained. She swept at hand out over the papers. "Nothing helpful so far."

"Come on, KayKay. Let the grown folks talk." Anthony appeared and beckoned to his little sister. "Got something to show you."

"No, wanna stay." Mikayla's brown eyes were bright with curiosity. "I'll see it later."

"Go finish your homework first then see what your brother wants to show you," Willa said firmly. She pointed toward Mikayla's room.

Mikayla pouted briefly then stood. She tucked her workbook under one arm. "Okay. Bye, Mr. Cedric."

"Bye, Mikayla." Cedric replied with a smile. He walked a few feet into the room then stopped. "No paper trail yet, huh?"

"Nothing except confirmation that he loved expensive wines and cheap women," Willa retorted. "And respect for the way Kay kept his office straight."

"Yeah, but give him his due. Jack had a rare skill for building networks and getting clients." Cedric sat down in one of two large recliners. Propped his elbows on both knees. "What I can do to help?"

"Go through a couple of these piles for me. I've got them sorted into receipts, paid bills, and so on." Willa frowned over one more credit card statement with hotel bills and lingerie on them.

"You okay? I mean, Jack took care of business but then he liked to play. Considering he was your husband this might be hard," Cedric said, his voice low.

"*Ex*-husband," Willa corrected.

"True." Cedric wore a sympathetic expression. "Still."

"Humph, I'm not learning much that's new. Well, this bill from a company called Smack That gave me a chuckle." Willa started to say more and then stopped. She held out a catalog of bondage accessories and let that speak for itself.

Cedric took it. "We didn't have a contract with a company called- Oh! Oh!" He cleared his throat.

"Put that one in my special file over there." Willa grinned at the way Cedric squirmed and avoided eye contact. She pointed to a plain brown folder.

"Gotcha. Anything related to an account of any kind?" Cedric appeared anxious to change the subject.

Willa suppressed a giggle. "Ahem, nothing but his personal checking and savings accounts. Both quite healthy I might add. So he wasn't exactly broke."

"Not to get too personal, but how healthy are we talking?" Cedric picked up a stack of papers and sorted through them like an expert speed-reader.

"Six thousand in the checking account. And..." Willa went back to that stack and plucked out the relevant bank statement. "Seventy-five thousand in savings."

Cedric moved on to another stack. "What's this big pile?"

"What I haven't gone through yet." Willa said.

They both worked in silence for a time; the only sound was from papers being shuffled. Mikayla stuck her head in the door in one last bid to be included. Willa took her down the hallway to her bedroom. On the way back to the den she stopped to pour a glass of wine for Cedric. When she returned she placed it on the table to his left.

"There you go. Might as well relax while we slog through this stuff." Willa smiled at him.

"Thanks." Cedric frowned at something he was reading. "Jack liked to travel."

"Didn't he though? Just ask MiMi. Took her all kinds of exciting places," Willa retorted. "One of their favorite destinations seemed to be the Caribbean."

"Really? It's good to be the boss," Cedric joked. "I haven't taken a vacation since... ninety-two, I think."

"Looks like Jack took trips alone. Business?" Willa showed the travel agency invoices to Cedric.

He read them. "Georgetown, Grand Cayman Island. Interesting."

"Jack was not into solitary recreation. My guess is he had a lady on that island. Probably more than one. No wonder he bought two of almost everything at those lingerie boutiques."

"Right." Cedric wasn't paying attention to her complaints about Jack. He was digging through more papers as Willa talked.

"I can see why he and Reverend Fisher hit it off. They're both addicted to chasing women." Willa shoved papers from her lap. This search had begun to put her in a really bad mood.

"Umm." Cedric laid out a set of papers and read them intently.

"Right. You're absolutely right. Why should I care? He was my ex-husband. It's just, it bothers me the way he could move on like that. You're a guy, explain it."

Cedric glanced up at Willa. "Don't generalize. Some guys don't know where they're well off. Don't lump us all together."

"Humph." Willa took a sip of wine and looked away from his dark gaze. Then she sat straight. "Off shore banking."

Cedric blinked hard at the sudden shift of subjects. "Say what?"

"Jack may have combined a little shady business with pleasure. He could have been hiding money to keep me from getting more child support." Willa let out a hiss as the thought made her breathe fire. "That no good—" Just then Mikayla entered. "Oh hey, baby."

"Mama, I can't find Binky Bear." Mikayla stood in the door rubbing her eyes and frowning at the same time. She'd gone from "big girl" to baby girl.

"I'll bet he's just hiding out in the closet or someplace around here. Let's find him." Willa stood and crossed to her.

"Maybe he's in the kitchen getting a glass of milk," Mikayla replied and giggled.

"Go back to bed, young lady. You're not going to play me and stay up late looking for Binky."

"But I always sleep with Binky," Mikayla protested, her little voice drifting into a whine.

"I'll round up Binky Bear. You just go get in bed. I'm not going to wrestle with you in the morning." Willa pointed down the hall then put both hands on her hips.

"Yes, ma'am," Mikayla replied in a pouting tone. She marched off with a backward glance at Cedric as though asking for support.

He waved. "Goodnight, sweet girl."

"Night," Mikayla muttered then kept going.

"That girl is looking for reasons to stay up and hang with us grown folks. Let me go find her bear." Willa ran through all the usual places Binky liked to hang out, or in other words where Mikayla usually left him.

"She's such a cutie. Hey, cut her some slack. She's a good kid." Cedric shrugged.

"Oh yeah, right. Then you wrestle with her in the morning. Trying to get her out of bed and dressed for school when she's been up too late is torture. I'll be right back."

Seconds later she found Mr. Binky Bear in one of the chairs at the breakfast table. Willa grabbed him, went to

Mikayla's room and tucked both of them in. Naturally Mikayla resisted simply turning in for the night. Willa finally had to get stern with her. After a firm "Go to sleep, young lady," Willa turned on the teddy bear night lights in Mikayla's room. With a flip of the wall switch Willa turned off the lamps on twin night stands. When she got back to the den Cedric had papers neatly lined up on the long cocktail table

"What ya got?" Willa stood over the table looking down at his handiwork.

"Just got things organized for you. You and the kids have had it rough. Concentrate on them and I'll run down this whole thing."

Willa glanced at him then back at the stacks. "You got all that stuff into these tidy piles?" She stopped and looked at her wristwatch. "Wow, I was only gone a little under twenty minutes."

"Yeah. These are receipts related to his house. These are general purchases. Here are car receipts like gas, oil changes, etc. Nothing special that I could see." Cedric stood up and slapped his large hands together. "Why don't you go get some rest?"

His words seemed to have some kind of magical affect on her. Suddenly the adrenaline that had pushed her for weeks seemed to drain away. Willa's eyes felt heavy and dry. Still a detail nagged at her. Willa pushed back against the fatigue wrapping around her.

"What about Jack's trips to Grand Cayman?" Willa eyed the stacks. "Which one of these stacks has travel receipts?"

"There are just a few of those. He also went to California and New York a few times." Cedric stood and rubbed his hands together. "Listen, I better get moving. I'll see you at the office Monday."

"Right." Willa drew the word out as she stared at the piles of paper. Between the wine and losing energy she had trouble putting a finger on what bothered her.

"Mama, can I have one more glass of water?" Mikayla yelled down the hall.

"No," Anthony yelled back from the hallway. "Go to sleep cause I don't wanna put up with you whining tomorrow morning." His response started a lively round of the dozens, sibling style.

"You two be quiet," Willa said. Her effort was drowned out by the dueling voices of her kids.

"I'll let you deal with World War Three," Cedric quipped.

Willa laughed as she followed him to the front door. "In spite of how it sounds they will be quiet soon. Trust me."

"I know you can deal, lady." Cedric stopped at the door and faced her. "See you at the office."

"Bright and early. Anything else?" Willa ignored the childish drone in the background. Cedric seemed poised to say something. Willa could have sworn he was leaning forward to kiss her goodbye. In a blink the moment passed though. Instead Cedric backed up and put his hand on the doorknob. Finally he huffed out a short laugh and shook his head.

"Have a nice peaceful evening," he said.

"Very funny. Bye." Willa pretended to shove him across the threshold once he opened the door.

She made sure the locks were engaged. Willa parted the curtains in the long window next to her front door. She looked out just in time to see him climb into his steel blue Mercury Mariner. The interior light came on. Cedric was already talking into his cell phone. Another shout from Mikayla interrupted her train of thought.

Willa let go of the curtain and headed toward her kids. "Okay, that's it. I want silence in this house. Now!"

Anthony and Mikayla must have recognized the "Don't mess with mama" tone because ten minutes later Mikayla was softly snoring, Binky Bear resting next to her. Even Anthony was in bed. With ear buds stuffed in both ears, Willa had no doubt that some junior rapper was lulling him to sleep.

Her job done whipping her little troops back in line, Willa went back to the family room. She stood over the tidy stacks. In the soft quiet of her home Willa's thoughts were finally able to click in place. Cedric had obscured her attempt to connect the dots that led to Grand Cayman.

"Now why would he do that?" Willa pushed out a breath. She hated to think of the possibilities. For some reason

Cedric was trying to distract her looking into Jack's trips to Grand Cayman. Which meant maybe he knew more than he was telling her. Willa swore and sat down to sort through the papers again. She was right back to not trusting Cedric's motives again.

***

The next day Willa kept to her office. Kay must have noticed something was up. She didn't say anything, but Willa noticed she watched her closely. A few minutes before noon Kay came into her office.

"Jai is here so I'm going to grab some lunch," Kay said.

Willa glanced up from her computer monitor for a second. "Fine."

"Did you bring lunch? I could get you something. Better yet come with me. You could use a break." Kay came inside the door and closed it behind her.

"Girl, I've got to learn to be the boss for real around here. I can't let Cedric do all the heavy lifting." Willa continued to scan the online regulations related to security agencies.

"You're doing great as far as I can see," Kay replied.

"Yeah, well that just means I've got you fooled," Willa joked.

"No way. Even some of the other employees say you're sharp." Kay sat down in one of the chairs.

Willa smiled. "Well, I sure needed that pat on the back. Thanks."

"Listen, women have it tough when we're in charge. Especially when a guy is used to being the big dog." Kay gazed at Willa steadily.

"Don't I know it." Willa thought about Cedric's hope of owning Crown Protection Services.

"I keep my eyes open around here. You get all important phone calls and mail."

Something in her tone made Willa sit up straight. "Really? Not to put you on the spot, but has Cedric asked you to do otherwise?"

"More like him not wanting you to feel… overwhelmed was the way he put it." Kay's expression made it clear she didn't buy his alleged altruism.

"I see. Any calls in particular?"

"Any problems with our job sites. Calls from our biggest clients. But you want to be the boss for real, right? So I've been sending you daily reports."

Willa thought about her words for a few seconds then laughed out loud. "So that's why Cedric was surprised that I knew so much."

Kay said nothing, but just smiled back at her.

"Thanks, Kay. I appreciate you more and more each day." Willa nodded. Having Kay watching her back made her feel less like a target.

"Mr. Crown obviously wanted you to be in charge. He loved this business. He wouldn't have left it to you if he thought you'd screw it up," Kay said, and sniffed. "He was a great guy. Ask any of the staff."

Willa got a bit teary-eyed herself. She got up and went around the desk to sit next to Kay. "Listen, sometimes I may say some raw stuff about Jack." Willa yanked a tissue from the box on her desk and offered it to her secretary.

"Oh I know he pulled some stuff on you. It's just…, well we saw a different side of him. You know?" Kay took the tissue and dabbed her eyes with dainty movements.

"Yes, I've come to understand that, sweetie." Willa continued to pat her secretary's shoulder, which seemed to make Kay cry harder. As she made soothing noises Willa thought about her late estranged husband. Jackson Phillip Crown had the rare talent of being loved and hated in equal measure, sometimes by the same women. He was a thoughtless philanderer. Yet he loved his children. He could have spent more time with them, but he never stayed away for long. He worked hard, and played just as hard. Played around to be accurate. Willa blocked the sarcastic train of thought and went back to concentrating on Kay's view of Jack.

"I'll try not to make too many negative remarks about Jack," Willa said, then wondered just how the heck she'd manage that. Especially when it looked like Jack had slipped into questionable business deals. Like father like son. Willa made a mental note to see if there was a family connection. The elder Crown and Jack's big brother weren't exactly squeaky-clean role models. Kay's throat clearing broke into her Crown family musings.

"Don't you worry, ma'am. I know he hurt you deeply. You just let it rip any time. I've been on the wrong end of a cheating man." Kay returned the favor by patting Willa's arm. She stood. "So, what should I bring you back?"

Willa stood as well. "I'm having lunch with my mama. You go have a relaxing break."

"At Best Burgers during the lunch rush? No way." Kay laughed. "But I've been good so I'm going to splurge on a big juicy quarter pound monster, with fries."

Willa glanced down at her own hips. "You're younger with the metabolism to handle it, girl. After two kids I'm done with rewarding myself with mega burgers and fries. I'll see you when I get back."

"Okay, boss. And don't worry. You lookin' fine for a mother of two. Just ask Reverend Fisher." Kay giggled at the scowl Willa gave her.

"Out." Willa pretended to growl in anger.

Thirty minutes after wrapping up a few phone calls and a short meeting with Cedric, Willa was on her way downtown to meet her mother for lunch.

Mama Ruby was in town on business with her manager in charge. Eric was Aunt Ametrine's middle child and totally trustworthy. Unlike her two youngest children. Mama had hired and fired them in quick succession, and with Eric's blessing.

Willa arrived at Serop's Lebanese restaurant after a short fifteen minutes of navigating Baton Rouge's downtown traffic. She quickly snapped up a parking space on the street before a black Corvette could beat her to it. Moments later she was easing her way into Serop's front door. The smell of garlic and meat cooking on their vertical rotisserie brought Willa's stomach to life. The place was crowded as usual.

"Over here, Willa," her mother managed to call over the hum of roughly three dozen voices. She waved a hand to make sure Willa saw her.

"Excuse me. Oops, sorry." Willa bobbed and weaved through other diners and waiters balancing hot plates of food.

"How you doin', baby?" Mama Ruby accepted a peck on the cheek from Willa.

"Okay. I'll be doing great when I get some food." Willa dropped down onto the chair next to her mother.

"Here comes Stephanie now. Hey, baby. Thanks so much." Mama Ruby gave a young redhead a smile of gratitude.

"You're welcome, ma'am. Y'all ready to order?" Stephanie put two tall glasses of tea on the table. She wrote down Willa's order for chicken shawarma salad and Mama Ruby's order for grilled shrimp shish kabobs.

"And we want an extra side order of that wonderful cucumber tahini sauce, Sugar." Mama Ruby took Willa's menu and handed both to the waitress.

"Yes, ma'am." Stephanie grinned at Mama Ruby then left.

"How did you manage to get a table, fast service and extra tahini sauce?" Willa said. She rolled her shoulders to ease the tension in them.

"I've been here a few times since they opened. Got to know Stephanie not long after she started working here. She's putting herself through community college. Her parents are no help. Mama drinks too much. Her rich daddy doesn't pay her any attention. Poor kid. Money or not, kids get mistreated by lousy parents." Mama Ruby shook her head.

Willa shook her head as well. Despite having no biological children, Ruby and Elton seemed to have been made to be parents. Fortunately they had no trouble loving children who didn't have their genes.

"Now how did you manage to get her life story while she served you lunch?" Willa laughed. She knew the answer, but liked teasing Mama Ruby.

"We got to talkin'. You know." Mama Ruby waved a hand and sipped from her glass. "Hmm, that's good Lebanese tea."

"Uh-huh. Nosey Ruby," Willa joked. She knew very well that Mama Ruby had an almost magical ability to inspire confidences. An aura of kindness and non-judgmental acceptance seemed to flow from Ruby Wilson.

"Oh hush. I didn't dip in her business. Poor child works so hard. But she's got backbone. She's not takin' one cent of her daddy's money. Too many strings attached if you know what I mean." Mama Ruby's voice dropped low.

Willa's smile vanished. A familiar sick feeling grabbed at her stomach. She thought about her half-sister. Jazz carried around scars because of those kinds of "strings."

"I hope Stephanie's scumbag daddy suffers some kind of special agony one of these days," Willa snapped.

"So have you heard from Jazz?" Mama Ruby had what seemed like a supernatural way of plugging into Willa.

"No. I'm not chasing her down either. Anthony has been confiding in her. Can you believe that? Oh yeah, she dropped that bit of news and now she won't return my calls. And she knows I'm worried that Anthony has been keeping secrets from me. I'm not going let her yank my chain this time. Well, she can kiss my assets, thank you very much." Willa flipped one hand as though chasing away a bothersome fly.

"Uh-uh." Mama Ruby pursed her lips.

Willa ignored her all knowing mama vibe. The waitress returned with their tea. She waited until the young woman left again. "I mean it. Jazz just wants me sweating after her. I'm over the guilty big sister syndrome."

"Uh-huh." Mama Ruby had an "I've heard that before" expression on her face.

"I'm serious, Mama," Willa insisted.

"Much as I care about the girl, you know how I feel." Mama Ruby smiled at the waitress approaching with two plates of food.

"You need anything, Miz Ruby, just wave." Stephanie gave Mama Ruby's shoulder a pat then darted off again.

"You have to rescue somebody's child, Ruby Wilson. And I love you for that." Willa pinched her mother's cheek.

"Go on." Mama Ruby beamed with pleasure.

Willa felt a rush of love for the tough talking, tenderhearted woman who had literally saved her life. Mama

Ruby's greatest joy was giving love and help to vulnerable people. Lord knows she'd given Jazz her best shot. Willa knew that Mama Ruby felt as though she'd failed with Jazz. Unlike the other ten foster kids who had come through her home, Mama Ruby had never been able to crack the Jazzmonetta Vaughn code. Jazz ran away at age fifteen. Seven years later she was unwilling to tell Willa where she'd been. But somehow Jazz managed to make Willa feel like whatever she'd been through was Willa's fault.

Willa chewed on a sliver of chicken rich with Lebanese spices. But her mind was across town on her half-sister. Maybe she should call her anyway. Jazz wanted affection and attention, even though she didn't know how to ask for it. Or receive it once given. Which only meant that she was lonely. Jazz had no real friends. She wouldn't let anyone get close. Including Willa or Mama Ruby.

"Tell her I said hi and she could call once in a blue moon," Mama Ruby said. "Yeah, I'm psychic. Got it from my grandmamma, Cille. Yeah, Lucille Langlois was one of them Creole women from Pointe Coupee Parish. She had second sight, cher."

"Aunt Ametrine better not hear you talking about hoodoo. She'd get too upset," Willa teased, eager to drop the Jazz subject.

"Wouldn't she though? I oughta wait until I see her with some of her other sanctimonious church lady pals and mention Granny Cille's fortune telling." Mama Ruby gave a sharp laugh at the very idea.

"Don't you dare get her all mad. I want her to give me some inside church gossip about Abundant Love Ministries and Reverend Fisher."

Mama Ruby dug her fork into a mound of her spicy salad. "I saw him on television a few times. Has a show that comes on every Sunday evening around four."

"Yes, and a radio broadcast of his church sermons Sunday mornings. Not to mention the CDs they sell, the church gift shop and Abundant Love Car Wash."

"Well, if anybody can clue you in its Ametrine." Aunt Ametrine walked into the restaurant seconds later. Mama

Ruby waved a hand to get her sister's attention. "Speak her name and up she pops."

"Sorry I'm late girls. How y'all doin'?" Aunt Ametrine looked flushed from an active morning. "Lord, I stopped to chat with Sister Isabelle and just couldn't get away."

"Really?" Mama Ruby shot a sideways glance at Willa.

Willa swallowed a giggle. They both knew Ametrine loved to gossip. Papa Elton claimed she held the world record for marathon gossiping.

"How is Miss Isabelle these days?" Willa managed finally.

"Poor soul is lonely. Her son and daughter ought to be ashamed. Hardly call her, bless her heart." Aunt Ametrine spent a few more seconds criticizing. She only paused to give the waitress her order.

"As usual you had a happy morning helping others," Mama Ruby said fast before Ametrine could resume. Again she gave Willa an amused glance. What she meant was her sister loved dipping in other people's business.

Aunt Ametrine went back to arranging items in her huge tote bag. She missed the joke as usual. She gave a dramatic sigh as she nodded. "The Home Mission Ministry really does have big job. As the president most of the work always falls on me. Still I'm blessed to carry the Lord's load."

"Yes, indeed. You've certainly got a load all right," Mama Ruby deadpanned and rolled her eyes.

Willa coughed to cover a bark of laughter then drank from her tea glass.

"Ahem, must be a cold coming on."

"And speaking of ungrateful children, have you talked to Jazzmonetta?" Aunt Ametrine arranging her tote bag finally.

She refused to call her Jazz, her stage name.

"She's probably busy," Willa said and swallowed more tea.

"Humph." Aunt Ametrine started to continue but stopped to accept her order. She watched the waitress leave then leaned forward and lowered her voice. "Should be on her knees in somebody's church. Half naked giving laps dances."

"Let it go, Ametrine. When she's ready to change her life she will." Mama Ruby's tight expression said she hadn't accepted her own words so easily.

"Speaking of church." Willa was determined to avoid more Jazz generated family tension. "I met Reverend Lawrence Fisher. Know him, Auntie?"

Aunt Ametrine blinked a few times then adjusted to the change in direction. She wore an expression of respect and envy. "Abundant Love Ministries. Of course. That church has doubled in size in just five years. They do radio and TV shows every week."

"Reverend Fisher is a little too slick for me," Mama Ruby said then savored a forkful of her lunch.

"Jack signed a contract to provide security to the Abundant Love Tabernacle. So he's a client," Willa said.

"That's funny. I think his congregation needs protection from him. He's got his hands way down in their pockets. And on their wives if I'm any judge of men." Mama Ruby pointed her fork to reinforce her words.

"He's an anointed man of God, Ruby. Maybe he's a bit theatrical, but he teaches Bible fed lessons." Aunt Ametrine frowned with disapproval at her sister.

"Two words, girl. False prophet. Another two words, scam artist." Mama Ruby had never been affected by her sister's righteous scolding.

"Maybe if you came to church more often you could afford to judge," Aunt Ametrine said with a sniff. She took a dainty bite of her gyros pita sandwich.

"Anyway," Willa said to break the usual argument cycle about to commence. "According to the good reverend Jack had gone back to church. His church."

Aunt Ametrine dabbed her mouth and swallowed. "Well, lift Holy hands. Jack died after getting right with the Lord. Reverend Fisher is truly a fisher of men if he got Jack into church."

"Oh he's reelin' 'em in all right," Mama Ruby retorted. She shrugged when Willa frowned at her.

"Just where did Reverend Fisher come from?" Willa didn't waste time or breath asking her aunt if she knew.

Aunt Ametrine rested both elbows on the table. "Came from New Orleans. He's got a powerful testimony of deliverance. Reverend Fisher ran with a murderous drug dealing gang in one of those projects. Broke his grandmother's heart with his lifestyle."

"Ha, served time in jail, too." Mama Ruby stopped her next comment at a dirty look from Willa.

"Go on, Auntie. You were saying about his testimony." Willa smiled at her aunt.

"He's never hidden his past," Aunt Ametrine replied with a sharp glance at her sister. "He says Hurricane Katrina swept away friends and relatives. The whole experience made him re-examine his sinful life."

"Interesting." Willa wondered who was right, her aunt or her mother. Then she remembered the suggestive glint in his dark eyes when he looked at her. Willa had a feeling Mama Ruby would come out on top this time.

"More than that, inspiring really." Aunt Ametrine went on to tell how he was born again during a church service in Houston, Texas where he had been evacuated during the storm. His grandmother died. Two of his brothers drowned because they had refused to evacuate. His mother, a drug addict, disappeared into the ghettos of Miami where she relocated. Fisher had three children by three different women by the time he was twenty-five. In true Sister Ametrine fashion, her aunt gave Willa plenty of back-story on Reverend Fisher. Willa figured Cedric would have an easy time filling in more details. After ten minutes Aunt Ametrine had moved on to the rest of the congregation.

"Do you know one of his deacons, Isaac Nelson?" Willa said to re-direct the flood of information back to relevancy.

"Isaac Nelson," Aunt Ametrine repeated. She dipped a sliver of pita bread in hummus, chewed slowly on it and the name. Then she shook her head. "Can't put a face to that name."

"Oh." Willa ate a tiny piece of chicken.

"Sorry, baby. Wait a minute. You can't think Reverend Fisher had anything to do with Jack's death." Her aunt's light brown eyes went wide at the very thought.

"I'm just trying to connect any dots that I can, Auntie. Especially in case Detective Miller starts looking at Anthony again." Willa thought about the beefy officer of the law. He did not impress Willa as a man who would roll over that easy.

"Looking at Anthony?" Aunt Ametrine's eyes grew wider. "Y'all didn't tell me that! Why the nerve of those officers. Anthony has his faults, but he would never hurt anybody."

"Well that's one thing I can say 'Amen' to," Mama Ruby added.

"So far Detective Miller hasn't been back." Willa pursed her lips. Somehow she felt like Miller had another shoe to drop though. Not to mention her fears that Anthony would slip from boyish mischief into more serious misdeeds.

"Don't forget that lawyer your brother told you about," Mama Ruby said, breaking into her thoughts. "No way we gonna let that child get caught up in nothing bad."

"And I'm gonna pray on it, too," Aunt Ametrine added.

Willa put a hand on each of their arms. These were two of her strong anchors. More than blood had forged her adopted family. Once again she felt a rush of love and gratitude to have them.

"Thank you. Y'all always make me feel like things are going to work out." Willa gave each woman a kiss on the cheek.

"We love you, too, sweetheart." Aunt Ametrine glowed from the compliment.

Willa felt a prick of guilt. Jazz had always felt like an outsider. She needed to find her sister and try again to bridge the gulf between them.

"I'm going to talk to Jazz again," Willa said. She saw her mother and aunt exchange a glance.

Chapter 7

Willa's head hurt from staring at numbers and reading reports. Cedric had taken over dealing with the contracts in a hands-on way. Easy decision since he had the experience in providing security services. Still he'd been forced to admit Willa knew about legal investigations. Her job as a paralegal meant she was very comfortable digging through records. Kicking it around online databases was second nature to her. Still she was getting sick of sitting behind a desk. She stood and did a few stretching exercises.

Kay knocked then entered. She carefully shut the door behind her. "This lady says she's your sister."

Willa stopped mid-stretch. "Jazz?"

"She wouldn't tell me her name, just said, 'Tell Willa her sis is out here.'" Kay wore a skeptical expression.

Willa exhaled noisily. "Yeah, that's my sister Jazz. I apologize."

"For what?" Kay blinked at her.

"She's all attitude, right? Sorry for whatever crap she tossed your way." Willa patted Kay's shoulder as she walked past her to the door.

"She's grown and should take responsibility for her own behavior," Kay replied.

"Have you been talking to my mama?" Willa wisecracked as she opened the door. With Kay on her heels Willa entered the lobby.

Jazz wore straight-legged jeans and a lime green tank top. Both clung to her curves like a second skin. Today she wore a short chin length blonde wig cut in a bob. Her sunglasses were huge and gold. A large gold metallic purse hung from her left shoulder. She jingled a set of keys on one hand and held a super-sized plastic cup of soda in the other.

"Hey." Jazz flicked a brief gaze up and down Willa. Then she turned in a circle to examine the office.

"Kay, this is my sister Jazz. Kay is our administrative assistant," Willa said, and then wondered why she bothered with the obvious.

"How ya doin'?" Jazz turned to face Kay. "Got a secretary. I could use one of them. You freelance?"

"Excuse me?" Kay blinked at Jazz then looked at Willa.

"You know, every girl could use some extra money. Least all the ladies I know. I'm startin' my own business. Gonna call it Girls To Go. My slogan is 'We can make your party rock hard'." Jazz tilted her head to once side. "What ya think?"

"Wow," was Kay's stunned reply. Her blinking no doubt could set speed records.

"Yeah. I have plenty of contacts from my work so I figure the phone's gonna be jumpin'. I'll need a good appointment secretary and stuff. Nothing too different from what you do around here." Jazz swept a hand out. "Bet you meet a lot of interesting people."

"No doubt," Kay blurted, then pressed her lips closed.

Jazz laughed. "Girl, for real. Listen, you could make some good connections. Some of the guys I know are pretty successful businessmen. Potential clients, I mean."

"I don't really have time to work another job. But thanks for the offer." Kay smiled at her then sat at her desk quickly.

"Okay, but you might wanna think it over." Jazz turned to Willa. "So what's up with you?"

Before Willa could recover from Jazz's performance Cedric strode down the hall from his office. Jazz's attention switched to him like a laser sight on an automatic weapon. She gave him a full body scan then smiled.

"How you doin'? I'm Jazz, Willa's sister. Nice suit." Jazz gestured at the charcoal gray suit he wore.

Cedric's gaze flickered to Willa for on an instant before he smiled at Jazz. He held out one hand. "Nice to meet you."

"Same here." Jazz shook it then briefly turned it over to stare at his ring finger. "Very nice meeting you."

Cedric's smile stayed steady as he freed his hand and turned to Willa. "Just call me when you're available. I have some results from that research we talked about."

His words hardly registered though Willa nodded at him as if she understood. The shock of having Jazz show up had twisted her brain and tongue. After a few minutes she realized Kay and Cedric were staring at her. Jazz was still staring at Cedric provocatively. Willa snapped out of her daze.

"My office is this way, Jazz." Willa moved to block Jazz's line of vision to Cedric and pointed the way.

"Right." Jazz looked past her anyway. "Maybe I'll see ya later."

"Have a great day," Cedric replied. He glanced at Willa but kept his expression neutral. Then he turned around and went down the hall to his office.

Though she walked ahead of Willa, Jazz glanced back in the direction Cedric had gone several times. "Girl, you got more like him up in here? Hell, I want a job with you."

Willa waited to reply once they were in her office with the door closed. "To what do I owe this totally unexpected pleasure."

"So you must be kickin' it with him. That's cool. Just make me happy and tell me he's got a brother, a cousin, or shit I'll take his daddy." Jazz let out a coarse laugh.

Willa led her to the seating area in her office. "Have a seat."

Jazz laughed again and dropped down into one of the leather chairs. Willa fully expected to hear the sound of fabric splitting. Yet Jazz looked quite comfortable. She even crossed her legs.

"This is a tight office. You got it sweet." Jazz looked around like an appraiser mentally adding up a price tag.

Willa could almost hear the word "again"added on the end of her sentence. "Hardly the way I wanted to own a business," she said crisply.

Jazz looked at her. "I know, I know. I was just sayin'. Anyway, I was over this way and decided to say hi."

"Possibly because of the dozen or so messages I left." Willa counted to five to keep her temper in check.

"Yeah, well. I've been busy. It's crazy at the club, girl. I mean, do you even know all the guys that are still in this city after that storm?" Jazz said, referring to the population boom in Baton Rouge since Hurricane Katrina devastated New Orleans.

"Right," Willa said dryly.

"Girl, Lorraine wants me to do three shows a day. I'm trying to be a partner in the business. She can't pimp me like I just got there." Jazz snapped her fingers to make her point.

"I didn't realize dancers had seniority," Willa answered. Some sarcasm must have dripped into her tone. Jazz's eyes narrowed.

"We're a business just like this place. Different product, but a lot of the same rules apply," Jazz cracked back. "Course I wasn't lucky enough to have a husband to leave me set up."

Willa sighed. Somehow they always arrived back in the same place. Jazz resented what she saw as Willa's good fortune. Logic, and Mama Ruby, told Willa the bad things that happened to her sister weren't Willa's fault. Yet their mother's words all those years ago stuck in Willa's head. "You shoulda been lookin' out for your baby sister" Vivienne had spat. Never mind that she'd never been much of a parent. Always chasing men and hanging in the clubs, Vivienne had never accepted any responsibility. She blamed the social workers, the police, the men, the drug dealers-- and Willa. A firm mental shove stuffed those memories back in the closet.

"So you had time to visit me. Nice." Willa gripped the arms of her leather chair.

"Yeah, well." Jazz shrugged. "You heard from the po-po again?"

"I haven't heard from Detective Miller lately, no. I did talk to Anthony. Jack offered Anthony a job, so that should show Detective Miller that Anthony had no motive to kill him."

"Right. Right. Good point. Yeah, Jack probably wanted Anthony to take over the business someday, huh? Probably told him about it." Jazz stood and walked around the office. She examined the prints on the wall. Then she went to the bookshelf in one corner and read the book spines.

"Anthony doesn't know any details, just general stuff."

"Still I'll bet Anthony would want to help out the family business. Work around here after school, right?" Jazz went to the window and gazed out at the scenery.

"Anthony has his hands full keeping his grades up right now. He can get a job next year." Willa studied her sister's profile. "You seem real interested in the business and what Anthony knows about it. What's up with that?"

Jazz turned to face her. "Me and Anthony just got kinda close, ya know? I understand what it's like to have people on your back all the time, wanting you to follow their plan."

Willa frowned. "Tell me again how y'all hooked up?"

Her sister shrugged and turned away. "You're gonna get on his case."

"Don't even tell me it was in the club." Willa grimaced.

"You didn't tell him I worked there," Jazz said over her shoulder. "So he was shocked to see me. Him and a couple of his boys slipped in with fake ID cards."

"He saw you on stage? Oh God." Willa flinched. The dull ache at the back of her skull kicked in full force.

Jazz twisted a lock of the fake hair. "I was in the bar hanging with a couple of regulars. Saw him and his partners havin' a good old time. Just kid stuff. Red-blooded teenage males with raging hormones. Whooping it up with beer and girls. When I could get away I rounded 'em up and kicked their little under age butts out of there." Jazz came back and dropped down into the chair without looking at Willa.

"Gee, thanks for finally telling me my son is involved in watching strippers and drinking," Willa snapped.

"I wasn't gonna let nothin' happen to him. Oh hell, don't give me that look like Ruby and her Amen Sisters." Jazz smacked her lips.

"You were looking out for him. Well that puts it in a whole new light," Willa shot back. "While I'm trying to keep him from being a statistic you're giving him a pat on the back."

"I told you I tossed 'em out," Jazz replied, her voice cracking loud enough to bounce off the walls. "They were bein' kids, not robbin' banks. Damn, no wonder he talked to me."

Willa rose from her chair. "I'd rather he be angry with me now if it saves his future, maybe even his life. Being a parent and being a buddy aren't compatible, Jazz. I realize you might have a tough time understanding that."

"Fine. I don't want to mess with you being super mama, all perfect and shit." Jazz spit out the words. She stood, purse on her shoulder again. "

"I'm no where near perfect, all right? It's just I have different values as a mother." Willa puffed out a sigh of frustration. She instantly knew her attempt to explain had come out wrong. "What I'm saying is— "

Jazz held up one hand, palm out like a cop stopping traffic. "Oh, I know damn well what you're sayin'."

"I'm screwing this up. Look, I really appreciate you throwing them out." Willa gazed at her baby sister. Jazz stood with both hands on her hips glaring at her. "I'm guessing you had a few choice words for them, too."

"I told them to stop bein' stupid. That they could get the club shut down and me unemployed." Jazz's hard expression eased a bit. "Better that than to say they were outta their league. That would have only made them pissed."

Willa nodded, understanding the psychology behind her actions. "Pissed enough to prove they're men by doing something even more stupid. Thanks, Jazz."

"Yeah, well." Jazz fidgeted with the tassel dangling from her purse. "At least you know where he was that night. I'll bet he went on home with his pal. I kinda acted like your aunt Ametrine and poured on the guilt."

Willa blinked hard at her. "What night?"

"The night Jack got killed. Anthony said he was gonna tell you. Anyway, Jack came in later and— " Jazz stopped when she saw Willa's expression. "What?"

"You saw both Jack *and* Anthony the night Jack was murdered? And you're just now telling me this?" Willa was in Jazz's face shouting.

The door to her office flew open. Cedric strode in with Kay right behind him. Both wore worried frowns.

"Is there a problem?" Cedric looked at Willa then Jazz.

"Nah, ain't no problem. Drama queen here is freakin' per usual," Jazz said. "I've had my daily dose of soap opera so I'm leavin'."

Willa grabbed Jazz's left arm and snatched her back as she tried to leave. "Oh hell no. Y'all excuse us a minute."

"Heffa, you best get control before I whip your ass up in here." Jazz pulled away then cursed when Willa's grip tightened.

"I need to talk to my sister. Leave us alone for a minute," Willa said, struggling to keep her voice down and her words polite. Out of the corner her eye she saw a curious crowd of employees and clients gathering in the lobby. No doubt they had ears strained to hear.

Cedric looked at both women as though making sure neither had weapons. "You sure?"

Willa only nodded. She and Jazz stared at each other as Cedric and Kay left. When the door closed Willa loosened her hold. Jazz jerked her arm free and stomped to the other side of the room.

"You better tell right now why the hell I'm just hearing this," Willa said.

"What you gonna do? Beat me down? Please. You couldn't whip me on your best day." Jazz tossed the challenge over her shoulder. She wore her tough hood girl persona like a suit of armor.

Any other time Willa would have seen through her, would have ached for the hurt kid she knew was inside. But now they were talking about Willa's son. Her baby.

"Tell me about that night," Willa replied in a controlled voice. Something in her tone seemed to crack through Jazz's defense.

"I was gonna tell you. I mean, I didn't realize it was the same night until a couple of days later. But you knew Anthony had been hanging with his friend that night. So I figured, you'd know." Jazz walked around the office picking up and putting down things. First an ink pen, then a framed photo of Jack shaking hands with the mayor.

"No. I'm not buying it." Willa blocked the path to her office door. She stood with her legs apart, arms at her sides. She was fully prepared to physically stop Jazz from leaving.

Jazz pushed out a harsh breath and faced Willa. "Okay fine. I was tryin' not to rock your perfect little bourgie world. But since you insist. Jack used to stop by the club. He was dating one of the girls, Nailah. When she left to work at Sugar and Spice Jack started hangin' there mostly. But every now and then he would come by to say hello. Him and his church buddies."

"Names?" Willa prodded.

"Some deacon. Liked me to call him Big Ike. Always braggin' about his size. If you know what I mean" Jazz rolled her eyes in a way that said she'd heard it all.

"What about a preacher?" Willa felt a nasty sick feeling grow in her stomach.

Jazz waved a hand. "We have a private entrance for the VIP section. The boss opened it two years ago for people who want to keep their partyin' habits quiet." Jazz's cynical smile distorted her pretty face in a way that made Willa's heart ache.

"Reverend Lawrence Fisher?"

"We don't have a damn guest book at the club. All them guys blend in to one big blur after awhile." Jazz shrugged. She sat down in the chair again.

Willa wasn't sure she believed her. "When did Jack leave that night and who was he with?"

"I got busy gettin' ready for my act. Maybe around ten. Jack came to my dressing room to say bye. Far as I know he was alone." Jazz fidgeted with her purse again. She concentrated on the leather as though the pattern fascinated her. "Anyway, doesn't matter. He was fine. Just happened to stop by that night. Ain't got nothin' to do with him being robbed by some crack head."

"Maybe someone from the club followed him. Jack wore an expensive watch. Dressed nice. He was driving his Jaguar. Jack could have been killed by one of your customers. You have to talk to Miller."

"I already have." Jazz's dark eyes sparkled with fear. Her long fingers clutched the purse until her long acrylic nails dug into it. "Somehow he found out Jack was at the club."

"So you told him all this." Willa felt a chill. "About Anthony, too."

Jazz stood and walked to Willa. "No. I left out a few details. Anthony went home with his friend. So him being at the club had nothin' to do with Jack showing up later. Nothin' at all."

Willa opened her mouth to speak, but couldn't form words. They both knew Miller wouldn't see it that way. And if Anthony was there, maybe he knew something about Jack's movements. Willa fought the urge to cry. Why couldn't she keep her kids safe, innocent of the dirty side of life? All of her efforts seemed pitifully inadequate. Willa felt as though her birth family's sordid ghetto lifestyle clung to her like a greasy fog.

Willa closed her eyes to fight the dizzy nauseous feeling. "I've got to do something."

"Listen to me, you don't do or say anything. You actin' like the police are our friends. Hell, I didn't even believe that in grade school when the cops would pass out candy. I knew better." Jazz pointed at her. "Keep your mouth shut."

"If Miller traced Jack to the club he's going to find out." Willa forced her mind to work around the fear taking hold. "Think, think, think."

"Anthony didn't kill Jack," Jazz said in a calm low voice.

"I know that. Hell, I don't need you to tell me my child didn't— " Willa started to shake. She dropped down onto the small leather sofa.

Jazz leaned forward. "Just be cool, awright? Miller can find out whatever he's gonna find out, but not so fast. Ain't nobody talkin'. That gives you time to be ready."

Willa gazed at her sister. "Right."

Jazz stood and crossed to Willa. She put a hand on Willa's shoulder briefly then pulled it back. "Anthony is gonna be safe. We'll make sure. Okay?"

"Okay." Willa felt numb as she watched Jazz walk to the door.

"I'll call you in a few days. Sooner if I hear anything about the police being back at the club." Jazz nodded once then went through the door.

Moments later Cedric came in without knocking. "Tell me what's going on, Willa."

For a panicked moment Willa thought she was going to throw up. She clamped a hand over her mouth. The sick feeling subsided. Cedric left the office, but came back moments later with a can of soda and a plastic cup.

"Breathe deep and slow, then drink this. It will settle your stomach." Cedric sat next to Willa. "Sip a little at a time."

Willa followed his directions. His solid arm was around her shoulder when Kay came in. The worry lines on Kay's forehead deepened when she looked at Willa.

"What can I do?" Kay said to Cedric.

"If we have any appointments shuffle them to later if you can," Cedric said.

"I can have Chris meet with Eric Harrington about the security at the high school games. You've got Mrs. Sandifer coming in at two-thirty." Kay didn't need to consult her computer.

"I'm okay," Willa said, fighting to regain her composure. She put down the cup of soda on the table nearby. "Business as usual."

Cedric and Kay looked at each other. Kay left at a discreet nod from Cedric. One of his big hands covered both of Willa's.

"Tell me what's going on."

"Just a bit of family drama. Nothing serious. Jazz and me have our moments like a lot of sisters." Willa sprang from the sofa and went to her desk.

"I can't help if you won't let me." Cedric stood. He stared at Willa hard.

"I promise to ask for your help when I need it." Willa smiled at him and hoped the effort didn't fail. His expression told her it had.

"If what went down between you and your sister just now has something to do with Jack's murder." Cedric stopped. "Don't wait too late to ask."

"Thanks. I want to meet more clients since I'm the boss, right?" Willa changed the subject.

"Right." Cedric gazed at her a few seconds longer then left.

Willa went to the office door and locked it. She punched in her mother's number first. Next she would call her brothers. Then she would call Brad Craft, her former boss at the law firm of Craft, Mouton and LaPlace. Legal advice seemed like a very good idea.

***

Hours later Willa had succeeded against the odds. She'd actually gotten work done at the office. On her mother's advice she hadn't raced to pull Anthony out of school to grill him. Mama was right. Anthony would likely dig in his heels in and refuse to talk. Or worse, he might lie to Willa. Besides, although Willa had skills interviewing witnesses for her old law firm, for rooting out the truth, when it came to family avoiding the truth was her main coping strategy. Long ago as a kid in the child welfare system Willa had learned to hate therapy. Or as she called it "Spill your guts until you cry and throw up." Those social workers thought a family sharing their feelings was a good thing. Bull. Willa very much valued the let-sleeping-dogs-lie problem solving method.

On the drive home her instinct to avoid bad news was in full force. By the time she pulled into her driveway Willa was rehearsing ways to let Anthony off the hook. She pulled into the garage and hit the remote. As the garage door slid down smoothly Mikayla peered through the window set in the back door. Seconds later Mikayla came into the garage. She hopped around on the concrete floor causing her thick braids to bounce.

"Mama, mama. Guess what? Guess what? Mrs. Anderson picked me to play fairy godmother in the play," Mikayla blurted out unable to wait for Willa to guess.

"Congratulations. You'll do a wonderful job I know." Willa kissed her forehead. Well, at least someone would be in a good mood in the Crown house tonight.

"Thank you. I have a list of everything I'm going to need. Mrs. Tate and Mr. Jenkins will make the costumes. Let's go." Mikayla tugged on Willa's hand urging her back toward the car.

"Go? I just got here. We're going to have dinner, I'll look over the list and this weekend we'll shop." Willa spoke in her steady "mama knows best" tone.

"Aw Mama," Mikayla replied in her well-practiced whiny tone.

"Aw daughter," Willa whined back. She grinned when Mikayla made a face that reminded her of Mama Ruby.

"Fine. Make me wait longer than the other kids. We start rehearsing in two days. I'm going to practice my lines." Mikayla stomped off like a diva.

"Hmm." Willa saw a bright red folder on the kitchen counter. In it was a letter from the Mrs. Anderson; the rehearsal schedule Mikayla had dramatically announced. Willa shook her head as she went through the kitchen and down the hallway to her bedroom. As she passed Mikayla's room she paused.

"This play is almost three weeks away. I think we can wait a few more days to gather up your fairy godmother supplies." Willa smothered a laugh when Mikayla gave a long-suffering sigh.

"Yes, mother," Mikayla replied drawing out the last word, a sign Willa was being unreasonable in her childish view.

Mikayla flipped one of her braids over a shoulder and concentrated on her script.

Anthony came down the hallway with his cell phone pressed to one ear. "S'up, moms."

"Hi, sweetie. Look, I'm going to get comfortable and start dinner. Then we need to talk." Willa watched his youthful face crinkle in a frown. "Yes, talk."

Anthony hit the mute button on his phone. "I told Cheyenne we were gonna meet at the library to study."

"This a new girlfriend I haven't met, huh? You know my rule. No hook up until I talk to her and her parents." Willa raised an eyebrow at him.

"Don't be embarrassing me, Mama," Anthony protested. "I'm sixteen."

"I want to know who you hang with, male or female. The rule will change when you hit twenty-one." Willa pursed her lips when Anthony's expression changed to one of horror.

"You're kidding. Please tell me you're kidding," Anthony pleaded, hands pressed together as if in prayer.

"Son, if I don't get the right answers to my questions you may not have a social life until then. In the den, forty-five minutes from now. So call Cheyenne and re-schedule."

Anthony flipped his phone open as he whipped around and headed for his room. He mumbled as he dialed. Willa didn't need to ask what he said. She had a pretty good idea of the general sentiments he'd uttered.

"So much for anyone being happy," Willa muttered. She thumped her bedroom door shut, grateful for a brief bit of sanctuary from parenthood. Twenty minutes later she'd showered. Willa put on her favorite pink lounge set. The supple cotton fabric hugged her. Her soft pink slippers completed her transition from her day to home life.

Willa padded into the kitchen. She took out a pan of her homemade lasagna. She defrosted it for a few minutes in the microwave then put it in her conventional oven. Minutes later she had a big bowl of tossed salad made and zucchini squash in the steam cooker. She took a deep breath, let it out and headed for the family room. Anthony was already there, sitting on the sofa bobbing his head to music from his MP3 player. He heaved a resigned sigh when he noticed Willa taking a seat across from him on the smaller sofa.

"What's the deal, moms?" Anthony took out his ear buds as he spoke. "Can't be anything at school. I've been nerdy."

"What?" Willa blinked at him, temporarily distracted from composing her opening line.

"You know, following the rules. Doing my assignments. Like a nerd, a geek." Anthony shrugged.

"Like a young man with a future you mean," Willa retorted. "Someone who won't be working in a fast food place at age thirty."

"Right." Anthony drawled out the word.

Willa felt her blood pressure rising. She would have to save her speech on the culture of under achievement for another day. The topic they needed to discuss was a lot more important.

"Jazz came to my office today." Willa watched him carefully. His left eyebrow twitched.

"Oh really? How's she doing?" Anthony cleared throat. He even managed to smile. "I'll bet Jazz made an impression in that bourgie office."

"She told me you were at the club. Which is something we don't need to discuss in detail, right?" Willa stared at him hard.

"Those places aren't for minors, I had no business being there and I'm grounded. Guess that sums it up." Anthony glanced at Willa then looked away.

"Perfectly. But beyond that you were there the same night Jack was killed." Willa leaned forward. Her chest tightened with tension. "Don't lie to me, son. This is too important. Did you see Jack that night?"

"For a minute." Anthony didn't look at her. "Not at the club though, at his office. Your office now."

"Why?" was all Willa could manage to say. Fear froze her tongue, but the need to protect him pushed her on.

"We hung out some cause he wanted me to be in the business. Keeping it in the family he said." Anthony smiled for a minute before it faded. "He wasn't all bad."

Willa swallowed the lump of emotion in her throat. "No, few people are. Did he say anything about somebody giving him a problem?"

Anthony looked at Willa. "He didn't say anything like that."

"Then tell me what y'all talked about." Willa could almost hear the wheels turning.

"He told me about contracts, how being the boss was hard work and stuff like that. That I needed to listen to you and work hard in school."

"Oh." Willa took a few moments to get over her surprise. Jack had usually schooled Anthony in the art of just getting by. Smart as he was, Jack had done as much partying in college as anything else. Unlike Willa, who had to work, Jack had a monthly check from daddy to sustain him while in school. He majored in business and minored clubbing. Jack had brains, but he also had the spoiled kid syndrome.

"Did he tell you anything about his plans later that night?" Willa tapped a foot nervously then stopped when Anthony glanced at it.

"No. Jazz gave me a lecture on staying away from clubs. At least until I'm legal." Anthony exhaled noisily. "Okay, I'm grounded until twenty-one or I get a job paying enough for me to move out."

Willa's temperature ticked up slowly at his impudent vibe. "Let me tell you one thing, youngster. Do not mess with me. You better be telling me everything that went on that night. Better me than homicide detective Miller."

"Say what?" Anthony frowned at her.

"That's right, sport. Detective Miller is checking you out for motive and opportunity," Willa said crisply. She crossed her arms and gazed at him steadily.

"He's crazy. I didn't have nothing to do with Dad's murder. He can question me. I'm straight." Anthony lost none of his defiant teenage cool.

"Boy, I haven't spanked you in a long, long time. Don't push me to put my hands on you tonight. Now tell me if you saw Jack again that night." Willa rose until she was standing over him, both hands on her hips.

"Mama, I'm telling you. Don't worry."

Willa was about to say more when the doorbell rang. She jabbed a forefinger at him. "Don't move."

She muttered to herself about the curse of parenting teenagers, her choice of a husband and Jazz as she marched to the front door. And who the hell was ringing her doorbell around dinnertime? She glanced out the window and cursed when MiMi waved with a grin. Willa clicked the locks with force. MiMi started talking the minute the door was open.

"Sorry, I know I should have called but honestly I didn't want you to refuse to see me. I think we really need to talk. Our lawyers are in a stand off. Let's cut to the real deal, the bottom line, the — "

"Not now. And how did you get this address?" Willa blurted out.

"Jack's address book in his PDA. He left it at the house, well our house. The police didn't search me. I'm surprised his mother didn't tell that detective Miller about me."

"Trust me, having Jack's mother ignore you is a blessing. Wait, Jack had a PDA?" Willa stared at the steel blue object MiMi was holding in her right hand. Her leather Dooney & Burke purse swung in her left hand.

"I'll tell you more once you invite me in." MiMi raised a perfectly shaped eyebrow at her.

"For a minute. I'm cooking dinner for the kids and—, " Willa stepped aside as MiMi swept past her into the foyer.

"Girl, I need to be taking notes for when I become a mother. Time for me to grow up. Can't be a glamorous rich man's plaything forever, you know. Ooh, love these colors." MiMi kept right on walking to the formal living room. "Where are those darling kids of yours?"

"Mama, you want me to check on the food? We're studying cooking at school." Mikayla stood in the door. She talked to Willa, but gazed at MiMi.

"Aren't you adorable. Your hair is so pretty. Did your mama style it for you?" MiMi beamed down at her.

"Yes, ma'am." Mikayla took a few steps into the room.

"I need to start studying up in case I have a girl." MiMi laughed.

"Mikayla, go back to your room. I'll check on dinner. You know the oven and stove are off limits." Willa moved to lead her away.

"I'm MiMi Landry. You can call me MiMi." Ignoring Willa's hint, MiMi stuck out a hand.

"I'm not allowed to call adults by their first name. Nice to meet you Miss MiMi." Mikayla shook her hand and gave her a polite smile.

"Hey, Mama. I have homework I can be starting on since you got company," Anthony said, peering around the door. "Hello."

"Hi, Anthony. So nice to see you again. Your kids have such lovely manners. I tell you it's a refreshing experience. You should see how some of my nieces and nephews act."

"Kids, Miss Landry was a friend of your father's," Willa replied, pushed into setting a good example in the etiquette department.

"Yeah, we met at Dad's office a few times." Anthony blinked when Willa glanced at him sharply. "Once or twice maybe I mean."

Mikayla's antennae seemed to pop up at the subtext. She looked at her mother then at Anthony. "You were daddy's latest girlfriend?"

"Real smooth, little sis," Anthony said low. He used his eyebrows and subtle hand movements to send her a non-verbal message.

Mikayla put a hand over her mouth then dropped it. "Sorry, Mama. But you knew about Daddy's other girlfriends."

"Oh Lord." Willa put a hand to her forehead. She'd done a poor job of keeping Mikayla out of her marital soap opera.

"Sweetie, your daddy didn't have any other girlfriends after me." MiMi smiled at her.

"But what about the nice lady who lives on an island?" Mikayla looked up at her.

"Oh no you didn't," Anthony blurted out. His eyes widened as he stared at his sister.

"What?" Willa and MiMi yelped in unison. The doorbell rang seconds later.

"I swear I don't remember mailing out party invitations," Willa muttered. "Nobody move or talk until I get rid of this person and come back."

She whispered a string of curse words to get it out of her system. Marching to the front door, Willa decided she would get control of her home. She swung open the door without checking. Detective Miller and his partner Detective Addison nodded to her. Willa's stomach lurched as fear slammed into her like a fist. Her throat tightened as though a noose had been drawn around it. No words could come out.

After waiting a few beats Miller spoke first. "Good evening, Mrs. Crown. We need to talk to you and your son."

Willa recovered quickly "What? I mean, no. He's a minor and you don't have my permission,"

"This will be easier if we can clear up a little matter soon. We're just trying to solve your husband's murder. I'm sure you want to help us." Miller's partner spoke in a calm, sympathetic voice. Apparently he'd drawn the straw to play good cop.

"I'm certainly willing to cooperate, but— "

"You see Anthony saw his step-father the night Mr. Crown was murdered," Miller broke in.

"Seems like an important detail to leave out. Your son was angry with his step-father and he saw him the night he was killed," Addison said.

Willa folded her arms and did not move from the doorway. "We'll come in and talk to you once I speak to my lawyer."

"Ma'am, this is a murder investigation and your son is a person of interest. Minor or not, we're going to talk to him." Miller's expression seemed to say it could be easy or hard, Willa's choice.

Chapter 8

The next day at the office Willa struggled hard to focus on work and not replay the previous night's events in her head. Miller's dire warning implying he was fully prepared to send shock waves through her world had worked. Willa allowed him to question Anthony. But she had interrupted her former boss, Brad, over dinner. Using her cell phone she let him listen in and advise her. Brad gave her terse instructions. Anthony gave the detectives a string of sullen "I'm not sure" and "I dunno" answers. Between that and Willa following Brad's excellent instructions, Miller and Addison left dissatisfied. Interspersed with that bad memory was her scream fest with Jazz on the phone later. Within a matter of about twenty seconds Jazz had used her total fund of cuss words to tell Willa where she could go and then hung up. Just the thought of that conversation made her heart pump double-time.

The phone on her desk rang and made her jump. Thankfully it was Kay, not the police. Her mama had stopped. Willa happily gave up the fight to concentrate on work. Kay showed Mama Ruby into the office.

"Yes, ma'am. I would love a slice of your sweet potato pie," Kay said as she opened the door for Mama Ruby.

"I'll be sure Willa brings you some." Mama Ruby patted her shoulder. Once the door was closed Mama Ruby grinned. "I can tell that girl's got your back around here. Whoa, this is a nice set up. Jack did right by you for once. Well, twice if you count giving you Mikayla. How you doin'?"

Willa accepted the light peck on her right cheek. She checked a small mirror in her desk. Sure enough Mama Ruby had left a smudge of crimson lipstick. "Oh I'm doing great. I just have to get over being lied to by my son, my sister and having Jack's hoochie announce she's pregnant."

Mama Ruby continued to examine the office. "A whole suite, too. Umph, umph, umph. Jack was a sorry husband, a so-so daddy, but he sure as heck took care of business."

"Is that a joke?" Willa sat on the edge of her desk and swung her legs like a little girl.

"What?" Mama Ruby blinked at her then chuckled. "I didn't mean takin' care of business as in the ladies. I meant this business. Anyway, back to your troubles."

"My troubles are giving birth to more troubles it seems. Literally," Willa said.

"The police should leave Anthony alone. Didn't his friend tell him they were together?"

"Yeah. But the girls invited over insisted they got home before nine. The boys have fuzzy accounts after that." Willa gazed at her mother. "I don't believe Anthony any more than Miller does, Mama. I just can't figure out why he keeps changing his story."

"He's a teenager. They do exactly what they're not supposed to then lie about it. It's what they do, Lord love 'em. I've lived through it more times than you can count. Girls are the worst."

"Gee thanks for giving me something to look forward to with Mikayla." Willa put off that stomach twisting thought though. "Anthony knows more than he's telling."

"Kid stuff. Nothing to do with Jack getting killed. But we better figure this out because the police aren't going to be so understanding." Mama Ruby frowned.

"We talked with the lawyer Dion recommended. She said far as she can tell the police don't really have anything on Anthony. Just want him, and me for that matter, to think they do. We should hang tight and not panic. The police won't talk to Anthony again without the lawyer now that they know he's represented. That would get them in hot water with the courts."

"Sounds like the right advice. If Dion says she's good then you can count on it." Mama Ruby nodded and smiled.

Willa tried to smile but didn't quite succeed. Not even having a sharp lawyer in the wings had helped her sleep last night. She chewed the inside of her bottom lip, a nervous habit she'd had since her first stay in foster care at age six. The prospect of separation from family still made her jittery. Even when Mikayla went on sleepovers a tiny sliver of anxiety could take hold in her gut. And somehow she felt as though Anthony was slipping away from her.

"Willa, I'm sure it's gonna be all right." Mama Ruby left her chair and sat next to her on the desk. She hooked a plump arm around Willa's shoulder. "You're doin' everything you can."

Willa shook her head slowly. "No, I'm not. Sitting here isn't enough. I need to be out doing... something."

"Tracking down your sister to whip her tail until she talks ain't the something. Besides, that tough little hellcat might just whip you instead," Mama Ruby said with a grin. "Come on now. We both know Jazz don't scare easy."

"Neither do I," Willa shot back. "No joke, Mama. I'm sick of playing with Jazz on this."

"Something is scaring her, baby. I got a bad feeling." Mama Ruby shook her head. "Let me talk to her."

"I don't know." Willa recognized how much Jazz resented the close relationship she had with her adoptive mother.

"She doesn't hate me like you think. Sure, to Jazz I always favored you. But every once in a while she'd let me in. I'm gonna try." Mama Ruby nodded as though she'd made up her mind. "I'm gonna talk to Anthony, too. That boy better come clean with me or else."

"Maybe you should let me handle Anthony for now. You'll have enough on your hands with Jazz."

Her mother would know how to approach Jazz. Anthony was another matter. Mama Ruby would be like warm putty in his hands. Anthony had been able to play her since he learned to bat his thick eyelashes on those big brown eyes of his. He was one year old when he mastered that trick.

"If you don't get that boy to talking soon I'm gonna deal with him." Mama Ruby slung her favorite tote bag over one shoulder and stood. "Now try not to worry. You got a business to run."

"Thanks, Mama." Willa gave her a tight hug, more to feel the comfort of her mother's support.

Mama Ruby had barely been gone for twenty minutes when Kay came back to Willa's office.

"Mr. Crown is here to see you, boss." Kay's eyes were big.

"Jack's dad?" Willa glanced up from the reports she was working on. "Wow."

"No, ma'am. His brother Ryan Crown." Kay breathed out his name as though close to being in a trance.

Willa laughed and shook her head. Ryan Crown, six feet three inches of gorgeous man, had been inspiring that look since he'd hit puberty. With jet black curly hair and skin the color of milk chocolate he looked mighty tasty. The Crown brothers had done serious damage to half the female population across two college campuses. Six years older than Jack, the two brothers had been competitive to a fault. Their father encouraged it as healthy. It wasn't.

"He's something else, huh? An older, taller version of Jack." Willa grinned as Kay fanned her face with one hand. Willa could have added he was even more handsome, but it was a close tie to be honest.

"My, my, my." Kay breathed in and out a couple to times as if to calm down.

"Show him in and just a word of warning," Willa said, careful to keep a straight face.

"Ma'am?" Kay continued to fan.

"He wears a subtle but seductive cologne. Try to not to pant and drool when he walks by you." Willa knew well the snares of the Crown brothers.

Kay let out one last long breath then pulled her shoulders back. "He's just another man."

"We'll see," Willa murmured.

"Mr. Crown, you can come in now." Kay gave him a cool, professional smile.

"Thank you, young lady. Appreciate it," came the basso voice smooth as warm caramel dripping down a heap of ice cream.

Kay stood holding open the office door. "No problem."

Out of habit Ryan dipped his head as he walked in. He favored Kay with a boyish half-smile. When his back was to her Kay slumped as though her legs had gone weak. She breathed in his scent then gave a shiver before closing the door.

Willa suppressed a laugh as she held out a hand to her former brother-in-law. "Hello, Ryan. Nice to see you."

Ryan grasped her hand and held it. "Hello, Willa. I hope you and the kids are doing well."

"Thank you. We're holding up. And the family?" Willa allowed him to hold her hand a few seconds longer before letting go.

"Mama and Dad are still shaken. You know how they felt about Jack." Ryan took a seat at Willa's gesture toward one of the larger leather chairs.

"Yes." Willa replied. She was too polite to mention Jack had been the favorite, that the other three kids had always resented it. At least the sisters didn't have the male sibling rivalry to negotiate.

"How is Chanelle?" Willa asked after his wife.

Ryan's expression remained neutral. "The same. My daughter will be graduating from high school this year."

"She's only sixteen, right?" Willa sat across from him.

Ryan sighed and nodded. "But very advanced. I told Chanelle she should stay in high school another year. One more argument I lost."

Willa thought about how much Chanelle reminded her of Jack's mother. Poor guy. Instead she smiled. "I'm sure she'll be fine in college. Like you said, she's ahead of most kids her age. Probably socially as well."

"Right." Ryan didn't appear to be confident of that at all.

"So," Willa said and waited to hear why Ryan had come.

Ryan seemed to shake off thoughts of his wife and daughter. "I just thought, well after everything that's happened we should keep in touch. I mean, it all seems so small in light of Jack's death."

"Meaning?" Willa gazed at him expectantly.

Ryan smiled. "Okay, so you don't have reason to make it easy on me. I know we weren't as open to you as we should have been."

"Hmm." Willa restrained herself from saying they'd considered her ghetto trash.

"Jack really did care for you, it's just-- well we all have our weaknesses." Ryan looked at a picture of Jack on the wall.

"So true." Willa struggled not to say more.

"And he dearly loved those kids. I know he'd want me to be an attentive uncle. Especially to Anthony. A boy at his age needs male guidance."

"Well, I, uh." Willa was truly speechless. She gaped at him as her mouth tried to work even though her brain was stumped.

"So I just wanted your okay to, you know, spend time with him. Guy time I mean. It's not all selfless on my part. I miss having a son to kick around with me. Lily isn't exactly a sports enthusiast, and definitely not into fishing."

"Uh, right." Willa thought of his girly-girl daughter so like her mother.

"Lily's favorite sport is competitive shopping to keep up with her friends. She's just like her mother." Ryan's tight smile implied he didn't find his joke all that funny.

"Yeah, ha-ha." Willa blinked at him and cleared her throat.

"Anyway, I saw how broken up he was at the funeral. I really think this will be good for our family." Ryan brushed a hand through his dark thick hair. "I'm not good at the whole warm, fuzzy thing. I just think this is the right thing to do."

Willa found her feelings toward him softening. "I have to say this is a big, I mean a really big, surprise."

Ryan gave a deep laugh. "I can imagine. I'm not saying my parents or sisters have changed. But you seem able to handle them."

"You mean I've learned to ignore their snobbish ways and swipes at my background. Yeah, I've had a little experience with being looked down on. But I won't ignore them being unkind to Anthony." Willa pointed a forefinger at him to drive home her point.

"Neither will I. Even my sister Tina backed me up on that one." Ryan nodded when Willa raised an eyebrow at his words. "And we had a little talk with our parents and my other sisters."

"Well, you took my breath away with that one, Ryan." Willa wondered at the eldest Crown child seeing the light. The Crown kids had always followed their mother's lead. Always.

Ryan laughed again then grew serious moments later. "Family is too important. Sad to say it takes a tragedy to drive that home."

"Thank you, Ryan. Anthony is dealing with being a teenager and losing Jack has just been..." Willa closed her eyes against the sudden wellspring of emotion. When she looked at Ryan again he wore an empathetic expression.

"I know, I know. Now I'm not trying to get in the way of your father or two brothers. Those guys are there for Anthony. I could see that at the funeral." Ryan smiled.

"Like I said, the more support Anthony feels around him the better." Willa reached out, took one of Ryan's large hands and squeezed it. "Thanks again."

"Hey, I'm looking forward to a few testosterone outings. I'm outnumbered by females," he teased. "So, how is the business going?"

"Pretty smooth actually. I was feeling lost at first, but Cedric stepped right up." Willa relaxed into the chair as she let go of his hand.

"Excellent. Of course even a right-hand man might not know everything. Jack and I talked business a lot. So if you need some advice, you know any loose ends, I might be able to help."

"Well, I really appreciate the offer. Cedric is on top of things. He's been great."

"I'm sure he has, but in my experience there's no substitute for family watching your back." Ryan smiled at her.

"I hear ya. Listen, if I think of anything I'll— " Willa blinked rapidly her mind working.

"What?" Ryan tilted his handsome head.

"You wouldn't happen to know anything about Stafford, Inc. and a contract Jack had with them?"

"Jack and I talked about the business in general. Sometimes he asked for my opinion on things. Maybe if you told me a little about it or let me read the file."

"That's just it, we can't find it. I'm going to get in touch with an employee who happens to attend Jack's church," Willa replied.

Ryan frowned at her. "Jack hasn't attended our family church in years."

"Uh, no. Apparently Jack had been attending the Abundant Love Tabernacle recently." Willa watched Ryan's expression turn from puzzled to faintly amused.

"Jack became a holy roller? I'm trying to picture it." Ryan shook his head.

"You don't believe he had a spiritual awakening inspired by Reverend Fisher?"

"More like he awakened to a business opportunity." Ryan laughed. "Let me know when you find out more."

"I will. And thanks for the thinking of Anthony."

Ryan stood. "We're family, right?"

Willa stood as well and looked up at him. "Yes, we are."

"I'll give Anthony a call this afternoon about the time he gets home from school." Ryan reached out and took one of Willa's hands into both his. "Are you okay?"

"I'm fine. Really." Willa smiled up at him. When he continued to hold her hand Willa gently pulled free. "I better get back to work. Being the boss is harder than I thought."

"I'm sure you're up to it. Well, I'll get out of the way and let you take care of business. Goodbye." Ryan headed for the door.

"Goodbye." Willa walked him out to the lobby. Cedric came out at the same time carrying folders.

"Cedric, have you met Jack's brother Ryan?" Willa said.

Cedric shook Ryan's outstretched hand. "No, nice meeting you."

"Same here. Thanks for being such a help to Willa. The Crown family appreciates your loyalty. This business meant a lot to my brother," Ryan said. "Good employees are a huge asset."

Willa pursed her lips. Ryan had expressed gratitude and reminded Cedric of his place. When she glanced sideways at Cedric his taut smile said it all. Willa wasn't imagining Ryan's condescending vibe. The Crown family superiority complex came through.

"Jack and I had a great partnership. I'm happy to maintain the high standards we set," Cedric replied without losing the smile.

"Glad to hear it." Ryan looked at Willa. "I'll be in touch soon. Maybe Anthony can come out to the club for tennis and lunch this weekend."

"I know he'll love that. Thanks again. Bye." Willa smiled at him and waved. Then she exchanged a glance with Kay, who sat at her desk pretending to be busy.

"What did Mr. Crown want?" Cedric said with enough salt in his tone to preserve a slab of beef.

"Just stopped by to offer his help. You know, I think he might give us a lead on the Stafford contract." Willa gazed at the door Ryan had just gone through.

"Can we talk?" Cedric said crisply. He marched into her office before she could answer.

Willa looked at Kay who gave a tiny shrug. She followed him in and shut the door. "What's the deal?"

"Are you close to your former brother-in-law?" Cedric crossed his arms.

Willa blinked at him rapidly. "Um, not especially. He's trying to extend himself now that Jack is dead. I mean he is Mikayla's and Anthony's uncle."

"But he didn't exactly act all 'we are family' before. Jack told me they clashed a lot. Barely spoke." Cedric frowned. "I'm just saying be careful. Jack and Ryan might have been brothers by blood but..."

"I knew they had a sibling rivalry thing going as kids. But you make it sound like they hated each other's guts." Willa raised an eyebrow at him.

"Look, I'm just saying don't be taken in by that thick layer of charm over the snakeskin," Cedric replied with heat in his voice. "I don't know the details of what went down, but Jack told me Ryan was a backstabbing SOB. His words, not mine."

"Oh." Willa stared at him, shocked by his vehemence.

"I do know that Ryan sabotaged three lucrative contracts Jack went after. I'm just saying the dude is bad news." Cedric stared at Willa. "And I think taking Ryan into your confidence about anything is a bad idea."

"Sheesh, don't hold back on what you think of ol' Ryan," Willa blurted out.

Cedric started to speak then took in and let out two deep breaths. He dropped his arms. "Sorry. I came on a little strong."

"Uh, yeah."

"But I don't take back anything I said about Jack's brother. Listen, we scrambled to build this business. That's right, Jack and me. Ryan tried to wreck Crown Protection."

"I know Ryan and Jack always tried to one up each other, but Ryan has his own successful company. Why would he go after Jack's business?" Willa tried to think back, to remember any outright hostility between the two men.

"I'm telling you what I know and what Jack said. Their old man was always bragging about Jack being in control. That family has some strange dynamics." Cedric shook his head slowly.

"Yeah." Willa could have said much more, but nasty or not the Crowns were family. Technically speaking. "Anyway, I tell you what. I'll get more information from Ryan than I give. At least until I sniff out any impure motives."

"That's all I'm saying. Be careful. Hope I didn't overstep too far." Cedric's intense expression relaxed. "I care a lot. About the business."

"Right. And don't worry, I appreciate the advice, I really do." Willa's smile of assurance covered her confusion. "Thanks."

"Just want to help. Really." Cedric took a step closer to her. "I've got a couple of phone calls to make, but I'm free for lunch. We can talk about two possible new contracts. One is security at a construction site."

"Um, sure. Sounds good." Willa went to her office door and opened it.

Cedric took the hint. "Great. We can go to The Great Wall for Chinese. Their lunch menu is something else."

"Okay. Let's meet up in the lobby at about twelve thirty," Willa replied.

Cedric smiled at her then strode away. The second he was gone Willa spun around to Kay.

"What the...?" Willa put both hands on her hips.

"All I know is Mr. Crown is *fine*," Kay blurted out. "Uh, that's not very helpful is it?"

"Having been married to one of the Crown boys, I can speak with much knowledge. Don't let a handsome face- "

"And delicious body," Kay cut in and gave a shiver.

"And delicious body make you stupid. A man's true character is what counts," Willa lectured. Kay's dazed, hungry female expression told her the advice was lost. "Okay. I tried. I'm getting back to work."

But the rest of morning was a wash out. Instead of working Willa sorted through the puzzle of Ryan's offer of help and Cedric's fervent suspicion of that offer. If what Cedric said was true, then Jack wouldn't have discussed his business with Ryan. On the other hand, Ryan seemed to imply Willa shouldn't rely on Cedric. Willa didn't know which man to believe. So she decided she'd keep an eye on both. Ryan was right about one thing, she should trust family. Her own, and that didn't include the Crown clan.

***

Sunday dawned into a beautiful day. Willa picked out a moss green suit to wear with a hat the same color. Church ladies worth their salt wore fabulous hats. Thanks to her aunts Ametrine and Beryl she had several to choose from. She got at least one from either of them each Christmas. Aunt Beryl would even scope out Willa's closet so she could find a hat to match.

Willa chose to drive Jack's Jaguar to Abundant Love Tabernacle. She figured it would blend in. She was right and then some. Rows of luxury cars, foreign and domestic, seemed everywhere she looked. The huge church took up half a city block in a section of southeastern Baton Rouge. Directly in front of the church was a green expanse of lawn. Three crosses towered against the blue sky, the tallest one in the center. Above huge front double doors of the church was a stained glass window with praying hands depicted. Elegantly dressed worshippers streamed into the doors. Willa forced herself to stop gawking and pay attention to driving. Directed by one of her own security guards, Willa found a space on one of two adjoining parking lots. She got out and locked the car. The guard walked over to her.

"Hi, Mrs. Crown." He tipped his cap with Crown Protection in gold embroidered letters on it.

"Hi, Gary," Willa said, after reading his nametag.

Gary laughed. "I know you don't remember all forty of your employees. Don't worry about it."

"Thanks for being understanding. But if I'm going to be a crack security business owner I need to work on that. Jack had a memory like a steel safe."

"Yeah, that party dawg could have a good time but he took care of business." Gary gave an appreciative laugh.

"Ah-ha." Willa gazed at him steadily for several moments.

"I mean he was a great boss." Gary tugged on his collar and looked around. He spotted a lady trying to park in a narrow spot. "I gotta go help."

"She just made it in. See?" Willa nodded at the white Cadillac. "Now tell me about Jack's party habits. Sounds like you two had some good times together."

"Um, well he'd treat some of the guys to a round of beers and hot wings. He didn't act all uppity. Sure he came from a rich family, but he was regular."

"Ah." Willa nodded and smiled at him. "Yes, Jack loved to mix and mingle. Ever went to any gentlemen's clubs with him?"

Gary rubbed his face hard with one hand, hitched his pants and looked around. "Ma'am it's Sunday, and we're outside the Lord's house."

"Which means you should tell the truth," Willa replied in a dry tone.

"I've heard a few after work parties were held there," Gary replied.

"Where, specifically, did they go?" Willa tilted her head back.

"Candy Girls over on Brookstown. They have happy hour for the working guys just getting off. Uh, that's what somebody told me." Gary glanced at Willa. "My wife is an usher here, ya know."

"Don't worry. She won't find out from me what you've 'heard' about Candy Girls." Willa smiled at him. "I'm not passing judgment."

Gary let go of the breath he was holding. "Thank you, ma'am. Have a blessed day, ma'am."

"You do the same."

Willa smiled and nodded to him as a cute, short plump woman wearing a dark blue dress approached. Two outside speakers rang with the sound of electronic bells. From out of nowhere seemingly MiMi fell in step beside her.

"Praise the Lord. We just happened to pick the same Sunday to visit Reverend Free Hands." MiMi wore a champagne suit. The peplum jacket accentuated her curves. Several church brothers beamed at her as they walked by.

"What the— " Willa caught the curse word about to come out when she saw the shadow of one of the huge crosses. "You're being here is no coincidence," she hissed.

"I called your house this morning to talk and Mikayla, sweet child, mentioned that she and Anthony were going to church with their great aunts, while you were going to the 'Lots of Love' church." MiMi smiled and dipped her head demurely at another flirting male.

"Sweet child indeed." Willa was going to have a chat with her little fountain of information.

"Reverend Free hands got Jack the hook-up with Strafford, Inc. So you're not here for the sermon I bet." MiMi spoke quietly as they entered the sanctuary.

"If we weren't in church..." Willa muttered through her tight smile. Another group of men hovered nearby glancing up and down at them.

"Remember we're practically family," MiMi said. "Let's sit here."

A tall gentleman impeccably dressed in a black suit and Kelly green silk tie strode down the aisle.

"Greetings in the name of the Lord, sisters. I'm brother Hilton Sanchez. Reverend Fisher invites you to our Honored Guests section." He pointed the way.

Willa exchanged a glance with MiMi and hesitated. "I, uh."

"Why thank you, Brother Sanchez. We are so thrilled," MiMi spoke up.

She cupped Willa's elbow firmly and propelled her along behind Brother Sanchez. They drew curious, even envious stares as they took the long walk. Moments later they arrived at the Honored Guests pew, three rows of cushioned pews upholstered in a deep red velveteen fabric. This in contrast to the deep blue fabric on the "regular people" benches.

"Let one of our ushers know if you need anything." Brother Sanchez pointed to a pair of women standing at the edge of the pews, apparently assigned to take care of that section.

"Thank you so much. Blessings, my brother," MiMi replied and beamed at him. When he nodded and walked away she looked at Willa. "Now this is what I call service."

"Yeah." Willa glanced around. She saw local politicians, several local television personalities and prominent black business people.

"They're on their game putting us in the big dog section." MiMi nodded at several women nearby. "How'd they know so fast that we were here?"

"Closed circuit television. The cameras are positioned in the foyer. Fisher must have his staff well trained to spot 'the right people'."

"You think?" MiMi looked at Willa steadily. "Wow. That's kind of creepy. Like a cult or something."

Willa looked at her in surprise. "Good point. Fisher evidently runs a tight ship."

Both looked around. The ushers, deacons and choir moved into their positions with military precision. Organ music rolled out from speakers playing a popular gospel tune.

"Smart though. Fisher identifies people with the deepest pockets. Makes them feel special and his collections increase," MiMi said close to Willa's ear.

"Yeah. Everybody may be equal in the sight of God, but Reverend Fisher sure doesn't see us that way," Willa retorted.

MiMi laughed. "Girl, you so crazy."

As the seats around them filled Willa and MiMi stopped talking. Willa looked at the imposing layout before her. A wide stage stretched almost the length of the huge sanctuary. The choir, dressed in deep blue robes with white sateen sashes, stood in back. Before them suited men and women in white sat in three rows of chairs. The pulpit had a row of tall chairs, the largest in the middle. Rows of chairs for the deacons and deaconesses fanned out on either side of the pulpit. After three hymns and a prayer by a deacon with a dramatic basso voice, Reverend Fisher appeared. He entered from the right of the stage. Wearing a solemn, reflective expression Fisher strode to his seat. He stood as the choir sang another hymn, clapping his hands to the tempo of the lively song. Fisher began to rock as he clapped. The crowd around them began to respond with more shouts of "Amen!" Suddenly Fisher grabbed a microphone and started leading in a strong baritone.

"Brother can sing," Willa said.

Indeed Fisher brought most of the crowd to their feet as he sang. Almost seamlessly he went into his sermon. The musicians punctuated his words. When he made a point the organist and pianist would chime in. Between Fisher's dynamic preaching and the musical background the atmosphere crackled with excitement. People began to shout, "Preach it, Rev!" Willa had to admit she felt the electricity. Fisher wasn't just handsome; he had a magnetism that radiated across the sanctuary. To blend in Willa stood and clapped with everyone else as his preaching reached a crescendo. Yet it wasn't all pretense. Fisher had tapped into her love of the call and response of the good old southern black churches. Aunt Ametrine had introduced her to them not long after Willa was placed with Mama Ruby. From the first stomp and shout service Willa had been hooked. Now as she watched Fisher wipe sweat from his face, Willa knew why Abundant Love Ministries had grown, and why the Abundant Love Tabernacle was so resplendent. Fisher had the power of personality. All eyes were on him.

The music swelled then died away to a quieter level. Fisher stood silent, head down for several minutes. Worshippers continued to shout out "Amen" and "Hallelujah," but still he kept silent. Suddenly he lifted his head and hands up. Then he brought the microphone to his mouth again.

"If you want to experience His joy, unspeakable joy that no man can take away. If you want to surrender all to a loving counselor, healer, provider and father, then come to His altar. You've been fighting this battle for too long. Come. Jesus is waiting to wrap you in his abundant love." Fisher paced back and forth as he spoke.

Willa felt the pull of his voice the longer he talked. She shook her head to clear it wondering if the man was some kind of hypnotist. MiMi must have felt it, too. She leaned close to Willa.

"Girl, that man almost had me up there. Look at this." MiMi nudged Willa in the side.

"Yeah," Willa said.

At least twenty or thirty people, mostly women, walked to the altar. Many had tears streaming down their faces. After a few moments of Fisher praying over them, the converts were led away by three ushers. Fisher sat down. A deacon handed him a bottle of water. While he drank and caught his breath, the choir broke into another song. Once they stopped Fisher made an impassioned speech about the power of tithing. MiMi nudged Willa again.

"I'll bet he rakes it in every Sunday. Has to. Can't be cheap keeping all this going." MiMi looked around the sanctuary with appreciation.

"Gotta admit one thing though. He works hard for the money." Willa gazed at Fisher. He was no ordinary preacher chasing after a religious empire.

The benediction and final hymn were just as impressive. Willa felt drained and overwhelmed by it all. She didn't think she could handle Fisher and his mega production on a regular basis. Not to mention being worried that she would end up one of the mesmerized faithful. The man had mad skills to be sure. Willa started to leave, but MiMi grabbed her arm and held her in place.

"Let's chat with some of the movers and shakers," MiMi whispered. "We might find out which one of the faithful is Isaac Nelson."

"You never came here with Jack?" Willa asked then nodded a greeting to several people.

"No. Jack said it was all business." MiMi waved to a woman wearing a wide brimmed lavender hat that matched her elegant suit.

"And you believed him? Please. Take a look at some of these church ladies." Willa nodded at the well-dressed and attractive sisterhood that surrounded Reverend Fisher.

MiMi sniffed. "Jack didn't go out for hamburger. He had filet mignon at home."

"I believed that line the first three years of our marriage," Willa wisecracked.

MiMi frowned at Willa and started to reply. Then she glanced over Willa's shoulder. Willa turned to find Brother Sanchez had returned.

"Ladies, Reverend Fisher has invited you to fellowship with him and a select group of the faithful. This way." Brother Sanchez swept out a hand dramatically and waited.

"What an honor," Willa said.

They followed him to a door set in the far wall. They made their way down a hallway, across a wide room bustling with activity and though another door. When it closed the sounds outside all but disappeared. They passed through a foyer then another set of open double doors.

"Whoa," MiMi blurted out.

"Amen," Willa said softly.

They entered into Reverend Fisher's inner sanctum. Red, gold and royal blue furnishings made the room look rich. When MiMi gasped and looked down, Willa followed her gaze. The wool Persian carpet beneath their feet took her breath away. Bordered in rich blue, a center medallion in sumptuous jewel tones pulled in the colors around them. A wide cherry desk sat to their left. Reverend Fisher stood in front of it. To the left was a seating area. Next to that was a round table with eight leather chairs circling it. Fisher's office had enough room for a small convention.

"Mrs. Crown, I am so happy you blessed us with your presence." Reverend Fisher clasped Willa's outstretched hand with both of his. "I hope our message and musical praise touched your spirit."

"Thank you, Reverend. I certainly was moved," Willa said with sincerity. When he turned his smile on MiMi Willa pulled free of his too warm grasp. "This is MiMi Landry."

Reverend Fisher glanced at MiMi then at Willa. His brow lifted for a second but he recovered quickly. "Nice to see you."

Before he could say more a group of middle-aged women swooped into the office. While they gushed and made a fuss over the preacher, Willa took in more details of the office. No expense had been spared. The smell of fine leather furniture and wood polish mixed with Fisher's cologne.

"Reverend Fisher knows how to work the ladies," MiMi muttered as she walked past Willa. She stood with her back to the room staring at a depiction of Jesus healing a blind man.

Brother Sanchez appeared after a few minutes. "Ladies, let me show you our new media room."

"So glad to see you," Fisher beamed as he nodded at them.

"Thanks again for taking time to visit with us," Willa said and started to follow the women out.

"No hurry." Fisher closed the door softly then turned to face them.

Willa felt a flash of anxiety, as though an escape route had just been cut off. The swish of MiMi's silk suit as she turned reassured her. A little. At least she wasn't alone with the man.

"What inspiring artwork. Who is the artist? I'm a collector of sorts." MiMi sat down and crossed her shapely legs.

"A young man of immense talent. We met him during our community outreach. He used to be a drug dealer. Now he's using his God given gift to glorify Him." Fisher swept a hand out at two other paintings. He pointed to the ceiling.

Fluffy white clouds on a sky blue background had been painted on the ceiling. Brush strokes of a golden hue lightened to white, became the robe of an angel. The face of the angel held a kind, loving expression.

"His interpretation of our journey to everlasting life," Fisher said in a hushed tone. "What a day of rejoicing that will be."

"Praise the Lord," MiMi sighed.

Willa glanced at her to find a dreamy look on her face. "Er, we really should let you get back to what I'm sure is a busy day."

"Ah, Mrs. Crown. Even on the Lord's day his servant takes time to rest." Reverend Fisher walked close to Willa.

Willa resisted the urge to step back. "Then we should allow you to relax."

Brother Sanchez appeared again. "Ms. Landry, would you like to see our sacred art gallery?"

"I'd loved to," MiMi breathed. She placed a hand on the man's arm and was gone.

Willa stared in disbelief at how smoothly she'd been played. Somehow Fisher orchestrated being alone with her. She calculated how she could drop her purse and execute defensive moves in her slim skirt.

"Don't worry. They should be right back. The gallery is small. Though we do have plans to expand. Coffee? I have a wonderful Columbian blend." Fisher didn't wait for Willa to respond.

"You're going to too much trouble for me. Really." Willa raised an eyebrow at him.

"No trouble at all. It's brewed and ready to pour." Fisher deftly poured coffee into two beautiful lapis blue cups. "Here we are. Ah, a moment of blessed peace at last."

"Yes." Willa accepted the cup and sat down in a chair.

Fisher sat on the sofa. "How are you and your children coping?"

"Day by day we're making it. Thank you for asking." Willa sipped some of the coffee. The rich flavor flooded her taste buds. She drank more.

"Wonderful isn't it? A member of my congregation imports it along with other products for high end food markets." Reverend Fisher sighed. "Our congregation has been blessed. Many of the most successful business people in the city attend our church."

"Which helps your ministry I'm sure."

Willa said and glanced at a set of ornate vases on a side table.

"We're able to do a lot of good, yes. The material things of this world can be used to advance the spiritual," Reverend Fisher said, repeating one of his famous quotes.

"Right. Sometimes even the Lord's work takes cash." Willa sipped more coffee and smiled at him.

Reverend Fisher let out a deep laugh. "That's true, Mrs. Crown. Willa. What a lovely name."

"Thank you, Reverend Fisher." Willa gave him a polite, and she hoped, distant smile. She'd roast in hell before letting him get too chummy.

He gave her a gentle, tolerant smile in return. "Your security services are top notch. Seems Jack taught you well about his business."

Willa sipped her now lukewarm coffee. "Not really. Jack and I were separated when his business really took off. Before that I had my hands full with kids and attending school."

"A well-rounded woman. I knew it." He let out an audible breath.

"You have multiple talents as well. Gifted preacher, singer and businessman." Willa felt her temperature rise despite her efforts not to be affected by his charisma.

"I'm indeed blessed, but I don't do this all on my own you know. Of course God is the foundation." Fisher's handsome brown face affected an earnest expression.

"Of course," Willa echoed.

"And my ministry leaders are some of the smartest folks around." Fisher tugged at the cuffs of his expensive dress shirt.

"No doubt picked for that reason." Willa set the coffee cup down on the end table nearest her.

"Jesus set the example when he carefully chose each disciple," Fisher smiled back at her.

"True." Willa nodded as though she was becoming one of his female converts.

"Each of my lay leaders has a defined role. Of course each has flexibility to be creative as well. We face the challenge of ministering in a complex, modern world."

"Still you seem to have mastered the difficult balancing act," Willa replied.

"Balancing act?" Fisher blinked at her.

"Yes. You stay in spiritual, close to scriptures. But you are very twenty-first century, using technology and running a successful business. No offense intended, but Abundant Love Ministries is like a corporation with many divisions." Willa knew she was speaking his language.

Reverend Fisher put down his cup of coffee. "Mrs. Crown, your level of understanding is refreshing. Most ladies look at me and calculate my net worth. You see beyond to what I'm really trying to accomplish."

"Definitely. You have a vision to create a unique ministry." Willa managed to spout that crap with a straight face. She just hoped his ego was big enough not to see it as obvious flattery. When he stuck out his chest and lifted his chin she stopped worrying.

"I've tried," he said.

"And succeeded. In my humble opinion." Careful, girl. Don't lay it on too thick.

"Thank you for that, Mrs. Crown. I hope to see you more and more at our services. We have a singles ministry that meets every Tuesday evening. I personally attend those meetings."

<u>I'll bet you do</u>, Willa almost blurted out. If his singles ministry was anything like it was at most black churches ninety-nine percent of the members would be lonely women. In this case they were likely well-to-do lonely women.

"I'll certainly consider that. Of course I'm so busy with the business and my family spare time is something I can only dream about." Willa smoothed down her skirt. Out of the corner of her eye she saw Fisher watch the movement of her hand. Did he actually smack his lips?

"Speaking of business, I wanted to meet Deacon Nelson and discuss the Strafford, Inc. contract." Willa looked up to find him gazing at her with a saintly demeanor.

"Of course." Reverend Fisher took out his slim cell phone. He hit the talk button. "Brother Nelson, come to my office please." A male voice replied immediately.

"May I freshen my coffee?" Willa stood.

"Let me serve you." Reverend Fisher reached for the cup at the same time Willa did. Their hands touched and he gazed into her eyes.

"No, no," Willa replied with a smile. "I can certainly do it myself. You've had a strenuous morning. Relax."

Fisher's eyes brightened. He sat back against the chair, a man used to being waited on. "You are a rare jewel, Mrs. Crown. I wonder how Jack managed to lose such a treasure."

"Some men are so busy chasing what looks good that they don't value what they have," Willa replied. She took his cup and poured more coffee for both of them. Without asking she added one spoon of sugar for him and a bit of cream.

When she handed him the cup Fisher gave her an appreciative smile. "Perfect."

After two respectful knocks on the door it opened. A tall bulky man came in. His suit was a copper brown. He wore heavy gold chain bracelets on both wrists.

"Reverend." The man nodded at his pastor then glanced at Willa.

"Mrs. Crown, this is my deacon Isaac Nelson. We just call him Ike." Reverend Fisher gazed at him. "This is Jack Crown's widow. She's taken over his firm."

"I know," Nelson rumbled.

Something about the way he said that gave Willa a chill. His black eyes seemed to be missing something. Willa chided herself for having an over active imagination.

"Nice to meet you finally. I'd mentioned to Reverend Fisher that I can't seem to find any paperwork on your company. So I'm not sure what we're supposed to do for Strafford, Inc." Willa's unease grew when Nelson gave her a sharp-edged and cold smile.

"That a fact? Well, I'm sure surprised my old buddy Jack wasn't more organized." Nelson seemed to relax into a better mood.

"Organization wasn't one of his assets," Willa said and smiled back at him with effort. The man gave her the creeps.

"So you don't know anything?" Nelson shot a sideways glance at Fisher.

"Not really. But if you could get me your copy of the contract that would be lovely. Frankly, I'm puzzled I haven't heard from your employer." Willa studied him.

"Yeah. Guess it fell through the cracks. I'll get with my bosses and let you know." Nelson rubbed his big rough hands together.

"You're not in charge of contract?" Willa said.

"Not exactly. But I did get Jack the hook up so to speak," Nelson said, baring his teeth in his scary version of a friendly smile.

"As the owner I like to take responsibility when we don't live up to our end of any agreement." Willa took out her PDA. "Just give me their names and numbers. I'll set up a meeting."

"Of course Ike can do that," Reverend Fisher said before Nelson spoke. The deacon grimaced and rolled his shoulders. He seemed to be holding back a protest.

"The project manager, Dean Haywood, is the guy you want to talk to," Nelson finally said. "I don't know. I think maybe he's out of town. I could talk to you about it."

"Thanks. I'll call him first thing Monday. After all I don't want Mr. Haywood to think Crown Protection doesn't value his business."

"Yeah." Nelson opened his mouth to say something, but the reverend spoke first.

"I'm sure he understands the circumstances." Reverend Fisher nodded gravely. "Thank you, Ike."

"No problem." Nelson didn't move toward the door. Instead he stared at Willa. His gaze slid down to her legs.

"If you need to deal with the van drivers don't let us keep you." Reverend Fisher stood and smoothed down his suit. In the process he blocked Nelson's view of Willa.

"Right. Right." Nelson rolled his bulky shoulders again then left.

MiMi appeared at the same time Nelson opened the door. Her flirty smile went stiff when she looked into his eyes. She hesitated, let him walk by then came into the office.

"You okay?" MiMi blurted out.

"Ms. Landry, your friend is perfectly safe here of course," Reverend said, his resonant voice boomed.

Willa stood up quickly and walked to her. "Thanks again, Reverend Fisher. Nice of you to take the time."

"I only hope you return soon. As we say here at Abundant Love Ministries, our hearts are as open as our doors. So come right in."

"How lovely. I must say you have a beautiful complex here and— " MiMi stopped when she glanced at Willa. "Uh, goodbye, Reverend Fisher. Lovely spending time with you."

MiMi and Willa were once again in the care of Brother Sanchez. He led the way out of the maze of hallways leading to offices and meeting rooms. They walked back through the sanctuary to the front doors.

"You ladies have a blessed day." Brother Sanchez nodded to them then spun around and walked away.

MiMi and Willa put on their sunglasses. They looked back at the church then at each other.

"Brother Sanchez is fine, but he is like one of those cyborgs from a sci-fi movie. Beautiful on the outside, but no human feelings. I like my men a bit more warm blooded." MiMi bit her lower lip, "Maybe he's gay."

Willa barked a laugh. Releasing the tension felt good. She walked down the sidewalk toward the parking lot. "What?"

"Yeah. You know, one of those find black men on the down low. Manly man on the outside, but..." MiMi shrugged. "Some of these homeboys are into that."

"What happened? He didn't respond to your long eyelashes fluttering at him or your silky seductive laugh?" Willa chuckled when MiMi pursed her lips.

"Exactly. And I always get guys to open up. I don't know. Maybe I'm giving off some kind of earth mother vibe. That could hamper our investigation."

"Our investigation. And you are no earth mother." Willa stopped and put both hands on her hips.

"Hey, feminine wiles are very handy when it comes to getting information." MiMi wiggled her hips and grinned from behind her designer sunglasses.

"One, *we* are not investigating anything. I'm trying to find out about a contract. I'll be contacting Strafford, Inc. Monday."

"Excellent. Please don't give me that modern women don't use sex nonsense. I saw how the good Reverend was all into you, and you used it." MiMi grinned. "Now we'll get to the truth about Strafford, the Cayman Islands and my money."

"Two," Willa continued, hands still on her hips. "We haven't established that you have any money. And finally, three."

When Willa paused MiMi tapped her clutch purse against one thigh. "Okay, spit it out."

"We are not pals. Don't follow me again and my lawyer will be in touch." Willa spun around and started for her car.

"That was more than three," MiMi called after her. "It's a free country. Besides, Mikayla and Anthony should get to know their baby sister. Or brother.

"Baby?" Willa stopped and spun around. She stared at MiMi's stomach. "No."

"Yes. I'm pregnant with Jack's baby." MiMi smoothed down the fabric of her dress. "And I'm still rocking this dress."

"Don't think this changes anything. I want proof. Even if you are pregnant I want a DNA test." Willa was waving her arms wildly causing people to stare at her.

"This does change things, I have proof. DNA test? Bring it on." MiMi grinned at her. "Let's be friends, Willa. It would make all this so much easier."

"Bull." Willa turned around and headed for her car, blood pounding in her ears.

Chapter 9

Two days later Willa sat in the spacious office of her former employer. Brad Craft, the senior partner of Craft, Mouton and LaPlace, was ready to deliver his verdict on Jack's will. He'd had it for the past week. Willa exchanged pleasantries with him trying not to appear impatient.

"Well, what do you think," Willa said.

"I have tell you, it's looking good," Brad said, looking at Willa over his reading glasses. "So far there is nothing in writing that confirms that there was a contract with Strafford, Inc., or that Ms. Landry invested in Crown Protection. The codicil says she's to be paid from those profits." Brad rocked his executive chair back and forth as he spoke.

"And since there are no profits MiMi Landry is SOL – So Out of Luck.. Hah." Willa gave a happy sigh.

"For now. But you have a duty as both the executor of Jack's estate and head of his company. You can't do anything to damage either the estate or the company, not until all claims are settled. If Crown Protection did provide services then you'll have to pay her." Brad wagged a forefinger at her.

"Of course. I have a meeting with these mysterious Strafford, Inc. guys Wednesday. I should know more then."

"Sounds good. In the meantime Ms. Landry is definitely out of luck. She has to wait until the succession proceeds. No debts can be paid until the court says so. She hasn't filed as a debtor yet."

"For a very good reason. She can't prove anything. I don't doubt Jack promised her money." Willa grimaced. "When he was in heat Jack loved to spend money on the object of his affection."

"Sure is easy for a guy to get caught up in the moment. Uh, so I've heard. Not that I've ever done it," Brad said when Willa glanced at him.

"Yeah. Anyway, I've got enough on my hands with Detective Miller still sniffing around Anthony." Willa thought about Jazz again. She wanted to shake her baby sister until the truth fell out. Jazz had more she was keeping secret.

"Do you think Anthony is telling you everything?" Brad looked at Willa as though he already knew her answer. When she hissed in response he shook his head. "You need to get ahead of Miller and get Anthony to open up."

"You don't have teenagers yet. In five years when your sweet little Ashley hits lucky number thirteen look out. Let's see how easy you pry info from her then," Willa replied. "Not to mention your son Matthew."

"Thanks for the good news. I'll be dealing with them and my wife's moods. What fun." Brad blew out a gust of air. Then he grinned. "Or maybe Anthony is telling you the truth."

"According to my sister."

"Well, there you have it. A responsible adult backs him up," Brad said.

Willa snorted. "Right."

His description didn't exactly fit Jazz, at least not in the usual way. Still Jazz could be very protective toward family, especially Willa's kids. Willa just worried about her sister's judgment and lack of predictability. Jazz simply didn't follow most rules. And the consequences could be bad.

"If you need a good lawyer for Anthony just say the word. He's underage so they have to deal with you. That's one big advantage. They can put a scare into a kid with no one to speak up for him." Brad flipped through Jack's will scanning the text again.

"They do a good job of putting a scare in grown folks, too," Willa said. "I've already talked to a lawyer with experience representing kids in trouble."

"Excellent. It's going to be okay, Willa." Brad took off his reading glasses.

"Thanks for the hand holding. I know you're right. Guess I've had one too many nasty surprises lately." Willa stood. "At least I can tell MiMi Landry to shut up and leave me alone."

"I'll communicate that message to her attorney as well." Brad smiled.

"She can just go back to selling lipstick at the mall. Or her daddy big bucks can support her and the baby." Willa turned to leave. "Either way she's not getting a dime from me."

"Wait a minute. She has a baby?" Brad leaned forward.

"Claims she's pregnant. She'll say anything to get sympathy." Willa waved a hand.

"Having Jack's baby?" Brad's eyebrows pulled together to form a single serious line.

"According to her. What?" Willa studied his expression, not liking the line of tension in his forehead.

"Children have a claim on the estate, born in wedlock or not. As the child's legal guardian Ms. Landry can assert those rights." Brad looked at Willa and nodded.

"But... but I don't even know if she's telling the truth. Or if Jack's the father," Willa protested.

"I'm sure her attorney has advised her to get the necessary proof, DNA and other documents." Brad stood. "Under Louisiana law a minor child is a forced heir. That means— "

"MiMi gets a claim of the estate no matter what," Willa finished. "I've had so much on my mind lately it just didn't click." She sat down hard.

"So we can't afford to play hardball with Ms. Landry. If she's pregnant, and if Jack's the father then technically speaking she's family. Sort of," Brad added when Willa stared at him open-mouthed.

"Speaking of nasty surprises." Willa rubbed at the sudden sharp pain in her neck.

***

Later that evening Willa and the kids had only arrived at Mama Ruby's house when Mikayla dropped a bombshell. She raced ahead of Anthony and Willa into Mama Ruby's living room.

"Nanna Ruby, I'm going to have a baby sister. Yippeee!"

"What the— I mean, Willa don't tell me you're..." Willa's father stared at her abdomen then looked up into her eyes.

"Lord have mercy." Aunt Ametrine shook her head and made tsk, tsk noises.

"Is it that handsome Cedric down at the office?" Aunt Beryl wore a wistful, and envious expression.

"Oh man, this is rich. Mikayla, I'm going to have a baby brother. No more girls," Anthony declared, made a chopping motion with one hand then marched off. He headed for the den to watch the sports channel.

Daddy Elton would have normally gone with him, but he was rooted to the chair staring at Willa's abdomen again.

Mama Ruby grabbed Mikayla by the hand and pulled her across the room to Aunt Beryl. "Auntie Bear is gonna give you some ice cream."

"But, but..." Mikayla tried to dig her little heels into the carpet. "I wanna stay and talk about my baby sister."

"Brother!" Anthony yelled from down the hall. He had just left the kitchen and held a big bag of corn chips. He leaned against the wall then stuffed his mouth. His jaws worked crunching the salty snack.

"Thought you wanted to watch some game," Willa said through clenched teeth.

"In a minute, Ma. I can stand some family time." Anthony grinned at her.

"Let Ametrine take Mikayla to eat ice cream." Beryl leaned close to Ruby. "I really want to hear this."

"No." Aunt Ametrine positioned herself deeper into the stuffed chair.

"Anthony." Papa Elton glared at his grandson, his expression and tone communicated even more.

"Come on, Mikayla. Let's go," Anthony jerked his head for her to follow.

"I don't wanna watch any old ball game," Mikayla protested. One look from her grandfather and she marched over to stand next to Anthony.

"We can play that rock band game. I'll let you be the leader of the band," Anthony said and held out the bag of chips. "Besides, the good game doesn't come on for another hour."

"Really? I can be the leader? Cool." Mikayla grabbed a handful of chips before bouncing down the hallway.

Willa waited for them to disappear. "I'm not pregnant. Let's get that out of the way. It's MiMi. Or so she claims."

"This is better than my favorite soap opera, As Our Days Turn," Aunt Beryl murmured and sat down hard.

"Get some proof she's pregnant," Mama Ruby said.

"And DNA proving Jack was the daddy," Aunt Ametrine added pointing at Willa.

"Lawd, but ain't this some drama." Papa Elton let out a low whistle and shook his head.

Willa shrugged. "Y'all got some of that cherry crème soft drink I like? You know that old fashioned brand made in New Orleans." She started for the kitchen.

Her family followed her, exchanging looks with each other. Aunt Ametrine raced down the hallway to make sure the kids were occupied. Moments later she scurried back joining the adults in Mama Ruby's large kitchen.

"We can talk. The children are into that video game," Aunt Ametrine huffed, breathless from rushing back. "What did I miss?"

"Nothing," Aunt Beryl replied. She sat on a stool at the breakfast counter.

"You're mighty calm considering," Mama Ruby said. She examined Willa with a concerned frown. "You feeling okay, baby? I know you've been working hard at that office. All this stress is just taking a toll on you."

"I'm okay. As okay as I can be." Willa got a bottle of soda from the big stainless steel fridge. "MiMi is no fool. With today's technology she wouldn't lie about having Jack's baby. She knows it wouldn't fly for long."

"Get the proof anyway," Mama Ruby repeated. "But you got a good point."

"Sure. But she knows me well enough to realize I wouldn't just take her word for it." Willa sighed. "No, I'm afraid Mikayla is going to get her baby sister."

"Or brother," Aunt Beryl said quietly. She blinked rapidly when the others glanced at her. "Or do you know for sure?"

"No," Willa said and sighed. She took a pull from the bottle of soda then sat down on a stool next to her aunt Beryl.

"Well, well. A new member of the family. Might as well invite the girl for dinner." Papa Elton rumbled.

"Yeah right," Aunt Ametrine said with a grunt. "What a fine role model that is for our children. A scarlet woman parading around with visible proof of her sin."

"What about Christian love?" Mama Ruby cocked an eyebrow at her sister. "You saved souls can be some of the most judgmental— "

"All right you two," Willa broke in, determined to block one of their head-butting sessions over religion. She looked at Papa Elton. "Daddy, you make a good point."

"I was just kidding about the dinner, but you could try being nice to her. She's got a claim on the estate." Papa Elton nodded.

"Exactly what Brad said." Willa put the bottle of soda on the counter. She rubbed the back of her neck. "I can't fight battles on all sides. It's wearing me down."

"I know, sweetie pie." Papa Elton walked over to Willa. He massaged her neck gently. "What with Jazz and Anthony, running a business, and settling Jack's affairs you got a hand full."

"Two hands full," Beryl agreed. She patted Willa's hand.

"Try six hands full." Willa sighed under her father's paternal nurturing. The tension eased from her shoulder muscles. "Thank you, Daddy."

Papa Elton kissed the top of her head. "You come see your daddy anytime you need a break. Speaking of kids, I'm going to check on my grandchildren."

Mama Ruby watched him lumber out. "He wants to play that game with them kids."

Willa laughed. "Daddy gave his advice and now he's tired of this serious stuff."

"So what are you going to do about this MiMi person?" Aunt Ametrine's wide mouth turned down in disapproval.

"I'm going to be nice to her. I mean after all Mikayla already thinks of this baby as part of her family. Anthony is even talking about a little brother."

"Well, just how are you going to explain this to those children?" Aunt Ametrine crossed her arms.

"They've already met her, Aunt A," Willa replied. She smiled at her aunt's scandalized expression.

"Where?" Aunt Ametrine spluttered.

"At my house. MiMi came over one day. Anthony met her before at Jack's office" Willa waved a hand in the air. "The point is I might as well accept it. MiMi now has negotiating power."

"Humph, I want to spend some time with this MiMi," Mama Ruby said. "I'll find out her game in hot minute."

"I'll bet you can." Willa laughed.

Mama Ruby had the warm heart of a loving mother. She also had the interviewing skills of a wily cop. She'd extracted more confessions and secrets than any group of FBI interrogators. Foster care workers respected her, but Mama Ruby would side with the biological parents of kids if she felt they deserved another chance. Willa trusted her sense of right. She just wished Mama Ruby could reach Jazz.

***

Three days later Willa sat in the lobby of Strafford, Inc. She glanced around the office and wondered if the place had been professionally decorated. Soft shades of blue, green and bronze made up the furnishings. Framed prints reflected the color scheme. The sleek model-thin redheaded receptionist fit right in. She handled phone calls in a clipped voice.

"Strafford, Inc. How may I assist you?" she said over and over.

Willa had given up trying to get information from her with chitchat. Ms. Icicle 2008 had no time or inclination to share. So Willa contented herself with flipping through a company brochure. Strafford, Inc. specialized in providing quality products that helped businesses and the environment, it read. Skimpy on details, the rest of the copy talked up Strafford and its highly qualified staff.

"Ms. Crown, Mr. Strafford will be able to see you in a few minutes. He's been tied up on an overseas phone conference." Ms. Icicle's frozen smile switched on.

"Excellent. Thank you."

So she would talk straight to the horse's mouth instead of his subordinate. Willa put on her game face. Inside her stomach churned. Maybe she should have brought Cedric with her, even if she didn't trust him. And she wanted to, very much. His broad shoulders invited her to lean on them. Having her family meant the world to her. But being around Cedric reminded Willa how long it had been since she'd snuggled up with a big, desirable man. One voice in her head said, "Girl, go for it!" The other voice, the one reminding Willa of all her past letdowns, said, "Don't be no fool!"

"Mr. Strafford will see you now," the cool voice said, interrupting Willa's thoughts.

"Thank you." Willa pushed her dilemma over Cedric on a back burner. She smiled and followed the administrative assistant into the boss's office.

"So nice to meet you, Mrs. Crown. Ike told me we've been something of a mystery to you. But let me say foremost how sorry I was to learn of Mr. Crown's untimely death. Horrible world we live in."

"Thank you. I appreciate you making time in what must be a very busy schedule on short notice." Willa tried not to stare at the unique looking man.

Strafford looked to be at least six feet four and had white hair all over. His eyebrows and mustache were white. More like platinum blonde. His dark blue suit had to have set him back a good two thousand dollars Willa judged. The light blue silk tie would have made Jack ask about where the guy shopped. It matched his cool blue eyes.

"Happy to do it. After all we were looking forward to working with Jack." Strafford rested his smooth hands on the back of a chair. "Please."

Willa smiled her gratitude and sat down. "As Mr. Nelson probably mentioned I haven't been able to find any paperwork. I'm in the embarrassing position of having to ask just what Crown Protection was going to do for Strafford, Inc.?"

Strafford smoothed down his tie unnecessarily as he sat down. The man looked so together Willa doubted even a strong wind would ruffle his look. He smiled back at Willa.

"My great-grandfather started our first family business back in nineteen thirty-seven when he was just a teenager. In Norway. He became quite successful dealing in scrap metals."

Willa thought, "What the hell?" but instead maintained her polite smile and said, "He was obviously hardworking and resourceful."

"Most of us business people have to be, yes?" Strafford nodded.

Willa noticed the lilt of a different accent for the first time. "Very true."

"Your late husband was the same." Strafford steepled his fingers and struck a thoughtful pose.

All well and good, but back to the present century. Willa nodded with him. "So you deal in metals, recycling?"

"To make a long family story short I've come back to metals, yes. But we have other ventures. Now we deal in futures, commodities of various kinds and moving money." Strafford seemed to be searching Willa's face for her reaction.

Though her pulse rate ticked up Willa didn't let it show. "I see. And Crown Protection's role would be?"

Strafford laughed. "Naturally I should get to the point, yes?"

<u>Hell yes</u>, Willa wanted to snap. She gave a little laugh worthy of any Southern "tea party" Belle. "Knowing your business is important."

"So refreshing to deal with Southerners. We have offices in New York. Here there is such charm. So European. Reminds me of home. I grew up in Italy you know."

Willa had a feeling that by the time she left she would know all about him. She was still cloudy about Strafford, Inc.

"Louisiana has deep roots in Europe," she replied.

"Indeed." Strafford pressed a button on his phone. "Elsa, bring us coffee and a pot of tea. I'm weaning myself off coffee. Drinking more green tea."

"I'll join you in being healthy then," Willa said. He was testing her ability to stay Southern Belle polite. Strafford might just find out how fast southern well-bred could shift to southern "get to the damn point".

Elsa slid in like she was riding on a cushion of air. She set a tray down then poured two cups of tea. "Sweetener?"

"No thanks," Willa said accepting the china cup. No crass foam cups for Strafford. Elsa left and Willa gave Strafford an expectant gaze.

"Crown Protection was going to help us in two ways. First, we do have three warehouses in Louisiana. We need security at them. One is here in Baton Rouge. Mr. Crown was going to hire staff in New Orleans as well."

"Really?" Willa blinked at him. Cedric would be just as surprised to hear that.

"Yes."

"Why would warehouses need round the clock security? Not that I don't want the business, but you could install alarms and security cameras."

"We do business overseas. As a result we are a twenty-four company. We have to operate in four different time zones." Strafford waved a hand.

"Which has what to do with the warehouses? What's in them?" Willa watched his thin lips tighten. She must have asked one too many questions. "Sorry to be so dense. I haven't been a business owner for very long. Lord, my head spins keeping up with local clients. I'm just not familiar with going global."

Willa spoke rapidly as she wore a confused, but she hoped, charming smile. She'd deal with the shame of playing the clueless female later. Right now she channeled her version of dumb blonde, minus the blonde. She even deepened her Southern accent. Strafford's mouth flexed into a smile. Willa stayed on guard because his blue eyes hadn't warmed up to match the smile.

"I understand how you must be quite taxed. And of course you have the children to think of." Strafford nodded slowly. "Working mothers face so many choices. Making the right one is critical."

Willa definitely felt a chill. She didn't like the way he referred to her kids. Was her imagination in overdrive, or was there a threat in his words? His polished looks and civilized accent threw her off balance. Then the hood rat in her rose up. She didn't like being threatened, however subtly.

"I manage quite well actually. My employees are top notch and my family is very supportive."

Strafford inclined his head. "Of course. One's network is so important. I'm glad you have others you can count on."

"You were going to tell me about the warehouse. Crown Protection can do a better job protecting property if we have information." Willa gave him her best chilled smiled.

"Actually we made other arrangements. With the tragic events and not knowing who would take over." Strafford shrugged. "In a global economy one must take decisive action quickly."

"I see. I'm just surprised you didn't contact Cedric Robinson. I understand you paid us. And then of course Jack did have a contract with you." Willa stared at him.

"Tragically Mr. Crown died before we could finalize the details. In fact, I hadn't returned my copy of the signed contract and no money changed hands. I've consulted our attorney. There is some question as to whether it is even binding. In light of that we made alternate arrangements." Strafford stood indicating their meeting was at an end. "Thank you for coming. Good luck with running your company."

What's the rush, big guy? Willa stood also. "Thanks again for seeing me. One more thing though."

"Yes," Strafford said, an edge to his tone.

"Are you sure maybe Isaac Nelson didn't pay Jack part of the contract fees? My late husband's girlfriend swears she got a call about money that should be returned."

"Jack's mistress called you? I didn't realize Americans were so like the French," Strafford replied coolly.

"Jack and I were divorcing. And don't forget Louisiana was a French colony. Maybe Mr. Nelson could join us and explain," Willa said with a "touché" smile.

"No. Not possible," Strafford snipped. "I'm very sure about our arrangements with Crown Protection, Mrs. Crown. Now if you'll excuse me I have other obligations."

"Well of course." Willa went back to being a flighty Southern lady. "I'm holding you up. I'll be on my way. I can always ask Mr. Nelson when I see him at church."

Strafford's administrative assistant opened the office door. She gave Willa a smile that looked more feral than friendly. "This way please."

"My, what service. Goodbye, Mr. Strafford. We may have business in the future." Willa waved gaily as she left.

"Perhaps," came Strafford's terse reply.

Willa kept up a stream of mindless chatter directed at the silent woman. The assistant practically pushed Willa out of the office suite into the hallway.

"You know what I— " Willa turned to in time to see the woman's back, but only for a moment. The door with Strafford, Inc. in burnished gold letters whisked shut. Wondering what to do next, Willa rode the elevator down. Outside in the sunshine she decided to forget about Strafford. If they didn't care about the contract then neither did she. The fact that MiMi wouldn't get that particular chunk of cash was lagniappe, a sweet little something extra.

***

The next day MiMi make another grand entrance into the lobby of Crown Protection. Kay rolled her eyes as MiMi swept through the door. "Hi, Kay. Girl, have you been working out? Don't stop what you're doing because you look great. I know how busy you are. Willa is expecting me." MiMi's gaze darted around.

"Mrs. Crown has a full schedule and I know it hour by hour. Your name isn't on here." Kay swung the flat screen of her desktop around to show MiMi.

"Oh we're not so formal." MiMi smiled back. "Wow, you guys have upgraded the equipment. Nice."

Kay stood in her path to Willa's office door. "I'll just let her know you're her."

Willa swung the door open after listening to the exchange on the other side. "I'm tempted to see who wins." She sighed. "But I did tell MiMi to come by."

"Oh." Kay's expression combined disappointment with irritation.

"Maybe we could get some coffee?" MiMi glanced at Kay. She backed into Willa and away from Kay's lethal scowl. "Maybe not."

Willa rolled her eyes and shut the door. "I'm going stop her from beating you down, but only until you have the baby; naturally."

MiMi patted her tummy. "One more benefit of motherhood."

"Do you ever wonder why so many women want to whip your butt?" Willa sat down at her desk.

"Not really. So how are my darlin' godchildren?" MiMi sat down, arranged her designer purse on her lap and smiled at Willa.

"Who?" Willa blinked at her, genuinely baffled.

"Anthony and Mikayla. I've always wanted to be a godmother" MiMi looked down.

"You have two nieces and a nephew, right?" Willa glanced at the screen of her new laptop.

"My sister lives in upstate New York with her husband and two kids. She prefers not to keep in touch. Long story. My other sister and I aren't close either. She's always been jealous of me."

"Y'all seem to have taken sibling rivalry to a new level. Your parents should have made all of you behave," Willa said.

"You'd think so, wouldn't you?" MiMi replied. She tapped a finger on the leather handbag for a few moments.

Willa recalled her mother's short history of the MiMi's family. The distinct stale odor of family secrets gave Willa a sour feeling.

"I know a few things about bad parents," Willa said to test the waters.

"They're not bad parents," MiMI said sharply. "Daddy sent us to the best schools. Mother always made sure we met the right people."

"The right people?"

"You know, like us. I mean— "

"I married into the Crown family. I know what you mean," Willa said in a dry tone.

"You don't have to say it like that. You want your kids hanging out with the right friends. True? Well, it's no different." MiMi shrugged.

"Yeah. I guess."

Willa decided not to argue the point. MiMi still hadn't broken the habit of making excuses for her parents or keeping the family secrets.

"What did your parents say about you having a baby?" With no wedding ring?" Willa raised both eyebrows at her. "The right families still frown on that stuff."

"They'll adjust. Once I tell them." MiMi patted her perfect hair. "They're busy, I'm busy. You know how it is."

"Oh yeah. I know how it is. They're going to trip; disinherit you or some stupid mess like that. You're grown. They can accept it or not. Bam."

"Hey, I need my own money. Until then I've got to handle the whole new baby, no marriage thing carefully." MiMi didn't seem quite so sure of herself.

"Humph. I take it they didn't know Jack wasn't officially free to marry. And maybe y'all weren't officially engaged." Willa blinked in the glare of a light bulb going off over her head. "So that's why you're going around calling Jack your fiancé. Now I get it."

"We were engaged. We'd talked more than once about spending our lives together," MiMi replied with a frown. She glared at Willa as though daring her to prove otherwise.

"That's your story and you're sticking to it," Willa quipped.

"Exactly." MiMi's sly half-smile matched the devilish twinkle in her greenish-brown eyes. "Anyway, back to my new family."

"S'cuse me?"

"Anthony and Mikayla. Hey, maybe Reverend Fisher can do the christening for us. I can get that fine Cedric to be the godfather." MiMi looked at Willa. "Not that I'm trying to make a move on him. I know that's your stuff."

"Let's start with the christening. No. As for Cedric 'being my stuff', no again." Willa squinted at her.

"Oh come on. Discussing the christening would be a great ruse to talk with Reverend Fisher again. You know, I had a chance to chat up Ike Nelson during that tour he gave me of the sacred art gallery. He's got a freaky mix of deacon on the outside and gangsta on the inside vibe. It's kinda sexy."

"You're pregnant and still flirting?" Willa huffed a sigh.

"To find out information," MiMi replied with patience. "I want to know who's got our money. I think they owe our company."

"We and our?" Willa grunted. "Please join the rest of us in reality, MiMi. This company is mine."

"Okay, that's true. However, I have an interest." MiMi nodded.

Willa hated to concede anything so she changed the subject. "Besides, according to Strafford we never did any work for his company. So Strafford, Inc. is not my problem."

"What do you mean it's not your problem?" MiMi said.

"You need to pay attention. Strafford didn't pay us anything and Crown Protection didn't perform any services for them. So I can't say they owe us money." Willa shrugged. "I repeat, your money is not my problem."

"But..., but that can't be true. Jack told me something about a joint venture with them." MiMi's mouth worked like a goldfish sucking in water.

"Then you should have gotten it in writing. Jack wasn't known for telling women the truth," Willa replied mildly. "Now I need to get some work done."

"Listen, this isn't just me wanting another pair of shoes. I have my baby to consider." MiMi twisted her hands together.

The mention of a baby tugged at Willa. She tried to be cold, but couldn't. She stopped tapping the lap top keyboard and gazed at MiMi. "Don't you have any money to live on?"

"Some, but it won't last for another six months. Not to mention the house note, baby things and the hospital bills." MiMi's party girl façade had disappeared. She blinked rapidly as a tear slid down one cheek.

"Damn," Willa whispered. She hadn't thought about medical coverage. "Maybe Jack has you on the company policy." She called for Kay.

Moments later Kay came in. "Yeah, boss."

"Look at the company policy coverage and see if Ms. Landry was added. Jack might have done that. He wouldn't need to tell you guys," Willa added when Kay narrowed her eyes.

"I'll check our records and with our agent." Kay glanced at MiMi then left.

"You need to tell your parents about the baby. Let them help," Willa said firmly.

MiMi shook her head. "No, no. I don't want to go to them."

"Wait a minute, where did you get that kind of money to invest? You have no job. In fact you haven't worked in a while."

"I had money saved up," MiMi said quickly.

"Uh-huh." Willa stared at her hard while she put two and two together. "Where did you get those 'savings', MiMi?"

"I earned that money, and it's not relevant how." MiMi crossed her arms and returned Willa's steady gaze. "And I need it back."

"Good luck getting it." Willa sighed. "I tried. Strafford won't talk. I don't have any paperwork. Besides you can always get more money where you got it before. Oh wait, you're pregnant so you can't hustle some rich old guy. Puts a cramp in your earning potential." Willa smirked.

"Don't underestimate the power of MiMi Landry, my dear." MiMi smirked right back.

Willa tried not to laugh but it broke through anyway. MiMi giggled and did a little shimmy move with her shoulders only. That made Willa laugh even harder until she bent double in her chair.

MiMi stopped laughing. She let out a long breath. "You should be thankful I've still got game. Ike Nelson is ripe for picking by now. I'm going to meet him for a drink and more conversation."

"You shouldn't be drinking. Not that it's any of my business," Willa added.

"I appreciate it." MiMi smiled at her with sisterly warmth.

Willa cleared her throat. "Yeah, well you're grown. But you better be careful with Ike. I got some funny vibes from his boss."

"Oh I can handle myself. Anyway I'm going to have red wine. My doctor says it's okay." MiMi frowned. "What exactly was Jack supposed to do for Strafford, Inc.?"

"Provide security at a large warehouse. Strafford was kinda vague on details. Which makes me think that wasn't the whole story." Willa thought about the cold blue eyes and the way he mentioned her kids. She crossed her arms tightly to deal with a sudden chill.

"What's wrong? You look like the guy creeped you out." MiMi shook a finger at her. "I told you these people are shady."

"At this point it doesn't matter to me. Strafford made it clear he doesn't care about the contract," Willa replied and looked out the window.

"Don't kid yourself that it's over."

"Have you gotten any more mysterious phone calls?" Willa looked at her.

"No," MiMi admitted after a pause. "But that doesn't mean they won't come after us again."

"Consider the money a business loss on your tax return. You could get a hefty refund." Willa waved a hand.

"Hell-to-the-no!" MiMi shrilled. "I'm not giving up my money."

"Well don't count on using your charm on Strafford. He's about as warm-blooded as a shark," Willa said with a grimace as she recalled his cold eyes.

"Please. When it comes to men there are two types. Men who give in to temptation quickly and men who take a few more minutes to crack." MiMi flipped one hand in the air. "But to save time I'll stick to my first game plan. Ike Nelson."

"Kinda rough around the edges for your taste," Willa wisecracked.

"Honey, please. I'm not going to date the man. I just need information." MiMi wrinkled her nose. "Then I'll ditch him like a bad habit."

"You better be careful. Ike Nelson doesn't look like the kind that would take being dumped lightly."

Cedric came in without knocking. "This Strafford, Inc. situation is getting deep... He glanced at MiMi. "Hello."

MiMi beamed at him. "Hello."

"Sorry to interrupt. Kay wasn't at her desk, but I assumed you were alone. Let me know as soon as you're free." Cedric gazed steadily at Willa as though trying to send a silent message.

"Did you mention Strafford, Inc.? We were just talking about that contract," MiMi said before Willa could speak.

Cedric glanced from Willa to MiMi then back at Willa. "Really?"

MiMi spoke up again. "Yes. I was just telling Willa that I planned to meet with Ike Nelson. We'll find out about this mysterious contract once and for all."

"You can consider that meeting cancelled." Cedric looked at Willa, then MiMi. The police found a body night a vacant lot last night. The victim was identified today."

Willa didn't have to ask by the expression on Cedric's face. "Ike Nelson."

Chapter 10

Cedric nodded. "Shot in the head. According to the news reports they're treating it as a robbery or carjacking turned deadly. His car was torched. The police found it across the river in a cane field."

"We start asking about his connection to Jack, and he turns up dead." Willa bit her lip and looked at Cedric.

"I say we forget about Strafford, Inc. Stop asking questions and let the police follow their leads." Cedric crossed his arms and glanced from Willa to MiMi.

"Holy sh—.You think I could be next? But I don't know anything. Not one thing about money or off shore accounts. Nothing." MiMi waved her arms around and paced in front of Willa's desk as she talked.

"Right. Cause of course it's all about *you*." Willa shook her head in disgust.

MiMi stopped to stare at Willa. "You know more than I do. I'll bet Jack left some papers or reference to money. You're just not talking."

Cedric marched forward with a scowl. "Hold on. Don't go blabbing that kind of crap around town or Willa will be next."

"That's her plan," Willa replied calmly. She returned MiMi's stare. "Isn't it?"

"No, no. I didn't mean— "

"Sure you did. And hopefully you could get control of Jack's estate," Willa continued.

"Well, I hadn't even thought of such a thing." MiMi blinked rapidly as though considering it then. She shook her head. "No, that's horrible. I would never do that. I sorta like you. Besides, you're practically family."

"Say what?" Cedric glanced from MiMi to Willa.

"Cedric, MiMi is pregnant." Willa watched his expression go from baffled to stunned. She nodded to him, as it appeared the implications sank in.

"Oh." Cedric sat down and rubbed his chin.

Willa gazed at him wondering what was going through his mind. He hadn't mentioned buying Crown Protection again. His expression cleared. Willa's gut told her somehow Cedric viewed this development as good news for him. But why?

"Then you need to think of Willa's safety, not to mention her kids," Cedric pointed out in a solemn voice.

MiMi faced him standing next to Willa's desk. "I know that. I'm speaking confidentially, just between us," she snapped.

"Yeah, sure." Cedric made a noise that fell somewhere between a grunt and a snort.

"And anyway, how do we know we can trust you? I mean, you probably thought you could get control of this company, what with Willa being clueless about running a security business and— "

"Excuse me, I lack experience not brains," Willa replied.

"That cheap divide and conquer trick won't work. But I guess you had to try. Cheap tricks being your blue light special," Cedric muttered.

"What the hell? You're nothing but hired help. Jack would never have sold this business to a dressed up hood rat." MiMi wagged a forefinger at him. "So there."

"Jack didn't want another kid, not one with her anyway. He was going to break it off and pay for an abortion." Cedric delivered his one two punch in a calm voice. The tight cords in his neck gave the only clue to his inner rage.

"Bull. We were picking out baby things. But you wouldn't know. You were just an employee," MiMi shouted. "Jack used to tell me about you. Hood rat makes good. But know this, homey, he had no intention of ever letting you be in complete control. And own a division of Crown Protection? Wasn't going to happen, baby."

"A division?" Willa looked to Cedric for an answer.

MiMi jumped in first. "Part of this Strafford deal was to expand, open up a cyber security division and start providing security even in foreign countries."

"I see. So you knew more about Strafford than you let on. Right, MiMi?" Willa continued to stare at Cedric. "And so did you."

"No," Cedric said quickly before MiMi could beat him again. "Yes, Jack and I discussed plans to branch out. But I didn't know about Strafford. Jack did that on his own."

"Because like I said you were only hired help. He didn't trust you with the important stuff." MiMi gave him a smug smile.

Kay came into the office with one of the uniformed security officers. The beefy man held his arms out as though ready to restrain someone.

"We got a problem in here?" Kay frowned at MiMi. "I've got a solution."

"Everybody calm the hell down," Willa burst out. She sprang from her executive chair and came from behind her desk. "Kay, I'll handle this. Cedric, would you excuse us?"

Cedric pursed his lips. Disapproval stamped his features, but he nodded. Staring straight ahead without looking at anyone he strode out, the good soldier following an order.

Kay started to say something to MiMi. She stopped when Willa held up one palm like a cop stopping traffic.

"Let's go, Ray. We'll be right outside though," Kay said looking at MiMi.

Once the door closed MiMi tossed her head. Her long hair bounced. "Guess we got them straight."

"We nothing." Willa shook her head slowly. "Drama follows you like a bad smell."

"What did I do? You need to be looking at Cedric. Something doesn't add up with him."

"Humph." Willa sat down at her desk again.

"No, I'm telling you, girl. You better watch that brother." MiMi nodded with vigor.

Willa had every intention of doing just that. She'd also keep an eye on MiMi. All of her talk about being one of the family was clever. MiMi was looking for a way to stick close to Willa to get information. Just how stupid did MiMi think she was anyway? MiMi seemed to read her mind.

"I know what you're thinking. Girl, you can trust me. I want this business to do well. And want to find my money. Jack's will is strong evidence to support my claim."

"Humph." Willa felt a headache coming on. She needed triple strength ibuprofen and a break from MiMi.

"I don't really want to fight you over Crown Protection. That would only give Cedric reason for hope." MiMi glared at the closed door as though she could see Cedric through it.

"Speaking of taking care of business, we need to. Goodbye." Willa grabbed MiMi by one arm.

"Okay, I understand. Call me if you hear any more about Ike's murder." MiMi talked fast because Willa's was marching her out double-time.

"Goodbye, MiMi." Willa pushed her past Kay's desk.

"Bye. I'll talk to you la— " MiMi's last words were muffled as the door closed.

"Yeah, yeah." Willa headed to her office. Before she could close the door Cedric was back.

"Okay, we need to talk about what just happened." He closed the door then stood with his arms folded.

Willa sat down at her desk. "Sure. Let's start with what else you haven't told me."

Cedric puffed out a breath as he sat down. "You were already overwhelmed. It didn't make sense to hit you with too much at once. Besides, you were trying to deal with one office. How could you have handled expanding?"

"That's a point. But you should have mentioned it by now," Willa replied evenly.

"Jack and I were still in the talking it out stage. We hadn't looked at office sites, talked about hiring or financing a branch office."

"MiMi could have been right. Jack might have had his own plans." Willa gazed at him steadily. His expression froze into what looked to her like a poker face, designed not to give anything away.

"Possible. He was the boss. Jack didn't have to tell me everything." Cedric shrugged after a few seconds. "At least not at first. Once he was ready Jack always relied on me to do a lot of leg-work."

Willa continued to gaze at him. She had to admit that sounded logical. Based what she'd seen in the files Cedric had a lot of responsibility. But Willa also knew Jack had a secretive streak. He liked being in control. And if he suspected Cedric might go out on his own Jack might have seen him as a potential competitor.

"Jack knew that I'd want my own company one day. The way Baton Rouge has grown since Hurricane Katrina there is enough for everybody. Not to mention opportunities in Ascension Parish," Cedric said.

Willa wondered if she was surrounded by psychics. More likely Cedric and MiMi just had reading people down pat. She smiled at him and sighed. His tight expression relaxed. A little.

"You're right. Why would I listen to anything MiMi might say?" Willa said.

"I guess in your position it's hard to know who to trust," Cedric said. His deep voice held the silken notes of sympathy.

Willa cautioned her soft side not to react. She was a sucker for a handsome man with a deep voice. In a perfect world she could just lean on one of those broad shoulders. Trouble was Willa had known since she was seven that the world wasn't perfect. Not even within shouting distance.

"I actually understand half of what it takes to run this place. But I didn't count on all the complications. Jack's mystery contract and even more mysterious business associates like..." Willa felt cold creep up her spine. "Ike Nelson."

Cedric's brow furrowed. He rubbed his forehead as though that would help him think straight. "Maybe it's just a coincidence. Could be a robbery gone bad."

"Another one you mean? That happens to take place after I start asking him questions about Strafford, Inc." Willa tapped a foot nervously. "I might have stepped in deep you-know-what."

"Don't get all dramatic on me. This isn't television or the movies. In real life crazy random events happen." Cedric leaned forward. "Until we know more that's all Ike Nelson's murder is."

"Another sign Baton Rouge has grown too fast, huh? More crime."

"Crime stats tell the story. Like that old saying goes, a sign of the times." Cedric stood. "Let's just wait and see before we get paranoid."

Willa could almost laugh at how much she wanted to believe it. Murder had a way of messing with her sense of humor.

***

That evening Willa went through her routine. The kids were in their rooms. Still thoughts of Cedric and just what she should do about him swirled around in her head. Fatigue and too many facts made her feel overwhelmed with it all. When the doorbell sounded Willa hoped it was someone bringing good news. Anyone. When she glanced through the peephole and saw Jack's brother, Ryan, she swore softly. Maybe she could pretend they weren't home.

"You want me to get the door, Moms?" Anthony shouted loud enough for the entire city to hear.

"No, thanks." Willa rested her head against the door for a second then opened it.

"Hope I'm not intruding. I just wanted to check on you and the kids." Ryan seemed hesitant. "I could come back."

"No, that's okay. Uh, come on in."

Willa motioned to him. He followed her to the kitchen. They sat at the breakfast table. A few minutes passed in awkward silence. Willa searched for something to say.

"How are Mr. and Mrs. Crown?" Not that she really gave a crap, but Mama Ruby had taught her manners.

"Pretty good considering, well you know." Ryan looked at her.

"Right." Willa knew exactly what he meant. Their parents were grieving the loss of their favorite child.

"So, y'all need me to help in any way?"

"No thanks. We're fine," Willa said automatically, not used to asking Jack's family members for help.

"You sure? I know how hard it must be for the kids, and you. I mean despite the problems between you and Jack. He really cared about you, Willa." Ryan paused, clasped his hands together then started again. "Fact is I think he loved you more than even he realized. No question he was devoted to those kids. I mean the way he left his estate in your hands proves it. Jack wasn't perfect,but…"

As Ryan spoke Willa unexpectedly felt full force of shock and grief. She'd been so busy with kids, the business and everything else. Now Ryan's words hit home. She remembered the Jack she'd fallen in love with years ago. Jack, the man who had embraced Anthony as his own; the man whose face had glowed with such joy when he held Mikayla for the first time, Willa covered her mouth with one hand to stifle the sob that threatened to come out. Tremors started in her shoulders and she squeezed her eyes shut.

"Willa? Are you okay?"

"I don't want them to see me break down," she rasped through her fingertips and shook her head.

Ryan nodded. "I'll check on them. Be right back."

Willa went to the kitchen sink. She got a glass and filled it with cold water. She drank a little hoping it would settle her stomach. Moments later Ryan came back.

"They're fine." He paused in the door. After a few seconds he walked closer. "Anything I can do?"

Willa drank more water then shook her head. "I'm okay."

"Sorry if I did or said anything to upset you. That's definitely not why I came over here." Ryan pulled out one of the stools at the extended kitchen counter. "Come on. Sit down."

Willa glanced at him and did as asked. When he sat next to her Willa moved back a bit. "Don't worry about it."

"But I do worry about you and the kids." Ryan sighed. "I apologize for the way the family has treated you."

"Like I said you've always been civil to me. As for the rest of your family, they're grown-ups. You can't apologize for them." Willa stared straight ahead. "Besides, they made it clear at Jack's funeral they still feel the same about me. Tell you the truth, I don't care how they act toward me. But when it affects my kids the game changes."

"I understand completely. I'd be angry, too," Ryan said with feeling. "Jack thought of Anthony as his son. We should have respected that."

Willa turned to face him. "He was just a kid. Human decency should have made them treat Anthony better."

"I know. Like I said my family has their own ideas about certain things." Ryan started to say more then apparently decided against it.

"Humph, that's one way to describe them." Willa stood. "Thanks for coming by, and thanks for the presents. My kids have everything they need."

"I know, I know. Jack left you his estate. Even left you the business." Ryan did not stand.

"Yes, he did. And?" Willa put both hands on her hips.

"He did the right thing, no matter what my parents or sisters think." Ryan wore an open expression. Apparently he wanted to impress Willa with sincerity.

"Right, he did. I have to get dinner started." Willa had been polite long enough.

"Sure. I understand. About the business." Ryan rubbed his face hard.

Willa noticed that his eyes looked red. Frown lines seemed etched into his handsome face. "Crown Protection is doing quite well. I've learned enough in the past few weeks to be a halfway decent boss. Of course having great employees helps, too."

"That's wonderful." Ryan cleared his throat. "Uh, I need to—"

Mikayla ran into the kitchen. She bounced up and down with excitement. "Uncle Ryan, come see the picture I made on the computer,

"Dang, girl. You must have been in the sugar. Let the grown-ups talk." Anthony came around her into the kitchen. "Since dinner is gonna be awhile I'm getting a snack then I'll be outta the way."

"Won't be much longer, Ant," Willa said, using the nickname from his baby days.

Anthony rolled his eyes. He mumbled something around the apple he was chewing. Then he handed Mikayla an orange. When he started pushing her out of the kitchen door Ryan stood.

"Growing kids need nourishment. I'll get out of the way. Just wanted to invite Anthony to a Hornets game. If he wants to go that is." Ryan smiled at Anthony.

"I'm there," Anthony said. He sprang away from Mikayla and pretended to shoot a basket. "Bam!"

"Six points. Yay for Anthony." Mikayla became her big brother's cheering section on cue.

"Three points. Girls." Anthony grinned at Ryan.

"Hey." Willa stared at Anthony.

"I meant little girls." Anthony shrugged at Willa. "I'm going to the NBA website."

Before Willa could say anything he was gone. Mikayla looked at Ryan. She crossed her arms. With her father's determined frown she lifted her chin.

"Where are you taking *me*?" Mikayla didn't question her right for a treat.

"Lily and I are going to a dance performance Sunday afternoon. Would you like to accompany us?" Ryan bowed to her then stood straight.

"Let me check my schedule." Mikayla pretended to turn pages. "Sunday afternoon, hmm. Yes, I'm free."

"Excellent." Ryan smiled at her.

Mikayla ran over, gave him a hug then flounced off. "I'll wear my blue and pink skirt set."

"You should have asked me first. I'm not sure Anthony should be going to New Orleans." Willa glared at him. "Suddenly you go from reluctant to even acknowledge us to Daddy Warbucks. What's up with that?"

"You're right. Absolutely. I was just so excited about the kids." Ryan stood. "I'll go let Anthony know right now the game is a no go. Same with Mikayla."

Willa let him get two steps before she stopped him. "Hold it. That's the first time I've seen him that excited since before Jack died. But going to New Orleans."

Willa didn't add the rest of what she was thinking. She had known Ryan for years, but not really.

"To tell you the truth I'm feeling guilty. About being such a fool about your marriage to Jack. About the stupid reasons Jack and I used to fight." Ryan shoved his hands in his pants pockets. He walked over to the breakfast nook and stared out of the bay window. "I can't get those years back."

"Yeah. What might have been. Your father raised you to compete with each other." Willa stopped herself from the litany of negatives about the Crown elders.

"But we were grown. As the oldest I should have had sense enough to end it." Ryan's voice broke. "Doing right by Anthony would make me feel better."

"I see." Willa blinked at him.

"So it's not totally noble of me. Bet you're not surprised. A Crown man thinking of himself." Ryan grunted and shook his head.

"You get it honest," Willa quipped then pursed her lips for a few seconds. "Sorry, that just slipped out."

"It's okay." Ryan looked at her. "You have a right after they way you've been treated."

"No, no. You're here being nice, extending yourself. I shouldn't be making backhanded comments."

"Considering the treatment you've had from us Crowns that was mild." Ryan rested both elbows on the countertop. "I sure as hell won't make excuses for us. My parents are-- I don't know where to begin on them, or my sisters for that matter. And then there's Jack's behavior."

"It's okay." Willa uttered the automatic polite response. His bark of laughter made her jump in surprise.

"Willa, you almost pulled off that lie." Ryan laughed harder until both his shoulders shook.

Willa caught it from him and soon they were both speechless from laughing so hard. They must have been pretty loud because Anthony poked his head in the kitchen door, looked at them like they were nuts then left. Finally, Willa was able to get control.

"More coffee?" she gasped.

Ryan wiped his eyes and nodded. "Yes, please. You know my wife can't be around my mother and sisters for five minutes without heading for the nearest exit."

"Really?" Willa felt relaxed in Ryan's presence for the first time since they'd met.

He must have felt the same because he assumed a casual pose, elbows resting on the counter. "She slapped baby sister Jeannie at the family Thanksgiving dinner last year."

Willa gaped at him and spilled the coffee she was pouring. "Oh Lord, please tell me you have video. Please! Cause if so name your price and I'll pay it."

That brought on more helpless laughter from both of them. Now Anthony and Mikayla stood looking at them. Willa spluttered, unable to speak. She waved at them to go away. The kids exchanged a glance then left, shaking their heads in wonder.

"No video, sorry. But that scene will live in my memory forever. I shouldn't be laughing. That day was awful." Ryan kept laughing despite his attempt to stop.

"I can't imagine your very etiquette conscious wife slapping anyone." Willa wiped up the spill then succeeded in pouring them both more cups of coffee.

"We're talking about my sisters, remember?" Ryan replied and tilted his head to one side.

Willa grimaced. "The patron saint of peace and forgiveness would want to whip their butts."

"Exactly. You can imagine the months of drama *that* generated. We finally had a peace conference. We have an uneasy family cease fire. My mother plays referee at family functions now. Even so we only get together three times a year. Easter, Thanksgiving and Christmas."

"Sounds like a decent compromise." Willa shook her head slowly. "I sure don't miss the Crown family gatherings."

"And I don't blame you. If I could get out of them I would." Ryan sipped coffee and stared into the cup as though looking for answers.

Willa started to blurt out "Get a backbone" then stopped herself. It was none of her business, she reminded herself. Ryan had always played the part of dutiful oldest son. He worked hard to win his father's attention and approval. Jack had no trouble getting both, being the favorite son. With Ryan seeming preoccupied Willa took the opportunity to study him. His handsome profile could still stop female traffic, but she noticed frown lines around his eyes. More lines were etched into his forehead. He was drop dead handsome, wealthy and had an ex-model, former black debutante for a wife. Yet here was another first, Willa felt a little sorry for him. He didn't look like a man who could count his blessings or enjoy them.

"Well, at least you don't live at home anymore. Right?" Willa joked and slapped him on the shoulder.

"Humph, right. Thank the Lord for small favors." Ryan lifted the cup and drained the last of his coffee. "I've imposed on you long enough. You haven't had a chance to fix dinner."

"Don't worry. I'm not a cook, as your mother so frequently pointed out to the world," Willa quipped. "I'll fix something quick and easy."

"No, let me order something for you. I've got it. Gourmet pizza and calzones from Angelo's." Ryan punched one button on his cell phone.

"No, really, Ryan. It's okay." Willa tried to go on but Mikayla's exuberance cut her off.

Mikayla yelled down the hall. "Yay! Uncle Ryan is ordering pizza, Anthony."

"Best news I've heard today," Anthony shouted from somewhere in the house.

"Come right in here, little miss," Willa said.

There was a ten second delay before Mikayla peered around the door where she'd obviously been standing. She shuffled in, head down. "Yes, ma'am."

"What have I told you about hiding and listening in on conversations that don't concern you?"

"I just happened to be passing in the hallway on my way to the den." Mikayla looked up at Willa. "I'm done with my homework, and I got an A on my quiz today."

"Excellent," Ryan broke in. "Now you guys like pepperoni or sausage?"

"Both," Mikayla bounced over to him and leaned against his knee. "Please."

"Anything you want, princess." Ryan went back to ordering. Moments later he hit the off button of his phone. "Done and done. They should be here in twenty-five minutes."

"Enough time for me to check that homework. For both of you," Willa said loudly. Anthony didn't answer and

Mikayla darted off. "So much for being through with her assignment."

Ryan stood. He smiled at Willa. "Your kids are a delight. Trust me. Their Crown cousins are trying. To say the least. Well, I better get going. I'll be in touch."

"Thanks." Willa followed him to the front door.

"I really mean it." Ryan faced her. "I'm going to spend more time with Anthony. Jack would want that. His last wishes made it clear how much he cared about you, too."

"Watch out. You're gonna ruin the Crown reputation for ruthlessness," Willa joked, feeling awkward in the face of his solicitude.

"And we can't have that," Ryan joked back. He leaned forward and pecked Willa on the forehead. "See you later, kid."

Shocked, Willa blinked at him with her mouth hanging wide open. All she could muster was a goodbye wave. He strode to his black Mercedes SUV. Willa closed and locked the door. Ryan being nice to her, telling stories that made the Crown clan look bad and wanting to spend time with Anthony. The world was upside down. Willa understood how Dorothy must have felt waking up in Oz.

***

Mama Ruby clicked her tongue as she peered at the newspaper through her reading glasses. "Says here he was thirty-six years old."

"Humph, so sad the way our young men are dying. Just killin' each other off," Papa Elton rumbled. He shook his head. "Humph, humph, humph. Doggone shame."

Willa sat in her parents' comfy kitchen. Decorated in green and yellow, the brightness combined with the smell of banana nut bread baking in the oven. Still Willa's childhood haven could not ward off the gloom caused by talk of murder. A second murder to touch their lives in a few short weeks.

"His car was found way down River Road in Iberville Parish. Somebody set it on fire." Mama Ruby rattled the paper as she turned pages to find where the story continued. "Probably destroying evidence."

"Which she knows from watching them forensic shows on television. You oughta call her Mama CSI," Papa Elton joked and poked Willa in the side with an elbow.

Mama Ruby shot him a dark glance then went back to reading. "Reverend Fisher is quoted in here. He's going to start a special outreach program to help fight crime."

"Really?"

Willa craned her neck to read over Mama Ruby's shoulder. Fisher knew about Jack and Ike doing business. Reverend Fisher would have to be very naïve to think the murders were a coincidence. And naïve was not a description Willa would ever attach to the good reverend's name. If Fisher was involved, which Willa had considered, then he'd want to keep a low profile. According to the article he planned to do anything but.

"Abundant Love Ministries, Inc. board of directors met in an emergency meeting. With approval from a grant source they will develop a new program," Mama Ruby read aloud. "Operation Lift Us Up, as it has been named, will not only reach out to troubled teens. In an unusual twist, young men ages twenty and older will be given opportunities for mentoring. 'We will talk to men who want to change their lives and help them do so', Reverend Fisher said."

"Ametrine might be right, baby. You judged him wrong. Seems like the man just wants to reach out and help somebody," Papa Elton said, echoing his favorite gospel hymn If I Can Help Somebody.

"Yeah, well." Mama Ruby pursed her lips. Her expression indicated she wasn't ready to change her mind just yet.

"I hope it was a carjacking," Willa mumbled. She picked at her slice of banana nut bread. Usually she inhaled the treat like a crazy woman. But not today.

"Of course it was. Nobody been bothering you or the kids. Jack might have had his faults but he wasn't a criminal. And you said that Strafford, Inc. is just a normal company." Papa Elton gave Willa a paternal pat on the back of her hand. "Don't let your imagination run away, darlin'."

"You're probably right," Willa said and gave him a weak smile.

"Now you listen to me. I got an extra pistol you can take and—" Mama Ruby started to rise.

Papa Elton pulled her back down. "What is the matter with you, Ruby Mae? This child is jumpy as it is. She don't need a gun. Too many guns in this country as it is."

"Yeah, well when that chump broke in here back in the day, and I popped off a round you wasn't complaining." Mama Ruby cocked a defiant eyebrow up at him.

"You lucky them social workers didn't take our children, too." Papa Elton shook a finger at her.

"Please. Y'all still arguing about that?" Willa broke in to head off one of their head-butting contests. She well remembered that wild night.

The violent parent of a foster child had somehow found out Mama Ruby's address. Determined to take his child back by force, he'd shown up one night. Terrified, the little boy had cowered in a closet screaming he didn't want to go. Few things could make Mama Ruby take such drastic action. A child being hurt was one of them. With lightening speed Mama Ruby had unlocked her gun, loaded it and aimed at him when he kicked in the back door. The man took off running. Willa wondered if he was still running.

"And no I don't want a handgun, Mama. Not with kids in the house. Besides, what kind of message would that send to Anthony?"

"Exactly," Papa Elton added. "She's working hard to keep that boy on the straight and narrow. No more gun play."

"Papa Elton is right. I'm overreacting. Now let's talk about something else." Willa broke off a tiny piece of banana nut bread and popped it in her mouth.

"Yeah, y'all can talk. But anybody mess with my family—" Mama Ruby snapped the newspaper and went back to reading. "Humph."

"Lord give me strength," Papa Elton muttered.

"Anthony knows right from wrong. He's just being a normal teenager. I've raised enough kids to know that. There's some that just too broken to fix. They've seen and suffered too much. Others get a taste of street life and decide it's more fun. Anthony ain't in either of them categories. I know," Mama Ruby said.

Willa also knew Mama Ruby was thinking of Willa's older brother in prison, and Jazz. "Of course I agree with you. But all it takes is one big mistake to ruin his life forever, just one time of being with the wrong kids in the wrong place."

"Yeah, like our church member's son. He was riding in the car with his buddy who shot a guy. Now he's sitting in prison right along with the boy that pulled the trigger." Papa Elton shook his head once more. "Umph, umph, umph. Broke his mama's heart."

"Poor Sharlene." Mama Ruby sighed and nodded.

The rear doorbell rang and Papa Elton got up. He pulled back the curtain to look through the window. Then he grinned and opened it. "Hey, Darrell. Hope they're not working you too hard."

A short and muscular UPS driver dressed in brown grinned back. "Afternoon, Mr. Elton. They sure are working me hard. Glad y'all are at home. I couldn't have left this one. Requires a signature."

"Sure thing." Papa Elton took the stylus from him and signed the electronic pad.

"My wife is to blame, always ordering something from that TV shopping channel."

Darrell handed him the box. "I'm not gonna complain too much. The ladies who shop give me job security."

"You got a good point, son." Papa Elton laughed at Darrell's joke. "Take it easy."

"Bye now." Darrell rushed off to his truck and his next stop.

"Now what have you bought, Ruby? I swear you don't need no more shoes or purses." Papa Elton passed the box to her.

"Daddy, scientific studies confirm that there is no such thing as too many pairs of shoes for women," Willa teased. She giggled when he rolled his eyes before sitting again.

"Or purses," Mama Ruby put in.

"Or earrings, bracelets and lipsticks," Willa finished.

"Amen." Mama Ruby frowned as she examined the outside of the box. "But this isn't something I ordered."

"Don't tell me I finally got a package in the mail. Better mark this on the calendar, Willa, so we can remember this day." Papa Elton peered at the package.

"No, it's addressed to me. From somewhere in the Cayman Islands. I don't know anybody down there." Mama Ruby put the box down then stared at it.

"Cayman Islands?" Willa leaned forward. "Open it."

"These days with foreign terrorists running wild, maybe we should call homeland security," Mama Ruby said. She pushed her chair away from the table, and stared at the long flat box.

"Don't be silly." Papa Elton gazed at the box for a moment then leaned back.

Willa grabbed it and tore open the seal. "Jack traveled to the Cayman Islands. He dropped a few bombs while he was alive. Let's see if this is one he's sent from the great beyond."

Chapter 11

Willa sat at her desk staring at the bright red USB drive shaped like a sports car. This cute small package held a lot of information and potentially big trouble. Big dangerous trouble. Which is why she didn't try searching the files on the USB drive while at Mama Ruby's. Willa wanted to keep her parents out of harm's way if she could. Now she could only hope no one knew the package had gone to their address. So she'd called MiMi, told her about the thumb drive. True to form MiMi didn't wait to be invited. By the time Willa had made it over to her office MiMi was sitting in the lobby patting her foot.

"Well what are you waiting for? Just stick it in," MiMi blurted out impatiently.

"Bet you've said that a few hundred times in your life," Willa tossed back at her.

MiMi lifted one arched eyebrow at her. "Jealous, huh? Now quit stalling and let's see what we've got."

"Maybe we should call the police." Willa chewed on one fingernail for a few seconds, remembered her manicure and stopped.

"Are you crazy? We don't know what is on that thing. The father of our children might have been involved in criminal activity. We need to know that before the police."

"So we can get killed, too?" Willa transferred her gaze from the USB drive to MiMi.

"No one knows it exists. I'm sure of that. Otherwise we would have been threatened before now." MiMi placed a hand on her stomach, and then sat down.

"You okay?" Willa stopped rocking.

"Yeah. This heavy feeling, is that normal?" MiMi yawned.

"You ain't seen nothin' yet, princess. Wait until you pack on fifty pounds." Willa smirked when MiMi shuddered.

"I'm going to start working with my personal trainer tomorrow." MiMi nodded.

"You got some secret stash of money I suppose. Designer maternity wear, personal pre-natal exercise guru." Willa shook her head slowly then looked at the thumb drive.

"Credit card Jack gave me. It has a high limit. But we must find that money. Now fire up that thing so we can get to it." MiMi leaned forward and reached for the USB drive.

"Stop," Willa commanded. "I'll do it."

"Fine. Sometime before I give birth would be nice," MiMi snapped back.

Willa mumbled and grumbled beneath her breath, but picked up the small device. She wanted to know, and didn't want to know. When MiMi let out another long-suffering sigh Willa glared at her.

"Sorry, it's just I'm dying to know." MiMi tapped her right foot. Then her impatient expression relaxed. "By the way I appreciate that you chose to call me. It means a lot to me. I'm not real close to my family, as you know. Anyway thanks. I mean you didn't even include your mama in this."

"I didn't want either of my parents in danger." Willa looked at the screen. All she had to do was tap the mouse pad on the icon. She didn't move.

"Great, but you don't mind putting me in the cross hairs. I'm with child, or have you forgotten? MiMi clicked her tongue to indicate disapproval.

"Okay, so which is it? You're eternally grateful to be included or ticked I put you in danger?" Willa put her hand on the USB drive. "I can always call Cedric."

"Well, you're a mother, too. Maybe handing this over to Detective Miller is the way to go. Mikayla and Anthony need both of us." MiMi wore a serious expression.

Willa blinked at her, mouth open. This crazy person had convinced herself they were actually family. Jack's mistress and love child? Then Willa gave herself a reality check. MiMi's baby would be Mikayla and Anthony's sibling, no question. Besides, Willa knew from experience that sometimes you have to fashion your own family to survive. The notion that a biological connection made a difference was wrong, totally wrong. Especially when it came to parents. So Willa decided not to argue with MiMi. At least not today.

"I know what Cedric would say, MiMi. We can't keep information from the police. Doing that could shut down Crown Protection." Willa tapped the mouse pad and held her breath.

"If we don't get some serious cash infusion that's going to happen anyway." MiMi got up and walked to the desk to get a better view of the computer monitor.

"What do you know about it?" Willa frowned at her.

"Jack left me an interest in this business. Your lawyer sent the financials my lawyer requested." MiMi squinted at the list of files.

"We're not broke. We have clients and new contracts," Willa argued.

"Right, but a huge chunk of operating capital is missing. I hate to say it, but maybe our darling Jack put that money in the Caymans. Open one of those documents."

Cedric entered the office. His dark tan skin contrasted in a delightful way against a crisp white shirt. He smiled, revealing that single killer dimple in his left cheek. "Excuse me, ladies. I have two new contracts for the boss to review and sign." Cedric strode in without waiting for an invitation. "More business means more money."

Willa gazed back at him without smiling. "Speaking of money, MiMi just shared some interesting news. Her lawyer says we have missing funds from the reserve account."

Cedric pursed his lips and let a few tense seconds tick by. "That's what Jack and I called it. One account was for operations, payroll and other expenses. Another was our reserve account for capital outlay, big ticket items and so forth."

"So you knew and didn't tell me?" Willa said and crossed her arms.

She speculated the reasons he'd do that. Maybe weaken the company then offer her a low-ball price. Or just damage Crown Protection, start his own outfit and take all the clients with him. Cedric rushed in with an explanation under Willa's pointed glare.

"I'm not keeping secrets, and I don't have a hidden agenda," Cedric said.

"Uh-huh, you just didn't tell me something super important," Willa snapped.

"The accountant called me this morning. I hadn't had a chance to tell you. She's doing an audit because of the estate fight Ms. Landry has initiated." Cedric waved a hand at MiMi. "Which is why I'm hard at work getting us more contracts."

"Estate fight?" Willa looked at MiMi sharply.

"Umm, my lawyer says the baby is entitled to at least one quarter of Jack's assets, not just a small interest in his business. Fight is too aggressive a word to describe it. We're opening discussions about Jack's estate." MiMi tried giving Willa a smile. Her lips turned down when Willa glowered at her.

Cedric looked from MiMi to Willa. "Your divorce wasn't final. What about the property settlement and your house, Willa?"

"Damn." Willa closed her eyes.

"Exactly. I'm no lawyer, but looks like you're going to be battling Ms. Landry here for what should be all yours. And your children's legacy, too."

"Give me the 'We are family' speech now, MiMi. I dare you," Willa said. "I could choke the life out of you right here."

"I'm pregnant." MiMi placed a hand on her stomach and backed up.

Willa huffed at her. "You better watch your back once that baby gets here."

"Anyway, I was going to tell you about the money at the right time." Cedric gazed at Willa.

"The right time." Willa stopped glaring at MiMi to glare at him.

"Yes, in private of course. You've had a lot to deal with lately. I wanted to have a game plan by the time I told you, so you wouldn't worry so much. I've just got to make sure we keep our cash flow solid. That means reliable paying clients." Cedric waved the contracts in the air. "Like these. I also wanted to talk to you about a couple that are shaky. We need to cut them loose and go after their overdue payments."

"Let's get back to the so-called reserve account," Willa said.

"We should talk later." Cedric gave a curt nod in MiMi's direction.

"I'm a part owner in Crown Protection, sort of," MiMi added when Willa growled like an angry cat.

"She's got a point," Cedric said rubbing his jaw, still gazing at Willa. "But it's not official until the estate is settled. Your call."

Willa looked from him to MiMi and back again. Mama Ruby had keen instincts about people, not that Willa had always followed her advice. But she sure needed those instincts right now. The urgent question wasn't who to trust, but which one of them she should distrust more. Willa channeled her mother and both aunts. She could hear all three voices chattering in her head at once. Then suddenly her father's wise voice broke through. Daddy always said when you're faced with tough choices take a break and a deep breath.

"Both of you leave right now. I have things to do." Willa raised a hand when Cedric started to speak. "I'll read and sign the contracts."

"What about that information we— " MiMi stopped when Cedric stared at her.

"I'll get back to you." Willa stood and herded them both toward the door.

"But this is very important," MiMi protested, still careful not to say more in front of Cedric.

"I'm sure after a nice talk with my lawyer things will be much clearer. Thanks to both of you for stopping by." Within seconds Willa had escorted them outside in front of Kay's desk.

Cedric gave a short nod. "Have Kay give me one set of the new contracts." He headed for his office with only a backward glance.

MiMi sputtered as she shifted from one foot to the other. "Willa, wait a minute. We've got some serious stuff going on, and I have a right to know."

"Don't get over excited, MiMi. Remember you're with child." Willa gave her a cheeky smile. "You go rest now. Bye-bye."

Before MiMi could sputter out another protest Willa spun around and marched to her office. She shut the door firmly then locked it. MiMi's voice came through in muffled tones followed by Kay's. Then silence. Willa's phone rang and she picked up.

"I will definitely be back in touch with you. This evening at the latest," MiMi blurted before Willa could speak.

"Fine. But as you pointed out not knowing what's in these files might be safer for you. Now get some rest. Bye." Willa hung up.

She stared at the whirling colors on her computer. Watching the screen saver soothed her jangled nerves after a few more seconds. Then she tapped the mouse pad once and a second time. After fifteen minutes of reading she hissed a few cuss words and picked up the phone.

***

One hour later Willa sat in the office of her former boss. Brad was a great attorney, which is why she thought of him first. Brad's experience defending white collar criminals and politicians was legendary in Louisiana. He knew a lot about white-collar crime. Willa had printed out the e-mails. Someone, maybe Jack or Ike Nelson, had saved them on the USB drive. Brad rocked his executive chair back and forth as he read. His handsome face looked just as good when he frowned in concentration. His colleagues teased him about his asset with female jurors.

He scanned the contents from the thumb drive and finally said, "These e-mails look pretty bland at first read, but then..." Brad shuffled back a few pages and examined one more closely. "I don't know."

Willa leaned forward with interest. "Yeah?"

"The more I read them, the more it sounds like some kind of code language. I mean they keep talking about storing the 'merchandise' and making sure it doesn't spoil."

Willa nodded. "Right. It's odd because Strafford isn't shipping any perishables. Strafford, Inc. deals with scrap metals and tech stuff. The scrap metal business has taken a beating lately so Strafford is diversifying, buying and selling metals for high tech products.”

“On the surface you don’t really have anything but supposition.” Brad dropped the stack of printed out e-mails. He held up a forefinger. “One, you know Jack visited the Caymans so you suspect he moved money over there.”

“But I don’t have anything except a safety deposit box key. Or at least I think that’s what it is. And a lot of receipts showing he traveled there at least six times.”

“Exactly. You also know Strafford has an office in the Caymans,” Brad put in.

Willa blinked in surprise. “As of this minute I know. How did you find that out?”

“Followed a complicated paper trail of shell companies, corporate filings. Trust me the details would make your head swim.” Brad waved a hand.

“Humph, the kind of trail some of your best clients used to leave.” Willa smiled at him.

Brad grinned. “Some of them were quite inventive I have to say. Electronic banking and the Internet helped a lot.”

“The police have also figured that out,” Willa said.

Brad’s grin faded into a serious expression. “Which is what I’ve explained to more than one client who was too clever for his own good.”

“And still they keep trying. Greed keeps the cops busy.” Willa looked at the e-mails. She picked them up and flipped the pages thinking of Jack.

“Yes, and rich greedy clients who get caught keep defense lawyers in business. God bless their rapacious hearts.” Brad rocked his chair back and thought some more.

“So I need to call Detective Miller.” Willa blew out a sigh of dread.

“Not so fast. What you have is innocuous business correspondence. Nothing directly related to Jack’s murder,” Brad said.

“Sounds like you’re rehearsing the speech you’ll give Miller just in case,” Willa replied.

“Yes, and it’s quite true.” Brad smiled.

“Agreed, but I also thought exactly what you did. Something is up with this.” Willa frowned at the puzzle.

"I have an idea. Why don't we let Ricki examine the files?" Brad tapped the keypad on his phone. The speaker phone buzzed and a female voice answered. "Ricki, it's Brad. Come to my office a minute."

Seconds later a tall young woman came into the office. Her eyes lit up when she saw Willa. "Hey, girl."

"Hi, Ricki. How are your babies doing?" Willa smiled when Ricki's smile grew wider. She loved talking about her two dogs.

"Excellent. Sinbad is still getting into all kinds of mischief." Ricki sighed, but her smile clearly indicated she loved the trouble.

"Before we spend the next few hours talking about Sinbad and Izzy," Brad broke in before Ricki could continue. "I have an assignment for you."

"Cool." Ricki loved computers almost as much as her dogs.

"Girl, you need a date," Willa teased. She and twenty-something had a running joke about which one of them needed a man more.

"Okay, let's double date," Ricki wisecracked. When Willa grimaced Ricki laughed. "That what I thought. So what's the new challenge, boss?"

Willa took the thumb drive from her purse and handed it to her. "This. Though I'm not so sure you won't fall asleep on this one."

"What's on it?" Ricki fingered the small drive attached to a key chain.

"That's precisely what we want you to tell us. On the surface it looks like some dull, dry business e-mails." Brad propped both elbows on his fancy desk.

"Ricki looked at the USB drive with interest. "Let me use your computer a minute, boss."

"Sure." Brad swung his slim laptop around on the swivel stand.

Ricki seemed to forget Willa and Brad were in the room. For about five minutes they watched her. The only sound was the click of the keys. Ricki's slender fingers moved quickly and lightly over the laptop's keyboard. Another minute passed before Ricki stood up straight.

"I'll know when I spend some quality time with this little puppy, but…" Ricki squinted at the computer.

"But?" Willa said to prod her.

"The size of the files looks off, like there's more to them than meets the eye. I have the right program on my computer." Ricki leaned over the laptop again. She closed the files then removed the USB device. Preoccupied with the task ahead, Ricki left.

Brad tilted his executive chair back. "Our next step depends on what she finds."

"Great. More waiting. I feel like one of those little computer hour glass icons is suspended over my head." Willa stood and slipped her purse over one shoulder.

"Everything is going to work out." Brad stood and smiled at her.

"That's what you told your last client, and he got three years for embezzlement," Willa said.

"He could have gotten twenty-five years, so look at the bright side," Brad said with a laugh. "Besides, he was guilty. You haven't done anything illegal."

"Yet," Willa said. "If the police go after my kid…"

"You're going to rely on good legal advice," Brad said firmly and wagged a forefinger at her. "Understood?"

"Right." Willa wondered if she should rely on the "normal" way or follow the street code. She knew what Jazz would say. She was about to leave when Ricki came back in wearing a self-satisfied smile.

"The files had hidden content. I cracked it open easily, so whoever did this wasn't that smart. Or he just wasn't smarter than me," Ricki quipped, and then her expression turned serious. "Back to this content, Jack and Ike were moving money around. Even in the hidden content they make it plain they don't want the authorities to know what they're doing. Even so they don't say *how* they got the money."

"Let me read those," Brad said with a sharp nod to Ricki. She plugged the USB drive into his computer and brought up the files. He put on his reading glasses again.

"Great. That's just great. If I tell the police Jack was running a money laundering operation the news will leak to the press in about two seconds. Then the kids will find out." Willa pinched the bridge of nose as she thought about dealing with the fallout. She barely noticed the background noise of Ricki and Brad voices.

Brad looked at her over his glasses. "Willa, this looks suspicious. That's the bad news."

"No kidding," Willa replied with a big sigh.

"The good news is the contents are too vague to indicate a crime has been committed. I mean Jack could have been moving legally obtained profits from his business in a bid to take advantage of tax loopholes." When Willa gave him a dubious look, Brad held up both hands. "Hey, I've made that exact argument at least twice in court. Quite successfully I might add."

"Those legal hairs you split are microscopic. But I'm okay with that, if it means I can keep the police out of this for a while longer." Willa gave Ricki and Brad a grateful hug before she left.

***

Frankie swung open the door to her condo with a flourish. Statuesque at six feet two, she wore a flowing leopard print caftan. Despite biology Willa had to admit Frankie's transformation to womanhood was successful.

"Girl, how have you been?" Frankie gave Willa a girlfriend kiss on the cheek. "Don't mind the mess. I'm cleaning up after that man again."

Willa glanced around looking for the "mess." The place looks fabulous as usual. You should see what my kids do to a room."

Frankie gave her a wistful smile. "Wish I had little rug rats around to get on my nerves." Then she seemed to shake off the blue mood. She smiled again, showing off a set of pearly white teeth. "What you doin' over here?"

"I've been trying to get in touch with Jazz. Have you seen her lately?" Willa dropped down onto a comfy leather ottoman the color of milk chocolate.

Frankie picked up a man's shirt and folded it. "Let me get this stuff out of your way. Howard leaves his clothes everywhere."

Willa shook her head and laughed. Frankie picked up the slippers and an empty glass. "I hope you don't nag that poor man of yours."

"I try not to be the typical woman," Frankie called back over her shoulder as she marched off.

"Mission accomplished," Willa yelled back, causing Frankie to bark out a raucous laugh.

Frankie came back into the living room and sat on the matching leather sofa. "We have our little moments, but trust me I know I'm blessed. Howard loves me for who I am, transsexual and all. Now back to your wayward sis."

"Jazz and I have our moments as well," Willa replied. "She hasn't been answering her cell phone."

"I haven't seen her since she moved. Try her new place."

"Moved when?" Willa finally stammered.

"Wait, I'm going to call the manager. She had to give notice because of the lease and all. Doris is a friend of mine." Frankie popped up and disappeared for a few seconds. She came back with a cordless phone. "Doris, when did Jazz move out? You know, the dancer in number 455, had the cops over there twice last year because of that crazy Latin boyfriend of hers."

"What?" Willa shouted then clamped a hand over her mouth.

Frankie pressed the mute button. "Yeah, child. Jazz has plenty drama. I like your sis and all but— wait a minute. Yeah, Doris I'm still here. Her sister is looking for her. I'll call you back, girl."

Willa gazed at Frankie's troubled expression. "What did she say? Did Jazz leave a forwarding address?"

"Doris says Jazz hasn't given notice that she was moving. She has four months left on her lease." Frankie shook her head. "Something ain't right."

"So why did you think she moved?"

"I saw some dudes loading up a bunch of boxes from her apartment in a truck then drive off. Then I saw Jazz throw some suitcases into her SUV and leave. Haven't seen her since."

"I want to see inside her apartment." Willa stood. She looked at Frankie. "Wish I had a key."

"Well I sure don't have one." Frankie shrugged.

"So her latest boyfriend was loading the truck?" Willa felt her stomach starting to churn.

"You kidding? Pretty boy doesn't get his hands dirty. Anyway I figured Jazz would call me with her new address."

"Maybe Doris could let me in." Willa gazed at Frankie.

"Doris probably won't do it, girl. I mean she could get sued. Knowing Jazz she could get her butt whipped, too," Frankie said and laughed loudly. Then she stopped when she looked at Willa. "Let me call her. Explain it's a family emergency."

Ten minutes later Frankie and Willa met Doris over at Jazz's condo. Doris, a former stripper back in the seventies, still looked good. Her short Afro had been dyed a bright blonde. She wore a camp shirt over white Capri slacks. The only nod to her age was the thick cushioned soles of her sandals.

"We have a clause saying if we think the tenant is sick or something we can go in. Still I don't want a mess on my hands. I told Jazz any more problems and she'd have to go, lease or no lease. Now this." Doris jangled the keys in her hand. She frowned at the door to Jazz's condo. "That boyfriend of hers might have done something to her."

"Shut your mouth, Doris. You're scaring her sister," Frankie snapped at her friend. She patted Willa's shoulder. "I'm sure Jazz is just pulling one of her little drama moves."

Willa thought about Jack and the unnatural ways the young could die. "Please hurry and open the door."

"Just make sure you back me up by saying you had reason to worry about her." Doris had already sorted out the master key. She opened both locks then pushed the door wide. All three peered into the small foyer that led into the living room.

After a few seconds Willa walked in. Frankie followed her inside with Doris bringing up the rear. "Nothing looks out of place. Jazz, you in here?"

"Jazz, holler if you here, girl." Frankie's voice boomed.

"Too quiet if you ask me," Doris muttered.

Willa went to the kitchen first. Dirty dishes were still in the sink. "Frankie, check down here and I'll go upstairs."

"Okay. Be careful." Frankie looked in the downstairs half-bath. Then she went into the dining room. "Her furniture is still here. Wonder what she was moving?"

Doris took another cautious step then another. Soon she seemed to relax. She opened the pantry and then the kitchen cabinets. "All her dishes are still here. Leftovers in fridge, too."

Willa had started up the stairs then paused. Frankie came up behind her and put a hand on her shoulder.

"Come on, I'll go with you," Frankie said firmly. "Doris, we'll be right back."

They went up the stairs to the master bedroom first. Jazz's clothes were tossed over the stuffed chair next to the bed. More clothes were on the floor. The walk-in closet had a lot of empty hangers.

"She didn't take all of her clothes and shoes so she must be coming back," Frankie said. She stood with both hands on her hips.

"Without these empty hangers I couldn't tell you what was missing." Willa picked up a tank top. "I rarely see my own sister."

"Honey, I could write a book on not getting along with family." Frankie pursed her lips. "My parents and brothers quit speaking to me years ago."

Willa chewed her bottom lip. "Looks like she left in a hurry. I'll call her boss."

Frankie nodded. "Good idea."

Willa dialed up the club. Jazz's boss answered on the second ring. What she had to say wasn't reassuring. Lorraine peppered her speech with a lot of expletives as she explained Jazz hadn't been at work. After listening to her complaints about losing money, being too nice to some people, etc., Willa finally managed to end the call.

"Child, I heard Lorraine way over here. I hope Jazz has another job lined up. Maybe that's what this is about. She just wanted out and took off for a few days."

"Jazz has been known to take off without saying goodbye." Willa looked around the condo. Nothing seemed radically out of place. But then Jazz was such a horrible housekeeper.

Frankie followed Willa's train of thought. "Yeah, if there was a fight up in here it would hard to tell. Her house cleaning service obviously hasn't been by in a while."

"You're telling me Jazz has a maid service?" Willa picked through some of the piles.

"Yeah. Her name is Debbie. I use her every once in a while." Frankie swept a hand out at the chaos around them. "Jazz gave her a few weeks off by the looks of this place."

"I can't believe Jazz let anybody in here. You know how guarded she is about her space." Willa shook her head. "Hell, this is my first time in her bedroom."

"And girl, she'd be ready to cut us both if she was here," Frankie said with a laugh.

"Call that cleaning lady and ask when she last talked to Jazz." Willa stepped over a heap of jeans on the floor. She peered at the vanity then carefully opened the drawer set into it. "Most of her cosmetics are gone."

"Bet she took her favorite thongs and dance costumes, too. A girl gotta earn a livin' no matter. Hey, Debbie. Girl, how are you?" Frankie walked out into the hall to get better reception on Willa's cell phone.

Willa looked around at a rare glimpse into her half-sister's life. Jazz had no family pictures around. She had one poster on the wall. The legendary black stripper from decades ago, Satin Doll, smiled alluringly, a huge fan of feathers hid most of what looked like a fabulous body. Was that Jazz's hero? Willa walked closer to examine the vintage poster.

"Debbie says she cleaned up last week. Jazz paid her for the month and said she'd be in touch." Frankie handed Willa the phone. "Satin Doll."

"Famous?" Willa faced her.

"Black folks say she had ten times more talent, beauty and class than Gypsy Rose Lee." Frankie's husky voice lowered in reverence as she walked to the poster. "Duke Ellington even wrote that famous song Satin Doll about her.

Damn, this is an autographed poster. Must be worth a small fortune. Now where would Jazz get that kind of money?"

"Good question. Let's search the two guest bedrooms and— " Willa froze. A beefy man stood in the bedroom door scowling at them. He wore his hair cut short. The part on one side was in the shape of lightening bolt.

"What the hell y'all doin' up in here?" The man said.

"Hi, Kenton. You remember me, I'm Jazz's neighbor. This is her sister." Frankie nodded in Willa's direction but kept her eyes on the man. "Willa, this is Kenton Turner, one of Jazz's friends."

Willa noted the inflection in Frankie's voice on the word friend. "Nice to meet you. I was worried about Jazz when I couldn't get in touch. The landlord said it was okay for a relative to make sure she's alright."

"She's okay. I came by to pick up a package, so y'all can go now." Kenton jerked a meaty thumb in the direction of the stairs.

"Maybe we can help," Frankie offered. "My husband is probably home from work by now and— "

"Don't need no help. Jazz don't like nobody up in her business so bounce," Kenton said with a sneer. He gave Frankie a head to toe glance and snorted.

Frankie stood straight to her full six feet two inches. "Don't be uncouth with me. I may be a lady, but I've still got enough muscle to— "

"Maybe we should just leave." Willa placed a restraining hand on Frankie's arm.

"How we know you're supposed to be here," Frankie said without moving.

"Frankie, I really think it's time to go, girl," Willa said through a tight smile. "Tell Jazz to call me first chance."

"Where did you say she was?" Frankie tossed in.

"She's going on vacation with her man, Felipe." Kenton looked at her. "Not that it's any of your damn business."

"Maybe we better call the po-lice," Frankie drawled out the word. "Uh-huh, cause both y'all got a history of violence against women. How we know you haven't done something to her? Huh?"

"Frankie, be cool. Jazz has taken off with a dude before," Willa said quickly. She looked at Frankie as though she'd lost her mind. "Let's just go."

"Y'all all right up there?" Frankie's husband yelled from the bottom of the stairs. "

"Kenton was about to tell us where Jazz is." Frankie really got an attitude now that reinforcements had arrived.

Kenton licked his thick lower lip and muttered a cuss word. "I'm the only one with Jazz's okay to be in her place. Everybody get the hell out."

"So you say," Frankie shot back without moving.

Howard's heavy footsteps made Kenton frown. Seconds later the hefty man appeared. With a shaven head and full beard Howard might have been intimidating except for his wide placating smile. "Look, pal, we just worried about little Jazz. Her sister here got a right."

"I said she's on vacation so ain't no need to worry," Kenton shot back. Still a sheen of sweat on his forehead indicated he was anxious.

"All right, man. It's cool. Let's go, ladies."

Howard gave Frankie a look that she obviously understood. With one last glare at Kenton Frankie swept past him and out into the hallway. Willa followed and in minutes the three of them were outside on the sidewalk. Only then did Willa let out a long sigh of relief.

"Frankie, you are real brave to challenge that guy. He looks like a dude who carries a gun," Willa snapped as she faced Frankie with both hands on her hips.

"He's tough with a bunch of his boys to back him, but alone he's a coward. You saw him break a sweat." Frankie wore a look of scorn.

"Yeah, well I'm glad we didn't keep testing that theory." Willa pushed Frankie ahead of her as they walked back toward the manager's office.

Once Willa returned the key they went to Frankie's condo again.

"Something was odd about Kenton showing up. You notice he still hasn't left. His raggedy car is still parked in Jazz's space." Frankie stood at her window. She stared out through a part in the curtains.

"Might be a good idea to call the police." Howard said and rubbed the smooth skin on his shaved head.

"You think he may have hurt her for real?" Willa felt as though a belt had been pulled tight around her chest.

"Real strange. Wonder what's taking him so long." Frankie planted a fist on one hip while the other hand held back the curtain.

"Put that curtain down. Kenton's going to see you," Willa said.

"I want him to know we're keepin' an eye on his chump ass." Frankie looked in another direction then turned around. "Did you call the police, honey?"

"No, it was still up for discussion." Howard joined her at the window.

Willa followed him. The flash of blue lights lit up the surrounding apartment buildings. "Oh crap. I wonder what's going on."

Moments later the manager hustled toward Jazz's condo. A uniformed police officer marched along side her. The officer guided Doris aside once she opened the door to Jazz's condo. Another office led her away to stand next to a nearby police cruiser. Shouts followed. More police cars arrived with officers running around the building that housed Jazz's condo and three others. Soon two officers came back dragging Kenton between them. Just then an unmarked car pulled up. Willa knew Miller and his partner the minute they emerged. The landlord pointed toward Frankie's condo. Miller and his partner turned and looked straight at them.

Frankie let go of the curtain. Howard sighed, and Willa felt a tension headache grip her head in a vise.

"Oh crap," all three in unison.

Chapter 12

"So when did you last see your sister?" Detective Miller asked again. Of course he phrased it differently, but it was the same question.

Willa tapped her foot nervously. She glanced around to see Miller's partner questioning Frankie. Howard was separated from her by several yards and was talking to a uniformed officer.

"Not for days and days. Maybe almost two weeks. What's going on?" Willa stretched to look around him.

Miller leaned with her. "How well do you know Kenton Turner?"

"Never met him before today. Look I'm worried about my baby sister. So if something has happened to her I'd like to know." Willa crossed her arms and looked at Miller.

He heaved a sigh. "We found a body inside her apartment."

Willa went to her knees, bent double. Her stomach clenched and the nausea was so strong she felt dizzy. Air seemed to have been sucked from the room. She covered her face with both hands as she gasped for air. Miller grabbed her elbow and led her to chair. Frankie ran to the door with a policewoman right behind her.

"Sir, I mean ma'am." The policewoman grabbed at Frankie's arm and missed.

Frankie moved too fast for the officer, despite being at least thirty pounds heavier. She rushed over to Willa and wrapped an arm around her shoulders. "Honey, what's wrong?"

Willa shook her head. "I should have tried harder to be close to her. She went through a lot as a kid."

"Had a rough time, huh?" Miller perched on the edge of chair.

"She had a worse stretch in foster care than I did. That's why she was so hard core on the outside." Willa swiped at the tears rolling down her face. "What happened to her?"

"Too soon to say. She worked at Candy Girls as a dancer. Pretty, uh, colorful place. Fights, drugs not good." Miller sighed again as if that explained it all.

Willa's head snapped up. "What's that supposed to mean? That it's okay she's dead?"

Frankie's arm closed into a hold to keep Willa from jumping up. "Take it easy, sugar. I'm sure the detective wasn't saying that." Frankie glared at Miller as if ordering him to fix his mistake.

"Of course not. I believe every victim deserves justice," Miller answered promptly. He didn't look at Frankie, but gazed intently at Willa's face.

"We'll see," Frankie mumbled.

Miller's partner came to the door and waved for Miller to join him.

"Excuse me for a minute." Miller strode out. Moments later he came back in.

"Your sister had a troubled life you were saying." Miller sat down again.

Willa rubbed at the numbness in her arms. She wondered if somehow her body was trying to deaden itself to the pain. "She made mistakes with men especially. Like that scumbag Kenton."

"And what connection did she have with your late husband?" Miller said, changing the subject.

Willa shook her head. "She said something about Jack dating some dancer she knew. I— " Willa stopped when Frankie gave a slight shake of her head.

"Take it easy, sugar," Frankie said quietly.

"That's all she told me," Willa finished, now on alert. "Why would you ask me that?"

"He hung out at strip joints. So did your son. Not a coincidence they both ended up at Candy Girls where your sister works. And now we're at your sister's place with a dead body, a known felon and she's run off." Miller took a small digital camera from his pocket.

Willa shook her head to clear the fog of grief. "What did you just say?"

"Recognize this person?" Miller showed her the LCD screen on the camera.

"Your sister left this behind in her spare bedroom. I can understand why she didn't pack *him* for the trip." Miller's voice drove home each work like a steel knife. "I want to know what brought you here."

Willa swallowed hard as she gazed at the picture. The digital photo showed a man sprawled out on a floor. The back of his head was bloody. She closed her eyes for a few seconds then she looked at Miller. "You let me think my sister was dead so you could pump me for information? You're even lower than scum."

"That's some cold-blooded shit," Frankie spat at him.

"I'm investigating two murders, and it looks like they're connected. I keep finding crumbs of information that lead me back to your son. Now why is that?" Miller stood and looked down at them.

His partner joined him. Both men frowned at the women with expressions that said they did what they had to and would do it again. Howard stood in the door making subtle hand signals to Frankie. He mouthed words that Willa understood to mean they should say nothing.

Willa rejected his advice. "What are you saying about my son?"

"We found a certain shoe print at the scene of your ex-husband's murder." Miller's partner rumbled ominously. "Then we dropped by his school to look around. Anthony happened to be coming out of class just as we arrived. He was wearing those very same pricey athletic shoes. Now how lucky was that?"

"You picked him up?" Willa jumped to her feet.

"Steady, honey. They can't interview a minor without his legal guardian." Frankie spoke fast in a low tone close to Willa's ear.

"Yeah, your baby boy is gonna need a good lawyer. Why don't we follow you home so we can all talk? " Miller's partner raised eyebrows that looked like twin wooly caterpillars.

"Down at the station," Detective Addison added.

"Oh my God." Willa found it hard to breathe. She seemed to be smothered under a wave of fear.

***

By eight o'clock that night they were home. Willa had hugged Anthony so many times her arms ached. Aunt Ametrine stirred a pot of her famous spaghetti sauce. Aunt Beryl was with Mikayla, distracting her with bedtime stories. Anthony joined them, so thankful to be home he didn't mind hanging out in his baby sister's bedroom listening in. In fact, the two had been inseparable. Mikayla had stuck close to her brother since they'd come home. She seemed to sense some force wanted to take him away.

Papa Elton sat on one side of Willa at the kitchen table, Mama Ruby on the other. Willa's twin brothers had their heads together for a time. Then Dion started working his cell phone.

Shaun joined them at the kitchen table. "Did you call the lawyer?"

"Sure did. She came to the police station fast. Thank goodness her office is downtown." Willa shuddered from the chill she felt. "Just the thought of Anthony sitting in jail."

When the doorbell sounded Shaun got up. "I'll see who it is."

Moments later Willa heard MiMi's familiar flirty laugh. She rubbed her forehead. "Why now, Lord?"

"What?" Papa Elton glanced at the kitchen door.

"Don't get your blood pressure up, Willa," Aunt Ametrine cautioned.

MiMi walked beside Shaun with a hand on his arm. Shaun nodded as she chattered. He glanced at Willa with a helpless expression until finally Willa decided to rescue her brother.

"MiMi, what are you doing here?" Willa got up and pried MiMi's hand from Shaun's arm.

MiMi brushed Willa's grasp off with a hurt expression. "Good evening to you, too. I'm sure your mama taught you better manners."

Mama Ruby stood and shot Willa a stern glance. "Yes, I did. How are you doing? You might not remember me from the funeral."

"Yes, ma'am, Miss Ruby. And how are you, Mr. Wilson?" MiMi beamed at Willa's father.

"Just fine, young lady. Have a seat." Papa Elton didn't look at Willa as he spoke.

"Fine. You've had my husband. Might as well take over the rest of my life, too," Willa mumbled. She growled when Shaun and Dion smothered laughs.

MiMi blinked as though hurt. "Uh, no thanks. I won't be staying. Maybe this was a bad idea." Her bottom lip trembled as she pressed her purse to her tummy.

"Sit down, child. How far are you along?" Mama Ruby took MiMi's arm and led her to one of the chairs around the breakfast table.

"Just over nine weeks. Thank you so much." MiMi accepted a glass of grape juice from Aunt Ametrine. "But Willa is right. I shouldn't stay long. This is family time. She's lucky to have y'all standing by her."

"Yeah, we hang tough." Papa Elton grinned at his foster sons and Willa. "Just like your people probably fuss over you. Especially now."

"Not really. My family isn't all that close," MiMi said in a tiny voice. Then she stood. "I've intruded for too long already. Y'all have a good evening."

Her parents, brothers and aunt shot glances at Willa. Aunt Ametrine made sharp jerking motions with her head while mouthing silently for Willa to speak up. Much as she hated to admit it Willa felt a prick of guilt. MiMi looked like the foster kids Willa had gotten to know; she wore a sad expression of loneliness, of wanting to belong but being isolated.

"Sit and drink your juice. It's good for you." Willa tried to smile, but gave up. Instead she just nodded. "I've had a hellish day."

MiMi recovered quickly. "Girl, I know what you mean. When I saw that news story about Jazz and the body I just about passed out."

"Did you say news story?" Willa broke in before MiMi's usual rapid-fire mouth got started.

"The five o'clock news. And when they mentioned Jack I was too upset." MiMi gaped at their shocked expression. "Y'all didn't see it?"

"Damn." Dion shook his head.

MiMi got up and went to the flat screen television in the kitchen. She grabbed the remote. "Let's find channel twenty. They repeat the Channel Two newscasts all day. Shoot they're on the sports section, so we'll have to wait for it to repeat in fifteen minutes."

Willa groaned in frustration. "Maybe I don't want to know. Just tell me what they said, MiMi."

MiMi hit the mute button. "The Police Beat reporter, you know that smart ass Barron Blanchard, was at the scene. He made some comments about black on black crime and young people. Then they talked to Miller. Blanchard says they'll have more details about a possible suspect in a related crime tonight on the ten o'clock newscast."

Dion rubbed his jaw. "I'll bet they're talking about Jack's murder and Anthony being questioned."

"But they can't say his name. He's a minor." Willa's heart skipped.

"If he's charged as an adult they can," Shaun said in a grave tone.

"Yeah." Dion nodded in solemn agreement.

"But that will stick to him like a permanent stain for the rest of his life," Willa whispered. She closed her eyes and fought off the urge to cry.

"Now we don't know all this for sure." Aunt Ametrine put an arm around Willa's shoulder.

"Can you boys find out some information from your pals on the street?" Papa Elton tilted his head to one side. "Things folks might not tell a reporter or the police."

The twins exchanged a glance. They had ways of finding out information from a network of sources, on both sides of the law. Their days of lawbreaking were long over, but they still knew people.

"Let us see what we can find out. In the meantime maybe don't let the kids watch the television news tonight," Shaun said.

"Or on the Internet," Dion added.

"Doggone. Back in the day it was easier to keep kids away from harmful stuff." Papa Elton shook his head.

"No it wasn't, Elton," Mama Ruby said. "Just seems that way with all the technology now. Kids always know more than adults liked to think."

"For sure," Willa agreed. "I always knew when something was up. Like I was about to be moved from a foster home, or my mother had relapsed again."

"That's why it's best to be upfront with kids, especially kids his age." Mama Ruby looked at Willa. "Might as well have that talk with him, baby."

"I just don't know if I can deal with one more thing today, Mama." Willa's voice shook despite her effort to be strong. "But I know you're right."

"We'll talk to Anthony, sis," Shaun said. Dion nodded and followed him into the hallway to find their nephew.

"So what's up with Jazz?" MiMi looked at Willa.

Willa winced at the mention of another problem family member. "That's the million dollar question."

"She's not in touch with us," Mama Ruby said to MiMi as a quiet aside.

"So you're not just protecting her from the police? You have no idea where she is? That's messed up." MiMi gave Willa a sympathetic glance.

Shaun walked in with one arm around Anthony's shoulder. Dion followed. All three were smiling and talking.

"Man, you're dreaming. My team can beat the Miami Heat this year," Anthony said. He gave his Uncle Shaun a playful shove.

"Hornets ain't just underdogs. They dogs, as in losers." Shaun slapped closed fists with his twin brother.

"You old dudes need to quit." Anthony shook his head.

"Since when did twenty-nine get to be old, man?" Dion looked at his brother.

"Since we stopped being sixteen," Shaun replied with a grin.

"That food smells good. Let's eat." Anthony went to the stove and lifted a lid from the big stockpot.

Aunt Ametrine tugged at his shirt. "Get away from that, boy. We got to bless this food first." Anthony, Mama Ruby and Aunt Ametrine teased each other.

Willa gave Shaun and Dion a discreet nod. They followed her to the hallway toward the front door where they could talk.

"He's cool," Dion said then glanced over his shoulder at his nephew.

"He's not upset?" Willa stared at Anthony. He seemed genuinely at ease.

"Nah. His friends are probably gonna think he's Mr. Big. I know what you're thinking, sis," Dion said, his hand help up.

"Yeah, but that's the way kids think. Anthony is like most teenagers, feels like he's indestructible. I don't think it's sunk in that he could be in serious trouble." Shaun shrugged.

"I hope he's right to be so confident." Willa rubbed her forehead. "I sure as hell wish I could be."

***

The next day Willa was in her office trying not to think about jail sentences, shoe prints and murder trials in connection to her son and sister. Willa huffed out a sigh and rocked back in her chair. The morning sunshine through her window seemed to mock her. There was nothing to be cheerful about. She'd spent the night alternating between punching her pillow hoping to find some way to sleep and getting up to pace in the bedroom. So she had tired feet to match her aching back and head. The knock on her door made her sigh.

Cedric opened the door, entered then closed it behind him. "Can we talk?"

"Might as well. I'm not getting much done." Willa looked at him. "What's up?"

"First, don't worry about Anthony. Shoe-print evidence is shaky. That brand of shoe is real popular. I guarantee a lot of gang-banging drug dealers wear them.

"Wow, I feel so much better knowing my kid is following their trend," Willa said dryly.

"I mean that hang around in Brookstown. Just as many good kids buy those shoes, too. Or at least their parents do. I wasn't implying that Anthony is a thug," Cedric replied.

Willa gave him a tired smile as she waved at him. "I know. Ignore my bad mood. So shoe-print evidence isn't all that solid. Thanks. Okay you said first, which means there is a second."

"Something interesting happened." Cedric wore a slight frown.

"Like I need more interesting events in my life." Willa opened her desk drawer and took out a bottle of pain reliever for her headache.

"Don't take too many of those. What you probably need is a neck massage. Much better than taking a lot of pills." Cedric pointed to the plastic bottle in her hand.

"Right, I'll just zip down to the spa," Willa quipped. Still she decided against taking three of the capsules. Instead she washed down one with the remains of her cold coffee.

"I learned massages when I played sports in college." He held up both hands.

Willa's body responded to the suggestion. She stared at his long, tapered fingers. The gold of his fraternity ring looked warm against his dark brown skin. She remembered being part of a couple and having someone to share the load. How wonderful would it be to be hugged by a man who wasn't a relative? To be comforted that way again? A tingling ache to be touched started at the base of her spine and spread all over. She sat straight and avoided his searching gaze.

"Forget it. You're not going to start rubbing my neck."

"Sure?" Cedric's mouth lifted at the corners. "I come dirt cheap."

"Positive. Now if that's all." Willa got busy with papers on her desk.

"No, there's more. What about the account in the Caymans? We need to find out if that is company money. Reviewing those records would be a start."

"I'd like to zip down to a tropical paradise, but I've got a few things going on here." Willa scowled.

"So let's examine your choices. You could let me go, but you're not sure of me. Wait, maybe MiMi Landry could go." Cedric raised an eyebrow at her.

"The account isn't a priority. Could be dirty money anyway. I'm worried about my family," Willa said.

"We need to find about one hundred fifty thousand dollars. I think maybe Jack diverted some funds to finance his other, uh, activities," Cedric replied. "We need that money for a few little things, like payroll, rent."

"You said we were fine. We have new contracts."

"The books were cooked. Jack must have had an accountant help him with this one. A crooked, but sharp one, too." Cedric grunted. "I wouldn't have believed he'd play that close to the edge of breaking the law."

"Jack studied accounting in college, Cedric. He probably didn't need much help. He owned this company. He didn't need to get anybody's okay to pull money out of it." Willa slapped the arm of her chair. "I'm not going to cry. I will not."

"You've been through hell this week." Cedric wore a sympathetic expression. He started toward her, but Willa stopped him with one raised hand.

"I'm fine," she said, fighting back tears.

"I'm not the enemy," he said quietly. When she only stared out the window. He sighed. "Okay. You're fine."

"So we have operating capital for how long?" She faced him, again in full control.

"Six months easy. The new contracts give us a cushion, assuming clients pay their bills on time. This is a challenging time for businesses, especially small and medium-sized firms. Which is the majority of our clients." Cedric shrugged when Willa frowned.

"We can't afford to play the 'check is in the mail' game. We need to get on any outstanding invoices fast. Got it?" Willa shot back.

"That's a tough line, but I got it," Cedric said.

"These are tough times. So what can we do?"

"Let's work up a strategy to get enough big accounts to balance the risk. We can talk about it later since you've been hit with so much." Cedric studied her.

"We can talk about it now. I said I'm okay," Willa said firmly.

"It's not that." Cedric cleared his throat. "I did a skip trace on your sister. Don't slice and dice me. I saw the news last night and figured maybe you'd want to know at least as much as the police before they catch up with her and— "

"You found her?" Willa stood and leaned on the desk with her palms flat.

"She used her gas card along I-10 through Lake Charles and Beaumont, Texas."

"Houston," Willa cut him off. She wanted to throw something but controlled herself. "That little witch is going straight to Houston. That's the last place our mama landed. Far as I know anyway. But Vivienne isn't exactly the 'bridge over troubled water' type maternal figure."

"Oh really." Cedric seemed to be trying to keep his tone neutral.

Willa glanced at him. "Don't act like you don't know my pedigree."

"No judgments from me. I climbed out of the hood myself." Cedric crossed his arms.

Willa looked at him in surprise. He had the solid, handsome look of a man women would want to trust. She was no exception. Maybe she was trying too hard not to trust him. She shook her head.

"Then you know the type. She had too many kids too young, never gave up hanging in the clubs. The usual ghetto rap song, same lyrics different beat."

"And daddy didn't step up. I recognize that song for sure." Cedric sat on the edge of her desk.

Willa waved a hand and sat down again. "Who knows which man floating in and out was daddy? I sure don't, and neither does Vivienne. Didn't matter because none of them was worth a damn."

"My father has always been missing in action. Paid child support sometimes, but he never wanted anything to do with me. Forget him." Cedric's tight jaw line indicated the subject was unfinished business.

Willa nodded in empathy. She had her own mama drama issues lingering. "Vivienne would let her hide out for awhile, for a price of course."

"Either your sister eats a lot or she's not alone on her road trip." Cedric added. "I lost her after Beaumont."

"Probably her latest man. That guy the police arrested at her place told me she was going 'on vacation' with him. I can't believe Jazz didn't figure out using the debit card would give her away." Willa rocked her chair back, the motion helping her think. "How'd you do that?"

"Databases I subscribe to, all legal. Called a buddy in Lake Charles. He's going to send me a store video. Maybe we can recognize the person she's with." Cedric rubbed his jaw. "I have an advantage over the police. I can get background information from you."

"Right, like my biological mother being in the picture." Willa nodded. "Okay. She'll be able to stay with Vivienne for a while. Jazz knows she'll need money to get the welcome mat."

"Touching."

"That's dear old mom. But she might not stay with Vivienne. Jazz ran away to Houston back in the day and survived on her own for almost a year. She might not need Vivienne."

"Okay, we've got two projects today: our strategy to increase business and to trace your sister." Cedric put both hands on his narrow waist. "It's going to be a long day. I could do most of the grunt work. That way you can get home to the kids."

"My family will take care of them if I have to work late." Willa looked at their picture on her desk. They'd spent hours last night surrounded by family. "I wouldn't have even come in today if I thought they needed me."

"Having strong family support is a blessing," Cedric said.

"Believe it or not, even Jack's family has been in touch. Ryan offered to spend time with Anthony. He's taking him to his sports club and for pizza. Male bonding, the old cliché." Willa grinned. "And Mikayla is being treated like a spoiled princess by Jack's mother."

"I'm sure Miss Mikayla is right in her element." Cedric laughed.

"Yes, and she'll be hard to live with for the next two weeks," Willa added. "So let's get to it. Let's meet in your office. I'll just ask Kay to help us prepare. We'll need snacks. Maybe even dinner like take-out pizza?"

"No pizza. I watch sodium, fat and calories." Cedric patted his tight abs.

Willa allowed her gaze to travel from the handsome face, down the broad chest to the rest of his fit body. "You're a good influence then. I should hang around you more often."

"Yes, you should. I'm a fresh fruit and fiber guy." Cedric walked close to Willa.

"Sweet and regular, huh? Every girl's dream."

His deep laugher sent shivers down her neck and to all the wrong places. Willa worked hard on ignoring the scent of his aftershave lotion and the heat from his body. Or maybe the heat came from her. To avoid danger Willa led the way out to Kay's desk in the lobby. Good thing they were headed to a public part of the office.

"What y'all need?" Kay looked up from a stack of papers in front of her. Like any good administrative assistant she was almost psychic in anticipating her bosses.

"Healthy snacks. We may be working late," Willa said.

"I'll hustle over to the Whole Foods deli." Kay dug through her desk drawer. "Ah-ha, here is their menu. Tell me what you want."

Minutes later they had ordered up enough protein to keep them going until midnight. Kay bustled off to make sure the fridge had enough room. Willa and Cedric headed to his office. Unlike her late ex-husband, Cedric's office was neat. Except for his degree and certificates from law enforcement classes, there were no pictures. Willa realized that Cedric rarely talked about his family.

"Lucky you. No family drama to drive you bat-shit crazy." Willa wanted to probe, but her comment was sincere.

"Oh I could have plenty of drama, but I don't play that. So how much information do you have on Jazz? A date of birth I'll bet." Cedric sat down at his desk.

"Sure, August fourth, nineteen eighty-one." Willa stood behind him as he signed onto a subscription search website.

"Now if we had her social security number…"

Willa rattled off the numbers before he could finish. When Cedric looked up in surprise she shrugged. "I'm real good at reading upside down. When we were in foster care the social workers used to have our files with them. Once I managed to read up on us, even stole a couple of forms."

"You were a little rascal, huh?" Cedric turned back to the computer screen.

"Hey, when you're a foster kid you become a survivalist. Anyway, that was my misguided attempt to find my biological father. I had this dream he would rescue me." Willa felt a sharp pang at the memory.

"I'm sorry about all the let downs you've had, including from Jack," Cedric said, his voice muted with sympathy. "All men aren't alike you know."

Willa waved a hand. "Don't reach for the box of tissues. No tears and no rage. My adopted father and uncles redeemed your gender. So thank them that I'm not a female serial killer taking my pain out on you guys."

"I will definitely thank Mr. Elton next time we meet," Cedric quipped as he pretended to wipe sweat from his forehead.

Willa laughed harder. This more relaxed joking side of Cedric made him look even more handsome. She wondered about the women in his life, not relatives. But that would be getting too personal.

"So what about your family? You got them handled, huh?"

"My mother is the original drama queen. Two of my sisters are just like her. The middle one, Daneese, has sense, thank the Lord. Mostly my brother and I just keep a low profile at family gatherings." Cedric grinned then turned back to his search.

"You don't have any pictures up. Nephews, nieces even?" Willa kept her voice casual.

"At home. Most of my family album is on a digital photo frame that holds over a hundred images. I'm not into a lot of clutter."

"Hmm, not the sentimental type." Willa watched the screens change as computer keys clicked.

"Not exactly a cold-blooded animal either. I'm loyal, trustworthy and dependable." Cedric looked at her

"A regular Boy Scout," Willa said, unable to take her eyes off his mouth, brown and tempting, like cinnamon. She felt that pesky tug he seemed to inspire at the wrong times. His deep laugh increased the pressure to move close. Willa leaned toward him more. Or maybe Cedric made the first move. His face was suddenly less than an inch from her breast. She could feel his warm breath through the thin cotton shirt she wore.

"Troop forty-nine at your service, ma'am," Cedric teased with a grin. His amused expression softened into something different.

"How many badges did you earn?" Willa tried looking away from his mouth and failed.

"A lot. I got two for knowing how to start a fire." Cedric raised an eyebrow at her.

Willa gazed back at him. "Oh I believe it."

"Knock, knock. Girl, where is that efficient assistant of yours? I've been wandering around this place forever." MiMi arched an eyebrow at the two of them. "Well, what's new in your world?"

Cedric's gaze narrowed when he looked at her. "We're into something right now."

"I can see that. Uh-huh." MiMi was about to go on, but one look from Willa stopped her.

Willa stood ramrod straight and marched across to her. "We're busy," she hissed.

"Y'all 'bout to get busy you mean," MiMi whispered low. Then she leaned to the right and waved to Cedric. "I'm afraid this can't wait. I'll have steal her for a minute."

"No you won't," Willa said, but MiMi pulled her by the arm into the hallway.

"I started to go get my nails done, but I got a call and I just have to tell you the news."

"We're working on something very important, MiMi. Seriously," Willa said through clenched teeth. She jerked free when they were almost to the lobby.

"This is me you're talking to, hon. I've used those moves myself a time or two. You had 'do me, baby' written all over you." MiMi gave Willa a stern look.

"You're lecturing me? This is a joke." Willa stood legs apart with both fists on her hips.

"Okay, I know it's been awhile since you've done the love monkey screech."

"What the hell are you talking about?"

"You know, when a fine man hits the spot, and you sound like a spider monkey on crystal meth." MiMi nodded and turned to walk toward Willa's office. "Girl, Jack used to do this thing. Oh, but you must know."

"If you weren't pregnant I'd whip your crazy butt," Willa said, her voice getting higher and louder as they reached the lobby.

"You'll thank me later for rescuing you," MiMi said.

Kay was back at her desk. "I told you Ms. Crown was in conference."

"Conference over, sweetie." MiMi flashed a grin at her and went into Willa's office.

"If you hear screaming it's me totally losing my mind. So hold my calls, " Willa said to Kay then went into her office and shut the door.

"Before you rip into to me— "

"Listen carefully, Ms. Landry. My son is a murder suspect, my sister is missing and my business is facing serious cash flow issues. So I don't have time for your spoiled princess games." Willa jabbed a finger in the air between them.

"Our business is in trouble? But, but I need us to be profitable. I don't have a job." MiMi gasped and sat down on the sofa in Willa's seating area.

"Try to break out of your usual 'it's all about me' mode," Willa snapped. "I'm scared about what might happen to two people I hold dear."

"You're right. Blame it on the selfish genes I got from my mother. You've been under a lot of stress, too. Here, sit and I'll fix us a cup of coffee." MiMi went to the pot set up in Willa's office and poured two mugs.

"MiMi you don't have to— "

"You'll need this because I have news about where Jazz might be. And I think she's got some kind of connection to Jack's shady deal with Strafford or whoever's involved."

"Number one, I already figured that out. Number two, stop playing The Preggers Detective." Willa sniffed the fragrant Louisiana dark roast in the mug then sipped. MiMi had put in just the right amount of sweetener and cream.

"Hey, I like that-- The Preggers Detective." MiMi grinned then grew serious. "But we need to sort out this mess quick. So I applied for a job at Candy Girls. Talked to the bartender and one of the other dancers. You okay?"

Willa couldn't answer because she was too busy choking on hot coffee.

Chapter 13

Willa hacked until she could croak a reply. "I'm speechless. Just talk."

MiMi looked around Willa's office, found napkins then mopped up the puddle of spilled coffee on the floor. She took the mug with the Crown Protection logo from Willa's hand and filled it again. She talked as she poured in more cream and sweetener. Willa still sat in a chair in the seating area working on recovering. MiMi patted Willa on the back then handed her the mug and sat down on the sofa.

"Well, I was worried about you, girl. I mean my sisters can be bitches and all, but if either of them disappeared with a dead dude left behind I'd be a little concerned," MiMi said.

"A little?" Those two words made Willa coughed again.

"Uh-huh. Of course if it were my oldest sister Raquel I'd totally believe she'd killed him. Tell you about her some time. Anyway, I went by Candy Girls just out of curiosity at first. I've never seen a strip club before. It wasn't as seedy as I'd imagined. Actually it's pretty nice. Must be a catering to middle-class guys."

Willa had recovered the power of speech after a few moments. In fact, she had to give credit where credit was due. "That was gutsy."

MiMi waved a hand. "Nah, not really. It was in the day time and that part of town isn't so bad."

"Yes it is," Willa corrected. "Easy Town looks deceptively quiet sometimes."

"I didn't see a lot of skuzzy types hanging on the corner." MiMi looked at Willa with skepticism.

"The city is trying to clean up the rough neighborhoods. But the dealers, wannabe baby gangstas and crack heads are there. Trust me. You just have to scratch the surface." Willa nodded at her.

"Wow, you describe it just like one of those Paula Woods mystery novels." MiMi stood and walked around the office. "Of course it would help if you had a seedy office in a tough neighborhood. The new décor makes it a bit too... nice. You ever think of writing a novel?

"No, now get back to the point." Willa crossed her legs and waited.

"I can understand why nobody is loitering around Candy Girls. That bartender Andre and the bouncer must weigh a ton between them. I mean they're both like seven feet tall. So when I went in Andre was like, 'We ain't open and you can't sell us nothin'. The words 'I'm applying for a job' just popped out before I knew what I was saying." MiMi laughed.

"Remind me to lecture you on making smarter choices."

"Yes, mother," MiMi shot back and rolled her eyes. "Anyway, Lorraine the boss wasn't there, but Andre called one of the dancers and— "

Kay knocked once then came carrying a folder. "Sorry to interrupt, but I need your signature on these purchase orders." She glanced at MiMi. You need anything?"

"We're fine. Really," Willa added when Kay looked at her with skepticism.

"Okay. It's almost eleven-thirty. Let me know if you want me to order lunch for you, or something." Kay lifted her eyebrows as a signal.

"Thanks so much," MiMi piped up and smiled at Kay. "You're such an asset around here."

Kay blushed. "Well, I— "

"No, I mean it. Willa is right to put so much trust in you. And anyone can tell that you help this place hum along like a well-oiled engine. Right, Willa?" MiMi

"Right. Thanks, Kay," Willa said and pressed her lips together. She signed the papers then at MiMi after Kay left. "That was laying it on a bit much."

"I don't want her to see as the enemy. Besides, I meant every word." MiMi sniffed.

"Now getting back to Candy Girls and your little escapade," Willa prompted.

"I talked to this dancer Nyeisha. She's sort of like Lorraine's assistant."

Willa nodded. "She's worked there the longest, almost six years now. She and Lorraine are tight."

"Yeah, she said the boss trusted her to do like a first interview. Anyway, we got along very well. I can put people at ease. Excellent people skills, which is why I'm good at sales."

"Right." Willa tilted her head to one side and pursed her lips.

"Okay, I'm getting to the point. We talked about twenty minutes then she gave me a tour. I did a few moves." MiMi frowned at Willa's expression. "What?"

"You did a little bump and grind?" Willa pursed her lips to keep from laughing.

"I can drop it like it's hot. Of course I didn't do anything too daring." MiMi put a protective hand on her stomach. "Nyeisha even said I was a little too chubby around the middle."

"With your charm school manners and designer rags Nyeisha must have known you were a sorority girl. She had to have been suspicious," Willa insisted.

"I told her I really needed the money, that I'd only just lost my job and my college degree wasn't helping pay the bills. I really poured on the desperate." MiMi sighed. "She was nice. I kinda feel bad about lying to her."

"Please." Willa put a hand to her forehead.

"Back to Jazz. Nyeisha and I ended up talking for almost two hours. They need another girl since Jazz disappeared and they had to fire another dancer. Drugs. Half the time she didn't show up. Plus her crazy boyfriend who would deal weed in their parking lot while he was waiting for her to get off work."

"Like I told you that's a rough neighborhood," Willa said.

MiMi nodded. "Point taken. As for Jazz, seems Nyiesha's theory is that she took off with her boyfriend. But get this-- Jazz met him through Ike and the good reverend."

"Reverend Fisher?" Willa's mouth dropped open.

"Yes, girl. Her Latin lover's name is Felipe Perez by the way. He and his buddy Kenton were part of this male mentoring program at Abundant Love Ministries. Ike was the program director. He and Felipe got to be buddies and started hanging at Candy Girls. They had a few private parties, too. And they were spending freely on good liquor and lap dances."

"So Reverend 'Spread The Love' has a taste for raunchy ladies." Willa snorted.

"Nyeisha didn't specifically mention his name, but you figure it out. I didn't try to ask for details about those particular customers in case she got suspicious. Plus I wanted her to talk about Jazz," MiMi said.

"Smart move."

MiMi looked pleased. "Thanks. So Jazz hooks up with Felipe and presto, she has a new car, expensive new clothes and they're traveling. They went to Costa Rica or the Caribbean whenever Jazz has four days off. Did you know that those girls work sort of like those offshore guys? Nyeisha told me that. And Jazz made good money dancing, too. Seems your sister is a local star."

"Lovely," Willa retorted. "Get back to the part about Jazz traveling to the Caribbean."

"Mention of the islands made my ears perk up. Of course Nyeisha wasn't sure which islands. She's jealous of Jazz. She just kept going on about Jazz thinking her you-know-what don't stink."

"To tell you the truth Jazz can be an uppity heffa. Mean and selfish, too." Willa had gone from worried about Jazz to being pissed off with her. "Let's check to see if the police have released the name of the dead guy."

"KeVon Latham, aka Von, aka Skim," MiMi said. She opened her handbag, took out her smart phone and tapped the tiny keypad. "Here's the Channel Two news website. Read for yourself."

"Thanks." Willa took it from her. "Twenty-four years old, been arrested for possession, aggravated assault with a deadly weapon and aggravated burglary. Nice people she's hanging with."

"I know she's your sister, but— "

"Jazz isn't a killer. She's got plenty of faults. I could list them, but we don't have all day," Willa muttered. "But like I said she's not a killer."

"What does Anthony say about all this?"

"He denied being there. A shoe-print isn't solid evidence according to Cedric, and he should know. That made me feel a whole lot better."

"Leaning on Cedric's strong shoulders these days, huh?"

Willa ignored her dig. "Besides, the police had to admit that it wasn't a clear impression. They got the insignia from a partial shoe-print. The fact that Anthony wears the same brand fits their neat little theory."

"You probably don't want to hear this, but we have to be realistic here. Anthony isn't telling you everything."

"I know my kid better than you. If Anthony knew more he would tell me." Willa felt angry that MiMi had hit on her secret fear just when she'd convinced herself Anthony had told her everything.

"He's been keeping secrets from you," MiMi said, pressing on in a firm tone. "You found out he saw Jack that night, which means that shoe print might be his. Then you discovered he'd been hanging out at Candy Girls."

"Shut up," Willa said. She went to the office window to escape the voice of reason from an unlikely source.

MiMi joined her at the window. "Being in denial can be even more dangerous for him, and for Jazz. We better get the straight story before the police."

Cedric knocked once and then came in. "Sorry to barge in, but I have to tell you something."

"Wait Cedric, you should hear this, too. Jazz got involved with some 'business deal' with Felipe. Nyeisha says everybody knows Felipe smuggles drugs." MiMi backed up as she talked. She inched behind Cedric as if seeking protection. "I'm just telling you what she said. I don't like saying it, but Jack might have been involved."

"This is crazy talk!" Willa waved her arms in the air. "Jazz wouldn't get involved in something that dangerous. And Jack was a lying skirt chaser. He liked being slick, but he was no criminal."

"Willa, you need to listen," Cedric said in a loud voice to get her attention. "I tracked Jazz's financials. She's been spending a lot of money, almost seventy-five thousand dollars in the last six months. Jazz also opened a savings account for Anthony."

Willa closed her eyes and opened them again. She looked at them both. "This nightmare just won't end."

***

An hour later all three of them were at Willa's house. She'd signed Anthony out of school early. Given the fact that the news of the dead body being found in his aunt's condo was all over his school, the assistant principal did not object. The ride home was tense. MiMi and Cedric were waiting for them when they got to the house. MiMi and Cedric exchanged glances as Willa led the way into the kitchen.

"Sit down." Willa pointed to the table. MiMi and Cedric took seats quickly. "I meant Anthony."

Still standing Anthony licked his lips nervously. "Something bad happen? I mean pulling me out of school early and stuff."

"Bad. Let's see. My soon to be ex-husband was murdered. I'm a suspect at first. My sister runs off and leaves another dead man in her apartment. Now my son is a suspect. Just what is your definition of bad, Anthony?" Willa's voice had risen to a shriek.

"All I meant was— "

"Don't even start with that wide-eyed 'what did I do?' act," Willa cut in shouting at him.

"Let's all take a deep breath and calm down." Cedric stared hard at Willa. "We need to know all of the facts. I'm sure Anthony can explain."

"I don't know what's going on, but y'all tell me and I'll try to help." Anthony looked to Cedric as if he sensed an ally.

Willa was about to talk, but MiMi pulled her aside. Cedric and Anthony continued talking to each other. MiMi dropped her voice low and spoke rapidly. "He's right, Willa. Anthony may be too scared or pissed to talk if we don't handle this right."

"Yeah. Sure." Willa steadied her breathing in an effort to calm her temper. They both went back to where Cedric stood with Anthony.

Anthony glanced at his mother nervously. "You pretty mad, huh?"

"I am. So if you know what's good for you start talking. It better be the truth, the whole truth and nothing but," Willa said, her voice rising.

Anthony fidgeted under Willa's hot glare. He looked at Cedric. "Okay. Dad... Jack said I could handle the responsibility so he opened a money market checking account in my name. He said we could invest the thirty thousand dollars together, but later on."

"Where did he get this big chunk of cash all of a sudden?" Willa snapped. "Didn't you think it was strange that he— "

"Of course he wouldn't think Jack having that kind of money was strange. Crown Protection is a very successful business," Cedric broke in. For the first time he glanced at MiMi for help.

"Sure. No reason for Anthony to question him," MiMi said as if on cue.

"I know my kid. He's smart," Willa shot back. "Spit it out, Anthony."

"He wasn't a crook no matter what anybody says," Anthony replied with heat in his voice. "I think he just got caught up."

"What the hell— " Willa felt MiMi's vise-like grip tighten.

"Start from the beginning, son," Cedric said.

Anthony took a deep breath and let it out. "Dad said he took on a new corporate client, Strafford, Inc, but those guys were too cut throat. So he wanted to protect the business and keep some money separate. That's all. He was handling it."

"Then he was killed," Cedric said carefully.

"I met that deacon from Dad's church, Ike Nelson. He worked for Strafford, Inc." Anthony faced his mother. "I always thought the dude looked shady. I bet somebody at Abundant Love Ministries know something."

"Why do you think that?" Cedric frowned.

"Mr. Nelson hired guys in a program he runs at the church to work for Strafford. Most of those dudes are hardcore gangsters. I could probably find out more from my boys on the street." Anthony looked at Cedric.

"You're going to stay out of this or else you'll have me to worry about. This isn't a video game. It's real." Willa's voice cracked.

"I know it's real. Two of my friends were killed in the last three years over stupid stuff. Dad understood how mean it is out here for a young black man. He told me to take care of you and Mikayla, and I will. For him." Anthony's mouth set in a tight line. At that moment he so resembled his stepfather. Willa could almost believe Anthony had Jack's stubborn genes.

"You'll do what I damn well tell you to do young man or— " Willa's threat was cut short when MiMi yanked her out of the kitchen and down the hallway.

"Let Cedric talk to him man-to-man because you're mouth is about to make him shut up completely." MiMi pulled a stuttering Willa into the family room, closed the door and blocked Willa's exit.

"Anthony needs a good kick in the behind right about now." Willa glared at MiMi for standing in her way.

"If you treat him like a little boy he's going to rebel. Now is not the time to play 'the mama' and order him around. Think," MiMi said in a firm tone.

Willa couldn't answer immediately. Instead she paced the length of the room. "If I hadn't paid so much for this crap I'd break something."

MiMi looked around. "Go ahead. You could use some updated stuff in here anyway. I like your red and green paisley jacquard sofa. But these lamps can go. And taupe drapes... what were you thinking?"

"I want to kick somebody. Since you're close by, you might do," Willa grumbled as she shot a heated look at MiMi.

"I'm a mother, so I understand. Your anger is motivated by fear for your child." MiMi placed a hand on her slightly rounded belly.

"Now she's a parenting expert." Willa continued to pace.

"We won't let anything happen to Anthony, girl. I think it's beautiful how he wants to protect you." MiMi winced then sat down in one of two large forest green chairs opposite the sofa.

"You okay?" Willa studied MiMi's expression.

"Just had to get off my feet for a minute." MiMi waved away her concern. "Back to Anthony. He's a good kid and loyal to his family. Honey, count your blessings. My family isn't full of warm fuzzies."

Finally Willa felt the energy drain from her anger. "Loyalty is all well and good, but he's making decisions that could put him in prison or worse."

"Well I— " MiMi stopped when the doorbell rang. "Crap. We don't need company right now."

"I'll get it. Lord, please don't let it be Detective Miller," Willa said and looked up to heaven. "A break, please. Just one today."

MiMi followed her. "Who is it?" she whispered as Willa looked through the window. Ryan looked polished as usual in a Perry Ellis white dress shirt, open at the collar, and charcoal gray slacks

"Thank you, Lord," Willa said as she opened the door "Hello, Ryan. How are you?"

"Doing great, and you?" Ryan looked over Willa's shoulder at MiMi. His amber eyes registered surprise "Good afternoon, Ms. Landry."

"Call me MiMi since we're practically family."

Ryan offered her nothing more than a cool smile as his reply. He faced Willa. "I hope everything is okay. I went by Anthony's school to pick him up, but learned he'd left early."

"We picked him up. Family matters," MiMi piped up first. She pursed her lips tightly when Willa gave her a look.

"He's fine. Why did you go to pick him up though?" Willa said.

"Not to worry. I planned to stopped by your office first and ask your permission to take him to one of my fraternity meetings. We mentor young men." Ryan kept glancing curiously at MiMi.

"Being involved in positive activities would be a big help." Willa let out a sigh of frustration.

"Anthony is okay," Cedric said as he walked toward Willa. His expression went stiff when he noticed Ryan. "Hello, Ryan."

"Hello, Cedric." Ryan barely glanced at him before speaking to Willa again. "What's going on with Anthony?"

"Jack opened a bank account with money from Lord only knows where. Anthony won't be straight with me about that, or anything. I don't know what to do. Cedric, did he say anything more?" Willa put a hand to her forehead and massaged her tension headache.

"Nothing." Cedric cleared his throat.

"A bank account," Ryan said quietly and rubbed his chin.

"Yeah, you know anything about Jack's deal with Strafford, Inc. or dealings with Ike Nelson?" Cedric asked.

Ryan seemed not to hear him. Instead he smiled warmly at Willa. "Let me talk to him. We've developed a rapport. And Anthony obviously feels more comfortable keeping this in the family."

"I'm hoping for any help at this point. He's in his room."

"You just relax. I'll talk to him." Ryan gave Willa's shoulder a reassuring squeeze. He brushed past Cedric without looking at him.

"Elitist chump," Cedric mumbled once Ryan disappeared around a corner.

"Don't be a hater, Cedric. Ryan obviously has realized that the Crown family should be more sensitive. I give him credit for being a support to Anthony." MiMi lifted her nose in the air.

"You snobs stick together," Cedric tossed back. While MiMi fumed he turned to Willa. "You think it was a good idea to tell him about the account? I don't trust the guy."

"I'm desperate for answers right about now. Jack and Ryan fought, but they did spend time together. Maybe he'll tell me something useful." Willa glanced down the hallway. "But just in case, we need to do some digging. See if that money is connected to Strafford, Inc."

Cedric nodded "Okay. What about Jazz? I can track her down and use my contacts in Houston to— "

"No," Willa said. "Houston is enough of a lead. My brothers can take it from there." Willa frowned at the space where Ryan had stood moments before.

"Okay. No problem." Cedric jammed his hands into his pants pockets.

"I appreciate your help, Cedric. Really I do. But I shouldn't have pulled you into my family mess." Willa tried to put an apology in her tone.

The deep furrows in Cedric's forehead stayed put despite his words. "I don't mind. In case you're wondering I have software on my computer that wipes clean stored keystrokes. So I don't have your sister's personal info. I'd better get back to the office. Goodbye."

"Thanks." Willa said.

She watched him walk out the door thinking she'd done something wrong. She could tell he wanted to help more, but Willa just couldn't be so sure of his motives. Or how much she was willing to open her heart to a man right now.

"That man has a serious love jones for you, girl. I was suspicious, but now I don't know. He seems sincere." MiMi walked to the window and studied Cedric as he prepared to leave. When he glanced back at the house before getting into his car, MiMi nudged Willa with an elbow. "Look at the sad puppy dog face. Oh yeah, he wants you."

"Oh please." Willa made sure the door was locked then went to the kitchen with MiMi following.

"What?" MiMi sat down at the breakfast table.

"I won't bother cause it would be wasted on you." Willa sat down at the kitchen table.

"Denial is your fave coping mechanism. Back to our brother-in-law. Something is up with Ryan." MiMi switched gears. "Funny how he shows up just at this moment."

"MiMi— " Willa broke off when she heard voices coming down the hallway. "We'll talk about it in a minute."

Ryan came into the kitchen. "Anthony's okay, and I don't think he knows much more than he told you. You have any indication that Jack was moving around large amounts of cash?"

"Why would you ask that?" MiMi jumped in before Willa could respond.

Ryan looked startled for a minute. "Jack put money in an account under a minor's name. People do that when they're hiding assets."

"Hmm, sounds like you know all about that kind of thing," MiMi said with a raised eyebrow. "Anyway maybe Jack just wanted Anthony to have his college fund early," MiMi replied.

Ryan glanced at MiMi only briefly before answering. "I seriously doubt that's why he opened that account. Willa, I have business and banking contacts all over. Give me a list of clients Jack dealt with in say the last six months before he died. Maybe all this is connected to one of them."

"Try Strafford, Inc." Willa tried to go on, but MiMi made wild hand gestures behind Ryan's back. When he started to turn around MiMi stopped gesturing and smiled at him.

"Strafford, Inc., huh?" Ryan nodded slowly.

"Yes, I believe you're familiar with the company and Ike Nelson," MiMi put in.

Ryan ignored her. Instead he gazed at Willa intently as though trying to detect some sign. "I'll check it out. Now this may sound crazy but Jack went to the Caribbean several times. Have you found any account information? If he was hiding money here, Jack might have put money in an island bank."

"I'll look through his papers and files again," Willa replied and wondered how Ryan knew about Jack's Caribbean trips.

"Right, right. I'll be in touch." Ryan turned to leave.

"I thought you were going to hang out with Anthony," MiMi said.

"Obviously this isn't the best time. I'll call you soon, Willa." Ryan gave her brief smile then left using the back door.

"Ryan is coming around here for more than quality family time." MiMi strode to the kitchen door and locked it once Ryan was gone. "He brings up Jack's trips, then asks about offshore accounts."

"Yeah. Something ain't right." Willa stood. "I'm through with this crap about a man being able to talk to Anthony."

"Lord, being a single mother is rough enough, but trying to deal with a half-grown male child? I hope I have a girl."

"Just ask Mama Ruby about trying to deal with me and Jazz as teenagers. Trust me, having a girl won't give you a free pass from big trouble," Willa tossed back over her shoulder.

"I'm going to take control the minute she arrives on this earth, baby," MiMi said.

Willa just grunted at her assertion. MiMi was silly enough to think she could control her kid. She'd learn. Then Willa decided it was time to turn her attention to Anthony. She walked down the hall. With only one sharp rap on his bedroom door Willa went in. Anthony was sitting on the edge of his bed. Both hands hung between his knees. He looked up at Willa after few a seconds. His cocoa eyes filled with unshed tears. Willa felt her heart skip, but then she put steel into her back and marched up to him.

"I want to know what is going on. No vague explanations. I've had it. You may be a couple of inches taller than me but I will whip your butt this day if you lie to me. Talk." Willa crossed her arms.

Anthony wiped his eyes with the back of one hand. "Do they think Jazz killed that dude?"

"I said talk, not ask," Willa replied firmly.

He let out a noisy breath. "Okay. I told Mr. Ryan the truth. I don't know where the money came from. Dad said it was from his business. He put it under my name so we could do some deals together."

Willa sat down on an ottoman that matched a chair in his bedroom. "What kind of deals?"

"You know, security jobs. I'm taking computer classes already, and I'm pretty good at it. A lot of private security work involves computer these days. Dad said we would be partners one day."

"Start from the beginning on how this whole account idea came about." Willa leaned forward.

"One day Dad came to school and picked me up before I got on the bus. We went to Smoothie King, you know, and just hung out. Then he told me about a business proposition. This big company was paying him a lot to help them find safe ways to transport their products."

"Transport their products," Willa echoed. A sick feeling grabbed hold of her stomach.

Anthony shook his head hard. "I know what you're thinking, but it wasn't drugs or anything illegal like that. This is legit biz. Jack wasn't into those kinds of games. You know him. Sure he liked being slick, but risk getting locked up? Oh hell no."

"Watch your language," Willa said on autopilot as she considered his argument.

"Yes, ma'am. But you know what I mean. Jack told me how it was when his dad went to prison. He never forgot how bad things were for his family."

Willa nodded. Jack had always spoken with bitterness about his father's jail time. The elder Crown had been convicted of malfeasance in office and mail fraud. He'd used his high-level job in state government to get kickbacks on contracts. Jack had never proclaimed his father's innocence though. Instead he'd spoken with anger about the double standard applied by the justice system. Mr. Crown had served almost two years in a federal prison back in the early eighties. He'd never been the same since. Neither had Jack.

"Anthony, I don't blame you. But you gotta see that this looks like Jack was hiding money. He took trips to Grand Cayman, a place where lots of folks who are up to no good stash money." Willa looked at Anthony. "You're old enough to hear some straight talk."

"I know it looks bad. But I think it went down like this-- Jack got in on some sorta business deal. He never gave me all the ins and outs. I guess he was protecting me. Anyway, I think he was planning to walk the line on something a little shady, find a loophole to avoid paying taxes. Some companies register in foreign countries to do that, right?"

"Yeah, but I'm wondering how you know so much about shady business deals, hiding money overseas and playing close to the edge." Willa placed a hand on one hip.

"Jack had this obsession about beating the system at their own game. He always said that anybody who thinks justice is blind is just plain dumb."

"Sure, and to hear him tell it his daddy was a saint," Willa retorted.

"No, mama, it wasn't right the way that went down." Anthony waved a hand. "His dad was the scapegoat 'cause he was a successful black man."

"Let me school you for a minute. A player is a player no matter what kind of social pedigree he has. If his daddy hadn't been dealing in dirt he wouldn't have gotten convicted. People who dance on the edge end up going down.”

“Yes, ma’am.” Anthony pressed his lips together.

“You better listen to what I’m saying, son. Why is the prison population about eighty-percent black men? The system doesn’t care about history or the plight of the Black man. You do the crime you are going to do the time.” Willa stabbed a forefinger at him. “Your best option is to not give them any excuse to get their hands on you.”

Anthony raked his fingers through his thick tight curls like soft wool. “I hear what you’re saying, Mama, but— ”

“Don’t give me ‘but’, Anthony. I’ve been at the mercy of judges, lawyers and social workers who decided about my life. I can’t rescue you for the rest of your life. You’ve got to make the right choices.”

Anthony stood to face her. “I get it. Really.”

“Then be straight with me. Is Jazz and her boyfriend part of the mix?”

“Jack and some other guys hung out at Candy Girls a lot, used to have business meetings there. I know because he caught me there one time, gave me hell. Pardon the expression.”

Willa waved a hand dismissing his lapse. “Ike Nelson, too?”

“Yeah, him and Felipe with his crew. I don’t know what they talked about and Jack never told me. I just wish Jack hadn’t gotten jammed up with those guys.” Anthony let out a heavy long breath, sat down and covered his face with both hands.

Willa heard the anguish in his voice. She sat next to him. “We’ll find out the truth. Between Cedric, your lawyer and I we’ll make sure *you* don’t get jammed up. You hear me?”

Anthony sat straight and lowered his hands putting on a brave face. At least he tried to. Willa saw the fear in his dark eyes. She wrapped an arm around him and pulled Anthony close. Now all she had to do was live up to her big words.

“I’m gonna work on my science paper,” Anthony said finally.

Willa brushed back a tear. Then she smiled at him. “That’s my boy. Don’t let this stuff worry you.”

"Mr. Ryan has been real nice, too. He says I should think of him as my uncle. I used to think he didn't like me at all." Anthony pulled out his books. "We're gonna be hanging out more. Funny how people change."

"Yeah, funny." Willa thought about Ryan's sudden interest in Anthony and Jack's travels to the Caribbean. She kissed Anthony's cheek. For once he didn't act embarrassed or too grown to be babied.

MiMi was on the phone when Willa returned to the kitchen. "Right, six egg rolls, and give me some of those spicy chicken wings. An hour? Guess it'll have to be okay, thanks." She hit the button turning it off. "I just ordered from Hong Kong House."

"Excuse me?" Willa blinked at her.

"Girl, you been through too much to be cooking this evening. I hope they get here faster than an hour 'cause I'm starving." MiMi rubbed her baby bump. Then she glanced at the door as though looking for Anthony. "Well?"

"We need to find out how Jazz, Ike and Strafford, Inc. are linked together." Willa frowned and went back to considering the puzzle pieces of what she knew.

"We will. Nothing a good team like us can't handle."

"Right, go team," Willa retorted with a roll of her eyes, but the sarcasm was lost on her target.

"Oh, there's the bus dropping off Mikayla. I'll go meet her. You fix us some sweet tea. I brewed it while you were talking to Anthony. It's cooling on the stove." MiMi went through the kitchen door and was striding down the driveway before Willa could react.

"I'm trapped in some weird Sci-Fi channel episode," Willa mumbled. Still she followed instructions and went to the large glass kettle that held brewed tea.

Chapter 14

Two days later Willa arranged for Aunt Beryl to baby-sit so she could meet up with her brothers. The twins had come through in a pinch for her again. Shaun and Dion found Jazz and brought her back to Baton Rouge. And Jazz wasn't happy about it either. Willa didn't mind facing her little sister's legendary wrath. At least Jazz was still alive. Once Willa got over being relieved she got mad. She was more than ready to tangle with Jazzmonetta Vaughn. Yes indeed.

Rush hour traffic had eased as Willa drove across town. She didn't take the quickest route to the Vel Rose Motel on Airline Highway. Instead she pretended to be doing errands like any normal single mom. She stopped at the Piggly Wiggly and emerged with a bag of stuff she didn't need. Next she drove to the drug store. This time she bought something she did need, pills to ease her growing headache. All the time Willa reverted back to her old street life habits, her cop radar working overtime. After more trips down side streets Willa took a circuitous route to meet her brothers and get answers. Thirty minutes later she pulled into the Vel Rose Motel parking lot. Two rows of single story rooms stretched out behind on either side of the scruffy looking office. The buildings formed a U-shape. She looked at the dirty orange doors with black numbers on them searching for number fifteen. She found it and pulled her car into an empty space. When Willa got out and knocked on the door Jazz pulled it open.

"You crazy? Get out of sight." Willa hurried into the room pushing Jazz ahead of her.

"You need a valium or something," Jazz quipped.

Shaun sat in a big chair, his long legs stretched out as he watched ESPN on the hotel television. Dion paced and twisted his hands together. He seemed to have taken on the nervous task of fretting for his siblings. Shaun gave off a strange vibe. He sat like a coiled spring ready to shoot into action at any moment. When Willa's cell phone rang she grabbed it after checking the caller ID and punched the talk button.

"MiMi, we're busy. Yes, we're all right and yes, we found Jazz. What are you doing at my house?" Willa groaned and looked at her brothers with a grimace.

"I kinda like her," Dion whispered aside to his brother, but Willa overheard and glared at him. "I mean, I'm not into the black princess type usually, but her heart is in the right place."

"Oh you were admiring her heart. I thought you were staring at her chest for some other reason." Shaun smirked at him.

"Shut up." Dion grinned back and pretended to aim a slap at his brother's head. "I'm hungry." He flipped open his slim cell phone.

Willa shook her head then turned her back on the pair. "Don't you dare let Mikayla polish her fingernails blue and gold. I don't care if you're both Southern Jaguar fans. And do not dress her in those ugly pink and green colors of your sorority either. Put my aunt on the phone." After instructions to Aunt Beryl not to let MiMi do anything stupid Willa ended the call.

Willa gestured to Jazz with a wave of one hand. "Tell us what the hell is going on."

"Good to see you, too, sis," Jazz said in a dry tone. She brushed back her long golden fake hair.

"The police found a dead dude in your spare bedroom," Willa shot back.

Jazz flinched at the blunt description. She sat down abruptly, her bravado tempered by reality. "Von."

"Von didn't die of natural causes. You and your boyfriends are on the short list of suspects in a murder. So don't give us any crap." Willa pointed a finger at her.

"Bet you ready to roll over on me, too," Jazz grumbled.

"You're in serious trouble and we're trying to help," Dion sat down next to her on the bed.

"Trouble? You don't know the kinda trouble y'all asking for taking me out of Houston. Felipe don't play." Jazz fidgeted with the metallic gold purse in her lap.

"Jack hooked up in some business deal with Felipe. You're not leaving this funky room until you say something that sounds close to the truth." Willa stared at Jazz who smacked her lips. "Jack was hanging out at Candy Girls. Is that where all this started?"

"Miss know-it-all big sister ain't got one clue. I didn't need to hook Jack up to anything. He was already in deep by the time I— " Jazz stopped when her cell phone lit up in a kaleidoscope of colors signaling an incoming call. "It's Felipe."

"Don't answer it," Dion said.

"Keep him guessing for a little while," Shaun agreed.

"We'll get more time if he hears my voice. Let me handle this." Jazz didn't wait for more debate as she hit the on button. "Hey, baby. I had to get some things from Walmart. You know we left in a hurry and I'm running out of underwear. Your ghetto thug friends don't have a washer and dryer. Man, you need to class up your associations."

Dion and Shaun exchanged a glance then both looked at Willa. They all had to count on Jazz's ability to shoot a line of bull to keep them out of serious danger. Jazz began with sweet talk to the dangerous man. She went to a far corner of the cramped room and said a few X-rated things to him. When Jazz gave a raunchy laugh Willa shook her head.

"I just hope Jazz has him whipped enough that he lets his guard down," Willa whispered.

"He won't for long," Shaun predicted. "Not that dude."

"Okay, baby. I'm gonna hang with my girl Toni tonight. You're right. Probably best if we split up for awhile. Kisses." Jazz turned the phone off and stared at it. "I need to got back to Houston."

"No way," Willa said.

"You don't understand." Jazz closed her eyes. She looked tired, and suddenly ten years older than her twenty-seven years. "Felipe killed Von because he stole money from him. I played on that and convinced Felipe that Anthony doesn't know anything about the missing money. If they think you or Anthony knows where that eight hundred thousand is..."

"Eight hundred thousand," Willa and Dion blurted out together

"Dollars?" Shaun asked. His mouth hung open.

"The offshore account," Willa whispered. "But the letter from Ike Nelson talked about seventy-five thousand."

"That was the first payment to Jack for hooking up Strafford with some shady guys who work at the port. Jack called it a 'consulting' fee. He didn't care what was going on. He just enjoyed sticking it to 'the man' as he called it. Jack talked like he was a hero in one of them old school black-exploitation films sometimes."

Willa felt a stab of sadness. "Yeah, he did. But back to this scheme."

Jazz rubbed her eyes and fell back in the chair. She kicked off the three-inch heel gold sandals she wore. "Just let me catch my breath. I hope you realize I'm not supposed to know all these details. But Felipe likes to talk when we... you know."

"Too much information, little sister," Shaun muttered.

"Aw, look at big brother blush," Jazz teased.

Willa frowned at her. "Listen, we got three dead men and my son on the hook for some crap you and Jack started. You can catch your breath later. I don't believe you. I'll bet you set up this whole deal with Felipe, Ike and Jack."

"What do you mean— " Anger made Jazz's light brown eyes flash golden.

"You've been lying about what you know since Jack got killed. That's what I mean." Willa stood over her.

"If you think you can whip my ass then try," Jazz shot back and stood.

Shaun stepped between his sisters in one long stride. "We don't have time for this."

"And we sure as hell can't draw attention to ourselves or have the police showing up." Dion stood on the other side of the women facing Shaun.

"This dump is the original No-Tell Motel. All the stuff going down here, the last thing anybody wants is to call the police. That includes the manager," Willa said. Still she unclenched her fists and stepped back.

"Damn it, Willa. I'm doing this to protect y'all. Felipe may be hot for me, but he's not stupid. I managed to get him outta Baton Rouge. If I don't go back to Houston he'll come looking for me."

Willa felt a chill flow through her veins. "He won't risk it. He must know the police are going to get the connection to him sooner rather than later."

"The police have that dumb ass Kenton. That fool probably led them right to my apartment. Besides, Felipe is not scared of the police. You gotta let me go," Jazz said.

"Not going to happen, Jazz," Shaun said before Willa could reply. "You'll end up dead for sure. He's probably got eyes all over anyway. He knows your first loyalty is to Willa. Don't kid yourself that you're safe."

"I'll take care of me like always. I gotta do what it takes to keep Felipe off my family."

Dion's smooth, easy-going demeanor was gone. Back was the street-hard expression he'd worn as a teenaged gang member. "We might be a mixed bag of nuts as far as families go. A collection of throwaway kids brought up on the streets, in foster care and group homes. But like you said we're family, and family sticks together. Besides, me and Shaun know how to handle our business, too."

Willa rubbed her forehead. The pounding headache building behind her eyes made her feel weak. She felt like there was no good choice to be made. Still she knew what they had to do. Her three siblings looked at her, waiting in silence for guidance.

"Dion is right. We'll face whatever goes down together."

Willa hugged Jazz, ignoring the way her sister stiffened at the touch. After a few moments Jazz relaxed a little. Then Dion and Shaun joined for a group show of support by putting their long arms around both of their sisters. Jazz broke away first.

"Okay, that was a real sweet moment. But group hugs ain't gonna help us when Felipe starts putting together the pieces, which should be any minute now. My game with men is good, but I'm not that good. Not when you're dealing with a coked-up gangsta who is mad about losing his money."

"We don't have a choice. Eventually he's going to come after Willa or maybe even Anthony the way I see it." Shaun looked at his twin brother and Dion nodded after a few moments of thought.

Willa sat down on the frayed bedspread. "I have an idea."

"Fantastic. Let's hear it," Dion said.

"Uh, part of it involves Jazz getting arrested," Willa said and cleared her throat.

Jazz's eyes narrowed as she stared at Willa hard. "I should have known you'd throw my ass to the pit bulls."

***

For the next three days life seemed to settle into a normal routine again, at least on the surface. Willa went to the office. She met with Cedric about contracts, payroll and cash flow like any other business owner. Shaun and Dion went to work during the day. The kids went to school each day. In the evenings Willa cooked dinner and helped them with their homework. Sure. They were all back into the same old everyday schedule. Almost. Willa's plan was for Jazz to surrender to Detective Miller and give him enough information to arrest Felipe, and have the gang leader indicted by the grand jury. With Felipe out of commission Willa figured both her son and her sister would be safe. What she hadn't planned was that Jazz would decide not to talk immediately for her own reasons. So Jazz sat in jail, a crazy gangster on the loose wanted his money back, and Willa's ex-husband's mistress was driving her nuts. Through it all Willa managed to hold onto her sanity. Just barely.

The dreary November day didn't help. Willa glanced out the window. So much for trying to see the sunny side of life, she mused. She shivered just looking at the steady drizzle of rain that had hung on since dawn. Most working people would be celebrating getting through half the work week. Back in the day Willa's father would call Wednesday "Hump Day," as in getting over the hump and closer to the weekend. To Willa it now meant visiting day at the parish prison where Jazz was being held. Willa had been watching the clock all morning counting down. Visiting hours were noon to one-thirty. At eleven Willa prepared to leave.

"Kay, I'm going to lunch early. Call my cell if something urgent comes up." Willa stared to say more when she saw

MiMi waving at her through the glass entry doors. "Call security, please."

"Hi ladies," MiMi said with her brightest smile. "How are you, Kay? Love the new do."

"Thanks," Kay said and smiled back. "Love those earrings. Gold looks good on you."

"Girl, show me a woman that doesn't look good wearing gold," MiMi quipped and both women laughed.

"I heard that. Now if you could just drop that tip on my man," Kay said and rolled her eyes in mock frustration.

Willa blinked at the exchange and shook her head wondering when MiMi had managed to charm Kay. "I can't visit, MiMi. I'm meeting someone for lunch."

"I know. I'm coming with you," MiMi looped one arm through Willa's and waved goodbye to Kay with her free hand.

Once they were outside the office suite Willa shook off her unwelcome companion. "I'm not playing around with you today. I have business to take care of, and you are *not* invited."

"You're going to visit Jazz at the Parish Prison. Dion told me, and don't you climb his butt about it either. Few men can resist confiding in me." MiMi lifted a shoulder and smiled.

"Seems Jack found you quite resistible. You didn't know about the money he stashed away or his extra trips to the Cayman Islands. *Without you.*" Willa hit the elevator button and smiled back at a now frowning MiMi. "I'm betting Jack had a woman on the big island as well, or two."

"That was downright nasty," MiMi snapped back. She fumed for several moments in silence. When the elevator door opened she followed Willa inside.

"So have a nice lunch," Willa said.

MiMi ignored the three people already on the elevator. "I'm already prepared to be searched. I've never been to a jail before. Kind of exciting."

"No." Willa clenched her teeth to keep from saying more.

"I'm not going to argue. This whole mess with the police affects me and the baby." MiMi patted her tummy. "I'm coming with you."

"No," Willa hissed.

The woman standing behind them leaned forward. The two men exchanged a glance with raised eyebrows then stared at the wall. All three seemed eager to learn more. When the elevator bumped to a smooth landing on the first floor the woman actually sighed in disappointment. Willa hurried off the elevator with MiMi right behind her.

"Hell no. No damn way no," Willa snapped and squinted at the woman who had exited the elevator right behind them. She stared at Willa and MiMi with interest. Once the woman left the building lobby, Willa gave MiMi her full attention. "Listen, they don't allow more than one visitor."

"That's not true. We're wasting time. Let's be green and carpool. I'll drive. You must be exhausted with everything going on. By the way, I talked to Mama Ruby and she cooked her special gumbo. We'll pick some up later." MiMi grabbed Willa's arm again and forcefully directed her toward the shiny BMW sedan parked in a handicapped space.

"What?" Willa blinked.

MiMi waved at one of the two building security staff, a male. "Charles said it was okay. I was only going to be a few minutes and of course I'm pregnant."

"Listen, Jazz won't talk in front of you, MiMi, so forget it. Besides, this whole situation is getting dangerous. I don't want you or that baby on my conscience. Now go."

Willa spun and marched off to a section where building occupants were allowed to park. She got in her Honda Pilot and drove off the parking lot. At the stop sign leading off the parking lot she looked in her rearview mirror and muttered a curse. MiMi waved to her from her BMW. For thirty aggravating minutes Willa continued to swear at the traffic and MiMi. She pulled up to the East Baton Rouge Parish Prison security booth with four cars ahead of her. MiMi's BMW was three cars behind. The small crowd went through the usual security process of making sure no cell phones or prohibited items were being carried in. Willa came prepared. She had put her purse in the trunk of her car and only carried her keys. After another fifteen minutes Willa entered the visiting room. Cement benches attached to the floor were scattered around. Two vending machines stood in one corner. A few visitors fed them coins to buy treats for inmates they would visit. Moments later a door opened and several women came through.

"Got here fast as I could. Where's Jazz?" MiMi sounded out of breath.

"You're like a rash I can't get rid of, you know that?" Still Willa eyed her closely. "Sit down over there before all the benches are taken."

"Thanks. I— " MiMi gasped and put a hand to her mouth as she looked past Willa.

Willa turned to see what caused her reaction. Jazz walked toward them. She wore a large white bandage across her left cheek and another was wound around her left right hand. Willa brushed past two people to hug her. "Oh my God. Jazz."

Jazz pushed back from Willa after a few moments. She shrugged. "Don't worry 'bout me. You should see the bitch that made the mistake of taking me on."

"Are you getting proper medical attention? Did they punish the inmate who did this? I will speak to the warden before the end of business today." MiMi blinked at Jazz as she whispered to her fiercely. "Don't you worry."

"Are you okay?" Willa had to catch her breath before managing to get words out. She felt shaky as she noticed the stitches on Jazz's cheek beneath the bandage. Her hand obviously had defensive wounds.

"I'm fine," Jazz said coolly as she glanced around at the other inmates entering the room. Then she looked at Willa. "Hey, calm down. I said I'm okay. The plan is rockin' along."

"Plan?" MiMi said, her voice low.

"Yeah, Willa will tell you about it later," Jazz replied and nodded to her.

"No, I won't," Willa tossed back and ignored MiMi's scowl.

"In the meantime don't worry about me. My girls are watching my back in here," Jazz continued.

"How did Felipe know so fast?" Willa demanded.

"I'm not sure it was him. Just so happens the girl Felipe had before me is in here. She's a crazy Latina, and he was cold-blooded the way he dumped her. Maybe Felipe's boys told her to get me. Maybe she doesn't know anything just wanted some payback for me taking her man." Jazz's gaze flickered around the room as she talked.

"Or maybe she wanted to score points with Felipe by taking you out," Willa said in a grave voice.

"Doesn't matter. She won't be coming back at me for a while." Jazz spat out a string of Spanish words.

"I don't speak the language but I know exactly what you said." MiMi blinked at her rapidly.

"Stop stalling, Jazz. Follow the plan and tell Miller what he needs to arrest Felipe fast, and get him off the street. Maybe I should pay your bail. I'm not sure that it wouldn't be less dangerous for you out on the street," Willa whispered to Jazz as MiMi leaned in to catch every word.

"Outside would be worse. At least here I can scope out and predict who is comin' at me. Felipe could have somebody I've never seen run up on me at anytime. No, until I get him first this is where I'll stay."

"The police are only dumb in cheap movies and bad cop shows on television. Miller will figure out you're playing him along." Willa glanced around to see if anyone was paying too much attention to them and their conversation.

"Not many visitors today," MiMi said as though reading Willa's mind. She nodded at the sparse crowd. "I think we're okay."

"About two dozen of these girls in here are either friends or friends of friends. I'm okay for sure. I checked out the other inmates before I surrendered in the interest of cooperation and justice." Jazz looked at Willa.

"Now I understand why you didn't kick, scream and cuss me out when I suggested it," Willa retorted.

"Sweetie, I always have a plan within a plan and a backup plan on top of that," Jazz quipped. "So once I do talk, Miller will pick up Felipe. And they'll take out the rest of Felipe's boys in town. Then I'll spill more of what I know and cash in my get out of jail card."

"But they could get out on bond and come after us," MiMi said. She gave a dramatic shiver. "We know they don't mind killing people."

Willa followed Jazz's gaze as she watched the last inmate say goodbye to an elderly couple. When all three were gone only one inmate with two visitors was left. Jazz nodded for Willa and MiMi to move even farther away to a bench on the opposite side of the room. Once they were settled Jazz looked even more laid back. Still she spoke in a soft undertone.

"They won't get out on bail. After what I tell them, they'll be held without bond. They're a flight risk and known felons. Even if the judge does set bail their cash is tapped out. That's why they were so pissed about the money falling through. They blamed Jack."

"Because he wanted to back out of whatever they were up to?" Willa said.

Jazz shook her head. "Jack wasn't in on Felipe's little operation. See these guys got the jobs at the warehouse through Reverend Fisher's program. Ike Nelson found out they were moving guns and drugs, but he wasn't going to cross Felipe. Besides he was making money both ways."

"I'm confused. Why would Felipe think Jack had his money?" Willa said.

"Felipe is paranoid. He probably thinks Ike and Jack decided to rip him off. I don't know. Doesn't matter because Felipe will soon have other things to worry about," Jazz said.

"So Jack was going to tell on everybody and Felipe killed him before he could," MiMi said. Her expression hardened. "I want Felipe and his crew to pay. Let's take them down hard."

"We're not taking anybody down. Jazz is going to tell Detective Miller what she knows, and then we'll let them do their jobs." Willa looked at Jazz. "You're not going to hold anything back or play games. No last minute surprises, which you're known to do."

"I said I was gonna take care of this." Jazz blew out a sharp breath.

"Don't start with the rebellious little sister stuff now. I'm not in the mood." Willa frowned as she stared hard at Jazz.

MiMi stood and looped an arm around Willa and Jazz pulling them into a group hug. "Girls, girls. Now is not the time to snap at each other. We have to pull together. Too much is at stake."

"Whatever. Anyway, show a little trust for once." Jazz told Willa, brushing free of MiMi's hold.

"Sorry. I shouldn't have snapped at you. I know you'll do what it takes to protect the kids," Willa said.

"I will," Jazz said then cleared her throat. "Okay, we've had our group hug. Now back to business. Felipe won't get out once they pick him up."

"But what about you?" MiMi leaned closer to Jazz. "You can't implicate them without getting yourself in trouble for being involved."

Jazz shed her streetwise tough exotic dancer persona. Like magic she became a scared young woman in over her head. Her voice trembled. "I was in fear of my life, Detective Miller. You've seen his record. Felipe has a long history of violence, including against women. He would slit my throat if I said anything."

"Wow, you're good." MiMi blinked at her as if seeing Jazz for the first time.

"Sure, she's got great acting skills. Plus the part about Felipe slitting her throat is true. This isn't a game," Willa said quietly.

"Willa, I got myself into something that got deeper than even I wanted to go. I should have followed my gut and avoided Felipe. But he's not the kind that takes rejection from women well, if you know what I mean." Jazz shrugged. "He wasn't all that bad, at first."

"I'm guessing he's super fine, was throwing around a lot of cash and has that hot, bad boy persona," MiMi added.

Jazz grinned. "Yeah, and I'm a sucker for a sexy Latino accent."

"Oh yeah, girl. I feel you on that one," MiMi said and fanned her face.

"Never mind the long arrest record and tendency to murder people who annoy him, huh? Jazz— " Willa shook her head.

"Lecture me later." Jazz waved a hand at her.

Willa started bouncing one leg, realized it and forced her leg still. Mama Ruby always said that was a dead giveaway that Willa was scared about what might happen next. When Jazz placed a hand on her knee Willa glanced up into her almond brown eyes

"I'm going to make this turn out right." Jazz spoke as though she were the older sister. When Willa nodded Jazz took her hand away. A devilish gleam lit her eyes making them sparkle as if in anticipation. "Miller is coming by this evening to 'interview' me. Shit ought to start hitting the fan not long after that."

"Let's just get this over with, little sister. No tricks," Willa whispered.

"Time, ladies," the female correctional officer said. The stocky woman unlocked the door leading to the cellblock.

Jazz stood and held up two fingers. "On my honor as a Girl Scout. I'll talk to you soon."

"Real soon. In twenty-four hours I'll get you out of here," Willa called after her.

Jazz didn't look back, just kept walking. She merely lifted a hand to acknowledge Willa's pledge. Once outside in the parking lot MiMi and Willa both slipped on their sunglasses. Neither left, but stood looking at the prison through the chain link fence topped with barbed wire. The gray sky had cleared to light blue with not a cloud in sight. The scene was deceptively peaceful in contrast to danger behind those walls. And outside of them.

"What now?" MiMi broke the silence though her voice was subdued.

"We all better keep our heads low cause like Jazz said, it's about to hit the fan."

***

By six-thirty that evening Willa stood in her kitchen tearing up lettuce leaves for the dinner salad. The television played in the background. She watched a re-broadcast of the six o'clock news. After the first few stories one made her drop the carrot she was about to peel and grab the remote. She hit the volume.

"Police arrested four men in a drug raid in Brookstown, a rough neighborhood that has been the scene of three drive-by shootings in the last two months. Sources tell us this raid is linked to the recent arrest in Houston of Felipe Perez. Perez is thought to have set up major cocaine and illegal gun operations in Baton Rouge. Perez is also suspected in a recent murder. We'll have more on this story during our ten o'clock edition."

Willa felt shaky, so she sat down on a bar stool at the breakfast counter. The phone rang four times before the sound registered in her brain. The caller ID read "Unknown." When she finally picked up the cordless phone a female voice spoke in husky drawl.

"Hey, what up? Got a message from your sis. It's all good."

"Who is this?" Willa said without thinking. When the woman gave a loud pointed sighed Willa got the stranger's second message. Anonymous was her name. "Right. Thanks."

"No problem. She's doing just fine." At that the call ended as abruptly as it had begun.

Moments later Anthony entered the kitchen. He still held one of the other cordless handsets. "Mama, what's up with Aunt Jazz?"

"You shouldn't be listening in on calls if they don't ask for you by name." Willa hit the off button of the phone and frowned at him.

"I picked up cause I thought you were busy fixing supper. Besides I'm concerned about Aunt Jazz. Sorry, but I couldn't just ignore it."

"Well try harder next time. The less you know the better." Willa went back to the salad bowl. She glanced down to find the carrot she'd dropped had rolled onto the floor. She picked it up and tossed it into the trashcan.

"Just tell me she's okay."

"You heard her friend, it's all good. Jazz is gonna land on her feet as usual." Willa had to admire her baby sister's ability to make it.

Anthony nodded. He sat down and watched Willa for a few seconds. "This has something to do with her boyfriend Felipe."

Willa spun around to face him. "What do you know about him?"

"Nothing, except he was at her apartment a couple times I went over there. And, uh, I saw him hanging at Candy Girls. Not that I've been there since you busted me," Anthony added quickly.

"I know. I'm not trying to treat you like a child, Anthony. The important thing is we're dealing with it."

"You, Uncle Dion and Uncle Shaun and Mr. Cedric. Even Miss MiMi is helping, huh?"

"I don't know how much Miss MiMi is actually helping, but we're doing what we can. Most important we're going to let the police deal with Felipe Perez and his crew. If there is anything else that Jack got involved in that was illegal— " Willa bit her lower lip. "We'll face it when we have to. If I can keep Mikayla from hearing any really negative information about her daddy I will."

"Good thing she doesn't care about watching the news. I can always distract her with one of those goofy kid cartoon shows."

"Yes. Thank goodness she hasn't grown up so fast like you," Willa said with a smile of affection. "Now let us old folks handle this mess, and let me get back to dinner."

"Just stay safe. I figured out Felipe was bad news when I met him the first time." Anthony's voice dropped deeper at the implied trouble Felipe Perez brought with him.

Willa suppressed the chill of fear. Instead she smiled as she opened the refrigerator. "Well, he's the Baton Rouge Police Department's problem now. So no worries. That's a direct order from your mother."

"Yes, ma'am."

Anthony said nothing as he watched Willa get another carrot and a cucumber for the salad. He followed her movements as she sliced through them on the cutting board. Willa could almost hear the sound of wheels spinning in his sharp mind. She also knew he had more to say, but decided to let him gather his thoughts.

"Mama?"

"Yes." Willa swept the sliced vegetables into the bowl with the green leaf lettuce.

"You think Felipe killed Dad?" Anthony's voice was quiet.

"I honestly don't know anything for sure, Anthony." Willa wiped her hands on a paper towel. Then she faced him again. "I don't even know for sure that Felipe ever met Jack."

"I know he worked at that warehouse Strafford, Inc. bought. Aunt Jazz told me," Anthony added when Willa's eyebrows shot up. "From what they said on the news Felipe was a big time drug and gun trafficker."

"Humph, you really are putting some pieces together. Warehouse, shipments, drugs and guns." Willa once again felt a chunk of his childhood innocence slip away. She had to remind herself that Anthony was not just bright, he could think ahead.

"Allegedly. Even scum bags are guilty until proven otherwise." Willa keep slicing and dicing until she had way more salad than they could eat.

"Sounds reasonable. Dad must have found out and didn't want to go along with it. But then Mr. Ryan should have figured it out, too, or Dad told him. Wonder how he didn't get hurt." Anthony's dark eyebrows pulled together as he concentrated.

Willa froze. "Why would you say Ryan must have known?"

"Dad told me Mr. Ryan's trucking company had a contract to move stuff from that warehouse. They both met with those dudes at Strafford, Inc."

Willa felt a piece of the puzzle click into place. So Ryan did have a contract with Strafford, a contract that involved the same warehouse Felipe used. And he didn't mention it to her despite his oh-so sincere Mr. Helpful act. She made a mental note to discuss that angle with Cedric.

"Ryan Crown is too prissy to get within miles of anything too dangerous," Willa said trying to shake him off that line of reasoning. "You're going to be a great investigator by the time you're out of college and ready to take over Crown Protection. Until then work out those math problems instead. Leave the mystery solving to Detective Miller. That's what I plan to do."

"Sure you will. You and Aunt Jazz helped hand over that Felipe character to the police slick as you please." Anthony grinned when Willa hissed at him. "That's what I thought."

"You're way to smart for your own good, *little boy*," Willa teased and tried to tickle him.

"Stop with that little boy stuff again." Anthony did fancy footwork to get out of her way.

"Anthony, don't repeat that stuff about the warehouse or Ryan to anyone else, especially not your grandparents." Willa said with intensity. "I want you safe, too."

"I'll be super careful, Mama. So don't worry." Anthony winked at her and left.

"Right. Don't worry."

Willa watched him leave with a confident adolescent male stride. Deep into counting all the reasons she had to worry, Willa was on number fifteen when the sound of the doorbell made her jump. She let out a string of curse words. Then in deference to Aunt Ametrine's Sunday school lessons she asked forgiveness. With the phone in hand ready to dial 911 she peered out the window. She cursed again and slapped the metal locks back then opened her front door.

"Good evening, Detective Miller," Willa drawled then crossed her arms. "Now what?"

He gazed at Willa without speaking for several seconds then looked over his shoulder. His partner got out of their unmarked gray Chevy Impala. Detective Addison opened the rear passenger door and held Jazz's arm as she got out. When she pushed his hand away the detective merely smiled at her.

"We wanted to bring your sister home to the loving care of her family," Miller said mildly. "And find out the real story so we won't go around thinking you ladies are obstructing justice."

Chapter 15

Detectives Miller and Addison stood on Willa's doorstep. Jazz took her sweet time getting from the car to the front door. The two men looked at Willa for a reaction. Jazz looked bored.

"I don't have any idea what you're talking about," Willa shot back with an irritated glance from Detective Miller to Jazz.

"Don't look at me. I wanted to stay with a friend of mine." Jazz tossed her head making her long weave bounce. Then she performed her "Bite me" strut of scorn past the two detectives, her leather purse swinging as she moved. As she brushed close to Willa on her way into the house she whispered, "They're bluffing."

"We need to talk. Seriously." Miller planted his six feet two inch bulky frame in front of Willa.

"I get the impression you'd shove your way inside if I refused. Don't try it, though. Not unless you've got a search warrant in your back pocket." Willa glared back at him.

"We're not opponents here, Mrs. Crown," Addison said over his shoulder.

"Following up on any leads is our job. And you want us to do our jobs. May we come in?" Miller said, his tone polite but firm.

"I'm more than happy to cooperate. Please, come on in detectives." Despite her tough act Willa had no intention of trying to get rid of them.

Addison, the shorter of the two men, was also short on civility as he stared at Willa. His bulk, packed into a dress shirt and brown slacks, made him look like an annoyed wrestler. He seemed psychic when he said, "You probably want to find out what we know and what we're doing anyway."

Willa led them into the living room. Moments later Jazz appeared with a can of cola in one hand. She stood next to Willa and took a sip but said nothing. "So you have Felipe Perez in custody. Is there any indication he was linked to my ex-husband's death?"

"Why would you think that?" Addison said. His dark gaze flickered to Jazz and back to Willa.

"Let's not waste each other's time." Willa waved for them to take a seat as she went to a chair and sat down. Jazz followed Willa but remained standing. "You know Jack had business dealings with the company that owned a certain warehouse. That warehouse was being used by Perez for illegal purposes."

"Allegedly. We have to verify this information," Detective Addison said gruffly. His gaze stayed on Jazz.

"You will if you look in the right places." Jazz returned his gaze with cool confidence. She smacked her lips and lifted her nose in the air. "I want some chips with this. Excuse me gentlemen."

"She's a real case." Addison watched Jazz's hip swaying exit.

"And she knows what she's talking about, so count your blessings," Willa tossed back at him. Miller, seated on the edge of the sofa, said nothing. He seemed content to wait for Willa to keep talking. "My sister is giving you information, solid leads to follow. Which means you know my son wasn't involved in Jack's murder."

Miller nodded. "Too many kids wear that brand of athletic shoe. The print at the murder scene led us nowhere. Your son is lucky."

"My son is innocent," Willa replied curtly.

"Every parent I talk to wants to believe that, Mrs. Crown," Miller replied evenly.

Willa winced at his implication, but didn't take the bait. "Detective, I appreciate your courtesy in giving my sister a ride. Now that Jazz had provided you with 'solid leads' I hope you solve Jack's murder. I just don't want her to get hurt."

"Bet that little lady can handle herself," Addison said with a grunt. He pressed his lips closed when his partner gave him a stern look.

"We don't want her to get hurt either. We can help her... and *you* for that matter, *if* we have all the facts. You both need to be straight with us." Miller leaned forward as he spoke.

Jazz stomped in the room with both hands on her hips. "I put my ass on the line telling you what I know so don't come up in here saying that sh— "

"What did I tell you about that dirty mouth in my house? My kids could walk in here." Willa cut her off sharply.

"Whatever. Let me get outta here before I trip on these dudes again." Jazz stomped out again.

Willa watched her sister's dramatic exit then turned to the detectives again. "My brothers dragged her back to Baton Rouge, and I convinced her talk to you. The truth is I agree with you, Jazz probably hasn't told you everything. But this time my kids are involved. Jazz wouldn't hold back on anything that might put them in harm's way." Willa gazed from Miller to Addison and back to Miller again.

Miller nodded. "Okay. Are you certain your son has told you everything?"

Willa's heart skipped. "Yes, unless you've uncovered something new about Anthony. In that case let me know."

Miller exchanged a glance with his partner then looked at Willa. "You must wonder why he keeps popping up in this case. First, he's hanging at the club where your sister works. Next thing we learn he's possibly at the scene of your ex-husband's murder. I know he's had a few scrapes at school."

"Plus he's hanging with a bunch of wannabe gangsters," Addison added, one wooly eyebrow lifted.

"He's had some problems at school, but nothing major or recent. As for the bad crowd, the worst they've done is to get caught in one or two petty thefts or slip into nightclubs with fake IDs. Anthony and I have had that talk. So far the only laws he's broken are mine." Willa stood to signal she wanted them to leave. Now.

"Kids have all kinds of ways of getting into stuff and keeping it from their parents," Addison stood first. He glanced at his partner.

Miller stood as well and smoothed down his tie. "Okay. But I suggest you ask him about hanging out with Felipe Perez's little cousin."

"D'Andre is like Perez's baby brother. They're real close. Another coincidence?" Addison gazed at Willa with an impassive expression.

The sharp words on the tip of Willa's tongue dissolved as their bombshell exploded inside her head. Willa stared at Miller trying hard not to look as shocked as she felt. "Like I said, Anthony and I have had a talk about who he hangs out with at school and elsewhere. If my sister or I can help you anymore we'll be in touch. Goodbye."

Addison and Miller merely nodded. Both men continued to glance at her as they walked out. Willa wanted to shove them out faster, but contained herself. When she went into the kitchen Jazz was perched on a stool at the breakfast counter munching on cheese puffs from a bag. She wiped her hands on a paper napkin.

"So those two finally stopped trying to play good cop, dumb ass cop. Like that act could work on us." Jazz gave a short laugh as she brushed her hands together.

"Anthony has been running around with one of Felipe's little thug relatives. You knew this and didn't tell me." Willa walked around the counter to face her.

Jazz threw the napkin down on the counter and planted a fist on one hip. "Don't start. I've been trying to keep the kid outta trouble for months. D'Andre goes to his school. Hey, you were the one that insisted he attend public schools."

Anthony walked into the kitchen. "It's not her fault, Mama. You already gave me the lecture on hanging with the wrong people. I cut D'Andre loose. I would have told you, but I didn't want you to worry."

"Was he one of those boys in my house? Big D is D'Andre, isn't he?" Willa said before Anthony could answer her question. The volume of her voice kept going up until even Jazz moved away from her, taking the bag of cheese puffs. "You must have totally lost your mind."

Mikayla rushed into the kitchen with wide eyes. "What's going on? Is Anthony in trouble again?"

"Go to your room," Willa and Jazz said at the same time.

"I never get to hear the good stuff." With a serious pout on her face, Mikayla spun around and left.

"I found out D'Andre was Felipe's cousin one night when the boys snuck into Candy Girls. I told Anthony right then he was in over his head. Obviously he didn't listen to me," Jazz said.

"D'Andre is all talk. He's not too bright either. Even Felipe didn't take him seriously," Anthony said.

"He's dumb, and he talks too much. Those are the kind of dudes that will talk you right into prison or the grave. D'Andre would give you up in a minute if he got jammed up. I told you so." Jazz clicked her tongue and munched another cheese puff.

"He just gave us a ride that day you came home early. Honest. I hadn't seen him for a couple of weeks before that," Anthony said to Willa.

"You know how many people end up arrested or dead being with the wrong people at the wrong time?" Willa felt like she would explode from frustration. She covered her face with both hands.

"Look how you got your mama all worked up," Jazz said. She went to Willa and led her to a chair. "You sit down. I'll get you something to drink."

Anthony followed them and sat at the table next to Willa. "Mama, what happened to Dad slapped me back to reality. All I want now is to get justice for him. I promise you gangbanging is not my goal."

Willa lowered her hands. She breathed in and out to steady her nerves then looked at her son. "At your age you're on your own more than ever. I have to rely on your judgment. After all I've taught you, the talks from Papa Elton and Mama Ruby, there's nothing new I can add."

"Jack gave me a good talking to also. He told me about his mistakes. He wasn't perfect, but I loved him," Anthony said, his voice pitched deep like the man he had become. Still his eyes went shiny with tears. "Now I gotta honor his memory."

"We both will, baby." Willa accepted a paper towel from Jazz and dabbed his cheeks dry. Then she kissed him and they held each other for a few moments. Finally Willa let him go. "So no more accepting rides from any of that crew. Walk, call your grandparents, or catch a bus. I don't care if you don't look cool doing it."

Anthony wiped his eyes then gave her a cocky grin. "No problem. I'm cool looking no matter what I do."

"Go do your homework." Willa smiled.

"See you later, Aunt Jazz."

Once he was gone Willa turned to glare at her sister. "As for you, Miss Jazzmonetta Vaughn."

"I thought you knew who he was hanging out with. Maybe I could have mentioned him showing up at the club but— " Jazz squirmed under Willa's continued silent glare. She sprang to her feet when the doorbell chimed. "I'll get that. Probably my ride."

"Hey!" Willa called out, but Jazz was already gone. Moments later MiMi walked in beside Jazz, both chattering away with ease.

"Girl, how can you come out of jail looking so good?" MiMi gave Jazz a playful shove.

"'Cause I look so good no matter what." Jazz pushed her back and both giggled.

"Good evening, MiMi. How is it you always show up when things are popping?" Willa squinted at her then glanced sharply at Jazz.

"Can we stop by my apartment? I need to pick up a few things." Jazz grabbed her purse. She looked at MiMi then jerked her head toward the door.

"This is your ride and the friend you're going to stay with? You have both lost your minds!" Willa yelled. Mikayla and Anthony called out to ask if everything was okay. "Keep working on those school assignments you two."

"I don't understand why you're freaking," MiMi said. "The bad guy is in lock-up, right? We're okay."

"Jazz, Felipe could have buddies looking for you. MiMi is pregnant," Willa clipped back.

"Those efficient detectives have scooped those dudes up, too. And I happen to know the other three got outta town to avoid ending up the same way," Jazz replied coolly. "I told you I was handling this."

"MiMi, you're going to a crime scene. And Jazz got kicked out of her apartment." Willa crossed her arms.

"Wrong again, sis. All is forgiven. The police have taken down the tape and the apartment manager is having my place cleaned up. I just gave her some extra money." Jazz managed to sound almost self-righteous.

"You plan to live where a dead body was lying for hours?" Willa stared at her sister wide-eyed.

"Hey, with some new paint and carpet— " Jazz shrugged. "Don't give me that look. Besides Frankie had this friend of hers clear out any bad vibes, a real spiritual medium."

"What she means is a voodoo woman. Girl, y'all better stop dabbling in that mess." MiMi gave a melodramatic shudder.

"Unbelievable." Willa shook her head.

MiMi waved a hand signaling it was time to leave. "Goodnight, Willa. Hey, Jazz, I picked up Chinese take-out for us. And yes, I got the hot and spicy shrimp dish you like."

"Sounds good. Excuse us a minute, MiMi," Jazz said.

"No problem. I'll just take a trip to the toilet, which I do a lot lately. Then say a quick hello to the kids." MiMi went out humming.

"She knows her way around my house like she lives here," Willa said and sighed. "And you— "

"Don't trip on me, okay? Felipe is taken care of in more ways that one." Jazz wore a street tough expression.

Willa figured she probably didn't want to know, but burning curiosity forced her to ask. "What exactly does that mean?"

"Let's just say his senior partners aren't happy with the way he bungled their operation. It should have been real sweet. First Ike picked the wrong crew. Then Ike got greedy and demanded a bigger percentage."

"So that's why Ike Nelson was killed?" Willa whispered then glanced around to make sure they were still alone.

"That's what I hear. Not to mention the missing money. Jack died before Felipe found where the money went, or even if Jack had it. I'll bet that's reason number two they'll go after his behind. But hey, live by the AK-47, die by the AK-47." Jazz shrugged.

Her casual attitude gave Willa chills. "But he was your man, Jazz."

"Felipe was always 'Mr. Right Now'. We had our moment and then it was over. This way I don't have to worry about that crazy-ass fool stalking me." Jazz's eyes flashed fire.

Willa hated to see how hard life had made her younger sister. "Don't be so cold-blooded."

"Life is tough. If you gonna survive you better be even tougher," Jazz replied quietly.

"Is it okay to come back in?" MiMi called out from the hallway.

"We're done talking. I'm ready for a hot shower, my favorite robe, and some Chinese food," Jazz said in a cheery voice. The steely street survivor had vanished in an instant.

"Then let's go so the kids can get a hot meal. Both of them are almost done with their assignments. I say put them in honors programs. I don't think they're being challenged enough at those schools they attend," MiMi said.

Jazz nodded as she followed her to the front door. "I told Willa to put them in private schools a long time ago, MiMi. She don't listen to me."

"We'll let ourselves out, Willa. Just remember to double lock the door and set the alarm," MiMi advised. Then both went out still talking to each other.

"Lord have mercy," Willa mumbled then followed MiMi's advice about the alarm.

***

The next morning Willa went to the office feeling as if a huge dead weight was gone from her shoulders. She entered the lobby of Crown Protection humming an annoying tune from Mikayla's favorite kiddie TV show. And she wasn't even annoyed that it was stuck in her head. The morning newspaper was tucked under one arm. As usual The Advocate had a full helping of bad news. Except when it came to one Felipe Perez. He would get a very long prison sentence with any luck.

"Hey, boss lady," Kay said with a wide smile. "Gorgeous day, huh?"

Willa laughed. "Sure, if you like clammy fog and clouds. Not usually my taste, but yes, this is one beautiful day."

Cedric came down the hall holding a mug with the company logo. "Good morning."

"Yes, it is. Give me an update on how we're doing with contracts. Haven't been able to concentrate all that well lately." Willa pointed to his mug. "I'd like to settle in with some strong, hot coffee first though."

Kay appeared at her elbow with a mug. "Done."

"You're priceless," Willa said with a grin.

"I sent you an e-mail with the spreadsheet on our budget breakdown." Cedric glanced at the newspaper she held. "I read the news online. Perez is in deep."

"Oh yeah, and the stinky solid waste is getting deeper for that sleaze bag. Thanks to our wonderful police department," Willa said. She went into her office with Cedric following.

"Whoa. Now you're a fan of the Baton Rouge PD. Big change from some of the names you wanted to call them not so long ago." Cedric grinned at her.

"I've had a change of heart, well sort of. Fan might be too strong a description. Let's just say I no longer think they're no-good, rush-to-judgment scum." Willa smiled at him.

Cedric laughed and lifted his cup to her. "So all is right in your world. I'm happy for you."

Willa stopped smiling. "Not quite. I found out some not so pleasant facts about people I thought I knew."

"Anthony will be okay, Willa."

"I have to learn to be a better snoopy parent and keep up with who he's hanging out with. But yeah, Anthony is going to be okay, and Jack helped a lot. What he lacked as a husband, he made up for as a father," Willa said.

"Speaking of people to keep an eye on, Ryan Crown is a great example. He owes a lot of people a lot of money. Neither his trucking company nor his moving service is doing well. I think the dude crossed over to the dark side more than once."

"Ryan always wanted to beat Jack in getting their father's attention. He never quite succeeded," Willa replied.

"He certainly couldn't impress the old man with his business acumen." Cedric shook his head.

"I guess Mr. Crown was right. He always said Jack had more skills. The problem is he'd say that in front of Ryan.

Competition and resentment about sums up the relationship between Jack and Ryan." Willa shrugged.

"Ryan is somehow connected to this little mystery about what Jack was really doing for Strafford, Inc., but I just can't put together how." Cedric frowned as though trying once more to figure it all out.

"Ryan is in this mess because of money, the main goal of the Crown clan. Trust me on that. My guess is the police will keep sniffing into Strafford, Inc. and get on his tail sooner or later." Willa shrugged

"I never really liked the guy, but still I hate to see the dude go down." Cedric sipped more coffee and looked thoughtful.

"I'm not going to feel sorry for him. Ryan should be grateful he got out of this alive. I hope the police make things hot for him," Willa said with an evil grin.

"What happened to 'family is everything even if they're not perfect'? Doesn't sound like the Willa Crown I know." Cedric tilted his head to one side.

"Family is more than blood, Cedric. Family is how you treat each other."

"At least he tried taking an interest in Anthony, and Mikayla, too," Cedric replied. "For that reason alone I hope he wasn't in too deep. The kids don't need another loss."

"Don't get too sentimental. Ryan thought Anthony might know where Jack stashed all that money. Let's see if he wants to play the attentive uncle once he finds out Anthony doesn't know anything." Willa grunted, sure she knew the answer to that one already.

"Even if Ryan goes back to being a SOB, Anthony will get on the right road again. He has a lot of love and guidance. Believe me that makes a big difference." Cedric walked around her desk and sat on the edge of it. "And what about you?"

"Me?" Willa shrugged. "I'm good."

"I know losing Jack hurt, even if you have moved on emotionally," Cedric added quickly when Willa started to speak. "He was a father to both your kids."

"Yeah. I always had to give him credit for that. He didn't deserve to die so young," Willa said softly.

"Losing him was losing part of your family. I understand." Cedric put down the coffee mug and leaned closer to her. "I'm here for you. When you need me that is."

Willa looked into his eyes. Without thinking she grabbed one of his large hands and squeezed it. "I'm glad to have you around. But right now I'm not sure I can..."

Cedric lifted her hand to his lips, kissed it then let go. "Understood. Take your time. I'm not going anywhere."

"No, let me be clear. I can't give you any promises or a timetable. And I don't expect you to wait around for me. I've got the kids to think about and— " Willa's voice trailed off.

"I see. " Cedric's rich brown eyes gazed at her. "You're not even close to being ready to try another relationship."

"Sorry," Willa said quietly. To her surprise, and relief, after a few moments of silence Cedric smiled.

"Nothing to be sorry about. Like I said, I'm not going anywhere in the near future. Maybe one of these days we'll be ready at the same time." Cedric winked at her then picked up his coffee mug and stood again. "Back to business."

"I'm glad you're on my team, Cedric." Willa smiled at him. "But what was that part about not going anywhere in 'the near future'?"

"You know I want to start my own business one of these days." Cedric nodded. "We did talk about that."

Willa sighed. "Not that I don't want you to succeed, but Crown Protection will lose a lot when you go."

"I won't be far away."

Willa cleared her throat then shook her head. "Thanks. Okay, for the first time in weeks I can concentrate on business, and I've got some ideas. We should draw up a five year strategic plan with clear goals."

Cedric nodded and smoothly switched to all-business mode. "I agree. Jack had great ideas and kept the business going strong, but we didn't have a long-range plan. The economic climate can change overnight."

For the next hour they brainstormed a vision and mission statement for Crown Protection. Cedric put his usual attention to detail to good use. Willa gaze at the outline on her computer. They had the building blocks for a solid strategic plan.

"We've still got a lot of work to do," Willa said as she read some of the goals. "I mean we need to increase business by fifteen percent in one year. Wonder if we can overcome the bad PR around Jack's murder?"

"We can expand outside this city, maybe even another state. " Cedric relaxed in his chair, long legs stretched out.

"Excellent point. Maybe I should work on a management degree. That would make me a better boss." Willa tapped the keyboard, sending the plan to Cedric's e-mail inbox. Then she rocked back in her chair. "Yeah, maybe I'll come up with my own personal strategic plan."

"Sure thing. I did exactly that." Cedric stood up and smiled at her.

"Why doesn't that surprise me?" Willa smiled back at him.

"Speaking of which, I updated the schedule for this month so you can see every event and job. Check the calendar." Cedric was about to go on when there was a knock on the door.

Kay came in seconds later then closed the door behind her. "Reverend Fisher is out front. I told him you were in a meeting."

Cedric spoke before Willa could answer. "If this is about his security contract I could talk to him. After this stuff linking Abundant Love Ministries to Perez and his crew— "

"No, Cedric," Willa said. "Something tells me he wants to talk about more than security guards at Sunday services."

"Even more reason I should stick around." Cedric's dark eyebrows pulled together.

"The bad guys are locked up tight. I'll do just fine on my own. Besides, surely a man of the cloth wouldn't pose any threat." Willa waved them both out as she came around her desk.

"Later." Cedric strode out wearing a stern expression.

Kay stayed behind and lowered her voice to a whisper. "As for this man of the cloth, take my advice. Keep at least three feet of space between you. I hear he loves to lay hands on ladies, and not for healing or prayer either."

"Go out there and show the man in." Willa struggled to control a fit of laughter before the door opened again.

Reverend Fisher strolled in wearing a beatific smile. He spread his arms wide. "Hello, Mrs. Crown. What a blessing to see you have come through all these trials and tribulations."

Willa smiled back at him as she gestured to one of the chairs facing her desk. "Thank you, Reverend. Have a seat."

"I'll bring y'all some coffee in a minute. I won't be gone long," Kay said with emphasis on the last sentence.

"Thank you, sister." Reverend Fisher beamed at her. He didn't see the grimace Kay aimed at his back when he turned around.

"How is the ministry going these days?" Willa sat behind her desk. The combination of space and a solid object between them would please Kay and Cedric.

"Ah well, the news that a few of my flock strayed has been a trial." Reverend Fisher's bright expression darkened.

"I understand the police visited your ministry office." Willa was being polite of course. Detectives Miller and Addison had interviewed at least fifty church members. They had examined the records of the work program as well. If she knew them they weren't through yet.

Reverend Fisher gave a long-suffering sigh worthy of a saint. He shook his head slowly. "That has been especially difficult. Of course they're just doing their job. But it's disheartening to have so many of the good, hardworking participants painted with the same brush."

"Most of them do have criminal backgrounds. I'm sure having the police around is, uh, uncomfortable." Willa gazed back at him.

"True. Of course knowing that Ike Nelson betrayed my trust docsn't help at all." Reverend Fisher folded his hands together as if he would start a prayer. Instead he rested them on the slight bulge at his waistline.

"I'm sure." Willa studied him. Reverend Fisher might be a minister, but he was nobody's fool. Not to mention he'd been a bit of a gangster himself back in the day. Willa had a hard time believing the good reverend had been so easily conned.

"I knew Brother Nelson, Ike, for twenty years. We grew up in the same tough New Orleans neighborhood, the Ninth

Ward. We found redemption at the same time you know." Reverend Fisher sighed again. He gazed off as though looking into his past instead of the skyline outside Willa's office window.

"Really?" Willa wanted him to keep talking so she stayed quiet.

After a few moments Reverend Fisher nodded. "Yes. We were in the same jail being counseled by Reverend Hezekiah Matthews. That man saved our lives. I wanted to be just like him."

"All it takes is one dedicated and sincere person." Willa thought about Mama Ruby and Papa Elton. They'd saved her in more ways than one.

"Exactly, and I wanted to be that person, Mrs. Crown." Reverend Fisher stood and walked to the window next to Willa's desk. "I'm to blame for all this."

"You? How is this your fault?" Willa leaned forward in reflex to catch every word.

"I expanded Abundant Love Ministries too quickly. I was so busy with the new programs that I relied on Ike, and others, too much. I took my eyes off the prize." Reverend Fisher twisted one of the gold rings around his finger. "I'm afraid the sin of pride took control."

"Hmm," was all Willa trusted herself to say. Obviously Reverend Fisher's new insight into the sin of pride didn't include getting rid of his bling.

"Still I didn't think Ike would hurt the ministry. Ike and me, we weren't just close. We were like brothers."

"You must have been shocked." Willa worked hard at keeping sarcasm from her voice."

"Wounded, my sister. Deeply wounded." Reverend Fisher shook his head slowly. "The Bible teaches us that even someone as close as a brother can betray us. Just look at the story of Cain and Able, or the way Joseph's brothers treated him because of jealousy."

"So you think Ike Nelson might have resented your influence and success."

"It happens, even in families," Reverend Fisher replied.

Nice act, Willa mused. There was one problem. She was from the 'hood just like Reverend Fisher. She knew a good game when she saw one. Fisher was laying the foundation for why he wasn't involved in Nelson's lucrative scam. That last part he tried selling was good though, even if it was a bit theatrical.

"How awful for you. So you didn't know about Jack and Strafford, Inc. either I suppose." Willa put empathy into her voice. At least she tried to anyway. Those gold rings and the Rolex watch made it hard for her to pretend.

"I knew they were doing business, the same way we had a contract. Now I'm reading about money laundering and possible import violations. I believe Jack's brother had some dealings in the same transaction?"

Willa nodded. "The sin of gluttony is still going strong, Reverend."

"Amen. I suppose he'll be questioned by the police. Or has he been already?" Reverend Fisher eyed Willa steadily. "Possibly even your own sister."

"I have no idea." Willa gazed back at him. A flutter of unease settled in her stomach.

"Terrible to find out someone so close could stab you in the back. Yes, truly a biblical parallel." Reverend Fisher walked over and took Willa's hand. "We have to be careful who we trust."

"Thanks for the advice." Willa pulled free of his hot grasp.

"I just wanted you to know that I fully intend to continue our contract. I have a lot of faithful church members who won't believe lies and false accusations about Abundant Love Ministries. Our contributions have even grown." Reverend Fisher's expression brightened again.

"Good for you. Thanks for coming by to show your support." Willa smiled at him, the effort straining her facial muscles.

Fisher had smooth moves no doubt about it. So far the police couldn't directly connect him or his church to any crimes. Willa thought about Crown Protection's contract with Abundant Love Ministries. They certainly couldn't afford to lose such a well paying client right now. Was this her deal with the devil?

"Have a blessed day, my sister." Reverend Fisher's sonorous voice rolled out as if he were an Old Testament prophet. With a flourish he pulled open her office door and swept out.

"Thanks," Willa murmured, feeling a chill as she watched him leave.

Big phony. She thought over his words trying to tease out the answer to a riddle, and a biblical one at that. For the first time in her life Willa regretted not paying closer attention in Sunday school.

***

Willa arrived at her parents' home trying to regain the good feeling Felipe's arrest had given her. Jazz had called and sounded quite confident. MiMi was back to dropping hints about owning part of Crown Protection. Well, she did have a kid on the way. And for some strange reason Willa didn't hate her guts quite as much as a month ago. Mikayla had already decided she was getting a new sister. Even Anthony seemed to be looking forward to the baby. So maybe MiMi was family. Willa was still laughing about the crazy twists and turns of her life when Mama Ruby opened the door. Warmth and spices flowed out to meet her. Papa Elton's deep laughter made Willa forget about hidden agendas and bad karma.

"You don't have to tell me. I can smell the gumbo and fresh hot cornbread. Now if you tell me you added oysters I'll do a back flip," Willa said as she took a deep breath in and let it out. She followed her mother down the hallway to the kitchen.

"Just for you, sweetie." Mama Ruby gave Willa a peck on the cheek then went back to her pots. The cheery green and yellow curtains, matching dish towels and gleaming white appliances said "home", and that everything would be just fine. "I made potato salad and French bread, too. Beryl is picking up the kids and bringing them over like I told you."

"I wanna see that back flip," Papa Elton said with a wink.

Before Willa could make an excuse the back doorbell rang. When she opened the door she blinked at Jazz in surprise. "Uh, hi."

"Mama Ruby says she's got gumbo so here I am," Jazz said abruptly as an explanation.

"Okay." Willa stepped aside as Jazz came in then peered out and got another surprise.

"Keep that door open," MiMi shouted through the window of her BMW sedan. She pulled up into the driveway behind Jazz's new tan Toyota Venza.

Huffing and puffing MiMi extricated herself from behind the wheel. She slung a large leather purse over one shoulder then waddled toward Willa.

"Don't worry. I'm not about to get between a hungry pregnant woman and food," Willa retorted as she watched her labored progress.

"Wise decision," MiMi shot back. "Hey everybody."

An hour later everyone was full and sitting around the big family room. Papa Elton had managed to ease the tension between Jazz and Mama Ruby, not that Mama Ruby didn't try. Being nurtured did not come easily to Jazz. Yet at that moment past conflicts didn't seem to matter.

"Come on, mister. Let's get the kitchen straightened up some." Mama Ruby gave Papa Elton an affectionate pat on the shoulder.

"Oh no," MiMi protested. "You should let us wash the dishes."

"Ruby likes getting me alone anytime she can. The woman can't keep her hands off me for more than an hour or so. She's been restraining herself since you girls got here. Isn't that right, honey?" Papa Elton laughed at the look his wife gave him.

"Get in that kitchen before I take a swing at you, Elton Conwell Wilson." Mama Ruby continued fussing as hoots of laughter followed them down the all.

"Let me call Aunt Beryl's cell and find out what's keeping them. The kids will love seeing their Aunt Jazz." Willa grinned at her sister who shrugged off the comment, yet still looked pleased. She tapped the keypad. "Hey, auntie, y'all don't get here soon the gumbo will be gone-bo."

MiMi let out a groan at the joke while Jazz shook her head. Willa listened to her aunt complain about traffic in Baton Rouge and incompetent drivers. Her usually sweet-tempered disposition vanished once she got behind the wheel. As she listened Willa held the phone out from her ear so the others could hear Aunt Beryl's strident rant.

"Yes, but just calm down. Remember to turn the other cheek, " Willa joked. "Say what? Alright, see you in a bit."

MiMi stared at Willa. "Something wrong?"

"Ryan picked up Anthony to take him out to eat." Willa squinted as she turned over the news in her mind. Something didn't strike her just right.

"Without calling to ask you first?" Jazz broke into her thoughts. She leaned forward.

"Well, he did promise to spend more time with Anthony," MiMi said.

Willa felt that troublesome unease start up again in her stomach. She took out her cell phone again. "I'm going to just check in with Anthony."

MiMi leaned over to Jazz. "I don't get why we're worried."

Jazz held up one hand and ticked off points on her fingers. "Ryan is desperate for money. Jack screwed up the barely legal deal that would have made him rich. Jack dies. Anthony was close to Jack. Jack has money in the Caymans, and Ryan doesn't know where it is."

"He wouldn't hurt his own nephew." MiMi blinked wide-eyed at Willa. "Would he?"

Chapter 16

Willa sat straight on Mama Ruby's brown leather sofa in her parent's family room. Jazz sat next to her looking worried. MiMi pushed down the footrest of the recliner that matched the sofa and frowned at the stony expression on Jazz's face.

"Anthony isn't Ryan's biological nephew," Jazz reminded MiMi.

"First Anthony's cell went to voice mail. Now the phone is off. Anthony never turns off his phone. Never." Willa stood and started pacing the hardwood floor. "Where would they go?"

MiMi stood up, found her purse and grabbed it. "Ryan belongs to the Camelot Club. They have a four-star restaurant on the top floor of the American Key Bank building downtown. They serve delicious steak and lobster."

"Thanks for the review," Jazz replied. "Let's go."

Willa pushed MiMi back down onto the sofa. "Uh-uh. You stay here pregnant lady."

"No way. Besides, I have daddy's Camelot Membership Club Card." MiMi searched her purse then waved the gold card at Willa. "I'm your way in past the security guy in the lobby. Let's roll."

Willa looked at her sister, who merely shrugged. "Hey, all we're gonna do is get Anthony and come home. Not like we're doing a drive-by."

Unwilling to waste time arguing, Willa led the way down the hallway to the kitchen. Jazz, nimble as ever, came up with a bland excuse as to why they were suddenly leaving. Mama Ruby and Papa Elton seemed to buy it because they went back to putting away dishes. Three minutes later they were in Willa's Honda Pilot.

"So what are we going to tell Ryan about why we showed up?" MiMi said from the rear seat, her legs stretched out.

"I don't need a reason to get my son." Willa clenched a fist against the rising tension in her body.

"No problem," Jazz said. "I can come up with something that won't make him get jumpy. We don't know what the dude might do." When MiMi gasped she waved a hand at her. " Relax, baby girl. I'm packing."

"You have lost your damn mind," Willa blurted out before MiMi could speak. Then she slapped Jazz on one arm. "You're not telling us something."

Jazz hissed softly then glanced at Willa. "Ryan and Jack got into a fight. I mean a real one, fists flying and everything. Ryan said he wanted to kill Jack for ruining this deal with Strafford."

"So why didn't you tell me this before?" Willa demanded without taking her eyes off the street.

"Ryan seemed like a wimpy frat boy, more talk than anything. Besides they were always getting into it about one thing or another. But now… I don't know."

"Hang on, MiMi. I'm going to hit the gas and get us to Camelot Club fast," Willa said.

Twenty minutes later they were in and out of the twelfth floor private dinner club. Anthony and Ryan weren't there. They stood in the lobby of the building deciding what to do next. Willa wrestled to control a growing sense of panic.

"I can get some of my friends to help us find them." Jazz waved her cell phone.

"We've had quite enough 'help' from your friends, thank you." Willa found Detective Miller's card in her purse and called him on her cell phone.

For the first time something went right. Miller was on duty and answered his phone. Willa explained her concerns in a rush until Miller forced her to slow down. He took some convincing, but Willa laid her cards on the table. Jazz and MiMi gestured wildly when she got to the part about the money, but Willa didn't care. She was going to find her son.

"How fast can you get here? Okay, thanks." Willa hit the button to end the call. "They're on the way."

"Five minutes to get our story straight," Jazz said, glancing at her watch.

MiMi blinked rapidly at Jazz. "What story do we have to get straight?"

"About the money, girl. We don't want the local cops and their cousins the Feds in our business." Jazz pressed her lips together and rubbed her chin.

Willa spun to face her. "I want to find Anthony and to hell with the money. Is that all this is to you?"

Jazz gazed back at her unfazed. "I already know where Ryan may have taken Anthony, which I'm going to tell Miller when he gets here. Anthony is going to be okay. He's got skills."

"Plus he's younger and can move fast," MiMi put in.

"Skills?" Willa ignored MiMi and glared at Jazz.

"You raised him to be a mild-mannered bourgie black boy, but Anthony likes the streets. He can handle himself in a fight when push comes to shove," Jazz said.

"Anthony is a thug and that should make me feel better?" Willa shot back. She headed for the security desk. "Plenty of thugs are in the grave. You've got it wrong, Jazz. The way I raised my son so far means he might live longer. I don't want him living your kind of life."

"So you finally came out and said it. You don't want your kids too close to me 'cause I'm ghetto. That's why you don't let them visit. And maybe that's why you don't visit too often either. You've got your cozy little middle-class life. Well news flash, sis. Life doesn't always go that smooth."

"I'm pretty sure Willa wasn't calling you her ghetto relative," MiMi said shaking her head.

"Don't play the victim. We've all tried from day one to be family to you. You're the one who keep us at a distance." Willa's voice rose with each sentence. She pointed an accusing finger at Jazz.

"Because I get tired of having you people judging me every minute," Jazz snapped. She pulled out her cell phone and walked away. Seconds later she was engaged in a deep conversation.

The security guard had left his desk and was walking toward them. "Ladies, what's the problem?"

Willa felt relief when she looked out the glass walls of the lobby. Outside Miller and his partner Addison pulled up to the curb in their unmarked car, blue lights flashing on the dashboard. They parked in the red zone right and seconds later were inside.

The security guard met them halfway across the shiny marble floor. He shook hands with Addison and then Miller.

"You guys showed up even before these two started swinging. Now that's good police work."

"Fight?" Miller glanced at the three women.

"Just a disagreement on strategy," MiMi rushed to explain.

"Uh-huh. So tell me again why you are worried about your son being with his uncle." Miller looked to Willa for answers.

"We don't handle family disputes," Addison said. He cocked at eyebrow at Jazz and MiMi.

"Ryan was part of a business deal with my ex-husband. He's desperate for money and was pissed when Jack backed out of the deal. He thinks my son knows where he can get his hands on that money, and he picked up Anthony without my permission." Willa spit the words out in an intense rush. "Please help me find them. Please."

"Jazz told us that Ryan got into a fist fight with Jack just days before Jack was shot. They never got along. So there's a motive, and where was he that night?" MiMi put in gesturing.

"S'cuse us a minute."

Miller pulled his partner aside. They stood several feet away talking in low tones. Both men took out note pads to consult them. Their deep mumbling conversation sounded ominous to Willa.

MiMi eased a few steps in their direction and craned her neck. When Addison squinted at her MiMi flashed a smile. When he didn't smile back she retreated again.

Willa squeezed her eyes shut, whispered a prayer and looked at the detectives. As the men started toward them her body went numb from tension. Jazz walked over to the two men, gestured to the detectives and extended her cell phone to him. He hesitated a few seconds then accepted it.

"What the hell is that about?" Willa tapped a foot on the polished lobby floor.

With a nod to his partner all three walked over to Willa and MiMi. Miller pocketed his note pad. "Okay, what kind of car does this guy drive?"

"He has a steel blue Mercedes, license plate number WER6709. Leather interior and walnut panels on the dashboard," MiMi said. When they all looked at her MiMi shrugged. "I notice the cars of well-to-do men. Sort of a hobby. And anyway, Ryan was always bragging about what he owned, trying to show up Jack."

"Uh-huh. I'm guessing he has one of those fancy GPS systems that does everything but wipe his nose when he sneezes." Addison looked at MiMi.

"Oh yes. He has the premium package with all the features. The company is NaviMate." MiMi nodded.

"Which means we can put out an Amber Alert and get his GPS service provider to track them." Miller nodded to his partner.

Addison walked away while dialing his cell phone. "Hey, we got a situation here and need to move fast."

"What's he doing?" Willa glanced at her watch. Precious minutes were ticking. "Can't we just jump in your car with the lights flashing and go find them?"

"We need to know where to go, ma'am. Look, I realize this is difficult for you. But we have a way to find them using technology. Racing around without direction just won't work," Miller said in his best combination of reasonable and reassuring tone. "Maybe Mr. Crown only wants to talk to the boy."

"I'm not so sure. Anthony would have checked in with me if he could." Willa's voice broke as she fought against the hysteria bubbling up upside her.

Miller must have seen it in her eyes. His huge hand hovered just above her shoulder. "Now let's not jump to the worst case scenarios. My lieutenant is going to call us when he gets a location from the GPS company."

"Hey, Armand. Come see a minute." Addison waved to Miller.

Willa put a hand on her chest. Her heart beat so hard it ached. "If we're too late and he's done something to my kid—"

"No, don't even say it out loud," MiMi cut her off. She put an arm around Willa and pulled her close.

Jazz glanced over at the two detectives then spoke low. "Listen, I think I know where Ryan might have taken Anthony. I'm betting he's at Ray J's Quick Mart in the old warehouse next to it. That's a corner convenience store over on Clay Street near Candy Girls."

"And near where Jack was killed," Willa said. "Why would Ryan go in that neighborhood with Anthony?"

"Because Felipe was tight with the owner. If Anthony was hanging out with D'Andre and Felipe I'll bet he's been there." Jazz kept her voice low and her eye on the detectives.

"Which might make Miller think Anthony is a viable suspect," MiMi whispered.

"Exactly. So maybe we can make a quick run over there. Get Anthony and then bounce." Jazz turned her back so that Miller and Addison couldn't see her face.

"Hell no," Willa hissed at her. "Anthony could be in danger. Not to mention some of Felipe's gang members might be on the prowl."

"I can have some of my friends meet us and— "

"We're not starting a shoot out with my child in the crossfire. I'm going to let the police handle it." Willa stabbed a finger at Jazz's nose. "Got it?"

Detective Addison studied the three women for a few seconds before walking over to them. "Y'all doing okay?"

"Yeah. What about the GPS?" Willa said sharply.

"The company is going through their chain of command, standard procedure. We've got patrol cars on the look out for them, too," he added when Willa huffed in frustration and fear. Before any of them could speak Addison left to join Miller again.

"We can't wait around for the system to finally do its thing. Let me drive and it'll take ten minutes tops to get to Ray J's. We could call the cops if Ryan is there." Jazz shook Willa's right arm. "I want to find Anthony fast, too, you know."

"But they're gonna wonder why we would leave," MiMi nodded toward the detectives.

"Or why we don't just tell them about Ray J's," Willa added.

"Because I'd have to explain how I know all about Felipe's office at Ray J's and a few other details, like how I know so much. The cops might panic Ryan and make him do something stupid. Hell with it. I'll go by myself." Jazz snatched Willa's car keys and spun to walk off, but didn't get far.

Willa reached out and jerked her back. "The hell you will. We do this my way."

The detectives noticed the commotion and strode over to them quickly. "Ladies we don't have time for the family drama. NaviMate got back to us and we know where to go, Ray J's Quick Mart," Miller said.

"We also talked to an informant about Felipe's office. We'll want to have a chat with *you* about that later." Addison pointed a finger at Jazz.

"But right now we gotta roll. You can follow us." Miller started walking off. We already got uniformed officers at the scene. Lights only. We don't want Ryan to get jumpy hearing sirens."

"You know the way," Addison added with one last piercing look at Jazz. Then he jogged after his partner who was already on his cell phone. Seconds later they reached their car. Suddenly a blue light flashed on their dashboard. With Addison behind the wheel the tires squealed. The police car made a sharp u-turn and raced off.

Without a word Willa ran toward the parking garage. Jazz followed while MiMi struggled to keep up. Willa slowed down only long enough to get her bearings. Jazz yelled out the row number where Willa had parked the SUV. Moments later Willa found her vehicle. She used the remote to open the locks. It took her a second to climb in the driver's side. Jazz was already in the passenger's seat with the seatbelt on.

"Where's MiMi? We can't leave her here alone," Jazz said looking around.

"Hold on."

Willa put the SUV in reverse at a speed that scared several people walking to their cars. MiMi leaned against a BMW. Willa hit the brakes, put the SUV in park and jumped out. She helped MiMi get inside. Seconds later they tore out of the parking garage.

"It will only take five minutes to get there," Willa said through clenched teeth.

She delivered on her words. The SUV passed slower cars, ran two stoplights and took one corner so fast Willa thought they must have been on two wheels. MiMi gasped a few times then sank down onto the back seat with her eyes closed. Willa was too scared for Anthony to notice the danger. Four minutes and thirty seconds later they arrived near Ray J's. They couldn't get too close because of the police cars.

"Please, Lord, let my son be safe," Willa whispered. She got out of the SUV. A police officer blocked her, but Miller and Addison intervened.

"Okay, this is the situation. They're in that old building behind Ray J's. They use that as a warehouse and office. Our aim is get everybody out safe and sound. You need to stay here." Miller spoke to Willa in a calm, deliberate tone despite the urgency of the situation.

"But what's going on?" Willa scanned the scene.

"That's what we're going to find out. These two officers are going to stay with you. Make sure the ladies are okay." Miller nodded to the two officers then strode off with Addison.

Jazz paced back and forth staring at the building. After five minutes MiMi's back started to ache so one of the officers let her sit in his cruiser. Willa fought the urge to scream and make a run toward the danger to save her son. Yet reason told her that hysterics wouldn't help Anthony at this point. When she saw Miller jogging toward her Willa's legs went weak.

"Come with us, Mrs. Crown. This is a hostage situation. Maybe you can talk to him," Miller said as he put a large hand under Willa's elbow.

"He's got a gun," Addison said bluntly.

"Mrs. Crown, I know this is hard on you. But I need you keep your voice calm when you're talking. Can you do that?"

Willa gulped air feeling as though she were drowning. Then she rubbed her cheeks hard and stood straight. "Yes, but Ryan never liked me that much. I'm scared he won't listen to me. We never got along."

Miller glanced at his partner then gripped Willa's arm. "Ma'am, Anthony is the one with the gun."

"What?" Willa felt the world spin around her. She blinked at Miller. "No. That can't be."

"Oh shit." Jazz rubbed her forehead hard with both hands. "Let me come, too."

"Uh-uh, his mother is the one we need to get through to him. Look, just get your son talking and let him know he has better options," Miller said as he pulled her toward the warehouse. Addison stayed behind arguing with Jazz.

Willa tried to process Miller's staccato instructions while she came to grips with Anthony holding Ryan Crown hostage. Police officers with automatic rifles parted to let she and Miller through. Willa breathed in the damp cool air in deep gulps trying to clear her head.

<u>Anthony has a gun.</u>

Those words swirled around until Willa felt rising nausea. She followed the detective through one of two gray metal doors leading into the building. Two dim, dirty lights set in the ceiling lighted the old warehouse. Just inside the doors Miller stopped, still holding onto Willa's arm. He gave an officer holding a rifle a signal. The man dressed all in black melted into a shadowy corner. Miller nodded to Willa then continued leading her through the open space. Boxes with the logos of liquor companies lined one of the walls. About twenty yards ahead was another door. A lamp spilled light onto the floor from what looked like an office in the corner of the building. When they were a few feet from the door Miller stopped.

"Anthony, it's Detective Miller again. We're in a bad place right now, but it's not something we can't fix. Using a gun isn't the solution." Seconds passed with no answer. Willa started to speak, but Miller squeezed her arm and whispered for her to wait.

"I've got a better idea, Detective Miller. Why don't you talk to my good old Uncle Ryan?" Anthony spat out the last words as if they were bitter pills. "Why don't you talk to the nice policemen, uncle?"

"Listen to me, Anthony. You don't want to do this, son. I— " Ryan's deep voice sounded hoarse from fear.

"Don't call me that," Anthony shouted. "I will shoot your ass right here and now if I hear one more lie. Now tell Detective Miller how you set up your own brother to be killed."

Willa ignored the hammer beating against her chest and used a firm maternal tone. "Anthony, stop this right now. You put down that gun and walk out of there."

"Mama?" Anthony's voice wavered then grew stronger. "You shouldn't be here."

"This is exactly where I should be. Now let Ryan go. The police will deal with him."

"Not before he tells the truth. Say it," Anthony snapped at Ryan. "Tell them how you and Mr. Nelson got greedy. See 'Uncle Ryan' isn't as good at business as Jack was. He got himself deep in debt. So when Felipe dangled the idea of big cash for them while he took all the risks 'Uncle' couldn't resist. But Jack wouldn't go for it."

"You got it all wrong, boy. Jack was your hero, but he was into the deal with both Strafford *and Felipe.* I tried to talk him out of getting hooked up with Felipe, but he wouldn't listen and— "

"What did I just say about lyin'?" Anthony shouted and there was a click.

"Anthony, don't," Willa said before her throat closed with terror.

"Calm down, young man, and let him tell the story," Miller said quickly. His huge arm supported Willa when she thought her legs would give way.

"Okay, okay, okay," Ryan rasped, his breathing so heavy he wheezed. "Everything was going just fine. We had the legitimate contracts with Strafford. My trucking company moved loads to the dock. Jack provided security at warehouses, and he hired guys to move merchandise for Strafford."

"Not strictly legit," Miller put in. "Strafford has a problem paying custom fees. But that's for the feds to sort out."

"I don't know what you're talking about. All I did was move merchandise," Ryan said quickly.

"You knew about Felipe and his crew," Willa said sharply. "Felipe decided to beef up his own enterprise using the warehouse, moving large cargo to the dock. So you decided to make even more money, right?"

"Jack was in on it, too," Ryan shot back. "But he turned stupid because of this boy. Right, Anthony? You're more responsible for Jack getting himself killed than I am."

"Oh God. Anthony, what is he talking about?" Willa said.

"Tell your mama about you and those thugs since you want everything out in the open. Go on," Ryan said. Scorn had replaced the pitch of fear in his voice.

"Anthony?" Willa glanced at Miller. The detective took a step closer to the door as though not wanting to miss one word.

"Me and the guys got into some petty stuff," Anthony added defensively.

"Don't be so modest. You got interested in Felipe's import and export enterprise. You should be proud, Willa. Anthony here showed real promise as an illegal drug and gun dealer." Ryan gave a nasty chuckle.

Anthony's voice broke. "Jack found out I was hanging with Felipe's crew, getting in too deep. Jack felt like it was his fault, that he set a bad example. He... he told me not to be like him. That's why he decided to get out of it all, the Strafford contract and everything."

"What an idiot. He gave up a lucrative business deal and you weren't even his blood. And that's what got him killed," Ryan muttered.

"Shut the hell up! He went to you first," Anthony said. "But you were in debt so deep you could lose everything, so you set him up to be killed. You told Ike and Felipe Jack would go to the police."

"That's a lie. Detective Miller, Anthony was the one close to those thugs. Maybe he wanted to avoid some jail time. He's just making all this up to save himself," Ryan said, the words coming out fast in an attempt to convince.

"Wrong again, chump. D'Andre lived up to his rep of having a big mouth. He told me Felipe was tipped off. You went to Strafford and Felipe to warn them, didn't you?" Anthony's words shot out fast, the rage in his tone building.

"Don't point that thing at me. No, don't please," Ryan screamed, the scornful bravado gone. "My family will give you money."

"Yeah, I want you to pay alright, but not the way you think," Anthony said. "Now get on your knees. You don't deserve to live after what you did. On your knees!"

Willa couldn't stand it any longer. Before Miller could stop her she was through the door and in the office. Anthony stood with legs apart, both hands gripping the revolver pointed at Ryan. "Anthony, listen to me. Jack didn't want you to end up in prison. If you hurt Ryan then Jack will have died for nothing, because that's exactly where you'll go. Baby please, give me the gun."

"Jack died because of me, Mama. I was stupid, and Jack paid the price. I've got to make it right." Anthony breathed hard as tears streamed down his face. His gaze never wavered from Ryan.

"Would Jack want this, Anthony? Is this the way he would want you to handle a problem, like Felipe Perez would?" Willa walked closer to Anthony and put her hand on his shoulder. She could feel the tension ease in his muscles beneath her fingers. When Miller slipped inside the door with his gun drawn Willa went dizzy with fear. Instead she kept walking until she stood between Anthony and Ryan. With both hands, out palms up, Willa gazed at her son. Seconds stretched into a lifetime. The only sound came from Anthony as he sobbed and Ryan's panting breaths. Sweat rolled down both their faces.

"Not like this, Anthony. Please. Mikayla needs you even more now that Jack is gone, baby," Willa said softly.

Anthony let out a ragged sob then backed up toward Willa. He bent down slowly and placed the gun on the floor at Willa's feet. Willa stooped down, picked it up and handed the gun to Detective Miller. Once he had the semi-automatic pistol the big man exhaled long and slow. Four uniformed police officers streamed into the room to secure it.

"Shh, it's going to be okay. You hear me? We're going to come out of this just fine," Willa murmured into Anthony's ear. She held him and cradled his head against her neck

Ryan recovered his upper-class tone of entitlement once the gun was gone. "Lock him up, officers. You and your little ghetto pals will get long prison sentences for this."

Willa blinked hard as one final puzzle piece clicked into place. "Ryan, Jack would never have gone into that neighborhood at night to meet Felipe, or any of his crew. But he would have shown up if *you* called him."

"What an obvious ploy, Willa." Ryan turned to Detective Miller. "She's trying to take suspicion from her son."

"Anthony is right. Jack would have told you he was backing out first. He'd try to protect you." Willa let go of Anthony. "Once again Jack stood in your way, blocking you from getting everything you deserved. So in a rage you killed Jack then moved his body to Brookstown. Either the police would think Jack had been robbed, or better yet, Felipe and his gang would get blamed."

"This is outrageous. I'm not going to be victimized a second time— " Ryan started to leave, but a beefy policeman blocked his exit.

"Check his phone records for that night, Detective Miller. See if he called Jack. Then compare Jack's cell phone GPS and see if it matches Ryan's cell phone ping location," Willa said, her voice razor sharp in the quiet.

"Mama, Ryan owns another gun," Anthony said.

"It was stolen," Ryan countered. A large drop of sweat rolled down is forehead. "Six weeks ago."

"So you reported that theft to us?" Miller's thick eyebrows went up when Ryan started to shake.

"The Crowns own a camp on Lake Solitude in West Feliciana Parish. Wonder what they'll find if they drag that lake, Ryan?" Willa smiled when Ryan's eyes went wide with fear.

"You... you can't take her seriously. She's a ghetto rat trying to save her brat' skin." Ryan gulped air like a fish out of water.

"If I were you I'd be speed dialing my lawyer right about now." Detective Addison strolled over to Ryan and clamped a beefy hand on one of his arms.

"We need to discuss your involvement in the murder of Jack Crown. Then there is a little matter of drug trafficking." Miller nodded slowly as he words hit home.

"Add gun smuggling," Addison said to his partner. He jerked Ryan's arm back.

"Just a minute, I'm the victim here. All I did was enter into a contract with an established business. I didn't know anything about any criminal activity. So take your hands off me." Ryan pushed hard against Detective Addison's grip on his arm. The big detective didn't even move. He merely smiled at Ryan.

"But we just heard you admit that you did know," Miller replied mildly. "Take him outta here."

Addison yanked a cursing, furious Ryan toward the door. "Yeah, I know. You'll have my job for this. I don't know who I'm messing with because your family has pull. Blah, blah, blah."

When Miller turned toward Willa she clutched Anthony close. "No."

"He has to come with us," Miller said in a gentle but firm deep voice. Two uniformed officers stood by with alert gazes fixed on Willa and Anthony.

Anthony pulled back from Willa. "He's right. I have to face up to everything. Jack would want it that way." He turned to Detective Miller. "I'm ready. No way is that chump going to tell the truth."

"But— "

"You can call the lawyer now, Mama." Anthony cupped Willa's face in his hands and kissed her on the forehead. "Don't worry. Like you said it's gonna be alright, remember?"

Willa looked at him for a few minutes. Anthony had a look of calm maturity in his dark brown eyes. After a few seconds the horrible ringing in her ears, the panic twisting her insides quieted. Willa continued to cry, but she nodded and watched her only son be led away by the police, a sight that had always been her worst nightmare.

"They arrested Anthony. Oh hell no. " Jazz marched forward as if ready to do battle.

MiMi waddled over as Anthony was guided into a police cruiser. "Willa, are you okay? Why are they taking Anthony? Ryan Crown kidnapped that child, and he had to protect himself." She glared at Detective Miller.

"They have to question him. There is a whole lot for the police to sort out," Willa said, surprised at how composed she felt. Jazz blinked at her rapidly in confusion but said no more. "MiMi, go home, get off your feet and rest for the baby's sake. In fact both of y'all go home and chill."

"No way," Jazz protested. "I'm going with Anthony."

"You're going to do what I ask," Willa broke in sharply.

"Don't worry, Ms.Vaughn. We'll be talking to you real soon about a list of interesting topics," Detective Miller said to Jazz.

***

The next ten hours was a blur of booking procedures, bail negotiations, legal advice and interviews. Dion and Shaun showed up at the police station. Despite not being able to do anything but pace in the lobby, Willa's brothers didn't leave until Anthony was released. By the time they got home Willa's parents and aunts were there. The aroma of food cooking flowed from the kitchen when Dion held open the door for Willa.

Mama Ruby grabbed Willa and Anthony in one tight hug before they got across the threshold. Mikayla ran forward to join in. Aunt Beryl dabbed at her eyes and fanned her face while Aunt Ametrine started a spirited thanksgiving prayer. After twenty minutes of sharing the love Willa steered Anthony away from the hubbub to his bedroom.

"Mama, I know you're mad that I was still hanging with D'Andre even after you told me not to, but I figured Big D would talk sooner or later, " Anthony said when they were alone. His eyes filled with tears. "Jack gave up his life because of me."

"Yes, he wanted to protect you, but his death isn't your fault, baby. Jack was killed because his brother was greedy. He was killed because a thug named Felipe is a cold-blooded murderer. Period."

Anthony rested his head on Willa's shoulder. She rocked him like she did when he was a toddler and needed comfort. Willa continued to murmur reassurances for another few minutes until he fell asleep in her arms. Despite his rangy adolescent size she managed to ease him down on the bed. She removed his athletic shoes, shirt and pants. He curled into a ball like a small boy. With one last kiss on his grubby face, Willa went out and closed the door. When she got to her bedroom she fell on the bed and cried until she drifted off to sleep, too.

***

After twenty-four hours of non-stop family attention, Willa felt a little better. At least the dead weight on her back that she hadn't realized she'd been carrying around for weeks was gone. Mikayla went off to school as usual. After Willa consulted with the principal and a school social worker both assured her that a return to routine would help Mikayla. Anthony, however, was a whole different ball of problems. Detective Miller said he would talk to the DA about Anthony's charges. Since Anthony had never been arrested before, Miller promised to advocate for a light sentence. Anthony's principal, vice principal and school guidance counselor all agreed that homebound instruction might be best for the time being. Willa fought back until they reached a compromise. Anthony would be temporarily assigned to an alternative school.

When the doorbell rang the familiar metallic taste of fear returned to Willa's mouth. Her aunts both sprang to intercept any intrusion but Willa waved them aside. Still they hovered protectively at her back as she went to the front door. For once Willa was relieved to see MiMi grinning at her through the window when opened the curtain. Jazz, unsmiling, merely stared back.

"We just came over to check on y'all. How are the kids? Who else is here? Hmm, girl, something smells good." MiMi walked in and followed her nose to the kitchen. Moments later Willa heard her aunts making a fuss over MiMi, exhorting her to sit down and eat as much as she wanted.

"Hey," was all Jazz said as she shut the front door behind her.

"Hi." Willa led the way to the kitchen. "Sure, MiMi. Make yourself at home."

"Thanks. I love lasagna and garlic bread, Aunt Beryl," MiMi said.

"We just dropped by to check on Willa and the kids, but we're going home now. Make sure Willa gets rest," Aunt Beryl said to MiMi.

"And you call us if anything else happens," Aunt Ametrine added as they blew goodbye kisses at Willa.

"Yes, ma'am. Don't you worry," MiMi replied hugging them in turn. She left the kitchen to escort the two women to Willa's front door.

"She gets along better with my family than I do," Jazz retorted. She perched on one of the tall stools at the breakfast bar.

"Yeah, well you could try a little harder at it," Willa cracked. "Forget I just said that. I'm too worn out for another battle."

"Like you didn't start it." Jazz snorted.

"Okay, okay. I'm sorry for making that remark." Willa sat next to Jazz on another stool and watched MiMi at the stove, putting food on a plate. When MiMi joined them Willa shook her head. "Right, help yourself."

"I have," MiMi said and licked a finger. "So Ryan is going to prison. Good."

"He's cutting a deal with the DA. He claims that he never meant to kill Jack; that he just wanted to talk to him. Things got heated and he blacked out. His lawyer is going for manslaughter," Willa said, the words dry and bitter on her tongue.

"Bull, he intended to kill Jack and blame it on Felipe. Not that Felipe ain't a killer, but at least send a dude up for what he really did. That's all I'm sayin'," Jazz replied. "Ryan says he blacked out, huh? Going for the insanity defense. Please."

"What else could he do once they found that gun in the lake at his camp?" MiMi sipped from a glass of soda.

"Mr. and Mrs. Crown are standing by him. They hired one of the best criminal defense teams in the state," Willa went the fridge and got a soda then sat down again. "I guess Ryan finally succeeded in getting all of his parents' attention."

"And I thought my family was messed up," Jazz retorted.

MiMi gave a sigh as she dabbed tomato sauce from her lips. "Ladies, we wrapped up this case quite neatly."

"We?" Jazz and Willa said in unison.

"Between the three of us we helped the police get at the truth. That last scene with Ryan and Anthony was so scary. All's well that ends well though." MiMi sighed then chewed on a piece of garlic bread.

"Ends well is not how I would describe what happened," Willa said. "My son narrowly missed being charged with felony assault, not to mention illegal possession of a weapon. As it is he'll be lucky to escape with probation and community service."

"He was holding a gun on a member of the Crown family," MiMi said. "Still Ryan is swimming in deep hot water right about now. His priority won't be pressing charges against his own nephew."

"Anthony is not his nephew in any sense of the word. I want to hurl every time I think how Ryan pretended to care about my son." Willa frowned.

"MiMi is right though. Miller and his partner explained the facts of life to Ryan. Actually what Anthony did was self-defense. And remember it was Ryan's gun." Jazz laughed. "I told you Anthony could whip his ass. Took that fool's own gun away from him."

"So you're proud that Anthony is good at playing the innocent and luring in victims-- that he acted like a mafia hit man?" Willa asked. "See that's what I'm talking about. Your values are all twisted up."

Jazz cut her off with a raised palm. "Hey, you were the one who married an upper-class player and inherited his slimy family. And you have the nerve to criticize my friends? Please."

"Stop," MiMi commanded with such authority that both sisters blinked at her in surprise. Willa and Jazz lapsed into sulking silence. MiMi sighed. "What am I going to do with you two? We've all made mistakes. But in spite of everything Jazz stepped up when you and Anthony needed her most. She put self-interest aside to do it, too. Mostly."

"At least somebody appreciates what I did." Jazz stared at the ceiling.

MiMi gave Willa's shoulder a shove. "A 'Thank you' would be appropriate about now."

Willa didn't answer right away. She gazed at Jazz's rigid back. Then she let out the breath she was holding. "Thanks, Jazz. You showed up on time for us."

"Jazz?" MiMi prompted.

When Jazz didn't move or respond Willa blinked back a tear. "It's just that I get so scared at the life you lead. I'd do anything to keep my family safe. Sometimes I go about it the wrong way. Like with Anthony. I screwed that up big time."

"You've got your faults, but being a bad mother isn't one of them. He's blessed to have you," Jazz said after a few seconds.

"Don't forget about his resourceful protective aunt," Willa added with a smile.

"Yeah, well." Jazz shrugged. Her shoulders relaxed and she turned a little toward them again.

MiMi put an arm around Willa and Jazz. "See? We're a team, like one of those old school singing groups. The Supremes, I'm Diana Ross of course."

"They split and ended up hating each other," Willa said.

"So forget that example. Now we have to figure out how to get the money Jack moved to those off shore accounts." MiMi switched gears quickly.

"Count me out. Those detectives are on my back as it is because of this mess. I think Miller is almost convinced I told him everything. I'm not going near laundered money, at least for a while." Jazz said. "Maybe a few months, and a new crime wave will keep the cops busy."

"True. The police have no evidence that money is dirty," MiMi replied quickly. "My lawyer told me so. They can't touch Jack's estate so we can proceed to— "

"I'm the executor of Jack's estate," Willa reminded MiMi. She carefully removed MiMi's arm from around her shoulder. "I'll handle the account at the proper time. I talked to *my* lawyer. I can't touch that money until the succession is complete. So don't either of you make plans to spend gobs of cash."

"Let me remind you that I own an interest in Crown Protection Services. Jack's little baby is an heir, and as her guardian I will manage her lawful share of his estate." MiMi smiled sweetly at Willa. "But we don't need to discuss all those complex family details now. Let's just enjoy this moment of sisterhood."

"That wave of nausea is coming back." Willa held her mid-section.

Jazz laughed. She stood and grabbed the tiny but fashionable purse that matched her three-inch pumps. "Much as I'm loving this warm moment I've gotta run."

"But you rode over here with me," MiMi said. "Where are we going so soon?"

"Don't sweat, girl. My ride is coming to pick me up." Jazz fluffed the long golden brown weave of hair hanging to her waist.

"Your ride?" Willa looked at MiMi who shrugged just as the doorbell rang.

"That's probably him now." Jazz went to the door, hips swinging.

"A man. Now why doesn't that shock me?" Willa followed her. "And I don't appreciate you giving some strange dude my home address, Jazz."

"Never fear. This is a man of good character, well respected in this city and one of your clients I might add."

Jazz winked at them then unlocked and opened the front door. Reverend Fisher gave Jazz an appreciative head-to-toe appraisal before his sanctimonious façade returned. He dipped his head to them then offered an arm to Jazz. Willa's mouth hung open as she stared at him wide-eyed. He seemed not the least bit self-conscious at escorting a single lady of dubious reputation.

"Hello, ladies. A pleasure to see you again."

"Lawrence, I mean Reverend Fisher is now my spiritual advisor. I'm trying to make changes in my life. Like you suggested, dearest sister. Kisses. I'll talk to y'all later." Jazz patted his arm as the signal she was ready to leave.

"Goodbye, ladies. Remember you are always welcome to receive spiritual renewal at Abundant Love Ministries." Reverend Fisher nodded to them then led Jazz to his white Lexus.

Speechless Willa and MiMi watched them leave then burst into laughter. In seconds Willa was gasping for air while MiMi fanned her face. They shut the door and stumbled into the living room still howling and trying to form words. They both fell on the sofa. Willa finally managed to speak.

"Those two have some nerve."

"One thing about this family is we're unique." MiMi wiped her eyes.

"What an understatement. You slept with my husband and got pregnant." Willa cleared her throat and sat up straight.

"You were practically divorced. Besides I wasn't dating Jack when y'all were together. I'm pretty sure," MiMi added in an undertone. She struggled to her feet and went to the kitchen. "I'm still hungry."

"Pretty sure?" Willa tossed back, but didn't follow her. "Geez."

"You said something?" MiMi called from the kitchen.

"No, not a thing."

Willa stretched her legs out and relaxed. She hardly cared at this point. Jack was dead, and their marriage had been just as lifeless for at least two years before he died. Besides if she had to put up with one of Jack's mistresses she could do worse than MiMi Landry.

"I'm staying so we can have a nice family dinner with the kids. Hey, let's have a girls' party this weekend. Just you, Jazz and me. She can give us the dirt on Reverend Abundant Love. And you can tell us the real deal between you and that fine Cedric." MiMi snickered at her own joke.

Willa rubbed her forehead at the thought of Jazz and MiMi around to make her life interesting. <u>Then again maybe worse is what I'm getting.</u>

ABOUT THE AUTHOR

Mix knowledge of voodoo, Louisiana politics and forensic social work with the dedication to write fiction while working each day as a clinical social worker, and you get a snapshot of author Lynn Emery. Lynn has been a contributing consultant to the magazine *Today's Black Woman* for three articles about contemporary relationships between black men and women. For more information visit:

www.lynnemery.com
www.facebook.com/lynn.emery.author
Twitter: @LEmeryWriter